WENDY PERCIVAL's interes
time honoured 'box of old docu
inspiration behind her Esme
novellas.

Wendy shares the intriguing, s
in her own family history on her ι  ͻ ....ϲ ιιαϛ nad several articles
published in *Shropshire Family History Society*'s quarterly journal and
in *Family Tree* magazine.

She lives in South West England with her husband in a thatched
cottage next door to a beautiful thirteenth-century church.

# The Esme Quentin Mysteries

*Blood-Tied*
*The Indelible Stain*
*The Malice of Angels*
*The Fear of Ravens*
*The Scourge of the Skua*

Novellas

*Death of a Cuckoo*
*Legacy of Guilt*
(An Esme Quentin prequel – FREE to subscribers)

# The Scourge of the Skua

### THE FIFTH ESME QUENTIN MYSTERY

## WENDY PERCIVAL

OLD KEY PRESS

Published by Old Key Press 2023

Old Key Press
Worlington, Devon, England

Cover design by Brian Percival
Cover Images © Brian Percival | Source unknown | Wikimedia Commons Dave
Wheeler / *Skua attack, Fair Isle*

ISBN 978-1-8380860-7-7

# Great Skua

(Stercorarius skua)

"The great skua is an aggressive 'pirate of the seas,
deliberately harassing birds as large as gannets
to steal a free meal."

R.S.P.B.

# Acknowledgements

Thank you to all the people who have helped me during the writing of *The Scourge of the Skua*. It's been a long journey!

Particular thanks go to Janet Few for allowing me to pick her brains on specific genealogical elements pertinent to the plot, and to Lorna Manton for her perceptive feedback on the final draft.

Thanks also to Alison Jack for her meticulous editing and scrupulous attention to detail.

I must also give huge thanks to all those readers who take the time to get in touch to share their enthusiasm for the Esme Quentin books or who've posted reviews. Such small things keep writers motivated when the going gets tough!

And last, but never least, my love and immense gratitude go to my husband Brian, not only for his magnificent cover design, but for his patience and unwavering support as I grappled with plot twists, toiled over story-lines and endured the usual agonies of the writing process. We got there in the end!

# 1

Murder?' Hester Campbell's cup of cappuccino clattered into its saucer, froth slopping over the edge.

Esme Quentin watched the colour fade from her client's face, waiting for the impish smile which usually followed a report about a scandalous family history story. It never came. Hester's eyes remained troubled, blinking as she processed Esme's information. She fiddled with the collar of her shirt, the crisp white edge becoming increasingly crumpled between her well-manicured finger and thumb.

'I'm guessing from your reaction,' Esme said, 'that you weren't aware of the story.'

Hester hesitated before shaking her head, her short bobbed hair flicking against her cheek. 'I knew nothing about it.'

'What about your partner,' Esme asked, 'do you think he knows his grandfather's story?'

Again, the shake of the head and a shrug. 'I have no idea.' She smoothed down the front of her grey pencil skirt, as though it might sooth her evidently fraught nerves.

Esme glanced down at her notes, uncertain how best to continue. Hester had engaged her to compile a family tree as a surprise present for her partner Frank's special birthday. Ordinarily, what she'd discovered would be all part of her final report, but Hester had been keen for an interim update. Did that suggest Hester had some idea of what Esme would find? Had she had a suspicion of something and wanted to establish early on whether there was any substance to that suspicion? But if Hester *did* have some inkling of what Esme might find, she'd have been more prepared, wouldn't she?

Hester's puckered brow and distant expression suggested she was still sifting through what Esme had told her. Perhaps she needed time to gather her thoughts. Esme cast her eye around the café, noticing that it was quickly filling up. Had the April showers threatened earlier finally materialised and visitors to Bideford's Victoria Park been forced inside out of the rain?

Esme pulled her attention away from the bustling café punters and back to Hester. 'Are you OK?' she asked.

Hester didn't give an answer, instead asking a question of her own. 'And you're quite sure about the details?'

'As sure as I can be,' Esme said, referring to the documents in front of her. 'I have a copy of the newspaper report of the trial.' She slid a print-out of the front page of *The Daily Herald* towards Hester across the table. 'As I mentioned, your partner's grandfather, Albert Philips, killed his cousin, Ernest Sanders, on the 3rd of March 1923 following some sort of argument.'

'An argument about what?' Hester said.

'Ah, well, that's just it,' Esme said. 'It seems Philips remained tight-lipped about the alleged dispute between him and Sanders throughout the trial and took his secret with him to the scaffold. He was hanged later that year without revealing any motive.'

Hester stared down at the newspaper image. Esme waited, allowing her time to read it. But after a few seconds, Hester stood up, her chair scraping the floor with a wince-inducing squeal.

'I'm sorry, I have to go.'

'What? No, don't go yet,' Esme said, scrambling to her feet. 'Maddy Henderson's on her way. She'll be here any minute. Can't you hang on for her? She's renovated the old photograph you gave me.'

Hester snatched her jacket off the back of the chair. 'I can't, I'm afraid,' she said, slipping on the jacket and picking up her oversized black leather handbag. 'I'd completely forgotten about another appointment.' She slid the chair back under the table, looping her handbag over her arm, and gave Esme a fleeting smile.

'I'll be in touch,' she said and wheeled away.

Esme stared after her as she weaved between tables and customers, her high heels clicking on the tiled floor, and hurried through the glass doors and out into the park.

# 2

Esme sat in the bubble of the noisy commotion in the café, trying to make sense of Hester's behaviour. There was something incongruous about Hester's response which she couldn't put her finger on. Had it been the expression on Hester's face? She tried to recall the image, but her memory failed her and the vision morphed into the stunned, shocked expression of later.

Esme was jerked out of her deliberations by the arrival of Maddy, a tote bag over her shoulder emblazoned with the words *There is no Planet B*. The colour of the logo matched the jade green and blues of her hooded sweatshirt and leggings.

'Phew,' Maddy said, pulling out a chair. 'I thought I was going to be late.'

'You are,' Esme said, sighing and slumping back in her seat. 'She's been and gone.'

'What? Already?' Maddy pushed up the sleeve of her sweatshirt to look at her watch. 'So what happened? Was she super early or something?' She sat down, dropping her bag on the floor beside her chair.

Esme shook her head and explained what had happened.

'You mean mentioning the murder freaked her out?'

'Looks like it, yes.'

Maddy rested her elbow on the table and tugged at her ponytail. 'People usually like a bit of scandal to spice up their family history. Too close to the bone, maybe?'

'Perhaps. Though it isn't her family. It's her partner's.'

'So who murdered who?'

'His grandfather killed his cousin in 1923. Some sort of dispute.' Esme shrugged. 'I dunno. Maybe it resonated with something she's known about, but hasn't taken seriously? Or maybe…' She rubbed her forehead. 'Or maybe I haven't the faintest idea.' She smiled. 'So, how did you get on with the photograph? I was really disappointed she didn't hang around long enough to see it. Did it come up OK?' The image Hester had given Esme was so faded, it was almost indecipherable. But Maddy's ability to digitally enhance old family photographs had produced some impressive results over recent times and Esme had been confident she'd be able to achieve a similar level of success with Hester's example. Frustrating as it was that Hester had not stayed to see what Maddy had been able to do, maybe her parting comment about getting in touch was genuine and once she'd come to terms with the shock of the revelation, she'd pick up the phone and they could continue from where they'd left off.

Maddy pulled her bag on to her lap and delved inside. She took out a small buff envelope and laid it on the table. 'It's a pretty early one – 1850s, I'd say. And you were right about it being of an old lady.' She took a printed copy of an image out of the envelope and slid it across the table to Esme.

'Oh, great job, Maddy – as always.' Esme picked up the photograph before glancing across at the counter. 'Did you want to get yourself a coffee while there's no queue?'

Maddy stood up. 'Yeah, sure. Good idea.'

Maddy made her way across the café while Esme turned her attention to the photograph. Maddy had worked her magic, transforming the image from the grainy, hard-to-decipher picture it had been previously into one with much greater definition.

The elderly woman was wearing a heavy Victorian dress, the folds of the skirt beautifully sewn into the waistband. Her hands rested in her lap. She wore a lace bonnet, its ties hanging from her chin over the bodice of the dress and hiding the detail.

When Maddy returned with her latte a few minutes later, Esme couldn't wait to express her admiration for her work. 'Wow, this is fabulous, Maddy,' she said. 'She's great. How old d'you reckon she is?'

'Got to be in her eighties, hasn't she?' Maddy said, picking up her coffee and taking a sip.

'Meaning she was born in the 1760s. Incredible.' Esme continued to stare at the photograph. There was something puzzling her about it, but she couldn't immediately work out what. Then she realised. 'Her eyes,' she said, almost to herself. 'They're a bit odd.'

'Well spotted,' Maddy said, folding her arms and leaning on the table. 'Probably painted on after it was developed.'

Esme looked up and blinked. 'You mean...?'

Maddy nodded. 'It's a mortuary photograph. Taken after death.'

Esme grimaced. 'Oh, creepy,' she said with a shudder. 'But then, Victorian society did have a fascination for death. Which was hardly surprising, I guess, given how common it was, what with TB, cholera, diphtheria and typhoid, and no antibiotics. I guess this was one way of coping with it.'

'*Memento mori*,' Maddy said. 'Literally, *remember you will die.* Mortuary photos gave a family a way to remember their loved ones. Something to display on the mantelpiece.'

'I'm not sure I'd want a mortuary photo of my nearest and dearest on the mantelpiece,' Esme said. 'But then we have the luxury of being able to take plenty of photos while they're alive.'

'Oh, nearly forgot,' Maddy said. 'There's a faint pencil mark on the back of the original, with what looks like a capital A. I'm guessing a name. Maybe Agnes? Have you come across an Agnes?'

'No, not yet, but I'd hardly got started. I sort of got sidetracked by the murder, if I'm honest.'

Maddy nodded at the envelope on the table. 'The original is in there, by the way. You might want to have a look for yourself before you give it back to Hester.'

Esme picked up the envelope and slid the restored photograph print back inside. 'That's assuming I ever see her again.'

'Oh, you will, won't you, surely? Once she's got over the shock.'

'Well, I'd like to think so.' Esme rested her elbow on the table and rubbed a thumb along the puckered scar on her cheek. 'You should have seen her face, Madds. It's like she'd opened up a Pandora's box and she was wishing she hadn't. I wish I knew what spooked her. Any ideas?'

'Don't ask me. Like I said before, it's usually the opposite. People want to find something scandalous or they reckon their family history is boring.' She frowned. 'You worried about getting paid?'

'No, that's not a problem,' Esme said, shaking her head. 'She paid a deposit which covers what I've done. But I'm intrigued now.'

Maddy laughed. 'Yes, I bet. Well, if I know you, you'll be taking a sneaky peep anyway.'

'No I won't,' Esme said. 'I've got far too much to do. You haven't seen the inside of my outhouse. The builders are due to start work to convert it to my office, and it's full of junk from the previous owners. That's my next assignment.' She stood up, collecting the envelope from the table and looking down on it. 'I'll give her a call later and if she decides she doesn't want me to go any further with the research, I can drop this off at her house.'

'Oh, she's local, then?'

Esme slipped the envelope into her bag. 'Yes, she lives in Appledore. We had been going to meet there, but then she phoned to change it and suggested here instead. I think she said she was in town for another reason and it was easier than going back home.' As she slung her bag over her shoulder, something flitted into her head about that particular conversation, but she couldn't catch it before it fizzled out.

'Everything OK?' Maddy said.

Esme gave her head a shake. 'Yeah, fine.'

They walked out of the café and into the park. Esme pulled her coat around her as the chilled spring breeze came around the corner of the building. She glanced left and right, instinctively looking for Hester, though why she thought Hester would be waiting outside when she could easily have returned to the café had she wanted, Esme had no idea. She pushed the bizarre notion out of her head and turned to Maddy.

'See you at the market on Saturday, then,' she said.

'Sure. I'll bring those little snuff boxes I got in that sale. They've come up a treat. Should bring in the punters. They're always popular.' Maddy had recently taken over the business of her late father, restoring small wooden items of furniture or paraphernalia and selling it on a stall at Bideford market. Esme helped out, covering the stall on days when Maddy was away at trade fairs to buy in new supplies for restoration, or as an additional pair of hands at busy times.

As Esme hurried back to her car, she wondered when she'd hear from Hester and how long she should leave it before getting in touch herself. What would Hester make of Maddy's assessment of the photograph? Given her reaction to the murder, perhaps the idea that the photograph had been taken after the old woman's death might be the final indignity.

# 3

The image of the dead woman in the photograph haunted Esme as she drove home. Who was she? Esme imagined 'Agnes' as a matriarchal character, whose family had been deeply affected by her loss. Even in death, she looked formidable. Had she wielded domineering control over those around her, leaving them rudderless at her passing? Or had she been a woman who'd engendered affection?

Perhaps if Hester allowed Esme to continue the task she'd set, answers to those questions might come to light. But the discovery of the murder appeared to have unsettled Hester to such an extent, Esme was inclined to think a termination of the arrangement was more likely.

Esme pushed open the front door of her cottage. Her two kittens Jeanie and Ally were waiting for her on the mat. She ushered them further inside.

When her friend Ruth had first brought her to view the cottage, she had tried not to fall in love with it, insisting that it was too small for her needs. The ground floor was one spacious room, a neat kitchen at one end from where the stairs climbed up to two bedrooms and a bathroom. On the opposite wall of the cottage, a substantial inglenook fireplace housed a cast-iron wood-burning stove. Facing the fireplace, Esme had installed a large squashy sofa, deep enough for her to curl up and lose herself in amongst its cushions. To one side of the hearth stood an ancient leather armchair and on the other side a television sat on a low cupboard. In the centre of the room, straddling the kitchen and the lounge, was a chunky dining table which at the moment served a multitude of purposes, including food preparation, eating meals and a temporary work desk.

Esme's initial objection that the cottage didn't have the

necessary accommodation was countered with Ruth's insistence that converting the stone building in the garden into an office would overcome all of its shortcomings. Esme relented and a few months later, she'd moved out of her rented accommodation and once more into a home of her own.

Ally, his fur as black as his mother's, turned left and headed straight for the kitchen. His sister Jeanie, black with white paws and flash on her forehead, took a detour, peering behind the log basket to see if the dead mouse she'd deposited there during the night was still there. It wasn't. Esme had disposed of it before going out. On finding nothing, Jeanie trotted around the sofa and joined her brother at Esme's feet.

When her charges were fed and watered, Esme put her duffel coat back on and headed out of the front door, down the stone steps on to the lane and down towards the beach. She'd got used to living on the coast over recent months and it had become a daily ritual to fill her lungs with sea air and gaze out across the water.

She passed the cottages which lined either side of the lane, bearing left as the road petered out and narrowed into a footpath down to the quay. The tiny stone building halfway down the hill ahead of her had once been an artists' studio. Its interior remained untouched and unchanged, a time capsule memorial to its owners, as though either of the two ladies had just stepped out and planned to return shortly to continue their creativity.

The studio was now managed by the National Trust, who opened it to the public at weekends and holiday periods. Visitors could squeeze into the pocket-sized ground-floor room, with its inglenook fireplace and shelves adorned with everyday bric-a-brac, and marvel at the view towards the sea, or climb the tight stair to see the narrow bed and dresser, a simple jug and bowl the only ablution facilities.

Esme hurried past the little building, pausing briefly to read the poster tacked to the notice board inviting visitors to Bluebell

Day in the grounds of the local Abbey, before continuing down the steep tarmac path as it turned left and became the slipway on to the beach. She crunched her way over the shingle down to the sea's edge and stood, hands in pockets, looking out to the horizon, breathing in the salty air, losing herself in the repetitive hiss of waves upon the shore and allowing the breeze to tug her hair out of its clasp at the back of her head.

For much of the time since she'd moved into the cottage, the wintry sea had been a muddy grey-brown as it churned up dark sand from the seabed, creating a forbidding mass of water. Today, with a promise of better weather, a hint of blue filled the sky, reflecting on the ocean's surface. It would never be the sort of beach which attracted throngs of swimmers or surfers, but a place for peaceful reflection, which suited Esme perfectly.

She wandered along the shoreline, coming to a halt where the cliff jutted out into the beach to look up at the remains of an old cottage perched precariously on the edge. Years of erosion had slowly undermined its foundations. It was predicted the next big storm would finish the job, and the cottage would come crashing down into the sea.

She wondered at its history. Who had lived there? What part had they played in the life of the village in days gone by? She'd intended to look up the census records for the area and find out, but with everything involved in the move and settling in, she'd had little opportunity.

Something caught her eye in the distance and she focused on a cove further along the beach, where a figure was clambering over the pebbles, away from the sea. It looked like a child, but it was so far away it was difficult to be sure. As she watched, the figure disappeared from view.

She thrust her hands in her coat pockets and took a deep breath charged with excitement. There was so much to discover here. She'd definitely chosen the right place to make her home.

She turned back the way she'd come, pausing to gaze beyond

the breaking waves to the horizon and over to Lundy Island, which lay just over 11 miles from the Devon mainland. A granite outcrop just three miles long and half a mile wide, its name was derived from the Norse for puffin and much had been done in recent years to increase the population of these charming little birds. For anyone seeking an escape from the 21st century, a stay on Lundy would suffice perfectly. In the summer, day trippers could board MS *Oldenburg* for a few hours of peace and tranquillity on the island. It was a trip she planned to take herself in the coming week.

She heard the crunch of footsteps behind her and turned to see Jim Watts walking away from his boat, which lay on the beach beyond the slipway. Jim's family had been associated with the village for generations, but he and his wife were the only residents left with ancestral links. To Esme, Jim was the personification of his heritage and, with his white hair and sideburns, he wouldn't look out of place in a Victorian setting.

Esme headed over to meet him.

'Grand evening,' Jim said, as they reached the slipway together. 'Been blowing away a few cobwebs, has ee?'

'Something like that,' Esme said, smiling. She turned back to gaze out to sea. 'Lundy's looking very inviting. You feel you could almost reach out and touch it.'

'Tis that, maid. Did you book yer ticket?'

'Yes, I'm going over next Thursday. I hope the weather's kind. I need a day with a nice flat sea.'

Jim chuckled. 'You'll soon get your sea legs.'

'I hope you're right. I don't want to feel too groggy to enjoy my trip. I'm looking forward to it. From what I've heard, the island's got quite a chequered history.'

'You'm right there. Wild and lawless place, it wore. Stories as'd make yer hair curl, 'bout renegades and pirates. And dangerous too. There be shipwrecks aplenty around its coast.'

Esme laughed. 'Another reason I'm hoping for calm

conditions. I don't want to end up going the same way.'

Jim shook his head and grinned. 'You'm not need to worry yerself about that. *Oldenburg* don't sail if the captain reckons it's too rough.'

'Pleased to hear it.'

They turned and began the steep climb back to the village.

'I see the derelict cottage up there survived another winter, then,' Esme said.

'P'raps. Still time, though. Spring tides and some wild weather and it could go yet. Wouldn't be the first. They reckon ther were three lost to the sea in the 1860s.'

'Really? I trust no one was inside at the time.'

Jim nodded towards the headland. 'I seed they'd cranked up the barriers around it. Guess they'm reckoning it's got more unstable.'

'Who used to live up there, I wonder. Odd that it's that bit further away from the rest of the cottages – you know, not quite in the village, as though it wanted to be on its own.'

Jim chuckled again. 'You 'istorians. Proper fanciful.' He glanced over at her and frowned. 'Now you wouldn't be thinking of poking around in there, would you? It's not safe.'

Esme shook her head. 'No, of course not. I don't want a quick way down to the beach, thank you!'

'Glad to 'ear it, maid,' Jim grunted. 'O' course, they do say,' he went on, a mischievous glint creeping into his eyes, 'that the old place was lived in by a famous smuggling family.'

Esme turned to him and grinned. 'Now you're just winding me up.'

Jim took on an innocent expression and held up his hand. 'Well, you'm did ask, me luvver.'

'OK. I did. So, what's the story?'

'Ah, a story is all tis. Nature of smuggling, b'aint it? No one zackly keeping records, like what you'd be after.'

'But there'd be rumours,' Esme urged him. 'Clandestine

21

landings on the beach. Secret places to hide the barrels of brandy and bags of tea.'

'Oh aye, there be that sort of caper. Bound to be.' Jim tapped the side of his nose. 'But word has it, it wore one of this family saved their gang from being rumbled by one of 'em custom officers.'

'Saved how?'

Jim leaned towards her conspiratorially. 'Bit like you wore saying just then. Showing 'im a quick way down to the beach.'

'They shoved him off the cliff?' Esme said, jerking her head to look behind her.

'Aye.'

Esme shuddered. 'Ruthless, then.'

'Oh yes. Certainly that.'

They'd reached the end of the slope and joined the road. Jim jerked his head towards his cottage.

'I'd better get back for me tea or I'll be in the dog house.'

Esme smiled. 'Yes, you better had. Thanks for sharing the story.'

Jim winked and turned on to the coastal path leading to his cottage, leaving Esme to trek back up the lane to hers while brooding over Jim's tales of homes claimed by the sea and the brutality of smugglers.

# 4

Esme stood in the open doorway of the stone building in her garden and stared despairingly at the junk and bits of old furniture and boxes which filled the space. The flagstone floor was piled high with an eclectic array of dining chairs, stools and occasional tables, many in a poor state of repair, damaged from years of being stored in a damp environment, a situation exacerbated by a leak in the ceiling through a broken roof slate.

When she'd bought the property, she'd agreed – rashly, as it was turning out – not to insist the couple selling it clear everything out before completion. The decision had been made partly for expediency – the transaction could go ahead more quickly if she didn't have to wait for the vendors to make arrangements to clear the building, so she could move in without having to rent somewhere in the interim – and partly because she'd been intrigued to see if anything of interest was buried amongst the old pieces. Perhaps she'd find a gem for Maddy to restore and resell on her market stall or something about the history of the cottage itself.

But now, the date she'd agreed with the builder to convert the outbuilding into an office was fast approaching and she'd not even begun the task in hand. She sighed. There was no getting away from it. She was going to have to give it priority and get stuck in.

She glanced at her watch. Today wasn't that day. She was due to take over from Maddy on the market stall in an hour and if she didn't get a move on, she'd be late. She closed the door and retraced her steps to the cottage.

\*

Bideford's historic Pannier Market had been built in the early 1880s at a cost of £4,200, commissioned by the town council after the previous structure had fallen into disrepair and its former owners had been unwilling to invest in its maintenance and improvement. The stone building, dressed with red and cream brick and supported inside by iron columns, derived its name from the wicker baskets known as panniers which would have carried produce to market, strapped to donkeys and pack horses. Esme felt privileged spending time in an environment with such a rich heritage and in quieter moments imagined the space bustling with Victorian tradesmen and women, crying their wares to potential customers.

When she arrived, Maddy was deep in conversation at the far end of her stall with an attractive man with short greying hair, wearing an Aran sweater and mustard-coloured waterproof jacket. Esme slipped in behind the display table at the opposite end, scanning the items Maddy had laid out for sale. There was a tell-tale gap towards the back of the stall, suggesting the Victorian mahogany sewing box, which Maddy had recently lovingly restored, had found a buyer.

Esme pulled out a bundle of old family photographs from her bag and took them round to the front of the display board at the end, where she began adding them to the other photos on there. She and Maddy had started *Photos Reunited* with the aim of finding the owners and returning the images to their personal archives. Maddy had built up a considerable collection over the years, acquired from antique fairs and car boot sales. As a photographer turned photograph restorer, she felt passionately that if only family historians had a way of locating discarded and lost pictures of their ancestors, they would love to have them back. Most of their successes had been made through social media and Esme had spent time researching any clues, no matter how small, that might help lead them to the family in question. The photos on display on the stall here in Bideford were those with potential local connections, perhaps taken by studios once active in towns nearby, or further afield in the rest of Devon and the wider South

West.

The project had stalled recently while Esme had been getting straight after the move into her cottage, leaving her feeling a little guilty at neglecting the cause. There were boxes of photos waiting for her to follow up on research and others which Maddy had already restored, ready and waiting to be uploaded on to the *Photos Reunited* website. But Maddy had flapped her concerns away, saying it was the same for her after her own recent house move.

Esme was pinning up a grainy image of a group standing beside a fishing trawler when she heard her name being called. She looked round to see Maddy walking towards her, followed by the man she'd been talking to when Esme had arrived.

'Esme,' Maddy said, gesturing towards the man, 'this is Aidan Garrett.'

The man smiled and held out his hand. 'Good to meet you, Esme. We share a passion for history, I understand.'

'Hi, how d'you do?' Esme said, shaking his hand, immediately conscious, as always when meeting someone for the first time, of the scarring on her face. 'So, what field of history interests you?' she asked, countering the urge to touch her cheek.

'Maritime.'

'Aidan goes looking for buried treasure on the sea bed,' Maddy said. 'Don't you?'

Aidan threw Maddy an indulgent glance before returning his attention to Esme. 'What she means is I'm a maritime archaeologist,' he said, slipping his hands into the back pockets of his jeans.

'Oh, old shipwrecks, that sort of thing,' Esme said. 'What a fascinating job.'

'Yeah, it is. Got to admit it's a great way to make a living.'

'Aidan was on the team diving on the *Mary Rose*,' Maddy said. 'A career highlight, you said, didn't you, Aidan?'

Aidan jerked his head towards Maddy, grinning at Esme. 'Anyone would think she was trying to get me some work. Unless you're looking to employ a maritime archaeologist?'

Esme laughed. 'No, I'm purely land based. Though since I've come to live in North Devon, I've felt quite connected with the sea and its history. Even more so now I've moved into a village right on the coast.'

'Must say I'm a tad envious. Wouldn't mind living around here myself.'

'You're not local, then?'

Aidan shook his head. 'Just here for work. I'm based in Dorset. Once I set everything up, I'll be around for a few weeks. Perhaps we could get together? Share our respective passions over a beer.'

Out of the corner of her eye, Esme saw a tiny smirk on Maddy's lips. She shifted her position to block Maddy out of her sight line.

'Working on the *Mary Rose* dive must have been incredible,' she said. 'I've been to the museum in Portsmouth. It's fabulous. I learned so much about the people who served on the ship. And all the artefacts they found. Well, *you* found.'

'Yeah, a once-in-a-lifetime opportunity, that's for sure.'

Maddy cleared her throat. 'Well, much as I'd love to hear you two natter on, I need to get back to Appledore. Still got a few things left to organise.'

Esme spun round. 'Oh, sorry, Maddy. Of course. You get on. I'll take over here.'

Aidan straightened up. 'Yeah, I should get going too. Assuming it's not still gridlocked out there.'

'Why? What's happened?' Maddy asked.

'Search me. It's not usually like that, then?'

'It can get a bit manic in high summer,' Maddy said. 'But not usually at this time of the year.'

He shrugged. 'Oh, well, perhaps it was a traffic accident or something. Great to meet you, Esme. Catch up with both you guys later.' He wheeled away and headed out of the market hall.

Maddy nudged Esme with her elbow. 'Well, you obviously

made an impression.'

Esme gave Maddy a half grin and rolled her eyes. 'Oh, give over, Madds,' she said. 'He was just being polite.'

Maddy laughed. 'Is that right? Well, we'll see, won't we, later this evening?'

'He's coming to your party?'

'Yes. Didn't you hear him say he'd catch up later?'

'I didn't think he meant it literally. So, what's your connection?'

'Dad knew him. He phoned up last week. Said he was coming down here on a recce for a job. Haven't seen him since Dad's funeral, so I invited him along.'

'That's kind of you. Nice for him to catch up with an old friend. Well, you know what I mean,' Esme added, feeling a bit foolish, being as Maddy's father Ted was no longer with them.

Maddy threw her bag over her shoulder and chuckled. 'Actually, I think he was probably more pleased to meet a new one.'

Despite herself, Esme giggled. 'Cut it out, Henderson. Get yourself away. You've got party preparations to attend to.'

Maddy winked and headed towards the exit. 'Oh,' she said, turning back, 'heard anything from Hester Campbell?'

Esme shook her head. 'No, nothing. I phoned, but she didn't pick up. Left a message, but...' she shrugged.

Maddy wrinkled her nose. 'Oh well. Early days,' she said, her expression thoughtful. 'Well, I'd better get going. See you later.'

# 5

When the market closed around lunchtime, Esme packed up the stall and heaped the unsold stock into the back of her car. After the final box had been stowed into the boot, Esme slammed down the lid and drove to Maddy's workshop, a short distance outside Bideford, to unload.

Maddy had taken on her father's furniture restoration and bric-a-brac business after he'd drowned in a boating incident. Ted had been teaching Maddy his trade and she'd decided it was a skill she was reluctant to give up. When Esme agreed to help out at the market stall, it gave Maddy the flexibility to attend antique fairs for finding new stock and restoration projects. The workshop itself had seen better days, but plans were in place for renovation of the old mill a short distance away and Maddy was looking forward to having more space, and to working in a building which didn't rattle alarmingly whenever the winter gales blew in from the Atlantic.

As Esme opened up the door, the wind caught it, snatching it out of her hand. She looked warily down towards the swirling muddy waters of the river below, noticing the rising tide. Something powerful was brewing out there.

With the stock back in place, Esme headed home to get ready for Maddy's house-warming party. Maddy and her partner Harry had recently set up home together, buying a place of their own not far from where Maddy's late father had lived. Maddy had invited Esme to stay over after the party, but a night away meant making arrangements for Jeanie and Ally to be fed. When she got home, Esme hurried down the lane to find her neighbour Libby who'd volunteered for the role. There was no one in the cottage itself, but Esme could see lights on in Libby's garden studio.

Esme went around the side of the cottage and down the steps

off the terrace and towards the tiny building where Libby worked, the wind flapping at her coat. When she reached the door, she paused. Perhaps she'd better not interrupt the sculptor in a moment of artistic muse. But before she could walk away, the door opened with a flourish, and Libby looked out, her customary denim smock over a roll-neck sweater and a cloth in her hand.

'Oh, sorry, Libby,' Esme said. 'I didn't mean to disturb you.'

'Don't be daft,' Libby said, flicking her long blonde plait over her shoulder. 'Saw you through the window. Come on in out of the wind. Gonna be a wild one, that's for sure. I'd just turned the TV on to watch the forecast.'

Esme stepped across the threshold, her eye drawn to the plethora of materials on the large table in the middle of the room – trays full of coloured liquid, saucers of mosaic tiles, pieces of cloth, mesh and chicken wire – along with a lump of wet clay Libby was in the middle of fashioning into shape. Many of her pieces were dominated by the colours of the pebbles of the village beach – slate greys, dark purples and oatmeal browns.

'This a commission?' Esme asked.

'I wish,' Libby said, wiping her hands on the cloth. 'No, just mucking about with some new ideas.' She dropped the cloth on to the table. 'So, what's new with you, then, Esme? You're off to that big bash tonight, aren't you?'

'Nothing quite so grand. It's just a house-warming party. But yes, that's why I came. Still OK to pop in and feed the cats?'

'Absolutely. My pleasure, bless 'em.'

'Thanks. I'll leave everything out for you. Well, you know the drill.'

Libby nodded. 'Yeah, no probs. Happy to help. Oh, here we go.' Libby picked up the remote and adjusted the sound of the TV.

'That explains it,' Esme said, as she saw Bideford Quay in the footage.

'Explains what?'

'Oh, a friend of Maddy's at the market today was saying town was heaving. It was probably due to that media circus. They're covering the new museum building.'

Libby peered at the screen. 'It's not open yet, is it? I thought it was months away.'

'Yes, it is, but it's some sort of satellite of *Treasures of the Sea Museum* in Bristol and it looks like they'd doing a bit of early publicity.'

'That's Isaac Maudesley, isn't it? Oh, I like him. He does a lot for history and for the arts. I actually met him once. Really nice guy. Oh, hang on. Here we go.'

Esme grimaced as the local presenter issued a Met Office amber weather warning of gales and heavy rain. 'Not a great night to go out, is it?'

'Well, I must admit there is something rather attractive about the thought of curling up on my sofa by the fire.'

'I think I'm inclined to agree with you.'

Libby shut off the TV. 'Well, at least you're staying over. And you'll be there before it really kicks off.'

'Yes, you're right. I'd better go and get my glad rags on, then, and get away sooner rather than later.'

'And I'll get back inside,' Libby said, switching off the lights and pulling her studio door closed behind her. 'And get that fire lit.'

They walked around Libby's cottage and parted at her front door.

'Have a lovely time,' Libby said, as Esme went to walk away. 'Oh, by the way,' she added. 'Did your friend find you?'

Esme paused and turned back. 'Friend?'

'Yeah. Scruffy bloke with a beard. He was peering in your sitting room window as I was walking up the lane a couple of days ago. I stopped and called out to him, like. Looked suspicious, as if he was casing the place. Reckoned he might have second thoughts if I let him know he'd been clocked. But turned out he knew you.'

'What did he say?'

'Well, that's just it. He said he was looking for you. No worries, he'd call again.'

'He used my name?'

Libby nodded. 'Which is why I dismissed him as being a random burglar. No bells, then?'

Esme shook her head. 'None.' She shrugged. 'Ah well, he'll be back, if he's kosher.'

'If I see him again, I'll get him to introduce himself. Didn't think about it at the time. Stupid, really.'

Esme thanked Libby and headed back up the lane, mulling over the identity of the mystery caller. As she climbed the front steps up to her cottage, she thought she heard someone behind her, but when she turned round, she realised it must have been the bushes on the opposite side of the stream being whipped by the wind. She pulled her coat around her and hurried inside.

# 6

The wind tugged at Esme's coat, flapping it around her legs as she walked from her car along the street to Maddy and Harry's new house. As she approached, she could hear the sound of music from inside. She stepped off the pavement and rapped the knocker. Maddy opened the front door and welcomed her inside, thanking her for the bottle of wine Esme put into her hand.

'This is wonderful,' Esme said, scanning around the room. Freshly painted whitewashed walls contrasted with the warm polished wooden floorboards, highlighted by brightly coloured cushions piled on the window seat overlooking the street outside. 'You've done an amazing job. It was pretty grim the last time I saw it, just after you'd got the keys.'

'Thanks,' Maddy said, wrinkling her nose. 'Still is pretty grim everywhere else, to be honest, but having done this bit, it seemed as good a time as any to have a party.'

Harry appeared from a tiny kitchen in the far corner of the cottage, a tea towel over his shoulder. 'Hi, Esme. Glad you could make it.'

'So am I. Looking forward to it. Looks great in here.'

'Yeah, bit different, eh?' He jerked his thumb back over his shoulder. 'Catch up with you later. Got a few things left to do.'

'Sure,' Esme said, nodding. 'You get on.'

'You'll want to dump your stuff,' Maddy said, nodding at Esme's overnight bag. 'Come on, I'll show you your room.'

Esme followed Maddy to the back of the room, past a patio door leading outside into a small courtyard garden and up a narrow set of stairs. On the next floor was a double bedroom, opposite which Maddy pointed out the bathroom before climbing another staircase which led up to an attic bedroom on the floor above.

'It's a bit basic, I'm afraid,' Maddy said, indicating the single bed and the chair beside it. 'But at least it's had a coat of paint.'

'Looks perfect to me,' Esme said, dropping her bag on the floor next to the chair. She slipped off her coat and threw it down on the bed. 'It's good of you to put me up.'

'Well, it's better than being on lemonade all evening, and then having to drive home,' Maddy said. She wandered over to the sloped roof-light window. 'Especially with the weather the way it's turning out.'

Esme joined her and they peered out beyond the rooftops to a glimpse of the sea. Street lamps had come on, and Esme could see rain being buffeted around in the pools of light.

'Perhaps it won't be as bad as they say.'

Maddy nodded. 'Let's hope.' She smiled. 'You look nice. Don't often see you in a dress.'

'Could say the same for you,' Esme said, grinning and admiring Maddy's floaty chiffon skirt, simple white sleeveless top and wide leather belt. She usually wore leggings and a hooded top. Esme glanced down at her own outfit, a V-necked navy jersey midi dress, flared from the waist. 'I bought this ages ago, but I'm not sure I can remember wearing it before.'

'Well, it looks fab,' Maddy said. She jerked her head towards the door. 'So, do you need a minute or two, or are you good to go?'

'Just a sec.' Esme unzipped her bag and took out a green batik silk scarf from inside, along with a small package. 'OK,' she said, draping the scarf around her shoulders. 'Ready. Lead on.'

They descended the steep stairs, Esme being careful not to catch the heels of her boots in the skirt of her dress. As they got closer to the ground floor, she could hear the sound of voices as party guests began to arrive. Esme scanned the room and noticed Harry by the window, talking to a man she recognised and a woman she didn't know. Harry said something to the couple, before crossing the room to join Esme and Maddy.

33

'Like your penthouse suite, then, Esme?' he said.

She laughed. 'I do indeed, thank you.' She held out the packet she'd brought with her from upstairs. 'While I've got you both here, I can give you this,' she said. 'House-warming present.'

'Oh, you didn't need to do that,' Maddy said, taking the package.

'Well, I couldn't resist it.'

Harry nudged Maddy with his elbow. 'Open it, then.'

Maddy unwrapped the paper to reveal a small wooden-framed sepia photograph of their cottage. Underneath was a short summary of the house's history and a list of its former occupants, which Esme had harvested from census records.

'Wow, Esme, that's fantastic.'

'What a great present,' Harry said, peering over Maddy's shoulder.

'Well, I can't claim it's my own idea,' Esme said, smiling at their reaction, 'but it seemed appropriate. And it was fun to put together. You won't be surprised to find a few mariners amongst the previous residents.'

'It's brilliant,' Maddy said, giving Esme a hug. 'It'll have pride of place.'

'Certainly will,' Harry agreed.

'Now,' Maddy said, laying her hand on Esme's arm, 'this is serious. You have no drink. What can I get you? White wine?'

Esme nodded. 'Perfect, thanks.'

'Right, back in a sec,' Maddy said and hurried away.

Harry turned back to the couple he'd been talking to when she'd come in and guided Esme over to meet them. 'You remember Jamie, don't you, Esme?'

'Of course,' Esme said. 'How are you, Jamie?' He was a volunteer at the local lifeboat station, a short jog away down the street, and was still sporting the RNLI baseball cap she'd seen him wearing when they'd met before. Jamie's evidence had been crucial a few months ago in solving a mystery involving Maddy's father and an unsavoury character associated with the family who owned the workshop Maddy rented.

'Great, thanks,' Jamie said. 'Good to see you again.' He threw a glance at the blonde-haired woman standing beside him, dressed in skinny jeans and a sparkly pink off-the-shoulder pullover. 'This is Beth.'

'Hi, Beth,' Esme said, with a nod. 'Nice to meet you.'

Beth smiled. 'Same here. I heard about what happened. Glad everything worked out.'

'All thanks to Jamie,' Esme said. 'So pleased he came forward when he did.'

Jamie coloured and shrugged, throwing a self-conscious glance at Harry. Harry had been the one who'd convinced him he needed to speak out about what he'd seen.

'Your glass is empty, Beth,' Harry said, holding out his hand. 'Top up?'

'Yes, please. Just tonic water.' Harry nodded and took her glass before peeling away towards the kitchen.

'So, how's life on the ocean waves?' Esme asked. 'Been busy at the lifeboat station?'

'Sure,' Jamie said. 'Been on quite a few shouts lately, haven't we, Beth?'

'You a volunteer, too, then?' Esme said.

Beth grinned. 'For my sins, yeah.'

Jamie jerked a thumb towards a small device attached to his belt. 'We're hoping these don't go off and spoil the party. Literally.'

'Amen to that,' Beth said, laughing. 'I really don't fancy going out on a night like this.'

'No, don't blame you,' Esme said. 'Let's hope all would-be sailors are either moored up in the harbour or have opted to stay put at home.'

Maddy arrived with Esme's wine and Beth's refreshed tonic water, before hurrying off to answer another knock at the door.

More people arrived, crowding good-naturedly into the living room and greeting mutual friends. Esme chatted to Beth for a while about how she'd got involved in the Royal National Lifeboat Institute. Her father had been a coxswain for years, and she'd grown up visiting the lifeboat station for as long as she could remember and had joined the RNLI at the earliest opportunity, on her 17th birthday.

When a friend of Beth's arrived, Esme left them talking and wandered into the kitchen to top up her glass. The party was well underway by now, laughter and chat almost drowning out the music playing in the background. In the kitchen, two women were in deep conversation about the woeful lack of childcare for working mothers. They smiled and acknowledged Esme's arrival before returning to their discussion.

Esme helped herself to a few roasted cashew nuts from the bowlfuls of snacks set out on the worktop and, after filling her glass from a bottle of Pinot Grigio in the fridge, wandered back into the living room. The patio doors were open and the party had spilled outside into the garden. She made her way across the room and peered out. The rain had eased, but the wind was still in evidence, eddying around the courtyard space, flapping hair around people's faces and skirts around legs.

Maddy was standing on the steps leading up to the small terrace, talking to someone. Esme realised with a jolt that it was Aidan. He was wearing a roll-necked sweater and a leather jacket. He must have arrived while she was in the kitchen.

'Ah, there you are,' Maddy said, spotting her. 'Come and keep Aidan company while I go and find him a beer.'

Esme climbed the steps to reach them, noticing as she got higher that she could see the sea in the distance. Maddy tapped Aidan's arm.

'You can tell Esme about this job of yours. She was saying only the other day that she's not been to Lundy.'

'You're going to be working on Lundy?' Esme said, as Maddy

disappeared inside.

'Not on the island. In the waters around it.'

'A shipwreck, then, I assume, given your line of work?' Esme said. 'How fascinating. What sort of wreck? I was reading the other day there are well over a hundred around Lundy.'

'One hundred and thirty-seven at the last count, I believe,' Aidan said, nodding.

'And is it one of those?'

Aidan gave her a knowing smile. 'Can't say much about it at the moment.' He winked. 'Sworn to secrecy.'

Esme grinned. 'Well, sounds all very mysterious and exciting. So, what are the chances of finding lost treasure round here?'

'Depends where you look. There was a discovery in Salcombe a few years ago.' A wistful smile settled across Aidan's face. 'Now *that's* a dive I'd have loved to have been a part of. A team of amateurs found it. They dived the site whenever they could over a number of years before it was made public, eventually bringing up hundreds of pieces of gold, which are now on display in the British Museum. The divers were convinced it belonged to Barbary pirates, though there's some speculation about that.'

Maddy arrived with Aidan's beer and shoved it into his hand. 'I'm going inside,' she said, shivering. 'It's getting cold out here. I'll leave you to it.' She hurried back indoors.

'You warm enough out here?' Aidan said, looking at Esme with concern. 'Or would you rather go back inside?'

Esme flushed under his gaze. 'No, I'm fine for the moment. Thank you.' She pulled the scarf tightly around her neck and took a sip of her wine.

Aidan looked up into the sky. 'Wind's picking up. Be gale force before long at this rate.'

She followed his gaze up into the blackness, dark shadows of cloud passing rapidly overhead. 'It's been building up to this all day,' she said, looking across to the patch of dark sea still visible in the distance between the buildings. 'I'm glad I'm not out there in a small boat.'

Aidan said something in reply, but his words were ripped away in a sudden gust which pulled at Esme's hair, threatening to dislodge the clasp at the back of her head. She put up her hand to grab it before the wind snatched it away completely.

'I think Maddy might be right about going back in...' she began, before the piercing sound of electronic beeping cut through the air, coupled with the shrill call of the siren from the lifeboat station in the distance. She saw Beth and Jamie hurriedly disappear through the patio doors in response. Harry came rushing up the steps past them and stopped at the top of the garden, staring out seawards, his face grim. Esme and Aidan followed, others joining them.

From the top terrace, everyone looked out across the roofs, the wind buffeting their faces. In the small pools of light from the street lamps along the edge of the seawall, Esme could make out the threatening, undulating swell of water in the distance. She shuddered, sensing everyone's trepidation, imagining what lay ahead for the lifeboat crew once it launched into the dark boiling mass of the sea.

# 7

Within minutes, the faint but familiar orange of Appledore's all-weather-class lifeboat appeared, its on-board lights oscillating alarmingly against the churning waves. The partygoers watched mesmerised as the boat disappeared out into the darkness, turning away when they could see no more, the atmosphere dampened now by events and concern for a launch in such horrendous conditions. Conversations became muted and the vibrancy of earlier in the evening fizzled out. Slowly, people said their goodbyes and the house emptied until there was only Esme, Harry, Maddy and Aidan left.

Harry stood up and began collecting discarded glasses. 'You can tell he works in a pub, can't you?' Maddy teased, getting up to join him. Esme and Aidan stood up together. 'No, you don't,' Maddy said, flapping a hand at them both. 'Won't take us long to clear the decks. You stay where you are.' She grabbed a handful of glasses and followed Harry into the kitchen.

Esme perched on the edge of the sofa and fiddled with the stem of her glass, feeling oddly conspicuous. She downed the last dregs of her wine.

'Want a fill up?' Aidan asked, leaning towards her and holding out his hand.

'No, I'm fine, thanks,' she said, shaking her head. She smiled. 'I'm sure I've had more than enough.' She cradled her empty glass, considering taking it into the kitchen, but didn't want to move. 'I think everyone had a good time, don't you?' she said. 'Despite the interruption.' She glanced out of the uncurtained patio doors, rain lashing against the glass, and thought about the lifeboat crew. 'I hope they'll be all right out there. I think it's extraordinary what they do, going out in all weathers because someone needs their help. True heroes.'

'*With courage, nothing is impossible.*' Esme turned to look at Aidan and he smiled. 'The institution's motto,' he said. 'Sentiment of its founder, Sir William Hillary.'

'I didn't realise. Says it all, really, doesn't it?'

'Yes, it does. It still takes guts to head out to sea in gale-force winds, despite the impressive standard of lifeboats these days.' Aidan rubbed his chin. 'Appledore have a Tamar. One of the best for safety. Self-righting and with the latest shock-absorbing seats for the crew. And they need it. Hitting a large wave full-on is like crashing into a wall of concrete.'

'You seem very knowledgeable,' Esme said, looking at him curiously. 'You ever been a volunteer?'

Aidan shook his head. 'No, doesn't really fit in with my work, being away from home a lot. I've always had an interest, though, growing up on the coast.'

'So it's in your blood, then, the sea.'

Aidan jerked his chin. 'You could say so. I always knew I'd have to find a career where the sea featured somewhere.'

Esme swivelled the glass between her fingers. 'I moved down here not so long ago from Shropshire, but I spent most of my childhood holidays in this area. It seemed the right time to come back and live here permanently.'

'But you'd never been to Lundy during those childhood holidays? Maddy mentioned something earlier.'

Esme shook her head. 'My mum wasn't keen on boats so it never happened. But it's something I intend to rectify – next week, in actual fact.' She glanced out into the inky black through the window and wrinkled her nose. 'I hope the weather calms down before then or it could be a bit too wild for my sea legs.'

Maddy came back into the room, yawning, Harry following behind. Aidan got to his feet.

'Well, I'd better get back and let you guys get some sleep.'

'Oh, sorry, Aidan,' Maddy said with a wry smile. 'I wasn't hinting, honest.'

Aidan grinned. 'No, you're OK. I need my bed too. It was a great party. Thanks for the invite.' He gave Esme a nod. 'Good to see you again, Esme.'

Esme smiled. 'You too.'

Aidan headed for the front door, Harry following to show him out.

'You two seem to have hit it off,' Maddy said, as soon as they were out of earshot.

'Yes, he's very easy-going.' Esme stood up, determined to ignore the tease she could detect in Maddy's comment. 'Thanks for a lovely evening. Both of you,' she added, as Harry returned.

'You're very welcome,' Maddy said. 'Glad you had a good time.'

'Want some help clearing up?' Esme asked.

'Nah,' Harry said, stretching. 'That can wait till the morning. You get yourself off to bed.'

Esme nodded and escaped to her room.

As she climbed into bed and turned out the light, the rattling of the rain hurling itself against the window sounded louder than ever. She snuggled under the duvet, thinking of the RNLI crew battling through the storm. Were Jamie and Beth out there? Who had needed their help?

She eventually fell into a fretful sleep, dreams dominated by images of rough seas, lifeboats climbing waves as high as houses, and with Aidan's words echoing in her head, *with courage, nothing is impossible.*

# 8

When Esme woke, she sensed it was well on in the morning. She picked up her phone from the chair beside the bed and squinted at the time. Just gone 9 o'clock. Not as bad as she'd feared.

She threw back the duvet and padded out on to the landing where she could hear voices coming from below. She peered over the banister, and seeing the bathroom door standing open, decided to grab a shower before joining her hosts.

By the time she'd got dressed and was on her way downstairs, the voices had gone quiet and she found Maddy on her own in the kitchen, sitting at the table, staring at her phone, a mug and a half empty cafetière beside her.

'Morning. Sleep OK?' Maddy said, getting to her feet. 'Coffee? Tea?'

'Tea, thanks,' Esme said, pulling out a chair and sitting down. 'Not bad. How about you?'

'So, so. Bit of a head, but nothing a couple of paracetamol can't fix.' She filled the kettle and switched it on before taking a mug out of the cupboard.

'And Harry?'

'Fine. He's gone out to get the low-down on last night's shout. Should be back in a minute.'

Esme looked out of the window at the heavy sky. 'The storm's passed, then. It was still pretty wild when we called it a night.'

'Sorry, your bedroom's on the worst side when there's a south-westerly.' Maddy dropped a teabag in the mug and filled it with boiling water.

'Not a problem, honestly. I dropped off pretty quickly, considering. Just dreamt about gales, high seas and lifeboats, that's all.'

Maddy slid the mug of tea across the table to Esme, along with a carton of milk, and sat back down. 'Yes, I don't know how they do it.'

'That's what Aidan and I were saying just before he went,' Esme said, turning towards the sound of the front door opening. A few seconds later, Harry appeared into the kitchen.

'Hi, Esme, how you doing?'

'I'm good, thanks. Did you find out what happened last night?'

'Some, yeah.' Harry took off his jacket and slipped it on the back of the chair next to Esme before taking a seat. 'Any coffee left?'

'I'll make some fresh,' Maddy said, standing up to flip the kettle switch. 'So, who did you see?'

'Jamie was down there, along with a few other crew members. You know how they all support one another after a difficult shout.'

'So, go on,' Maddy said. 'Tell us. What happened?'

Harry rested his arms on the table. 'They'd had a report of a boat in trouble, heading for rocks. Engine failure, probably. Coastguard said people had been spotted on board.'

'Who called it in?' Maddy asked.

'A guy out walking his dog.'

'I'm surprised he could see anything last night.'

'Well, that's just it. It wasn't that far out at that point.'

Maddy put a mug and the fresh coffee pot on the table and sat down. 'So did they find it?'

'They found the boat, yeah. But no one in it. They did a sweep as best they could – well, you know what the conditions were like – but no sign of anyone. They assumed they'd been swept overboard and had gone into the water.'

Esme shuddered, thinking of the storm of the night before. 'How terrifying.'

Maddy chewed her bottom lip and gave her head a shake. 'Oh, that's never good. That would have piled on the pressure for the crew. Chances of dying of hypothermia are massive once you're in the water.'

'Yeah,' Harry agreed. 'Seconds mean everything. But then, just when they were thinking it was going to be like last time, one of the guys saw a figure in the water. And then another.'

Maddy put her hand across her chest. 'Thank God. How many?'

'Three all told. A fella, his wife and daughter.' Harry grabbed the cafetière and poured some coffee into the mug. 'They hauled them into the lifeboat and made it back to shore pretty quickly. But they weren't in great condition. They're waiting to hear back from the hospital.'

'God, that's awful,' Maddy said, echoing everyone's thoughts.

'How are the crew?' Esme asked.

'As you'd expect,' Harry said, cradling his mug. 'Jamie and Beth were both pretty subdued with things still hanging in the balance. Saving lives is what they train for. It's hard when a shout doesn't have a good outcome.' He took a sip of coffee.

'Well, there's still a chance it will,' Esme said, picking up her mug of tea. 'They got them out of the water and they're now in the best possible place. We just have to keep our fingers crossed.'

\*

It was late morning before Esme got back home, the fate of the RNLI casualties preying on her mind. She dealt with the kittens and phoned Libby to thank her for looking after them. After a bite of lunch, she wondered whether she should spend the afternoon tackling the old outhouse.

She wandered down the garden path, unlocked the door and stood on the threshold, her good intentions evaporating at the sight of the chaos within, the many years of accumulated junk. If she'd been sensible and tackled the job weeks ago, as intended, she wouldn't be under so much pressure to get it done. She could have taken some pleasure in browsing the eclectic mix of old furniture, books, bric-a-brac, paintings, newspapers, magazines and bundles of papers, hunting for an intriguing find or perhaps some small item for Maddy to renovate and sell on her market stall. As it was, a leisurely trawl through the contents of the building was out of the question, with the builder's starting date rapidly approaching. She must give the task priority over the next few days.

But where to start? There was hardly any space, nowhere to move A to B, to order what was needed. A large wardrobe dominated the centre – goodness knows what was hidden behind that – and the heaped items sitting on top of tables and desks needed to be off-loaded to somewhere. And that somewhere didn't exist, or it was similarly covered in other heaps of rejected household bits and pieces, chipped crockery, enamel plates, a rusted-out barbecue, a cobweb-covered bag of charcoal sitting on top of the broken grill.

She picked up an old print of a sailing boat, brushing the dust away with the sleeve of her coat, prompting the memory of the lifeboat crew being called out and wondering how the casualties were faring in hospital. As if her thoughts had conjured up the answer to her question, her phone rang. She put down the painting and pulled the phone out of her pocket, glancing at the screen with a stab of concern.

'Maddy. Any news?'

'Yes, and it's all good,' Maddy said, relief clear in her voice. 'They're going to make it. All three are out of danger. '

'Oh, that's so good to hear,' Esme said, letting out a long sigh. 'Thanks for letting me know.' She dragged a small stool out from underneath a table piled high with dining chairs and cardboard boxes, and plonked herself down on it. 'Another success for the crew. They must be delighted.'

'Yes, they are. On a real high. The coxswain said when they'd seen the empty boat, they'd worried it was going to be the same scenario as a few months back.'

'Was that the one they decided must have pulled free from its moorings?'

'Eventually, yes. But it didn't stop the anxious wait, expecting a body to wash up, feeling they'd failed.'

'No, it can't be easy to return to the station having not achieved what they set out to do.' Esme knew Maddy would be thinking of her father, who'd drowned while negotiating the infamous and dangerous Bideford Bar, a sandbank in the Taw and Torridge Estuary.

'Anyway,' Maddy said, 'I knew you'd be waiting for news.'

'Yes, I was.' Esme glanced at the painting she'd discarded when Maddy's call came in. 'In fact, I was just thinking about them the minute you rang.'

'What are you up to?'

Esme groaned. 'I'm about to tackle the nightmare of converting my junk-filled outbuilding into a slick and aesthetically pleasing office space.' She scanned the dusty piles of unwanted jumble around her. 'I'm sure there's more here than there was before. It's going to take ages.'

'You have my sympathies. I remember what it was like when I cleared Dad's place out. Well, you know. You were there.'

'The worst of it is it's not even my junk.'

'Yes, but look at it this way. If you hadn't agreed to take it on, you might still be waiting to get in your cottage. Which is worse?'

Esme sighed. 'Yes, you're right. It would be very frustrating to have had to delay the sale.'

'Did I hear you tell Aidan that you're visiting Lundy next week?'

Esme stood up. 'You did, yes. And if I'm giving myself the day off to go, I need to earn it by making a start on this hell-hole.'

Maddy laughed. 'Yes, you better had. Good luck!'

# 9

Sunday afternoon's session in the outhouse made minimal impact on the overall task, but Esme cheered herself with the thought that filling two bin bags with rubbish must count as some sort of progress. She got up the following day determined to make further headway, but after a hard morning's work, her expectation that she'd have broken the back of the job by now was looking over optimistic. As she looked around, it was difficult not to be disheartened at how much was still left to do.

She brushed off her grubby fingers and picked up the next consignment of bin bags, aware her stomach was grumbling. She took the bags to the dustbin, before going into the cottage to clean herself up and fix herself something to eat.

After she'd eaten, she decided she'd earned herself a break. She grabbed her coat and went back outside, pulling up the hood against the stiff breeze as she descended the front steps into the lane. As she turned down towards the coast, her thoughts drifted away from the chaotic outbuilding and back to her client Hester Campbell, who'd still not returned her calls.

Esme revisited her theory as to whether Hester's reaction to the news of the murder indicated she already knew about it, had perhaps previously dismissed it as an exaggerated family story. Now, to discover it was true had come as a shock. And yet Esme felt that didn't quite fit Hester's reaction. It had been astonishment rather than shock, as though it was the last thing she'd expected. There was a subtle difference. But even that wasn't completely convincing and no matter how many times Esme had gone over the conversation, she couldn't identify what message she was missing.

One thing Esme *was* certain about, though, was the more time passed without Hester getting in touch, the less likely Esme was to hear from her again.

She sighed and, thrusting her hands in the pockets of her duffel, strode on down the lane, the wind buffeting around inside her hood. She passed the cluster of cottages at the bottom of the hill and continued down the footpath, beyond the artists' cabin and on towards the beach.

The tide was coming in, waves a churning swirl of teal green and foam as they crashed on to the dark pebbles, powering their way up the shingle. She descended the ramp and crunched on to the beach. Ahead of her near the overhanging cliff, someone in a bright yellow coat was bending down, gathering stones and dried seaweed from along the high tide line. When Esme got closer, she saw it was Libby.

As Esme walked towards her, Libby looked up and waved.

'Find anything interesting?' Esme said, when she got within earshot.

Libby opened her palm and held it out. 'Couple of quite nice stones,' she said, smoothing the surfaces with her fingers. She slipped them into her pocket and looked out to sea. 'Not that I was looking, particularly. Just force of habit. I really only came out for a breath of air.'

'Same here. Needed to blow the cobwebs away – literally. And the dust. I've made a start on the outhouse sorting.'

'Oh, brave, very brave.' Libby smiled and shuddered. 'All those spiders.'

'I don't mind the spiders so much, they run away. It's what they leave behind that's the problem. Flies' bodies and strands of web which stick to everything. Yuk.'

Libby laughed. 'Sounds revolting.' She looked out to sea. 'Good, the storm's eased.' She hugged herself. 'I was thinking about those brave souls on the lifeboat. Rather them than me. It amazes me how they go out in all weathers. And all volunteers, too. I'm in total awe of what they do.'

'Me too. I was so relieved to hear the casualties pulled

through.'

'Oh, before I forget,' Libby said. 'Did that friend ever get in touch, the scruffy guy?'

Esme shook her head. 'Reckon he was having you on that he knew me.'

'He knew your name, though.'

Esme shrugged. 'Probably been poking around in my recycling bin. That'll teach me to put addressed envelopes in there, won't it?' Something caught her eye to her right in the distance and she turned her head to focus on it.

Libby followed her line of sight. 'What are you looking at?'

'That's the second time recently I've seen someone in the far cove over there. Where is it? Looks an interesting little beach.'

Libby peered in the direction Esme indicated. 'Not sure. I didn't think those coves were accessible other than by sea. You saw someone?'

'Well, I thought I did.' Esme blinked and pinched the bridge of her nose, before turning back to gaze out at the horizon. 'Perhaps it's my eyes playing tricks on me. Too much screen time, probably. I'm sure it gets worse as I get older.'

Libby looked at her and smiled, her eyes wide. 'Maybe it's a ghost?' She gave a soft laugh. 'Funny, this beach always makes me think of a ghost story I once read. Can't remember the title. Something about the waves being haunted. Oh, no, wait a minute. *The Children of the Waves*, that was it.'

'Spooky you should say that,' Esme said, glancing towards the cove. 'I'm fairly sure it was a child I saw, a little boy, I think.' She turned back to Libby. 'So what happened in your story?'

Libby chewed her lower lip. 'I can't quite remember the details, but it had something to do with the current pulling a girl down under the water.'

Esme shivered. 'That must happen a lot along this coast. The rip tides around here are notorious. Terrifying if it happens to you, I'd imagine.'

'There was something about her being taken to atone for something,' Libby continued. 'A sacrifice, something like that. The rest of it escapes me, but it was quite creepy.'

'Sounds like one of those stories you share with a group of people sitting round a fire on a dark, cold night.'

Libby laughed. 'Yes, you're right there.' She turned to look back along the coast. 'Perhaps you should do some of your digging, Esme. Find out if a child *did* ever drown in that cove. Then you'll know it's an apparition. Now that *would* be spooky!'

# 10

'Did she recognise someone?' Maddy said, as Esme said goodbye to an elderly lady in a tartan headscarf at Tuesday's market.

'She thinks so, yes.' Esme pointed to a photograph pinned to the *Photos Reunited* display board. It was of a young woman with 1920s-style cropped hair, dressed in a servant's uniform. 'She's given me a name, Ethel Murray,' she added, glancing down at her notepad. 'Not a relative of hers, though. Someone she knew as a child. She remembers seeing a photo like this on the lady's sideboard. Apparently, she was always fascinated by the frilly apron and oversized mob cap.'

'So, was Ethel in service?'

'Worked in a large hotel, apparently. She said she'd love to know where. It was somewhere local, she thinks.'

'Well, it'd be nice to have another success,' Maddy said, leaning back against the stall. 'They've been a bit thin on the ground of late. By the way, keep meaning to ask. Anything from Hester yet?'

'Not a thing.'

'Mmm. It is odd, isn't it? Had any more thoughts about what freaked her out?'

'Not really.' Esme rubbed her finger along her scar and peered up at the photograph of Ethel Murray. 'The 1920s seem more in touching distance than, say, something that happened in the 1800s, don't they? Maybe that's it.'

'Yeah, but we're still talking 100 years ago. I can't imagine that'd be the issue.'

Esme dropped the notebook into her bag. 'No, it seems unlikely. Well, if she does ever get in touch, you can be sure I'll ask her. It's an interesting case, though.'

'You said it was about a family dispute and that Philips was very tight lipped about the reason for their disagreement.'

'Yes, I think it was probably that which made it such a cause célèbre.'

'So, what's your theory? You must have thought about it.'

'I did wonder whether he thought it might prejudice his own defence if he'd owned up to what had been going on between the two of them.'

'Between a rock and a hard place, you mean. Even so, bit of a gamble to keep schtum.'

'A huge gamble, yes,' Esme agreed. 'Which he lost, as he was found guilty and hanged.'

Maddy tugged at her ponytail. 'So, without knowing what he was trying to hide, it's hard to judge if it would have made any difference to the outcome.'

'The jury clearly took his silence as a sign of guilt, and as he didn't present any mitigating circumstances, there was only one way it was ever going to go.'

Maddy looked thoughtful. 'I wonder if anyone else in the family had any idea of what it was all about?'

'If they did, they weren't saying. Or they knew anything they did say wasn't likely to have improved his situation.'

Maddy grinned. 'So, are you all fired up to find out? You don't need Hester to come back to you. Surely your inquisitive little brain would just love to get to the bottom of it.'

Esme rolled her eyes. 'Oh, don't tempt me. But I daren't. Not at the moment, anyway. I'm under too much pressure to get that outbuilding cleared. I have to give that priority or I'll lose my builder's slot. If I put him off, I'll have to wait months before he can fit me in again.'

'I can come and give you a hand clearing, if you like.'

Esme frowned and shook her head. 'Oh, I couldn't do that, Madds. It's very good of you to offer, but you've got plenty to do yourself, with having just moved in. All that decorating you were telling me about. I can't steal your time like that.'

Maddy flapped her hand. 'Oh, one day's not going to make any

52

difference to my long list, whereas the two of us could probably sort your outhouse out in that time. Break the back of it, anyway. Besides, it would reciprocate for when you helped me sort out Dad's house.'

Esme considered. 'Well, if you're absolutely sure. Thanks. I can't deny it would be a great help. And who knows,' she added, gesturing at the display on the market stall, 'we might even find something for you to renovate and add to the stock.'

'There you are, then,' Maddy said. 'Win-win.'

\*

Esme woke on Wednesday morning with a sense of anticipation for the day ahead and Maddy's help in tackling the contents of the outbuilding. The weather forecast looked promising – not sunny, but muted cloud giving a mellow light and no rain expected, which was perfect, as they needed a dry day. Any chance of making meaningful progress depended on being able to offload everything which was blocking their way on to the path outside, giving them the space to sift through the rest of the Aladdin's cave of junk.

Maddy arrived early and they decided the sooner they started, the sooner they'd finish.

'It's such a pretty little garden you've got here, Esme,' Maddy said, as Esme led the way down the path to the stone building. 'The primroses are absolutely gorgeous.'

Esme stopped and looked across at the border Maddy was admiring. 'They're beautiful, but they're getting rather out of control.' She laughed. 'That's another job I must find time for. But I can't think about it yet. Not until this outhouse is sorted, anyway.' She stepped on to the grass and stared down at the tiny flowers, splashes of sulphur yellow zinging brightly in the dull day. 'I'll split you some, if you like, when I get around to it?'

'Oh, yes please,' Maddy said. 'And anything else you've got going begging,' she added, looking round. 'Those little blue flowers there, if you've got any spare, under the bush. Oh, poor things. Looks like someone's trampled all over them.'

Esme peered across to where Maddy was pointing and frowned. 'The builder, probably, when he was standing back to appraise the roof.' She turned back to the path. 'Well, we'd better not get distracted or we'll never get started.' They continued down the path and Esme slipped the key into the lock. 'Oh great. The perfect start,' she groaned.

'Why, what is it?'

'Lock's jammed. Oh, no, hang on. It isn't. It wasn't locked. I must have left it open last time I was here.' She remembered being desperate for a break from the dust and cobwebs, so she must have forgotten to lock up when she'd gone back to the cottage for something to eat. 'Not that there's much here that's going to be of interest to any burglars,' she said, pulling the door open to show Maddy. 'See what I mean?'

Maddy laughed. 'I take your point. Then again, who knows what we'll find? All part of the fun.'

They decided to begin with the furniture closest to the door to give them access to one half of the floor space. As they worked diligently, dragging things outside on to the flagstone path, Maddy picked out a couple of small side tables on which she thought she could work her restoration magic. The rest, she said, might find a home with an associate of hers who dealt in second-hand furniture. By the time they'd cleared a small area of floor, only a pine farmhouse kitchen table with a wonky leg remained, along with a roll-topped desk, both of which Esme hoped might be salvageable.

'Well, it definitely feels like we're making headway,' Esme said, looking round. 'With more room to move about, it makes it easier to see what's left to do.' She nodded towards the wardrobe and a large chest of drawers creating a wall in the middle of the room. 'That lot can wait for another day. But apart from that, it's not looking anywhere near as daunting as it was. So thanks, Madds.'

'You're very welcome.'

They decided to pause for a well-earned coffee. Esme took her drink over to the pine table and began picking through the numerous cardboard boxes sitting on top. Most were filled with discarded household items: saucepans, chipped crockery, and bags of faded curtains and cushion covers, many of them with holes in the fabric, suggesting mice had used them to harvest nest material.

'Nothing very exciting in there,' she said, wrinkling her nose at the smell.

Underneath the table were more boxes, this time full of dusty old books. As she bent down to take a closer look, her eye was caught by a stack of pictures and empty frames leaning up against the side of the desk. She crouched down and flipped through the stack. Most were faded paintings, water damaged and probably past saving. One, larger than the rest, seemed in better condition.

She put down her mug of coffee on the floor and pulled it out for a closer look. It was a print of an old map and, although it had lost much of its definition, she could see that it showed the village and its ribbon development running down to the sea.

'Anything interesting?' Maddy said, coming over.

Esme held it out for her to see. 'Map of this area. Might clean up enough to keep.'

'Looks 17th century, to me,' Maddy said, 'judging by the writing. It's wonderfully pictorial, isn't it?'

Esme looked around the room. 'I could hang it up over there, maybe,' she added, indicating the opposite wall.

'I'll clean up the frame for you if you like,' Maddy said, running her finger along it. 'Nice bit of oak, there.'

'That'd be great, thanks. But no rush. It'll be a while before this place is habitable enough to be thinking of pictures on the wall.'

Maddy propped herself against the desk and took a sip of her coffee. 'So, what are you going to do with this lot?'

Esme scratched her head and sighed. 'I can't imagine there's much here of interest to anyone. It's mostly junk.'

Maddy nodded at the frames. 'I know a guy in Bideford who'd be happy to take those, I'm sure. He'll clean them up and reuse them for framing other pictures. He'll give you something for them, too, as long as they're in reasonable condition.' She picked up one and inspected it. 'Can't see any sign of woodworm, which is good. I'll give you his number.'

Esme nodded. 'That'd be great. All helps to add to the coffers for paying for the building work, too.'

'Right,' Maddy said, downing the last of her coffee. 'I suppose we'd better get back to it.'

*

By the end of the day, Esme was encouraged by their achievements. Smaller items had been sorted into boxes – a few for keeping, some for charity shops and the rest destined for disposal at the local recycling centre. Dealing with the larger pieces of furniture, they'd concluded, would need use of a van and an extra pair of hands. Maddy was sure Harry would be happy to help and before she left, she called him and made the necessary arrangements.

After feeding the kittens and eating her own evening meal, Esme fetched the framed map from upstairs where she'd put it for safekeeping and laid it down on the kitchen table. She carefully wiped the glass with a damp cloth, revealing the detail of the map as it emerged from behind the dust, before sitting down to study her find.

On the left hand side were the words *THE FAMILIES THAT HAVE BENE DIGNIFIED WITH THE TITLE OF DEVONSHIRE*, but there it ended, suggesting that Esme's version was only a section of the complete map. Villages in the area were denoted by the icon of what she assumed to be a church, their names alongside. Her own village wasn't marked, having only become a settlement worthy of the name considerably later than the date of the map in front of her. But she was intrigued to see a name in the bay where the current village met the sea: *Chalacombe Mouthe*. The name Chalacombe appeared again, in an inlet a little further along. It was approximately in the location of the cove she and Libby had talked about only a couple of days before.

Intrigued, Esme grabbed her laptop and, after booting it up, negotiated her way to the National Library of Scotland's website of old maps. She typed in the name of the village and looked at the options. The oldest map available to view was dated 1884. She clicked on the image and watched as it filled the screen.

She scrolled along the coast to where she'd seen the named inlet. But nothing appeared there which had been on the older map. As she pondered on this omission, she noticed a narrow track leading inland, indicated by a dotted line. She scanned out so she could see the bigger picture and followed the track until it came to a black shaded outline of a building, surrounded by woodland. Its name echoed that of the inlet and the bay, denoted in cursive script as *Chalacombe House*.

She went over to the bookcase and pulled out her current Ordnance Survey map and opened it out, running her finger along the coast until she came to the corresponding place to the screen display. Like the map of 1884, neither the bay nor the cove was named. The house was marked still, but it now had no name attributed to it. She must take a walk along the coast path sometime soon and investigate.

But now, she thought as she glanced up at the clock, it was time to put away the maps and explore the Chalacombe mysteries another day. Tomorrow was her visit to Lundy and the chance to learn about the island's fascinating history. She couldn't wait.

# 11

Esme hurried out of the cottage into the brisk chill of the dawn, pulling the front door closed behind her. She needed to be at the offices of the MS *Oldenburg*, Lundy Island's ferry and supply ship, at 7.30 am, half an hour before it sailed.

As she walked over to her car, she saw Jim striding up the lane and called good morning to him.

'Looks like them weather gods have smiled on you, maid,' he said, chuckling. 'Flat calm and blue sky, just like you wanted.'

'I know,' Esme said, throwing her rucksack into the boot. 'I can hardly believe it, given what it was like earlier this week.'

'Ah well, that be the British weather for you. Now, you be having y'self a good time.'

She arrived in Bideford ahead of schedule, parked her car and made her way along the quay to join the queue waiting to board. No doubt the large number of passengers were taking advantage of the benign weather. According to Jim, the ship had the capacity to carry over 200 people. As Esme stepped on to a metal gangway displaying a banner emblazoned with the ship's name, she could easily believe every ticket had been sold.

Once on deck, she found herself a seat on a slatted bench with a good view over the rail and out to sea. She sat down beside a silver-haired man dressed in olive-green waterproofs, a large-lensed camera around his neck, guessing he and the rest of his group, similarly equipped, were bird enthusiasts. Esme learned that there had been reports of a Great Skua being spotted off the island and he and his fellow birders were hoping for a sighting.

'It's rare to see the notorious pirate of the seas in our neck of the woods,' he said. 'He'll be on his way to the Scottish islands. That's where they breed.'

The boat headed down the estuary, over the infamous

Bideford Bar and out into open sea. Jim had told Esme she may see dolphins on her way, but although she kept her eyes on the waves, scanning the surface, she saw no sign.

About halfway across, a patch of fog appeared from nowhere, enveloping the ship and bathing the passengers on deck in a damp chill. Esme was thankful she'd dressed warmly, despite the promise of the favourable day. She dug into her backpack and fished out a woollen hat, pulling it over her head as the crew distributed blankets to those not so well prepared.

By the time they arrived at the island, the fog had lifted, revealing the clear blue sky of earlier, allowing Esme to look up and see the granite cliffs above as the ship sailed into the landing beach and tied up at the quay. The passengers disembarked and began climbing the steep, rough track, passing a large, plain-but-elegant classic-styled house, its tall sash windows offering stunning views down the wooded valley and out to sea. Esme overheard someone say it had belonged to the Heaven family who'd purchased the island in the 1830s.

The track finally reached a cluster of stone buildings linked by cobbled paths. The stream of visitors slowed and Esme realised they'd arrived at the village.

By now, people were beginning to disperse in different directions, some heading for the island's pub, *The Marisco Tavern,* and others striding off along paths leading away from the settlement. Esme continued ahead, wandering along between the buildings, and discovered the island store which, she found on going inside, sold everything from gifts for day trippers to an impressive range of provisions for residents and visitors staying in the many historic buildings on the island or at the campsite nearby, hidden behind a wall built with granite boulders.

She bought a book on the island and an Ordnance Survey map before emerging back into the sunshine. In the distance, she could see St Helen's church against the skyline, its clean, crisp edges seeming strangely incongruous compared with the wild ruggedness of the landscape in which it sat. Esme decided it was as good a place as any to begin exploring and set off along the path in the direction of the church.

Wide steps under a Gothic arch led up to a large solid door. Inside the church, an earnest young woman with flyaway blonde hair scraped back in a scrunchie stood beside a series of display boards, talking to an elderly couple about the many shipwrecks which lay strewn around the island's coast, a testament to the wild weather conditions Lundy had seen over the years. An older woman, owlish and bespectacled, wearing jeans and a chunky chenille sweater was pinning extra photographs to the board. Esme paused to read how the church had once been nothing more than a tin shack before being rebuilt courtesy of the Heaven family, and how recent renovation work to the roof had repaired damage caused by 100 years of gales and exposure.

Esme drifted away down the aisle, admiring the patterns of different coloured brickwork forming the roof and upper walls, giving the space a bright, airy feel, enhanced by light coming through the stained glass window at the far end. In one corner of the church, an exhibition board told visitors about the new Education Centre. Leaflet dispensers full of flyers extolled what the island had to offer in terms of art, history, science, geography and sustainability. Photographs of smiling schoolchildren enjoying day trips exploring the island's charms were pinned up beside a teachers' guide to what their pupils' visit would entail.

Esme retraced her steps back down the aisle, pausing at the doorway to admire the view out to sea, punctuated by mounds of bare granite and undergrowth dotted with pink thrift. She returned to the path, considering whether to visit the old lighthouse on the opposite side of the island. She slipped her rucksack off her shoulder, but as she pulled out the OS map she'd bought at the shop, she realised she was hungry. Breakfast had been an early meal and the bracing air had only heightened her appetite. Perhaps she should go back to the village and grab a coffee and a bite to eat at *The Marisco* while she wasn't too far away.

As she debated, she heard the throb of a helicopter's rotary blades and looked up to see a dark brown aircraft fly over her and land in the adjoining field. Esme sensed someone standing beside her and turned to see the younger woman from the church, also watching the helicopter's arrival, holding up her hand to shield her eyes. She glanced at Esme.

'We're going to be on TV later,' she said with a coy smile, nodding towards the activity. 'That's a film crew.'

'About your restoration work?' Esme asked.

'No, not this time. It's our new Education Centre. We're collaborating with the *Treasures of the Sea Museum* in Bristol.' She gave a half laugh, blushing. 'That's to say, Isaac Maudesley's taken an interest in our little venture.'

'Congratulations,' Esme said. 'I suppose it ties in quite nicely with his museum's maritime theme. Must be quite a coup to get him on board.'

'Yes, we're very lucky. He's been very generous.'

As they watched, the door of the helicopter slid open and half a dozen passengers disembarked, aided by three men dressed in high visibility jackets who'd been waiting beside a vehicle parked on the track on the other side of the field. Most were dressed appropriately for a visit to such a rugged location, in walking boots and waterproof jackets. One man, who Esme assumed must be Maudesley himself, was wearing a suit. As he hurried away towards the waiting Land Rover, others stayed back to unload silver cases and other boxes, which Esme took to contain filming equipment.

'Well, I'd better get back to my post,' the young woman said, turning towards the church.

'You're not in the welcome party, then?' Esme said.

'Not this time. Clara's doing the honours today.' She gave Esme a sheepish grin. 'I'm better with kids and your everyday visitors than celebrities.'

Esme laughed and wished her well, before hoisting her rucksack over her shoulder and setting off back towards the village.

*

Replenished with a latte and an egg mayonnaise sandwich, Esme came out of *The Marisco Tavern* eager to make the most of the remaining time of her day trip. She homed in on an empty picnic table outside the pub and opened out her OS map. Should she retrace her steps to the church and cut across to the old lighthouse, or should she take the right hand path out of the village, which ran along the coast, and explore the other end of the island?

She decided on the latter, folded up her map and slipped it back inside her rucksack before turning north and passing the island stores. As the path stretched out ahead of her, she sensed, rather than saw, two figures standing in the shadow of the gable end wall of the last building in the group.

As she walked past, she turned her head, noticing one of the pair was dressed in a suit, and immediately recognised Isaac Maudesley. He was deep in conversation with another man in a mustard-coloured jacket. She couldn't hear what was being said, the pair were too far away, but Maudesley's body language told her he was agitated about something. His hand was clenched and he was pumping the air, as though to emphasise his message.

Maudesley's companion glanced round and looked at her. Esme turned away, uncomfortable at being caught eavesdropping. But as she hurried away, she realised with a jolt that she knew the man Maudesley was arguing with.

It was Aidan Garrett.

# 12

Esme trudged along the path, brooding on what she'd witnessed. She knew Aidan was working around Lundy, he'd told her himself at the party. So it was hardly a surprise to see him on the island, but she wondered at his connection with Isaac Maudesley. Could Maudesley be Aidan's client? Perhaps it had something to do with the museum's collaboration with the Education Centre, given the numerous wrecks around Lundy's coast. But an alliance between visiting schoolchildren and scuba diving seemed unlikely.

She pushed away the unease at witnessing the dispute and focused on the way ahead. The landscape opened out to reveal a wide expanse of heathland, splashed with yellow gorse growing haphazardly against the wall of granite boulders, its fragrance hanging on the air. As she pressed on along the path, buffeted by the breeze off the sea, she thought she heard her name on the wind. She turned to see Aidan hurrying towards her, the coat tails of his mustard waterproof jacket flapping around either side of him.

'I thought it was you,' he said, when he reached her, grinning as he tried to catch his breath. 'I wasn't sure at first, but then I remembered you'd said at the party you were coming over this week.'

She nodded. 'It worked out well, weather-wise. It was a nice, easy crossing.' She wondered if he'd say anything about his run-in with Isaac Maudesley. He must know she'd have seen them arguing. Would he give an explanation? 'You're here for work, I take it? I didn't see you on the boat.'

'No, I took the chopper.' Aidan jerked his head along the path. 'If you fancy a bit of company, we could walk a while before you're due back at the boat. I've done everything I came here to do.'

'Yes, why not? You can give me a history lesson if you like,' Esme said, smiling. So, he wasn't going to mention Maudesley. Well, that was fine. Whatever they were arguing about was probably confidential, anyway.

Aidan shoved his hands into the pockets of his cargo trousers. 'Well, I know a bit of history, but I'm no expert.'

Esme laughed. 'It's got to be more than I know,' she said, as they began along the path. 'Since I arrived, I've learned about St Helen's church and the Heaven family who paid for it to be rebuilt. And their beautiful Millcombe House of course. They obviously weren't short of a bob or two, given the costs and logistics of getting materials and labour to the island.'

'No, they weren't. Thanks to William Heaven inheriting his godfather's Jamaican plantations.'

'Oh, that's where his wealth came from, is it? The slave trade.' Esme did a quick date check in her head. 'So it would have been just after the abolition of slavery, when former slave owners got compensation for loss of income?'

'Yeah. That's right. Heaven got close to twelve grand, apparently, and spent nearly ten grand to buy the island, and then invested more on the buildings.'

'It's mind boggling to get your head round the whole slave compensation thing. No compensation to the slaves for years of exploitation, just to the people who'd made money from them. Didn't the loan the government of the day took out only get paid off in 2015?'

'So I believe.'

'It's unreal,' Esme said with a shake of her head. 'It's uncomfortable to think of people getting rich in such circumstances.'

'Well, Heaven didn't stay rich. How often do people buy a rambling old property with a view to renovating it to its former glory, only to run out of cash, as the place eats up every penny they've got? Lundy was a bit like that for the Heavens. To cut a

64

long story short, William's descendant was forced to sell up in 1917.'

They arrived at a drystone wall, at right angles to the path and stretching out to their left, across towards the opposite side of the island. 'This is called the Quarter Wall,' Aidan said. He pointed ahead. 'Further along there's Halfway Wall.'

'Is there a Three-Quarter Wall, as well?' Esme asked.

Aidan grinned. 'Certainly is. Nothing like stating the obvious. If you follow the Quarter Wall, it leads you to the earthquake.'

'Sounds dramatic.'

Aidan shrugged. 'It's a series of fissures that for years was thought to have appeared during the Lisbon earthquake of 1755. But that's since been discounted. More likely it was caused by mining activity during Victorian times.' He gestured towards some ruined stone buildings in the opposite direction. 'The Lundy Granite Company came into existence in the 1860s. Our Mr Heaven thought there were some bucks to be made from the island's resources. He ploughed lots of money into various buildings, including these cottages for the workers. There was even a hospital.'

'And were there any bucks to be made?' Esme asked, grabbing a wayward piece of her hair being blown across her face.

Aidan shook his head. 'The whole thing folded almost as soon as it started. Part of the reason the family's finances fell apart.' He stood with his hands on his hips and gazed out to sea. 'Hard to imagine on a day like today how treacherous it can be around this stunning island, isn't it? Though perhaps not, when you look at those unyielding granite rocks down there.'

Esme came over and stood beside him, following his line of sight. 'You thinking of all those shipwrecks out there?'

'I was, yes. Not surprising, the names of the places. *Hazardous Head*, *Skeleton Cove* or *The Rocks from Hell*.' He turned to look at her with a wry grin. 'And *Dead Cow Point*, of course.'

'Oh, poor cow,' Esme said, adopting an expression of mock

concern. 'Must have been a pretty important cow to get an outcrop of rock named after it.'

'No doubt,' Aidan said, as they resumed their walk.

'My neighbour told me that the island has a pretty lawless history.'

'They reckon it's been inhabited for at least 3,000 years and in that time it's been a fortress, a sanctuary, a base for marauding pirates and smuggling, as well as having a diverse number of owners. There's even one story that the island was won in a game of cards.'

'Ouch,' Esme said. 'Someone's luck ran out then.'

'And they probably had a big hangover in the morning, too,' Aidan added.

'It's easy to see why it was a fortress. Easy to defend.'

'Not always, though. It didn't save the island from falling prey to Algerian pirates in 1625. They rounded up the inhabitants and shipped them back to Algiers to be sold as slaves. They then used to island as a base for raiding ships bound for the Irish Sea and the Atlantic.'

'They actually came ashore and carted people off?'

'Yes. Coastal villages were always vulnerable to being raided by Barbary pirates for the white slave trade. Though, not so much in the south west. Most were captured from ships out on the high seas, rather than from the land, but for other places like Ireland and particularly countries bordering the Mediterranean, raids were a constant danger.'

Esme gazed out at the distant horizon. 'Must have been pretty scary seeing pirate ships heading your way and not being able to do anything about it. You can't exactly *escape to the hills*, can you? You're trapped.'

'Indeed you are. Then again, the pirates didn't have it all their own way. A few years after the raid, the islanders successfully warded off a similar attack by pelting the incomers with boulders.'

Esme grinned. 'Good for them.'

'But you're right about the island's fortress credentials. One unpleasant individual, Pirate Captain Thomas Salkeld, decided he'd claim Lundy as his own in 1610. He declared himself king and used captives under threat of death to build a quay, a gun platform and repair the castle ruins to defend his so-called kingdom. "A reign of terror" is how those seamen lucky enough to escape described his rule.'

'Charming,' Esme said, wincing. 'How long did this "reign of terror" last?'

'Only about a month. He ran short of gunpowder.'

'Ah yes,' Esme said, nodding. 'Might be easy to defend, but by contrast, vulnerable to being laid to siege.'

'So, with no guns,' Aidan continued, 'Salkeld and his motley crew were seen off by their captives who threw rocks at them. Salkeld fled, hotly pursued by the navy. Not that they caught him. Word has it he later got into an argument with another pirate who threw him overboard and he drowned.'

'Wow, that's some story.'

Aidan looked at his watch. 'Much as I'd love to wander along with you all day, I think we may have to call a halt and return to base or you'll miss your boat and I'll miss my flight.'

They turned round and headed back the way they'd come.

'You seem very well informed on Lundy's pirate history,' Esme said, after they'd walked along for a while.

'Isn't everyone fascinated by pirates? The romantic idea of swashbuckling heroes, adventures at sea and buried treasure.'

'So it seems, judging by the huge box office success of a certain pirate fantasy film series. But real pirates were – and still are, it has to be said – of the ilk of your Captain Salkeld. Ruthless, lawless and with a cruel streak to boot.'

'You're right, of course. But people don't think about that. They'd rather indulge in the fantasy. Or, at least, the lure of hidden gold and the chance to find it.'

'That must be a prerequisite in your line of work,' Esme said, looking round at Aidan, but he avoided her gaze and stared ahead.

'Oh, I don't know. I'd say an inquisitive nature is the most important qualification.' Now he did turn to look at her, amusement on his face. 'Much like yourself in your line of work.'

Esme responded with a smile and a nod of her head. 'Naturally.'

'Of course, some might say it's an addiction.' He seemed lost in his thoughts for a moment before adding, 'But that's because people don't really understand. Can't grasp what drives us. Don't you find that?'

Esme hesitated, thinking of friends and family who'd worried for her as she'd pursued a trail they felt she should have left well alone. 'Yes, perhaps.' But there'd always been a specific reason for such an endeavour, to come to someone's aid, to uncover the truth for justice. She'd never seen it as an addiction. But maybe others had.

The path arrived at the village. Ahead of them was a throng of people gathered on the edge of the cobbled area near *The Marisco Tavern*. When they got closer, Esme realised what was attracting everyone's attention. The media were filming an interview with Isaac Maudesley. She couldn't hear what he said, but a ripple from the crowd as they arrived on the margins suggested he was in his usual good spirits and indulging in his customary teasing of his interviewer. By the time they joined the back of the group, the interview was over and the film crew had begun to pack away their equipment.

Aidan touched Esme's elbow. 'I'm going to have to shoot.'

'Yes, of course. And thanks for the guided tour.'

Aidan smiled and nodded. 'You're very welcome.'

As Esme watched Aidan walk away, she glanced over towards Maudesley who was now striding in the direction of the heliport. In moments, both men were out of sight. Esme wondered whether they'd settled the differences she'd witnessed earlier.

She turned away and joined the flow of boat passengers

heading back down to the quay where their vessel awaited them. As she trudged along the path, her mind drifted back to Aidan's comments about their respective occupations sharing similar traits. Certainly, they both needed to be curious, disciplined, analytical and even imaginative. For Aidan, she might add adventurous, bold, courageous. But what of Aidan's perception that they risked slipping into dangerous waters, that their fascination could become an addiction? Did she believe that? No, of course not.

But as the path turned on the headland and the harbour came into view down below, a troubled notion floated into her mind. Had Aidan's observation been meant as a warning?

# 13

John Ford's antique establishment, specialising in old prints and maps, was located near the top of Bideford High Street. The man himself was the dealer Maddy suggested might be interested in the frames Esme had found in the outbuilding.

As Esme entered the shop, a metal bell on the door jangled noisily. By the time she'd manoeuvred inside with the bundle of frames and closed the door behind her, the shop's proprietor had emerged from an anteroom in the corner. A small, thin man in a charcoal grey suit, wearing a classic school-style red and blue striped tie, removed his horn-rimmed glasses and regarded her curiously.

When she gave her name, his inquisitive expression softened and he broke into a smile. 'Ah, yes,' he said, slipping his glasses into his jacket pocket, 'Maddy's friend.' He hurried across the shop floor towards her. 'Let me help you with those.' He took the frames from her and propped them against the ornate leg of a table on which stood a stuffed pheasant under a glass dome.

Esme thanked him and looked around. The shop was filled with highly polished dark oak furniture, desks and tables adorned with lamps with fringed shades and jardinières of aspidistras, giving it the air of a Victorian drawing room. Pictures of every size and type hung on the walls, all but covering the elaborate burgundy flocked wallpaper.

'Quite a treasure house you have here,' Esme said.

'Thank you,' he said, inclining his head. 'It has been a passion of mine for many years now. And the fascination for such items has not waned during that time, I'm happy to say.'

Esme gestured towards the frames she'd brought with her. 'Maddy seemed to think these may be of interest to you. I've moved house recently and I found them while I was clearing out.

I don't have any need of them, so if you can reuse them in some way, that would be great.'

'Yes, indeed. *Reuse, reduce, recycle.* The mantra on everyone's lips these days.' His eyes twinkled. 'Something I've been doing for many a long year in one form or another. Shall I take a look through your little collection?'

'Yes, of course. Be my guest.'

Ford gathered up the frames and took them over to a small table next to the anteroom from where he'd appeared earlier. Esme wandered over to look at the many paintings, prints and maps displayed on the back wall. Miniature portraits in oval frames jostled with large gilt-framed landscapes, scenes of stags in Scottish glens and others of still-life.

When she reached the end wall, she noticed something familiar. Set in an ornamental gold frame was a large map, the top section of which she recognised as the print she'd found in her outbuilding. Now she could read the family crests which weren't visible on her copy, and she wasn't surprised to find listed amongst them the name Chalacombe.

'Seen something you like?' Ford said, appearing beside her.

'I've got a print of the top section of this map,' she said, looking back at him over her shoulder. 'I found it with those frames I brought in.'

'Ah yes, a particular favourite of mine,' he said. 'Created around 1611 by arguably the most famous and influential British cartographer of the early 17th century, John Speed.' Ford slipped his glasses on and peered at the framed image. 'Speed's county maps were generally acknowledged as the finest geographical documents of their time and were used as reference for over a hundred years.' He turned to her with a smile. 'Which tells you a good deal, don't you think?'

Esme acknowledged his comment with a nod. 'I was intrigued by the name Chalacombe, there in the bay,' she said, pointing, 'and again in that little cove. It's not on modern maps. I see the

Chalacombe crest is illustrated here, too.'

'Ah, yes. The family were once major landowners in the area. They have a long history, as you'll have surmised from their mention here. Let me show you something.' He led Esme to the opposite end of the shop and pointed to a painting hanging high up on the wall of a woman dressed in a sumptuous embroidered gown adorned with jewels, her ringed fingers resting on its skirt. 'Elizabeth Chalacombe,' he said, 'wife of William Chalacombe.'

'What a fabulous outfit,' Esme said, admiring the stunning brocade of the sitter's dress. 'Obviously a wealthy family.'

'Indeed.' Ford moved along to a smaller, less ostentatious painting, the sitter dressed in a blue satin gown trimmed with lace, a simple row of pearls around her neck. 'And her daughter, Amelia. Painted much later, of course, when fashion was very different. Amelia was born in the late 1600s, so this would be the early 1700s, before she married Richard Venner.' Ford turned to look at Esme. 'Do you know the story of their son, Thomas Venner?'

Esme frowned and shook her head. 'No. I don't.'

Ford nodded at the painting. 'Thomas Venner was captured by Barbary pirates in the early 18th century and sold as a slave. We know that, because he eventually came home to tell the tale.'

'I'd imagine it's quite a story. Actually, I was on Lundy yesterday and I was hearing how Barbary pirates feature in the island's history.'

'Yes, though most of the pirate activity on Lundy was in an earlier period to the time when Thomas was abducted.'

'So, was he taken in a land raid, like the poor island inhabitants were in the 17th century?'

'No, not like that. It was more common in this part of the world to happen on the high seas.' Ford removed his glasses and began polishing them with a large white handkerchief he took from his jacket pocket. 'Young Thomas and his brother were serving on his uncle's merchant ship. The south west had

72

important trade links with Mediterranean countries, and lucrative ones, at that. Everyone knew about the risks, of course, but needs must, and all that.'

'Risks of piracy, you mean?'

'Just so. Most captives were seized from ships on those trade routes. I'm sure William Chalacombe,' again he gestured towards the painting, 'Amelia's elder brother, who'd inherited the merchant shipping business from his father, would have been well aware of potential pirate dangers – all ship owners and their crews were – but trade was their livelihood. They had no choice but to go to sea and take their chances.'

'So pirates captured the ship and its crew?'

'Indeed. They were taken back to the north African coast and incarcerated, as happened to hundreds of others during the period, and were subsequently sold into slavery. Conditions were horrendous and many didn't survive beyond their initial capture. For those that did, their next challenge was enduring the hardship of being a slave. Many became labourers, building palaces and other grand edifices commissioned by the sultan of the time, working in searing heat with little food. Unsurprisingly, there were many deaths.'

'And Thomas?'

'He was chosen to work in a household. And from Thomas's own account, his owner wasn't a tyrant, unlike others. By comparison to some, his life was relatively benign.'

'But still always a slave?'

'Oh, yes. Which is why when the opportunity presented itself, he took it and escaped back to England. Piracy was something of an epidemic, you see. Quite well-to-do British subjects were falling victim, perhaps on ships travelling back from other parts of the world. Ransoms were the order of the day for these wealthy captives and some were paid with monies raised within the communities from where these people came. The church was often at the heart of such fund-raising efforts, though in latter years, pressure was put on the authorities and parliament sent envoys to negotiate the release of captives, with some success.'

'Was Thomas one?'

'Apparently not. He was an escapee. Whether that's because a ransom attempt had been made and failed, I've no idea. As I mentioned, Thomas maintained that his master was fond of him, so perhaps he wasn't prepared to release his favourite slave, ransom or no ransom. Thomas, understandably keen to secure his freedom and return home, might have realised the only way to achieve it was to abscond.'

'How long was he in slavery?'

'Ten years. And he was a young lad of 14 when he was captured.'

Esme chewed her lip, thoughtfully. 'Ten years on, having lived his formative years in such strange circumstance, he must have found it hard to readjust to life back at home.'

'For some, their time away was even longer, to the point where their families hardly recognised them when they returned.'

'I suppose it would have been a shock to Thomas's family to see him again ten years later, as a grown man. I wonder what they made of what he told them?'

'He wrote an account of his adventures, as I mentioned,' Ford said. 'A number of former captives became travelling storytellers, touring the country recounting their experiences. It was a way of spreading the word to help raise funds for ransoms for those still in captivity, not to mention using the opportunity to make an income out of what had befallen them.'

As they concluded their deal for the sale of the frames and Ford handed her a receipt for their transaction, he said, 'I believe you can find a copy of Thomas's story on the World Wide Web.'

'Thank you. I'll take a look.' Esme dropped the slip of paper into her bag. 'You said his brother was captured too? Did he escape as well?'

Ford gave a philosophical shrug. 'I'm afraid we know nothing about his brother's fate. It seems likely that, like hundreds of others, he succumbed to the squalid conditions of his incarceration and died in captivity.'

The shop's telephone rang. Esme thanked him for everything and left him to take the call. She went out into the street, pulling the door closed behind her. As she made her way towards the car park, she felt her own phone buzz in her pocket and pulled it out to check the screen, noting she had three missed calls. She stabbed at the screen and listened as the line was connected.

'Libby? It's Esme. You've been trying to get hold of me.'

Libby sounded breathless. 'He's been here again.'

'Who?'

'That so-called friend of yours. The scruffy one. I take it he didn't get in touch?'

'No, he didn't. Are you sure he was after me?'

Libby sighed. 'I don't know what to think any more, Esme. But I think you need to get back home pronto.'

'Why, what's happened?'

'I saw him actually coming out of your outbuilding, Esme. He must have broken in. I challenged him, but he ran off.'

'I'm on my way.' Esme severed the call and hurried back to her car.

# 14

Esme stood next to Libby on the garden path, warily scrutinising the outbuilding, half expecting someone to burst out of it, despite Libby's assurance that the intruder was long gone.

'I'm so sorry about this, Libby,' she said. 'It must have been pretty scary.'

'Oh, I'll live.' Libby chuckled. 'Wouldn't be the first time I'd chased after a dodgy bloke.'

'You shouldn't joke,' Esme said, grinning despite herself. 'He could have been dangerous.'

Libby flapped her hand dismissively. 'I doubt it. Too desperate to get away after being caught in the act to think about taking me on.' She dug down into the pocket of her trench coat and pulled out a scrap of paper. 'Here. I'd better give you this, before I forget.'

Esme took the paper and looked at it, puzzling over the letters and numbers. 'What's this?'

'Police incident log number. I called it in. Not that it triggered the blue lights brigade, once I'd explained that he'd run off.'

'Even so, they should have responded. You'd have felt a bit more reassured, for a start.'

Libby shrugged. 'Well, to be fair, even if they had sent a patrol car, it was all over by then. He'd already scarpered. Waste of resources, as far as they were concerned.' She tapped the paper with her forefinger. 'They said to get back to them and quote that when you've checked whether there's anything missing.'

Esme looked up at the building, recalling when Maddy had come over to help. 'I'd left it unlocked the other day. At least, I thought I had. Now I'm beginning to wonder.' She strode over to the door and examined the lock. No evidence of it being forced or even any attempt to force it. She looked round at Libby. 'Isn't this where on TV police dramas, they get forensics to check for fingerprints?'

Libby folded her arms. 'You need some of those cute elasticated bags to go over your shoes and a pair of latex gloves.' She cocked her head in the direction of her cottage. 'Can't help you with the shoe bags, but I can do the gloves, if you want. I use them all the time in my art studio.'

Esme grinned. 'That won't be necessary, detective. But thanks for the offer.' She looked back at the door and took a deep breath. 'Well, I suppose we'd better go and take a look.'

She grabbed hold of the door knob, hesitating for a moment, wary about what they'd find inside. She turned and looked at Libby over her shoulder.

'I'm going to get the builders to change this so it opens inward, rather than outwards. Less like a shed, then, don't you think?'

'Yeah, makes sense.'

Esme nodded. 'Yes, I thought so.' She swallowed. 'Sorry. I'm dithering,' she added, with a nervous laugh.

Libby put a hand out and squeezed her arm. 'It's OK. He won't be there any more. And anyway, I'm here. Black-belt karate, me.'

'Really?' Esme said, looking at Libby in surprise.

'No, not really,' Libby said, with a wry smile. 'I went to Judo classes when I was six, though. That's got to count for something. Right?'

Esme laughed. 'I appreciate your optimism. OK, let's get this thing over with.' She turned back to face the door and yanked it open.

They stood on the threshold and stared inside. Nothing looked any different to the way it had before Esme had gone out. And why would it? What had she been expecting to find? As she'd already told Libby, there was nothing worth stealing anyway.

She stepped inside, Libby at her shoulder.

'Hey, you've made a great start,' Libby said, walking into the middle of the space which Esme and Maddy had cleared.

'Actually,' Esme said, scanning around, 'coming to it fresh, I'm pleasantly surprised. Maddy said she reckoned we'd broken the back of it and I think she's right.' She looked over towards the wardrobe and chest of drawers, stacked high with dusty dining chairs, their tapestry seat cushions long rotted away. 'Shouldn't take long to get rid of the rest of it.'

'What's left behind the wardrobe?' Libby asked, wandering over.

'Oh, more of the same, but not anywhere near as much, thank goodness.'

Libby craned her head to look round the side of the wardrobe. 'Oh, hell.' She spun round, looking back at Esme in alarm.

'What?' Esme said, tapping into the anxiety in Libby's voice. 'Don't tell me there's more there than I thought.'

'That's not what I mean,' Libby said, shaking her head. She jabbed her finger towards the corner of the room. 'What I'm looking at explains everything.'

Esme strode across the room and peered towards where Libby was pointing. On the floor between the wardrobe and the stone back wall of the outbuilding, scrunched up and discarded, lay a grubby orange sleeping bag.

Libby grabbed Esme's sleeve. 'Looks like you've got an uninvited guest.'

# 15

'So, what will you do?' Libby said as they sat in Esme's living room, discussing the situation over a mug of tea. 'You have to report it back to the police.'

Esme shrugged. 'Don't know. What are they going to do about it? I'm sure they'll just tell me to change the locks. And give me a lecture on crime prevention.' She slumped back on the sofa. 'Perhaps I should bag up the evidence, in case we get a spate of burglaries, and hand it over when the time comes to get the perpetrator's DNA.'

'I'm not sure you're taking this seriously enough, Esme,' Libby said, tickling Ally's chin as he scrambled on to her lap. 'If you really think there's any chance he was using your place as a base for criminal purposes, the police should know about it. I'm sure they'd rather be ahead of the game, wouldn't you say?'

'You think?' Esme gave Libby a quizzical frown. 'Like you said, he's long gone by now. You scared him off. His cover's been blown, so whatever his plans were, he'll have had to abandon them. Even if I was to speak to the police, what would I tell them? Nothing's been stolen so they'll just write it off. No crime has been committed, they'll say, won't they?'

'Breaking and entering?'

'Can't be sure of that,' Esme said, thinking back to the day she and Maddy had begun clearing out. 'I could have forgotten to lock up. And it's only the equivalent of a shed at the moment. It's not like he's broken into the inner sanctum of my house.'

'Even so, finding someone bedding down in your property, whether it's a shed or your front room, isn't to be taken lightly.'

Esme stared down into the dregs of her tea and sighed. 'No,' she said, with a nod. 'You're probably right. I shouldn't try and second guess the police's reaction. I should call it in.' She jerked her head back towards the table behind her. 'I've got the incident number you gave me. I'll give them a call later, or email them or something.'

After Libby had gone, Esme wandered back to the outhouse. She peered round the furniture which had done such a good job of hiding the intruder's nest and stared down at the crumpled sleeping bag. The corner of a camping mat poked out from underneath and there was a discarded water bottle lying alongside. She withdrew and scoured around for the bin bags she and Maddy had used to get rid of the rubbish while clearing out. She found the roll and tore one off, giving it a shake to open it out.

Had she and Libby jumped to conclusions about the trespasser? Perhaps he wasn't a burglar with criminal intent, but a homeless man looking for a harbour in a storm, a sanctuary, somewhere to stay safe and warm. It seemed an odd place for someone to choose as a refuge. Surely towns had more opportunities for the homeless – finding food would be easier, for one thing, not to mention access to hostels and charity assistance.

Food. She hesitated. Had anything gone missing from her fridge? She didn't think so.

The image reminded her of a scene from the film *Great Expectations* where young Pip is threatened by escaped convict Magwitch in a churchyard. Pip steals food from his aunt's larder to give to Magwitch, under threat of having his throat cut. As a child, she'd been terrified and the scene triggered nightmares for weeks afterwards.

Esme shuddered and told herself to stop being so dramatic. She took the bin bag over to the wardrobe and hesitated. Perhaps she should leave well alone until she'd spoken to the police. If the sleeping bag did come to play a crucial role in solving a crime, they'd not thank her for contaminating the evidence.

She left the bin bag on top of the desk on the other side of the room and went outside. Her eye drifted to the overgrown butterfly bush opposite, where Maddy had spotted the soil and grape hyacinths under its canopy had been trampled. Had her intruder been using the shrub as a screen, watching her as she trotted down the path? She dismissed the thought. No chance. It didn't offer enough cover at this time of year. But the idea of it made her shudder as she turned back to lock up.

As she grasped hold of the keys, she paused. Would her intruder be back to retrieve his belongings? She'd not moved any of the furniture, so if he looked in, he could easily conclude his hide-out hadn't been discovered. In which case, she might get a chance to sneak up on him and find out who he was. But should she take the risk?

She withdrew the key from the lock without turning it, slipped the bunch into her pocket and hurried back to the cottage.

# 16

By the time Esme had settled down on her sofa for an evening in front of the fire, the book on Lundy Island's history in her hand and the kittens curled up contentedly beside her, she'd already abandoned her madcap idea for finding out the identity of her unwelcome visitor. Did it matter, anyway? Nothing had been stolen and, despite her ruminations, he must know that, having been chased off by Libby, he'd been rumbled. Even if he returned to collect his sleeping bag, it seemed likely as not he'd abandon his post and leave her in peace. Besides, he must have realised by now she'd begun the clearing operation and his hiding place was no longer viable.

She glanced over at the key to the outbuilding hanging on its hook on the wall beside the front door, regretting she'd not locked up. Well, it was too late now. She wasn't about to venture down the garden path in the dark and risk bumping into him.

She pushed the idea out of her mind and turned her attention back to the book about Lundy's history which she'd bought on the island, returning to the fascinating, if gruesome, story Aidan had told her of Captain Thomas Salkeld, who'd landed on the island in 1610 and declared himself king. Salkeld insisted that his prisoners – seamen captured from ships sailing in the Bristol Channel – renounce the crown and swear allegiance to him instead, threatening them with being shot or hanged, and having their heads shaved.

Lundy gained a reputation in its history for lawlessness and piracy, particularly during the sixteenth century. There were accusations that a blind eye was turned in the case of certain English pirates who used Lundy as a base. Esme read of the raiders from North Africa and was reminded of John Ford's tale of the unfortunate Thomas Venner who'd been captured by

Barbary pirates and forced into slavery. Authorities, it seemed, struggled to keep such predators of the rich traffic of the Bristol Channel under control. And while the island itself had little to commend it in the form of resources, it had other attractions in the form of a lookout, a place of shelter and a pirate landfall.

Esme felt herself growing sleepy. The wood burner was little more than a bed of red-glowing ashes, soon to fade and chill. She closed her book and prepared for bed, thoughts of the outhouse conundrum jolting her as her eye caught sight of the key hanging beside the front door.

She toured the cottage, ensuring that windows were secure both upstairs and down. When she turned out the bedside lamp, she lay in the dark waiting for sleep to come, forcing herself to focus on something cheering and regretting her choice of reading matter. After the discovery of the intruder, she should have picked something more soothing. A romance, maybe. Certainly not the antics of pirates and cruel treatment of their captives.

When sleep finally came, it was peppered with dreams of the angry faces of men jangling chains or waving cutlasses, her laboured breathing as she ran through the wild tussocky grass of an abandoned graveyard surrounded by a raging sea. She woke with a start, blinking into the inky darkness as she tried to gauge what time it was. She propped herself up on her elbow and checked the clock: 4 am. Well, it could be worse, she decided. At least it wasn't the middle of the night. She dropped back on the pillow and let out a long sigh.

Inevitably, her mind drifted to the subject of the outbuilding. Had her unwelcome visitor returned to his den? She turned over and tried to get back to sleep, but she knew it was hopeless.

With an exasperated grunt, she threw the bedclothes back and wriggled to the edge of the bed. A surreptitious peek through the window would do no harm. She wasn't looking for confrontation.

She pulled on her dressing gown and padded downstairs to find her Wellington boots, a small voice in her head asking her why she needed to do this. Hadn't she convinced herself last night that it didn't matter? That the most important thing was to ensure whoever it was didn't come back?

She snatched up her duffel coat to put over her nightclothes and, grabbing a torch from the small table beside the front door, she undid the bolts and stood on the mat, hesitating. Well, was she up for it or not?

She pushed the doubts to the back of her mind, snatched open the door and stepped outside.

The breeze coming off the sea tugged at her coat and whipped her hair around her head. She pulled the door closed behind her, switched on the torch and tentatively set off down the stone path, the torch beam swaying in front of her.

When she reached the end of the outbuilding, she extinguished the torch and stood for a moment, letting her eyes adjust to the light. Above her, clouds played games with the moon, throwing muted shadows down on to the ground around her.

If she was being realistic about this, she told herself, she wasn't going to establish anything by aiming her torch though a window to sneak a look. She'd see nothing from out here. She'd have to open the door and go inside, walk across the room and look behind the wardrobe. That's what she'd need to do to satisfy her curiosity. Was it worth it? It wasn't too late. There was still time to turn back and forget the whole idea.

The clouds parted once more and a shaft of moonlight lit up the path in front of her. She strode to the door and, holding her breath, closed her hand around the handle and gently pulled it open. As she stepped across the threshold, the sound of a snore shot a stab of fear through her.

She froze.

So, now what? Retreat? But if she did, she'd never know. It would be the coward's way out to run now, having come this far. Besides, if he was snoring, it meant he was asleep. She only needed a quick look.

She switched on the torch and marched boldly across the room, shining the shaft of light around the side of the wardrobe, aiming it on to the floor in the corner.

The sleeping bag moved, the figure within it struggled to a sitting position and a head emerged. The intruder lifted his arm to shield his eyes from the light.

'Is that you, Ez? For Chrissake, turn the bloody light off, can't you?'

Esme stared at the face caught in the beam of her torch, fear turning to fury.

'Max Rainsford,' she said, her voice shaking. 'What the hell are you doing in my shed?'

# 17

Esme bustled around the kitchen, the sound of running water from the shower in the bathroom above an irritating reminder of Max Rainsford's presence in the cottage. As she threw the rashers of bacon into a frying pan, she asked herself what she thought she was doing, given everything she'd said to Max the last time she'd seen him. How could she even deign to look at him after that devastating occasion, when he'd exposed her to the truth about her husband's death in such a cruel way?

She was well aware Max hadn't seen it like that. He'd been under some sort of delusion that he was actually helping. *Hadn't she wanted to know the truth?* he'd asked. Yes, of course she had. But not at the price he'd paid for it on her behalf.

Max and her late husband Tim, both journalists, had been close colleagues for years before Tim was killed. She blamed Max's journalistic mindset as the reason she'd fallen out with him so vehemently. He just didn't get it. Couldn't see it from her point of view. She'd never forgiven him. And now, here she was, making him breakfast. The world had gone mad.

Above, the flow of water stopped and a few minutes later, Max came downstairs in his stockinged feet, dressed in a pair of crumpled jeans and threadbare sweatshirt, the towel she'd lent him thrown over his shoulder. She assumed his change of clothes had been in the moth-eaten rucksack he'd had with him.

'Smells good,' Max said, rubbing his damp hair with the corner of the towel. It was greyer and longer than the last time they'd met, his beard thick and unkempt. He jerked his head upwards. 'Thanks for the shower. Appreciated.'

Esme flicked off the kettle. 'It wasn't for you,' she said, filling the coffee pot with boiling water. 'It was for me. You smelled like the inside of my dustbin.'

Max chuckled. 'So would you if you'd been living rough for the past week.'

Esme took the coffee pot over to the table and put it down. She gripped the back of a dining chair and threw Max a steely glare.

'Well, I hope you realise that my hospitality is only so you can tell me *why* you've been living rough in my outhouse.'

'Sure, Ez. No worries.'

Esme turned back to the kitchen. 'You'd better sit down, then.' She snatched up two slices of bread from the breadboard and put them on a plate, before adding the rashers of bacon from the pan. The kittens were sitting on the back of the sofa which divided the sitting room from the kitchen-diner, eyeing Max warily.

'They not used to visitors, then,' Max said, nodding towards the cats.

Esme handed the plate to Max and sat down opposite him at the table. 'They certainly know who to treat with caution,' she said. 'Cats are very good judges of character in my experience.'

'Oh, thanks for the vote of confidence.' Max piled the bacon between the slices of bread. 'You not having any?'

Esme shook her head and reached for the large jar of granola. 'Cereal's fine for me.' After tipping a portion in her bowl, she looked at the clock. 'I've got to go out in half an hour,' she added, picking up the milk jug, 'so you better get to the point.'

'Don't your little fellas get any breakfast? Don't reckon it's me they're interested in, but that jug of milk.'

'They've had theirs.' She poured coffee from the pot into two mugs. 'And anyway, the milk thing is a myth,' she added, picking up her spoon. 'Seventy per cent of cats are lactose intolerant.'

'Always amazes me what stuff you know,' Max said, grinning. 'Good to see you haven't changed.'

Esme frowned. 'Stop stalling, Max. Why are you here? And why not just check into a local hotel? There's a perfectly good pub down the road, you know.'

'Oh, come on, Ez. We're not in the anonymous big city now. Strangers stand out like a nun in a brothel in the countryside.'

'As proved by you being spotted by my neighbour,' Esme said with a fleeting smile. 'You must be losing your touch, Max.'

Max grunted and picked up his knife to slice his bacon sandwich in two. 'There's always that risk when working undercover.'

Esme stared at him, a quizzical expression on her face as his words sank in. Part of her cautioned it might be better to turf Max out without learning anything about the reason for his subterfuge. But the other side of her scoffed at the notion. If Max was up to something, she needed to know what it was. Especially if it was on her patch.

'Aren't you getting a bit old for this sort of thing, Max?' she said.

Max ignored her jibe. 'The thing is, Ez,' he said, resting his elbows on the table, 'working undercover means you can't just go around telling all and sundry what you're up to. That's the whole…'

'Don't patronise me, Max. I'm not suggesting you tell the world. It's my shed you're using. Don't you owe me an explanation?'

'You'll just have to take my word…'

Esme snatched up his plate and stood up. 'If you want this, you're going to have to give me more than me taking your word for it. Your word doesn't account for much any more, remember?' She turned away and headed over to the bin and put her foot on the pedal, flipping open the lid.

'OK, OK, you win. But don't say I didn't warn you.'

She frowned and returned to the table, plonking down the plate in front of him. 'Warn me about what?'

'About getting involved.'

'I didn't say anything about getting involved. And if this is some elaborate hoax to get me to do something for you, it won't wash. Got it?'

Max held up his hands in mock surrender. 'Sure, Ez. Loud and clear.' He grabbed his sandwich and took a bite.

Esme looked at the clock again. 'Time's running out, Max. Give.'

Max nodded and swallowed his mouthful before taking a gulp of coffee. Esme sat back down and resumed her own breakfast.

'Truth is,' Max said, 'I'm on a hunch. Nothing more. Hence my reluctance.'

'Hunch about what?' Despite her bias towards his behaviour in her own case, Esme knew Max was a good journalist. After all, Tim, her late husband, had rated him highly. That said, Max's diligence could be misplaced, in her opinion. She'd accused him on more than one occasion of 'digging for dirt' and twisting the so-called evidence once he found it to suit his purpose.

'Great bacon butty, by the way,' Max said, giving her the thumbs up.

Esme pressed her lips together and put down her coffee mug. 'I should perhaps point out here,' she said, leaning across the table towards him to emphasise what she had to say, 'that the police have been alerted to your antics. My neighbour called it in when you legged it yesterday. I even have an incident log number. They're waiting for me to let them know if anything's been stolen. So I could quite easily mess up your entire assignment by reporting back to them.' Esme folded her arms and stared at him.

Max popped the final piece of his sandwich into his mouth and fixed his eyes on her, chewing. After a moment, just when Esme thought she'd have to carry out her threat and was about to get up to find her phone, he brushed off his hands and sighed.

'I'm trying to get some intel on Isaac Maudesley.'

Esme blinked. 'Maudesley? The museum owner?'

'The very same.'

'And? What about him?'

'Like I said, it's all a bit hazy. There've been rumours.'

Esme shrugged. 'So, why here? He's based in Bristol, isn't he?'

Max plucked at his beard. 'He's got a place down here. Where he keeps his private collection, so rumour has it.' He cocked his head backwards. 'It's just over the fields. In amongst a load of trees. Not easy to see and not easy to get to.'

Esme sat upright. 'Not Chalacombe House? Land runs alongside the coast path. Between here and the combe?'

'No, it's called Dowell Lodge. Monstrosity of a place. Victorian Gothic.'

'But there once was a Chalacombe House, though. I found it on a map from 1884.'

Max rubbed his beard. 'Well, maybe there's a connection. It was a Chalacombe who founded the museum. Word is that Maudesley's related in some way.'

'To the Chalacombes? How?'

Max scoffed. 'How should I know, Ez? You're the family historian.'

Esme scowled. 'I knew it. This is your convoluted way of getting me to research him, isn't it?'

'No, it's not,' Max protested. 'You've got it all wrong.'

Esme stood up. 'You knew if you asked me directly, I'd say no,' she said, clearing away the breakfast things, the crockery clattering as she ferried it between the table and plonked it down on the kitchen worktop. She looked round at Max and shook her head. 'You take the biscuit, Max, you really do.'

Max got to his feet. 'That wasn't in the plan, Esme, I promise you.'

She turned on him. 'No? Then why choose my place to doss down in?'

'Why not? It was perfectly placed.'

She glared at him. Her head spun at the implications. Had he chosen to investigate Isaac Maudesley *because* he'd discovered she lived so close and thought he'd take advantage? And how had he found her anyway?

'You must have thought it was your lucky day when you found out where I lived,' she said, bitterly.

Max grinned. 'Yeah, I did. Fate, eh?' He picked up his boots from the foot of the stairs and put them on.

Esme dumped the dirty dishes into the bowl in the sink and looked about for her coat. 'Time for you to leave, Max.'

Max snatched up his jacket and rucksack, which were hanging over the newel post. 'Yeah, sure, Ez.' He slipped the rucksack over his shoulder. 'Look,' he said, taking a step towards her, 'any chance I could use your place – the shed, I mean, not in here, obviously – for another couple more days?'

'Are you serious?'

'I need time to find somewhere else, don't I?'

She wanted to say no, to scream at him to get out of her life and not come back. But one more day wouldn't make much difference. It would be easy enough to avoid him.

'You've got 24 hours, and then you're out. Or I'm making that report to the police.'

Max lifted his hand. 'Sure, you're the boss. I'd better get out your hair.' He strode over to the door before turning back. 'Thanks for breakfast and the shower. I hope I haven't dragged you into anything.'

And he was gone before she could work out what he'd meant.

# 18

Maddy looked up from the box she was unpacking on her stall as Esme arrived at Bideford market hall.

'I thought you were running late?' Maddy said, straightening up.

'I was. Well, I could have been. But in the end I wasn't.'

Maddy laughed. 'Obviously.' Her smile faded. 'Are you OK? What's happened?'

Esme pulled a box towards her and began unloading the items from it on to the table. 'Max Rainsford,' she said, her tone of voice conveying her sour mood on the subject.

'What, the journalist?'

'The very same.' Esme explained everything that had happened as they set out the stall ready for the punters' arrival. 'The stupid thing is,' she said finally, pushing the last of the empty boxes underneath the table out of sight, 'I was so quick to react when I thought he was trying to outmanoeuvre me, I didn't press him on any detail.'

'Knowing Rainsford, you're probably better off not knowing. How did he find you, anyway?'

Esme wrinkled her nose. 'That's another question I never asked him.' She folded her arms and leaned against the edge of the table. 'I shouldn't have kicked him out until I had all the answers. Stupid of me.'

'You know as well as I do, Esme, that anything involving Max Rainsford is bad news. Perhaps you'd be better off out of it.'

'Yes, I am aware of that, don't worry. It's just that...'

'Yes, I know. You can't resist a mystery. You are your own worst enemy – you know that, don't you?'

Esme raised an eyebrow and gave Maddy a wry grin. 'It has been said before.'

'Talking of mysteries, I assume you still haven't heard from the elusive Hester Campbell?'

'Not a thing. She hasn't answered my emails or responded to messages I've left on her mobile phone.'

Maddy tugged her ear. 'So, what will you do?'

'I thought I might go round and see her after the market.' Esme reached down for her bag and pulled out the old photograph of the matriarch that Hester had left with her, the one which Maddy had digitally restored. 'I could return this to her at the same time.'

'You'd think she'd have been in touch, if only to get that back,' Maddy said. 'I'd love to know who it is. Perhaps we could display it on our board here. See if anyone recognises it.'

'She'd have to agree to that, obviously. I'll ask her, shall I?'

'Yes, do. She might have got over the shock of everything by now and put you back on the case.'

Esme dropped the photograph back in her bag. 'Yes, that'd be nice.'

'Hey, don't forget the *Antiques Roadshow*'s on tomorrow,' Maddy said.

'No, I haven't forgotten. The recorder's all set,' Esme said, dropping her bag behind the stall. She and Maddy had attended the filming of the TV programme, where members of the public brought furniture, jewellery, bric-a-brac and memorabilia for expert analysis and valuation, at nearby Hartland Abbey the previous summer. Maddy had taken a small tortoiseshell casket and Esme had gone along with her out of curiosity. Now, months later, their episode was being aired on screen. 'I thought I ought to make sure we had a copy for prosperity. I wonder if we'll be able to spot us.'

'Let me know if you do. I'll have to catch it on iPlayer later. Me and Harry are out with friends.'

'Are you still OK for Monday?' Esme asked. They'd planned to use Maddy's van to take the larger items of furniture from

Esme's outhouse to the charity shop opposite the Pannier Market.

'Sure. All sorted.'

'Oh, that'll be a great help. Thank Harry, won't you? It'll be useful to have the extra muscle.'

Maddy stood upright. 'Oh, looks like we're on,' she said, as two women headed purposefully towards the stall.

\*

After the market finished, Esme went with Maddy back to her workshop and helped her unload the stock. With the last box stored, and reassuring Maddy she'd report back later, she got in her car and headed towards Appledore.

The village was bustling as ever with visitors and parked cars lined the road running parallel with the quay on both sides, but she managed to grab a space as someone pulled out to leave. She crossed the road and hurried up Meeting Street, turning left past the chocolate shop into Market Street. She could see Hester's cottage ahead of her on the right hand side, close to the café, and was relieved to see lights on inside, suggesting Hester was at home.

When Esme reached the cottage, the front door was ajar and the drone of a vacuum cleaner boomed out on to the street. She knocked hard on the half-open door and peered round. Inside, a woman dressed in denim dungarees, who was definitely not Hester, was vigorously hoovering the hallway carpet. Esme pushed the door open a little further and took a tentative step into the hall.

'Hello?' she shouted, above the noise of the vacuum.

The woman threw a puzzled look over her shoulder and put her foot on the machine to switch it off. She pushed a strand of hair off her face and smiled.

'Can I help you, dear?'

'I was looking for Hester.'

'Hester?' The woman cocked her head to one side, questioningly.

'Yes, is she in?' A sudden thought. 'Oh, perhaps I've got the wrong house. I was looking for Hester Campbell. I thought she lived here.'

The woman nodded. 'Oh, I see. Hester. Of course. Yes, I do know who you mean. But she's gone, I'm afraid.'

'Gone?'

'Yes, it was only for the week, you see.'

'Oh, right.' Esme frowned as the truth hit her like a slap in the face. She swallowed. 'So this is a holiday cottage?'

'Yes, that's right,' the woman said. She grabbed the handle of the cleaner and pulled it towards her. 'And I must get on, I'm afraid, dear. Got another lot of holidaymakers coming in this afternoon and I need to finish up here.'

'Of course. Sorry to hold you up.' Esme went to go, but an idea struck her. 'I don't suppose you have Hester's home address, do you?' she added, turning back.

The woman shook her head. 'I don't do the bookings, dear. Just the cleaning.' She threw Esme a stern look. 'But even if I did, I'd hardly be telling you, would I? I don't know you from Adam. Data protection and all that.' And she turned back and returned to her cleaning.

# 19

If it hadn't been for the evidence of the dirty dishes sitting in the sink when she got home, Esme might have believed she'd imagined the dawn breakfast session with Max. So much had happened since. The discovery that Hester Campbell hadn't been honest with her seemed to accentuate the peculiarity of her reaction to news of the murder. Had she had some inkling of it? Had it made her cautious from the beginning? So why the subterfuge? What was she hiding?

As Esme washed up and tidied the kitchen, she thought of Libby. She was almost certain to ask whether Esme had been in touch with the police about the intruder. What could she tell her? It was hardly reassuring to admit it was someone she knew. More to the point, it raised more questions than answers. But if she said nothing, Libby would continue to worry. Perhaps it was better to face it head-on.

She pulled on her duffel coat, went out and headed down to Libby's cottage. The unanswered knock on the door and a quick check on Libby's studio, which was empty, told her Libby was not at home. But her battered old Volvo was in its usual parking space, which suggested Libby wasn't far away, and the most likely place she'd be was wandering along the shoreline looking for flotsam and jetsam for her artwork.

Esme hurried down the lane and on to the steep footpath leading to the beach. As she rounded the final bend, she saw Libby leaning against the wall of the slipway, gazing out to sea. At the sound of Esme's footsteps, she turned round.

'Oh, hello,' she said, as Esme came to stand beside her. 'I was just thinking about you.'

'Oh yes? Why's that?'

'I got chatting to the new couple who've moved in at the top of the hill. They seem very nice. I've invited them round for a meal next Saturday evening. Wondered if you'd like to join us, if you're free.'

Esme smiled and nodded. 'That would be lovely, thank you.'

'Good. Say 7.30, then?'

'Perfect.'

Libby straightened up and turned to Esme. 'That wasn't the only reason you were on my mind, though,' she said, an expression of concern on her face. 'What happened about your unwelcome visitor?'

Esme gave her a watery smile. 'That's why I'm here. Thought I'd better call in and update you. I guessed you'd be down here when you weren't at home.'

'So, did you speak to the police?'

Esme took a strand of hair being flicked across her face by the wind and tucked it behind her ear. 'No, I didn't. But only because I found out who was camping out in there.'

Libby's eyes widened. 'You did? So, who was it? Oh, hang on. It was that guy I saw, wasn't it? The scruffy one who said he knew you?'

'Yes. Yes, it was.'

For a moment, Libby seemed reassured, then she frowned. 'So, what the hell was he playing at?'

Esme gave a half laugh. 'That's exactly what I asked him.'

'And what did he say?'

'It's all rather embarrassing,' Esme said, stalling. She'd spent the time walking down the lane preparing her answer, but now it came to it, she found herself fluffing her lines. 'It's all a bit odd, really. Well, *he's* a bit odd, if I'm honest.'

Libby nodded, knowingly. 'Oh, I see. Suffers from mental health issues, does he?'

'Something like that. He's a bit unpredictable.' That was certainly no word of a lie.

'Well, it's good he's got a friend like you. Not everyone would

97

be so supportive.'

Esme flinched, alarmed at the potential for Libby's imagination to drift into fanciful territory and the narrative to get out of control. 'Well, it's a bit more complicated than that, to be honest.'

'These things often are,' Libby said with a sympathetic frown.

Esme swallowed. 'Anyway, the thing is, we've come to an understanding. He's accepted he can't bunker down in my outhouse indefinitely, so he's going to explore alternatives.'

'Right. Good. And he'll keep you informed, I assume.'

'Oh, I'm sure he will.' Esme shoved her hands into her pockets. 'So, how's everything with you?' she asked, eager to change the subject. 'Any new projects on the go?'

'A possible commission. Plus,' Libby turned her gaze back up the path to the tiny stone building above, 'I've been asked to do an "artist in residence" session next month at the cabin. Should be fun.'

Esme smiled. 'Good for you, Libby. I hope lots of people come and visit.'

'Be nice to think so. I'm looking forward to it.' Libby pulled out a pair of gloves from her pocket. 'Well, on that note, I'd better get back and get on with some work,' she said, slipping on the gloves. 'Oh, by the way. Your ghost.'

'My ghost?'

'Yes.' Libby pointed along the beach to the distant cove. 'The little lad you were telling me you'd seen on the shoreline the other day.'

'What about him?'

'I've seen him too. Yesterday afternoon when I came down looking for driftwood.' She grinned. 'So he *is* real.' She laid a hand on Esme's arm and chuckled. 'Either that or we're both being haunted.'

# 20

As Esme walked back to her cottage, mulling over what she'd told Libby about Max, her irritation with him surfaced once again. She climbed the steep steps to the front door, pausing at the top and gazing down the path towards the stone outhouse, wondering if he'd managed to find himself another hideout yet. As she did so, a niggling question wormed its way into her mind. Had he genuinely planned to use her building without her knowing to carry out his clandestine mission before slipping quietly away, unseen and unchallenged? Or had he secretly hoped she'd discover him, giving him the perfect excuse to draw her into his investigation? Despite his protestations to the contrary, she was inclined to think the latter.

She pushed open her front door and went inside, her mind still unable to let go of the subject. Why was he so interested in Isaac Maudesley, anyway? On the face of it, Maudesley seemed an unlikely candidate for Max's attention. Affable and popular, knowledgeable in his field of history, generous with both his time and financial backing of projects close to his heart.

*It's all a bit hazy,* Max had said. *There've been rumours.*

Esme slipped off her coat and hung it up, scoffing at the memory of Max's vague statement. Really? Or was Max at a loose end and had been drawn to Maudesley like a wasp to sugar, determined to make something out of what didn't actually exist? It wouldn't be the first time.

She fixed herself a coffee and set up her laptop on the kitchen table before looking up Isaac Maudesley on the Internet. His entry on Wikipedia was rather thin and bland. His connection with the *Treasures of the Sea Museum* was cited, but nothing was said about his so-called link to the Chalacombe family, the museum's founders. Perhaps he or someone on his publicity team had put the story around for PR purposes to boost his association with the museum. Born and raised in Bath, he'd attended a middling red-brick university to study archaeology, professing a particular interest in Mediterranean history. He'd dabbled in a number of areas, including finance, media and communication. He'd been married, but had since divorced and there were no children.

When he'd become involved with the *Treasures of the Sea Museum* a few years ago, the BBC had taken an interest and he'd been the subject of Radio 4's *Profile* programme. Esme searched for a recording of the episode and, picking up her coffee, settled back to listen. But she learned very little more from the friends and associates the presenter had persuaded to contribute. Maudesley was considered a hard worker, knew how to get the best out of people, was partial to a good wine and enjoyed classical music, particularly Bach. No one had any revelations to offer, or if they did, they weren't prepared to share them. Whatever rumours Max was acting upon, it was unlikely she'd find them mentioned here.

If she hadn't been so quick to accuse him of setting her up, she might have had the opportunity to learn why Maudesley was in Max's sights. But perhaps it was just as well that things had gone the way they had. As Maddy had pointed out, nothing good ever came out of getting caught up with Max Rainsford and one of his investigations. Esme would only regret it. So instead of speculating, she should be congratulating herself for not falling into Max's trap. OK, it didn't satisfy her curiosity, but she'd have to live with that.

Esme pushed the subject out of her head, drank down the last of her coffee and closed the lid of her laptop. She had better things to do than second guess what Max was up to. But as she swilled her coffee cup under the tap, she again wondered if Max had moved out of the outbuilding. She knew she'd find it much easier to disregard the whole subject if he'd actually gone.

She snatched up the key to the stone building from its hook

and went outside, striding down the path until she reached the door, where she hesitated. Perhaps she was expecting too much too soon. Her 24 hours' notice to quit wasn't yet up. Max may not have had time to find an alternative hideout. Maybe she'd give it until the following morning.

She told herself to stop prevaricating and pulled open the door, before marching over to the wardrobe screening Max's hiding place, holding her breath and peering around the side. She found herself staring into an empty space. Any evidence of Max's presence had gone – no camping mat, no orange sleeping bag and no water bottle.

She let out a long sigh. Good. Now she could relax. She and Maddy could finish clearing the building and have it ready for the builder to start its transformation.

*

With Max and his belongings gone, Esme spent the next day, Sunday, cleaning the outbuilding and ensuring there was a clear passage to the door in readiness for the following day, when Maddy and Harry were coming to cart away the larger items of furniture. By the time the evening came, she was ready for a rest. She lit the wood burner and settled down to watch the episode of the BBC's *Antiques Roadshow* which she and Maddy had attended the previous year. The weather had been mixed and they'd spent much of the time huddled under an umbrella, Maddy clutching her tortoiseshell caddy.

Despite the frequency of blustery showers, the event had been well attended, which meant the queues to consult the antique experts had been long. But they'd been rewarded for their patience by learning that Maddy's tortoiseshell caddy was a rare Victorian needle box. The downside was that by the time their turn had come and gone, they'd had little opportunity to see much of what else was on show that day, so Esme was looking forward to learning what items of interest they'd missed, as well as seeing if they'd been caught on camera.

The signature tune of the programme began and Esme curled up on the sofa with the kittens. The presenter gave a brief introduction of their location, along with a tour of the Abbey grounds and interior. Then the first item was a large landscape painting of a beach and cliff, in oils. The artist wasn't well known and Esme suspected the owner was disappointed by the expert's valuation.

Next came a 19th century pocket watch, in silver with an engraved case. Esme gazed longingly at the screen as the specialist opened the back to reveal the intricate workings of the mechanism. There was something about clocks and watches which she found captivating. Perhaps it was to do with her fascination with the past, they being instruments of time. She loved the ticking of her old longcase clock on the wall and found it soothing. A friend who'd once come to stay had found it distracting and she'd had to still the pendulum to accommodate her.

The cameras had turned now to pottery and Esme pulled a face at the vulgar green vase on display. She decided to take the opportunity to put another log on the fire and fetch a glass of wine from the kitchen. When she returned, the focus had shifted again, this time to jewellery. The camera homed in on a gold ring, fashioned into a heart with clasped hands either side. The owner, a middle-aged woman in a print dress, wearing an apricot scarf draped around her neck, was responding to the expert's question as to what she knew about the piece.

'I inherited it from my grandmother,' she said. 'And it was passed down to her from her grandmother.'

The expert, a portly man in dark-rimmed glasses and dressed in a flamboyant waistcoat, nodded. 'That fits with the tradition of this type of ring. It was the custom to pass it down from mother to daughter.'

'How old do you think it is?' the woman asked.

But Esme was oblivious to the expert's reply. She'd seen something, someone in the crowd, watching on with interest. Someone who she recognised. She grabbed the remote control, paused the TV and rewound the footage.

There, at the back of the group, stood Hester Campbell. And standing right beside her was Max.

# 21

Esme switched off the TV. The sighting of Hester and Max was too distracting for her to concentrate on the rest of the programme. Had Maddy also spotted them? But Maddy was going out and hadn't planned to watch it until later. Besides, she hadn't met Hester and hardly knew Max, so she wouldn't notice either of them unless Esme pointed them out.

Esme slumped back into the sofa and let her thoughts run. The kittens, who'd had a rude awakening at her abrupt reaction, crawled back on to her lap. She picked up Jeanie and cuddled her. Assuming it wasn't just a fluke that Hester and Max were standing next to one another in the same shot, what did it mean? That they were working together? But on what? Was it connected to Max's interest in Maudesley? But the filming had taken place during the previous summer. There was no reason to suspect it was anything to do with his current investigation.

Then again, some enquiries could go on for months, even years. And who was Hester Campbell, anyway – assuming that was her real name? A journalist colleague of Max's? And what were they doing at the event? Obviously Esme had not seen them that day, but that wasn't surprising. There'd been hundreds of people milling around the grounds, and she and Maddy had spent a long time merely standing in a queue to consult the antiques expert. Besides, she wouldn't have known Hester back then, and as for Max, if he'd spotted Esme, he'd have made sure he stayed out of sight.

So, if this wasn't about Max's current fixation on Isaac Maudesley, perhaps it was about Hester's mystery research. Which immediately suggested Max was behind Hester's employing Esme in the first place. So, where did Max fit in to Hester's investigation? Whatever his interest, it was a sneaky way of using Esme's services without showing his hand. He'd have known she'd never agree to doing the work if he'd approached her himself.

The more Esme thought it through, the more holes appeared in Hester's story. The 'special birthday' narrative had to be a complete fabrication. And who was Frank Stone anyway? Was he really Hester's partner? Esme didn't think so for one minute.

But what if there *was* a link between Hester's enquiries and Max's? Given Max was sniffing around in this area, allegedly looking into Isaac Maudesley's affairs, only a few months after they were standing together at Hartland Abbey, it had to suggest it was more than sheer coincidence, didn't it?

On the other hand, Max had been evasive about Maudesley. He'd talked about *rumours* and how it was *all a bit hazy*. Was he using Maudesley as a smokescreen, when he was really interested in what Esme had uncovered for Hester? It would explain why he couldn't say anything or he'd have had to admit his involvement in Hester's enquiry, confess that it was he who sent Hester Esme's way.

She pushed the thought away and sighed. Did it really matter? Hadn't she decided she wanted nothing more to do with whatever Max was up to? Hadn't she accepted Maddy's assessment that she was best out of it, that nothing good ever came from getting caught up with Max Rainsford and one of his investigations?

The image of Hester's initial shock at discovering the murder in the family story floated into her head. The niggle of not knowing what was behind it had not gone away. It seemed unlikely that Hester was going to get in touch and explain it herself, so if the mystery was to be solved, it was down to Esme's own initiative.

She kissed the top of Jeanie's head and put her down on the end of the sofa. She gave herself a wry smile as she thought of Max's smug expression if he knew he'd piqued her interest. Thankfully, he never would know.

She fetched her laptop and put it on the kitchen table. As the machine booted, Esme worked out what route to take. Hester had been keen to know about Frank Stone's ancestry. That had been the starting point, so perhaps the answer lay there. She needed to dig further back. Maybe the mortuary photograph was key too? Esme felt the excitement growing, reminding herself that this was merely an academic interest, that she mustn't get carried away.

Esme opened Hester's file and read her notes to reacquaint herself with the facts of the case. The man convicted of murder, Albert Philips, was the grandfather of Hester's so-called partner, Frank Stone. As Esme had explained to Maddy, newspapers of the day had reported that Albert and his victim, Ernest Sanders, were cousins. Esme had established that Ernest's mother, Betsy, was the younger sister of Albert's father, John. According to reports of the trial, Albert's mother Eliza, his wife Hannah and his brother Frederick had attended every day, watching events unfold from the public gallery. The victim's father Roland Sanders had also been present.

Esme wondered at the impact of the crime on the two families and how it had affected relationships. Had they been close before or distant? Had it driven a wedge between brother and sister, John and Betsy? And the argument between the cousins which had resulted in so tragic an outcome – had either side been aware of it? Was it, as Esme and Maddy had speculated, a family dispute? Certainly, if the family had known anything about it, they'd not shared it with the court or the journalists covering the trial. Albert Philips in particular had appeared reticent about offering anything substantial on the subject. His explanation of a falling out over 'a trivial matter' but not elaborating further only served to mystify those present.

Why so evasive? The evidence against him was compelling – the discovery of Ernest Sanders' battered body in an alley and Albert arriving home, agitated and covered in blood. Everyone must have wondered what the point was in being so reticent and perhaps concluded, as the jury clearly had, that there were no mitigating factors which he could present in his defence or he'd have done so. She imagined the conversation between Philips and his defence counsel, the latter exasperated that his client was doing little to help his cause.

For Hester's report, Esme had drawn up a simple family tree, following the Philips line using census returns and parish records. Albert's paternal grandfather had been George Philips, born in 1824, and his grandmother was Lucy Hannaford, born 1834. George's father had also been called George, born around 1794, married to Ann Turner. According to his baptism record, his father was another John and his mother was Mary. There Esme had paused, awaiting further instructions from Hester, which, of course, had never materialised.

She sat back in her chair. She was wasting her time, wasn't she? Randomly gathering information on Albert's ancestors was no guarantee she'd uncover anything meaningful, and with a common name like Philips, she was likely to encounter an insurmountable number of potential connections. Even if she continued down the line, there was nothing to suggest she'd ever be able to satisfy her own curiosity. How could she justify such a trawl?

She rested her elbows on the table either side of her laptop and scowled at the screen. She idly considered whether learning more about the victim of the crime, Ernest Sanders, would give up more information. But she knew she'd only encounter similar issues. Sanders was as common a name as Philips. It wasn't impossible, just exceedingly time consuming. And for what? It was just a futile fishing expedition.

It didn't mean there *wasn't* anything out there in the family histories of Albert Philips and Ernest Sanders which would explain Hester's behaviour, but how likely was it that Esme would find it? She'd have to trawl along every branch and unpick a lot more than names on a tree. And even if she did inadvertently come across what Hester appeared to be reluctant for her to discover, would she even recognise its significance?

She realised with a jolt she was in serious danger of again falling into Max's trap and getting dragged into one of his grubby little investigations. She slammed the lid of the laptop down and pushed it away. Forget Max and his devious ploys. She needed to put the whole thing out of her mind and divert her energies into her own endeavours.

# 22

'Are you sure it was Max?' Maddy said, when Esme told her about the *Antiques Roadshow*. They were taking a coffee break in Esme's kitchen after they'd loaded Maddy's van with the furniture Esme didn't want. She'd kept the desk and the large pine table, but had no use for the huge wardrobe and the 1960s-era sideboard.

It was good to see the space cleared. For the first time, Esme could begin to imagine how the room might look when the builders had finished and she could set up her office. It had been the right decision to earmark the building for conversion. By the time everything was completed, decorated and heated, it would be a pleasant place to work.

'Who are we talking about?' Harry said, joining them. He sat down at the table and slid a set of keys across to Maddy. 'I've locked up,' he said. 'Can't be too careful round here, so I'm told. Shady characters camping out in outhouses.'

'That's precisely who we're talking about,' Maddy told him. She nodded towards Esme. 'Esme saw Max Rainsford in the crowd at the *Antiques Roadshow*.'

'What? When you were there last year?' Harry said, turning to look at each of them.

'No, not then. On the tele last night.'

Harry cocked a thumb in the direction of the garden and looked at Esme. 'This is the journalist guy who'd been using your shed, right?'

'The same,' Esme said. 'And that's not all. There was a woman with him. A recent client of mine.'

'Is that a problem?' Harry said, dragging a mug of coffee towards himself.

'I'm not sure. But given she's gone AWOL since I gave her my interim report, it's looking a tad suspicious.'

Harry pulled a face. 'Yeah, take your point. Any theories?'

Esme glanced at Maddy. 'I've already been told I should give it a wide berth.'

'That means nothing, believe me,' Maddy told Harry, with a wry smile.

'Oh, come on,' Esme said, protesting. 'I've been very good, I'll have you know. I've gone nowhere near Max's investigation.'

'Not even a little bit?'

Esme gripped her mug. 'Well, I had a quick look at Isaac Maudesley, but that's all.'

'Isaac Maudesley?' Harry said. 'Where does he fit into all this?'

'Don't go there, OK?' Maddy said. 'If you knew Max Rainsford like Esme does, you'd know anything he is into is merely a figment of his imagination.'

'So, your client's brief didn't match up with Max's, then?' Harry asked.

'No,' Esme said. 'Someone different entirely. So, the two are probably totally unconnected, which is why I refuse to read anything into it.'

'So, what were they doing?' Maddy asked. 'On the footage, I mean.'

Esme shrugged. 'Just standing there. Listening in.'

'To what?'

Esme stood up. 'Oh, you know. When they do the TV close-up bit. There's always a few people from the crowd in the background. Hang on a minute, I'll show you.' She put down her mug and went over to the television, switching it on and clicking through to the list of recorded programmes. She selected the previous night's episode and brought it up on the screen, pressing fast forward until she reached the right place.

'There,' she said, pressing play and perching on the sofa arm. Maddy and Harry carried their mugs over to join her. When Max and Hester came into view, Esme paused the recording to point them out.

'I couldn't believe it,' she said, looking over her shoulder. 'I grabbed the remote and just stared at them. That was it, then. I couldn't concentrate on the rest of the programme after that. My brain went into overdrive, trying to work out what I should read into it.'

Maddy sat down on the other arm of the sofa. 'Run it and let's see what they do next.'

Esme restarted the footage. The owner of the ring was answering the expert's question about how she'd come by it.

*'I inherited it from my grandmother,'* the woman was saying. *'And it was passed down to her from her grandmother.'*

Esme fixed her eyes on Max, watching as he turned away and melted into the crowd.

Suddenly, Harry interrupted. 'Stop it a minute, will you, Esme,' he said. 'Wind that back a bit.'

Esme pointed the remote at the screen and did as he asked. 'Back to where?' she asked.

'There!' Harry said, pointing to the screen. 'The bit you showed us at the start.'

Esme stopped at the point she'd seen Max and Hester together and froze the screen, looking anxiously at Harry. 'What have you seen?' she said.

Harry jabbed a finger in the direction of the television. 'Her. I've seen her before. I served her in the pub the other day.'

Maddy grabbed his arm. 'Who is she, then? Do you know her? Is she really called Hester Campbell?'

Harry shook his head. 'No idea. Aidan might know, though.'

'Aidan?' Esme said.

Harry nodded. 'Yeah. He was talking to her.'

# 23

'Thanks so much, both of you,' Esme said, as Harry opened the passenger door of the van and climbed inside. 'I owe you one.'

'No worries,' Harry said. 'Glad to help.'

Maddy pulled the van keys out of her pocket. 'I hope what you've seen isn't going to set you off on another magical mystery tour.'

Esme flapped her hand against Maddy's arm. 'Stop fretting, Madds. I've already sent Max off with a flea in his ear, so he's long gone. As for Hester, I can't deny I'd love to know what she was up to, but I'm probably never going to find out now she's made it perfectly clear she doesn't need my services any longer. I've just got to live with that.'

Maddy raised an eyebrow. 'I could always ask Aidan about Hester when I see him next?'

'Don't be silly. Just because he was talking to her doesn't mean he knew her. They could have been discussing the weather.'

'Good answer,' Maddy said, chuckling. 'That was a test, in case you hadn't realised.'

'Go!' Esme said, pushing her towards the van. *The Refurnish Centre* is expecting you. I'll give them a ring anyway to let them know you're on your way.'

Maddy joined Harry in the van and, with a farewell toot of the horn, pulled away up the hill. Esme turned back to the cottage. As she reached the front door, the spring sun broke through the cloud, promising a hint of warmth. She paused to breathe in the fresh air. With so much progress made on the outbuilding, she could allow herself some time off. Perhaps she'd explore the coast path and maybe find a way down to the cove where she, and now Libby, had seen the young boy on the shoreline.

After phoning the charity to alert them to Maddy and Harry's arrival, she laced up her walking boots and grabbed a coat, swapping her usual duffel for a lightweight waterproof jacket. She set off down the lane, turning up to the right on to the South West Coast Path before the road became a dead-end. The path passed in front of the unstable cottage, where mesh barriers stood along with a warning sign. *Dangerous structure,* it read. *Do not enter.*

*No fear of that*, Esme thought, as she joined the coastal path. Had it not been threatening to crash on to the beach below, though, she would have been tempted to explore inside the cottage and imagine past residents. Had Jim's story been true about the family who'd lived there, how one of them had pushed a custom officer off the cliff? As Jim pointed out, most smuggling tales survived through being passed on by word of mouth, often embellished for the pleasure of tourists' imaginations. There was little written evidence of such deeds.

She strode up the hill, leaving the derelict cottage below her as the narrow coast path plunged into deep woodland. Beautiful though it was, she found it a little frustrating only to catch intermittent glimpses of the sea to her left. On her right, she could just make out an occasional field stretching away inland on the other side of the margin of trees and bushes which lined her way. But she could see no obvious path down to the beach below, certainly not at the point where she estimated the cove she'd looked back at from the village beach would be. She was far too high up, for one thing. Any route down would be too precipitous, unless you were equipped with ropes and climbing tackle and could abseil to the shoreline below. Perhaps a path existed a little further along, one which zig-zagged its way down.

She pressed on.

Just when she was about to retrace her steps and head back home, the trees on the seaward side parted and, for the first time since she'd started her walk, she was able to stop and embrace the view from her elevated position. In the near distance ahead of her, she could see the distinctive features of Green Cliff, and beyond the extensive sandy beaches of Croyde and Woolacombe. She took a few moments to study the stunning vista.

By now, the path was beginning to descend and she knew she was as far from the cove as she'd been at the village in the opposite direction. Too far along for any hope of locating the track down to the cove she was looking for. The next beach was accessed by a narrow lane which cut through the steep wooded valley from the main road above. While she might continue down the combe and walk back along the beach from this end, she wasn't confident she'd be able to get through.

She turned and headed back the way she'd come. When she reached the point where she'd expected to find the seaward path, she slowed. Perhaps she'd missed something. But the gorse and trees, gnarled and bent over by the prevailing winds, lay thick and tightly packed against the ground and there was no evidence of any pathway other than the one on which she stood.

So, how had the young lad got to the cove? What other way could he have used to reach it? By boat? By rope? Surely he wasn't old enough to do either. Perhaps there'd been an adult nearby, out of sight, hidden by the rocks. Or, she thought, smiling to herself, he had truly been a ghost.

She dragged her gaze away from the thicket and back to the path. As she did so, something caught her eye through the trees on the landward side – a flicker of light in the distance, sun reflecting on glass. She reached out and pulled aside a curtain of ivy to peer through the gap between the branches of the trees lining the boundary between the track and the land adjoining it. There in the distance she spied a building, grand and austere, with a steep roof and ornate chimneys. It could easily be the Victorian Gothic property that Max told her belonged to Isaac Maudesley.

She shivered and let go of the dangling ivy. She had no intention of spoiling a beautiful spring day speculating on Max's agenda.

She strode back along the track until it turned and opened out on to her lane, where she saw Jim on his way up from the beach. After they'd passed the time of day, Esme gestured back the way she'd come.

'Does Chalacombe House still exist back there somewhere?' she asked him. 'I found it marked on an old map I came across amongst the junk in my outhouse. But it doesn't seem to appear on modern maps.'

'Yes and no,' Jim said, rubbing his chin. Esme waited. 'You'm see that there gert monstrosity through them trees?'

'Yes, I could. Ugly looking place. But that's not Chalacombe House, is it?'

'Not no longer, it int, no. But it wore on same spot yer ago. Remodelled when old Queen Victoria wore on the throne. They give it another name, too.'

'Dowell Lodge, right?'

Jim nodded. 'Bout sums it up, if yer ask me.'

'Sorry?'

Jim leaned towards her, a hint of mischief in his eyes. 'Dowell, maid. Old Devon word for the Devil.'

# 24

When Esme got home, she went in search of the old map, manoeuvring her way between the piles of boxes and office furniture in the spare bedroom, currently being used as a store room until her new work space was complete. The framed map was propped up against a filing cabinet. She carried it downstairs and laid it on the kitchen table.

As she'd seen before, the Chalacombe name appeared on the bay, the cove and the house. Given the Victorian penchant for restoration, she wasn't surprised Chalacombe House had been remodelled in the 19th century. She wondered what the house had been like before the Victorian architects got their hands on it. Of course, it was possible that by then, the Chalacombe family no longer owned the property or its land. Perhaps renaming it had seemed appropriate at the time. If Maudesley did have a Chalacombe family connection, as Max had suggested, had he purchased it because of the link? It seemed unlikely he'd be unaware of its history.

John Ford seemed to be very knowledgeable about the Chalacombe family. Perhaps he also knew something about the house. She might call in his shop and ask him. Max's words echoed briefly in her head – *How should I know, Ez? You're the family historian* – after which she'd accused him of trying to trick her into investigating Maudesley's ancestry. But she dismissed the coincidence as tentative and pushed the concept away, instead turning to Ford's tale of Thomas Venner and his terrifying experience of being captured by Barbary pirates, a full account of which, Ford had informed her, was available on the Internet.

Esme pushed the map to one side and fetched her laptop. While it booted, she recapped what she remembered from Ford's account of the family. Amelia, whose painting Esme had admired, had been one of three children born to William Chalacombe and his wife Elizabeth, the woman wearing the sumptuous dress and jewellery. Amelia had a younger brother, John, and her older brother, William, his father's namesake, had inherited the merchant shipping business. Amelia had married Richard Venner, and both their sons had served on their uncle's ships. It was while sailing into dangerous waters that they had been taken by pirates.

A brief search brought her to a summary of Thomas's experiences, his life as a slave and subsequent escape. Thomas's account spoke of men being held in filthy and squalid gaols, before being sold off as domestic slaves, often purchased by cruel and vindictive owners. But, as John Ford had intimated, Thomas was fortunate to have been bought by a master who treated him kindly. For a while, Thomas appeared to have accepted his new life. He'd been allowed, perhaps even encouraged, to marry, and after a year or so a daughter was born. Sadly, though, both Thomas's wife and his child had died of fever. It may have been the loss of his family, probably the reason he'd remained in Barbary as long as he had, which had changed his outlook. Maybe his grief spurred him to look for opportunities to finally escape captivity and return to his homeland.

So, what had happened to Thomas on his return to England? His memoir ended with arriving back with his family, but said no more as to his life beyond. What had it been like after everything he'd been through for so long? Had he ever remarried?

Esme returned to her genealogy databases, but could find no record of a marriage. She located his baptism record, citing Thomas's father as Richard Venner, and his mother, Amelia. The couple had married in 1713.

Esme discovered another earlier baptism attributed to Thomas's parents, which she concluded was for the brother mentioned by John Ford, who'd been captured at the same time as Thomas. His name was Henry and he was 7 years Thomas's senior. She found a marriage for Henry in the parish records for

1736, the same year the brothers went missing. His wife, Felicity Davey, must have already been pregnant when her husband was captured, as their son Josiah was born the following year. So, had Josiah ever seen his father again?

Esme returned to the summary of Thomas's adventures and confirmed there was no mention of Henry. Perhaps they'd been split up and Thomas had never known what had befallen his brother.

So, what had become of Henry's wife, Felicity? Esme entered her name into the search engine and as she scrolled through the list of options, her eye alighted on a baptism record for a Matilda Felicity Venner, dated 1749. It hadn't taken place in the parish Felicity and Henry had lived, but elsewhere in the county. Esme clicked on the name to bring up the detail. The mother was listed as Felicity Venner and Matilda's father Thomas Venner.

Esme frowned at the screen, puzzling over the information as she rubbed her thumb down her scar. Could this be the same Felicity Venner as was married to Henry? And the same Thomas Venner as had returned from captivity as a Barbary slave? It certainly suggested that Henry had not had the fortune of his younger brother and had lost his life somewhere in the harsh reality of slavery. It also appeared that once it was clear that Henry had not survived the ordeal, Thomas had taken on the responsibility of his brother's widow. Did that suggest Thomas had been aware of his older brother's fate?

Thomas mentioned in his account one of the most cruel and dehumanising roles imposed on the strongest and the fittest of the captives: galley slaves. An arduous and odious system where men were chained to their rowing benches and never allowed to leave. If they succumbed to exhaustion, they died where they sat, still shackled to their bench. If the ship sank, the unfortunate galley slaves sank with it.

Esme shuddered at the chilling description. Maybe Thomas, seeing his brother, 7 years his senior, as a tough and able seaman, believed this had been Henry's destiny. It would, perhaps, explain why he'd felt the need to tell the shocking story of the men who rowed the sultan's boats.

# 25

'You did what?' Esme said, staring at Maddy with astonishment as they finished setting up Tuesday's market stall.

'I phoned Aidan and asked him whether he knew Hester.' Maddy looked at Esme with raised eyebrows. 'Well, why not? You wanted to know, didn't you?'

'Yes, but…' Esme frowned. 'Didn't he think it a bit odd?'

'Wasn't odd at all. It was all very casual. I was phoning anyway to offer him the use of our spare bedroom while he's working on this job of his. Harry suggested it and I thought, why not? Better than a hotel or B & B, isn't it?'

'Yes, yes, I suppose it is. So, how did you manage to jump from offering to be his landlady to asking about Hester?'

Maddy grinned. 'You'd have been proud of me. I said Harry had seen a woman on the *Antiques Roadshow* programme and recognised her from the pub. Well, it's no word of a lie, is it? He *did*, after you'd pointed her out.'

'So, what did Aidan say to that?' Esme asked.

'He said he knew her from the museum.'

'What museum?'

Maddy pulled her phone from her back pocket and scrolled through it, before holding it out for Esme to see. 'The *Treasures of the Sea Museum*. Her real name is Chalacombe, not Campbell.'

'Chalacombe?' Esme echoed, squinting to bring the photograph on the screen into focus.

'She's one of the trustees. According to the blurb, she's a descendant of the founder.'

Esme stared at Hester's image smiling out at her from a website page, her thoughts a jumbled mess as she struggled with the implications. It certainly explained Hester and Max being together. Maudesley was the obvious link. But where did Max's interest and Hester's cross over?'

'So, there you go,' Maddy said, returning the phone to her pocket. 'You can leave it alone now. Mystery solved.'

'Well, not all of it,' Esme said. 'It doesn't explain her reaction to the murder, does it? Or where Max fits in.'

'No, true,' Maddy admitted. 'But at least you know who she is now. She's clearly quite legit, not some suspicious shady character.'

'Well, I wouldn't go that far,' Esme said, not sure whether to be relieved to learn something or irritated she'd been misled. 'Why all the pretence?'

Maddy folded her arms. 'Does it matter?'

Esme shrugged. 'I guess not. I'd still like to have understood what spooked her, though.'

'Well, you might just have to write that off to experience.' Maddy regarded her sternly. 'Unless you're going back on your promise to give Max a wide berth?'

'No, of course not. You don't need to worry about that.' Esme noticed a woman in a bouclé coat studying a recently restored wooden box on the end of the stall, giving her the excuse to change the subject. She nudged Maddy. 'Looks like someone's got their eye on your little tea caddy.'

Maddy looked round. 'I'll go and have a chat,' she said, moving away. 'She might be interested in its history.'

'Show her your photos,' Esme said. Maddy always made a photo diary of her renovation workings. She'd originally adopted the practice for clients who'd engaged her to renovate a prized family heirloom, presenting the photographs as part of the piece's history.

'Yes, I will,' Maddy said, pulling out her phone again. 'Oh, something else I meant to say,' she added, turning back to Esme.

'What's that?' Esme said, bracing herself for another reminder about the wisdom of letting go of the Hester conundrum. But it seemed Maddy had already said as much as she intended on that subject.

'There's a sale on in town next week,' she said. 'Been meaning to mention it.'

'What sort of sale?'

'One of those fabulous Captain's houses in Appledore has just gone on the market. The old guy who lived there was an avid collector of all things seafaring and everything is being sold off at the sales rooms in Rope Walk. It's bound to be a fascinating collection. I'm going along and thought you might like to come, too.'

'Yes, I'd love to. Let me know the details.'

\*

After the market closed, Esme helped load the stock into Maddy's van before heading into the centre of town to carry out a few errands. By the time she left for home, the afternoon had almost disappeared.

As she drove out of the town, her thoughts returned to the connection between Hester and Max, the museum and Isaac Maudesley. But no matter how much it churned around in her head, she couldn't come up with a scenario where Max's interest in Maudesley tied in with Hester's genealogical queries. Clearly, she was missing the vital link.

As she arrived at the junction where the main road met the lane leading down to her cottage, a 'Road Closed' sign blocked her way. A police officer stood beside it and as Esme turned into the lane, he gestured for her to stop.

Esme came to halt in front of the sign and wound down her window. 'What's going on?' she asked.

'I'm afraid you can't go down here, madam. If I could ask you to…'

'But I live here,' Esme protested.

'Ah.' The constable nodded. 'Then you may proceed. My colleagues will direct you further down.' He stood back and waved her on.

She considered pressing him for more information, but decided she'd quiz one of his colleagues in the village instead. She put the car into gear and carried on down the steep winding lane. The tips of the trees in the woods on either side swayed against the drama of the dark skittering clouds. Debris from the beech trees flew like petals across her path, bouncing off the windscreen, giving her a sense of being under attack.

Another policeman was waiting at the entrance to the car park, his vehicle positioned in the centre of the lane, its hazard lights flashing. Like his colleague at the junction above, he flagged her down.

'What's going on?' Esme asked again.

The constable, fresh-faced with thick hair swept back off his forehead, bent down to speak to her through the car window. 'Are you a resident, madam?'

'Yes, I am. Look, can someone tell me what's going on?'

'The end of the village has been cordoned off due to a dangerous structure.'

'You mean the cottage on the cliff?'

He nodded. 'That's right. Looks to be on the move. A resident alerted us to it. You won't be able to drive right down to the bottom, I'm afraid.'

'That's not a problem. My cottage is about halfway down. So, can I carry on, then?'

He straightened up. 'Yes, go ahead.'

Esme squeezed past the police car, continuing down the lane and round the corner. In the distance, she could see a crowd of people in the road, and beyond, in the gathering dusk, the stark flashing blue light of another police vehicle. She pulled into her driveway and got out of the car. What was the plan? They couldn't expect to keep up this sort of vigil indefinitely, so something must have happened to move the threat from potential to imminent. As she'd discussed with Jim the other day, the cottage had been designated a dangerous structure for months and she'd expected it to topple in dramatic fashion during the winter gales. Yet, still it clung to its perch, as though determined not to be written off so readily. But perhaps the recent storm *had* undermined its precarious grip and its time had come to finally let go.

Esme strode out into the lane and saw Libby standing talking to Jim.

'The cottage is on the move, I understand,' Esme said, as she joined them.

Jim nodded. 'I seed rubble on the beach earlier. Reckoned it was about to shift, even afore I seed rocks coming down.'

'Jim called it in,' Libby said, 'and the boys in blue descended a short time later.'

Esme turned and looked ahead towards the cordon at the bottom of the hill, where the residents of the cottages beyond were assembled beside the police vehicle, presumably evacuated from their homes as a precaution.

'So, do the experts think it's about to go?'

Libby shrugged. 'Only a matter of time, I think.'

'Yes, but do they know how much time?'

Libby turned to Jim. 'Did they say anything to you, Jim?'

Jim pulled a face. 'They b'ain't know, maid. Tis all guess work when it comes down to it.' He lifted a finger. 'Scuse me, ladies, I'z need to have a word.' He shuffled off down the lane towards one of the police officers standing by the cordon.

'I wonder if they've plans to move all of us out of our homes,' Libby said.

'I can't see the need for the whole village…' Esme's words were overtaken by a low grumbling sound, followed by the sharp crack of stone landing on stone.

Libby nodded towards the cottage. 'Bits have been falling off like that all day. I can't see how it can last much longer.'

They walked down the lane as far as they could. Barriers had been set up to prevent access to the beach and the coast path on

124

either side. Esme looked across and saw Jim still talking to the police officer. On the other side of the barrier, another police officer was deep in conversation with a man in an orange waterproof jacket. They had their backs to the crowd, and the civilian, who Esme assumed must be the engineer advising the police, was gesticulating towards the cottage.

She looked up at what remained of the structure, the jagged profile of its gable end silhouetted against the sky. As she watched, a piece of masonry tumbled from the wall and disappeared beyond.

'They think it's the cliff that's crumbling below it,' Libby said, 'rather than the cottage itself. I don't think it would be falling, otherwise.' She glanced over her shoulder. 'We can't see a lot from here. Let's go back to mine. We should have a better view from my garden.'

They hurried up the lane to Libby's cottage. She led Esme round to the back and pointed up the steep garden path on to the terrace above, which looked out to sea.

'You go on up,' she said. 'I'll go and get the bins.'

Libby disappeared inside the back door and Esme climbed the path to the terrace, wrapping her coat around her against the wind which was strengthening now. Libby emerged from her cottage and joined her on the terrace.

'There you go,' she said, handing Esme a pair of binoculars before looping the strap of a second pair over her head.

Esme peered through the eyepieces and adjusted the focus, her hair flapping in the wind. As she did so, another section of wall plummeted backwards and disappeared. She heard the crowd below gasp and as they watched, the low growl they'd heard earlier grew to a roar as the cottage finally gave up its fight. The end gable crashed backwards off the edge of the cliffs and the remaining cottage walls collapsed in on themselves, creating a billowing cloud of dust which surged into the air and settled over the immediate area, followed by shocked cries from the cluster of people below.

Esme lowered the binoculars and stared at the empty space.

'Well, that was a bit dramatic, wasn't it?' Libby said, blowing out a long, heartfelt sigh. 'Just as well it didn't happen in the middle of the night. It would have been terrifying for those who live nearby. At least we know everyone is safe.'

'Yes, you're right, there.' As Esme watched while the dust settled, her eye caught a fragment of fabric in the debris. She raised the binoculars and homed in, gasping at what she saw.

'What's the matter?' Libby asked, peering in the direction Esme was looking. 'What have you seen?'

'There,' Esme said, pointing. 'There, right in the middle. That orange.' She swallowed. 'It looks like Max's sleeping bag.'

She clasped her hand across her mouth and closed her eyes. He must have used the derelict cottage after she'd kicked him out. Was his body buried somewhere in the rubble? Had she been responsible for Max's death?

# 26

Esme sat in Libby's kitchen, still turning the various scenarios over and over in her head, only vaguely aware of Libby clattering around at the sink. Surely Max wouldn't have been inside the cottage when it collapsed, would he? He'd be out and about, spying on Maudesley's country house, trying to find out whatever it was Max thought he could learn from such surveillance.

But what if his vigils had been at night? Might he have been asleep during the day?

Libby had tried to reassure her, saying he'd have been alerted by activity outside when the police arrived and would have come out of the cottage. But given that Max would have not wanted to make his presence known, he might have stayed where he was, trapped and unable to get out without being spotted. But none of this Libby would appreciate until she knew the truth about who Max was and what he was doing here.

Earlier, as Esme had stood, fixated on the sight of Max's sleeping bag caught in the rubble, Libby had tugged at her arm. 'We need to tell the police about your friend.'

'No,' Esme said, snapping her head around. If Max *hadn't* been caught up in the incident, he'd not thank her for breaking his cover. But when she saw Libby's horrified face, she added, 'What I mean is, yes, we do need them to check, but...' She took a deep breath. 'There's something I ought to tell you.'

Libby frowned and looked at her curiously. 'About your friend?'

'Yes. But before I do, you're right. We must get the police to take a look.' She made her way down the steps, Libby following behind. When they came around the end of the cottage, Esme looked down on the scene below. One police officer was talking into his radio, the other addressing the gathering of people at the barrier. There looked to be more there than earlier. Had word got around? Had the press got hold of the story?

Esme stopped and caught hold of Libby's arm. 'What I said, up there,' she said, jerking her head back the way they'd come. 'It's best the police don't know who he is. Not unless...' She shuddered, not wanting to contemplate the worst scenario. 'Well, you know.'

Libby hesitated for a moment before squeezing Esme's hand. 'Look,' she said, concern showing in her eyes, 'I definitely don't know who he is. So, how about I tell them I think I saw someone in the cottage earlier? I could point out the sleeping bag. You stay here.'

Esme watched Libby as she hurried down the lane, moved that her friend was able to trust her, despite everything she'd said, which must have sounded highly suspicious. She knew she had to respond to that trust and tell Libby everything.

When Libby returned a few moments later, she assured Esme that the officers had taken her sighting seriously and would seek advice on the safety of the site before attempting any search. Libby suggested she and Esme convene to her kitchen and warm up, as by now, dusk was falling and the air was chilling.

Now, sitting at Libby's kitchen table, Esme realised Libby was talking to her and she dragged herself out of her pondering as Libby slid a hot mug of tea over to her.

'OK,' Libby said, sitting down opposite Esme, cradling her own mug of tea. 'Truth time.'

Esme gave her a watery smile. 'Thank you for accepting things at face value,' she said. 'I know it must sound very dubious.'

Libby raised her eyebrows and returned her smile. 'You're right, it does. So I'm intrigued to hear the simple explanation.'

Esme stared down at the dark liquid in her mug, wondering where to start. 'My unwelcome guest,' she began, 'is an investigative journalist. I've known him for years.'

'Your late husband was a journalist, wasn't he?'

Esme nodded. 'Yes, he and Max used to work together.'

'So you're good friends, then.'

Esme gave a derisory laugh. 'No, we're most definitely not.' She stared down at the table top. 'Max is a good journalist, but not always ethical in his methods. We never really kept in touch after Tim died, but a couple of years ago, we fell out big time because Max…' she hesitated, choosing her words carefully. 'Well, let's say that Max uncovered something which was very important to me, but his lack of scruples soured our relationship. I haven't had anything to do with him since.'

'Until this week.'

'Yes, until he turned up out of the blue on some undercover investigation.' Esme looked up at Libby. 'I'm furious with him, Libby. The gall of the man. After everything he did, just to turn up and help himself to my hospitality.'

'What's he investigating?'

'Ah, well. I never quite got to the bottom of that. I kicked him out before he could say much. In one way, I'm annoyed that I did. On the other hand, it's probably best I'm out of it.' She lifted her mug and took a sip of the strong tea before carefully replacing it on the table with a shaking hand. 'But if my kicking him out caused him to search for alternative accommodation…' She looked towards the kitchen window, which faced the now demolished cottage.

Libby reached across the table and took Esme's hand. 'Don't think about it. You don't even know he was in there.'

There was a loud rapping on the front door. Libby went out into the hall, closing the kitchen door behind her. The sound of voices filtered through to the kitchen, but Esme couldn't make out what was being said.

After a few moments, Libby returned to the kitchen. 'That was the police,' she said, resuming her place at the table. 'You'll be pleased to hear they've not found anyone in the rubble of the cottage.'

Esme let out a long sigh. 'That's a relief,' she said. But Libby's face still looked troubled. 'What?'

Libby hesitated. 'They did say they hadn't checked the beach below yet, but I don't think you should read too much in to that. You don't know for sure your friend was in the cottage.'

'But we saw his sleeping bag.'

Libby shook her head. 'They found a bunch of rags, the officer said. My guess is it was probably some old curtains.' She gave Esme a reassuring smile. 'So, that's looking hopeful, isn't it?'

It was dark by the time Esme left Libby's house. She hurried up the lane, knowing the kittens would be wanting their tea and wondering where she'd got to. Behind her, there was still activity at the end of the lane. Lights had been set up around the ruined cottage and she assumed that residents had been allowed back into their homes.

She fished in her pocket for her keys, pulling out her phone as she climbed the steps for the flashlight to guide her way. As she slid the key into the front door, she heard footsteps on the path. With a jolt of alarm, she spun round, pointing the phone in the direction of the sound.

In the beam of light was Max. And his face was covered in blood.

# 27

Esme steered Max inside and sat him down in the kitchen. He had a nasty cut on his cheekbone and one of the lenses of his glasses was cracked. She took his glasses off and put them on the table. He seemed dazed and she was concerned he was suffering from concussion. She washed her hands and grabbed the first aid box from under the sink.

'You really need to go to A & E, Max,' she said, sponging the blood from his face. The cut continued to seep as she cleaned it up. 'This could do with a couple of stitches, for a start. Why don't I call an ambulance?'

'No.' Max grabbed her wrist. He looked at her. 'No medics. Stick a plaster on it. It'll be fine.'

'It won't be fine, Max. It's way beyond a sticking plaster.'

'Try.' He let go of her arm. 'And thanks for this, Esme. Appreciate it.'

She glared at him for a few seconds and sighed. 'Here, hold that,' she said, guiding his hand to the wad of cotton wool she'd pressed against the cut. 'I think I've got some steri-strips upstairs.'

She hurried up to the bathroom and fetched a pack of the medical tapes. As she closed the cupboard, she glanced at her reflection in the mirrored door, her eye falling on the scar on her own cheek. She shuddered and turned away. No time to get maudlin.

Max hadn't moved. He sat staring vacantly into the middle distance. She realised she was still wearing her coat. She slipped it off and threw it on the end of the table.

'Are you sure you're OK?' she asked.

He looked up at her. 'I've been a lot worse,' he said, with a weak smile.

'I can quite believe it.' She dropped the steri-strips packet on the table and pulled out a chair, turning it to face him. 'I saw you on TV the other day,' she said, opening up the packet. If he was incapable of holding a normal conversation, it'd give her the excuse to override his wishes and make that emergency call.

He looked at her, curiously. 'What are you talking about?'

She took his hand and gently lifted it away from the cut. 'What's it doing? Is it still bleeding?'

'You tell me.'

She wrinkled her nose. 'I think it's slowing.'

'See? Told you, you didn't need to get the blue-light brigade.'

She grunted. 'Don't get too cocky, it might not last.' As she assessed the damage, it was obvious he wasn't going to be in any fit state to go on his way. Not for a while yet, anyway. She wondered where his car was parked. But if he'd had a car, he'd have used that to hole up in, wouldn't he? He'd have no use for her outhouse.

'Well, get on with it,' Max said, jolting her out of her thoughts. 'You were making out I was bleeding to death a minute ago.'

'Sorry.' She reached for the first steri-strip and peeled it off its backing, before lining it up on his cheek. 'Now, keep still, for goodness sake.'

They both fell silent as Esme concentrated on attaching the tapes across the wound. After a few moments, she sat back and admired the result.

'Well, I'm not sure I'd pass any nursing exams with it, but it's doing a job, I think. No, don't touch it!' she added, snatching Max's hand down. 'I don't know how secure it is. Anyone ever tell you, you make a terrible patient?'

'Frequently.'

'Well, you're going to have to be careful. And I still think you ought to get someone more qualified than me to look at it.'

Max flapped a hand dismissively. 'What's this about me being on TV? Been watching some old documentaries, have you?'

'Oh, so you did hear me, then. That's a good sign. Not quite brain dead yet.' Esme collected up the empty packets off the table and stood up. 'No, it wasn't a documentary. *Antiques Roadshow.*'

'What?'

'The one at the Abbey they filmed last summer. I didn't think you were into antiques, Max?'

He looked at her suspiciously, but said nothing.

'I was there too, as it happens,' she continued. 'But I never saw you.' She threw the litter in the bin under the sink and turned round, leaning against the worktop, her arms folded. 'The BBC cameraman did, though. I watched the programme the other day and spotted you in the crowd.'

'How d'you know it was me? Could have been just a look-a-like.'

'So, are you saying you weren't there?'

Max rubbed his chin and stared at her. Esme stared back, waiting for his answer, guessing he was weighing up whether to admit it or pretend she'd made a mistake.

'Yeah, you're right. I was following a tip-off. Waste of time in the end, as it turned out.' He sat back in his chair. 'Didn't see you there, though. Did you go along for the hell of it or did you take something to show the experts?'

Esme looked at him from under her brow and ignored his question. 'So, who was the woman with you?'

'What woman?'

'The one standing right next to you.'

He gave her a pitying look. 'Oh, come on, Ez. You said yourself, there was a crowd. She could have been anyone.'

'It won't do you any good pretending, Max. You know who I'm talking about. And I know who she is, too. What I want to know is what you and Hester were up to. And why she was calling herself Hester Campbell when it's not her real name. That would be good to know, too.'

He regarded her for a moment. 'Can't say, you know that.'

'*Won't* say, you mean. You're the one who sent her to me.'

Max put his hand to his head and pulled a face. 'Isn't there something in the nursing code against berating a patient? You told me a minute ago you were concerned about my health. Now you're giving me the third degree.'

'I'm pretty sure it doesn't apply to journalists who are being less than truthful to their rescuers.' She inclined her head. 'You did, though, didn't you? Go on. Admit it.'

Max closed his eyes and exhaled. 'OK, you're right.' He held out his hand in a gesture of appeal. 'Well, I had to, didn't I? You wouldn't have given me the time of day.'

Esme shook her head. 'I can't believe the cheek of you, Max Rainsford. After everything you did.' She bit her lip as her voice cracked. She swallowed and allowed it to steady before continuing. 'So, are you going to tell me where Hester fits into this or not? I'm assuming it's something to do with your Isaac Maudesley investigation, given their joint interest in the museum.' Max shot her a wary glance. She raised her eyebrows. 'Didn't think I'd worked that one out, did you?'

Max laid his hands on his knees and sighed. 'Look,' he said, peering up at her, 'I get that you've made the connection. But it's not in my gift to explain Hester's interest. You'll have to speak to her about that.'

'Well, tell her to answer my emails, then,' Esme snapped, turning away from him and busying herself tidying the sink.

After a moment, she heard Max take a deep breath behind her. 'I'll tell her, OK? Can't make her, of course. But I'll pass on your message.'

Esme nodded, not trusting herself to speak.

'So,' Max said. 'My turn to ask the questions. What's with all the police?'

Esme spun round. 'You know why they're here,' she said, with sudden concern. Perhaps he was concussed after all and his memory was playing tricks on him. 'The cottage you were dossing down in crashed onto the beach.'

'What?' He winced. 'Ouch,' he said, touching the back of his head. 'You got any paracetamol, Ez? My head's throbbing like a sixties disco.'

Esme opened the kitchen drawer and found a pack of painkillers. She filled a glass from the tap and handed it over with the medication.

'Thanks.' As she watched him take out two tablets from the pack, something struck her. Why hadn't it occurred to her before? Max wasn't covered in dust.

'You didn't get your injuries when the cottage collapsed, did you?' Esme said.

Max shoved the tablets in his mouth and took a gulp of water. 'Course not,' he said, wiping his lips with the back of his hand. He looked at her quizzically. 'I wondered why you never asked what had happened. Thought it was unlike you.' He grinned, which turned into a grimace and again his hand went to the back of his head.

Esme folded her arms. 'So what did happen?'

'Some joker sent the dogs after me. Had to throw myself over a fence to get away. Ended up head first into a pile of rocks.' He pointed to the cut on his face. 'And got this for my trouble.'

'Dogs?'

'Yeah. Never seen them before. Must be new.'

'You've been over at Maudesley's place?'

Max nodded, then winced. 'Oops, bad idea.'

'Look at you,' Esme said. 'You need a doctor.'

'Nah, I'm fine. Look, I'd better get off.'

'You're in no fit state to go anywhere.' She couldn't believe she'd just said that. But she didn't like the pallor of his face. At the very least, she must stop him from rushing off prematurely.

'Stop fussing, Ez. I'll get out of your hair in a minute, then you won't have to worry about me any longer.'

'That'd suit me perfectly. But not just yet, OK?' Maybe keeping him talking would buy them some time. 'So, how about

135

you tell me *why* you were poking around Maudesley's place?'

Max slumped back in his chair. 'If you're sure you want to know?'

A distant echo of Maddy's words played somewhere in the back of her head. *You know as well as I do that anything involving Max Rainsford is bad news.* Why did she ask him that? Why not ask something innocuous, like was he planning a holiday any time soon?

But knowing what Max was up to wasn't at all the same thing as getting involved. She let Maddy's words fizzle out.

'Go on, then,' she heard herself say. 'Tell me.'

# 28

Max rested his elbow on the table, peering at her with bloodshot eyes. 'You sure about this, Ez?' he said again. 'You said you didn't want to know.'

Esme pulled out a chair and sat down at the table. 'It's a bit late for that now, though, isn't it? Now you've dragged me in by getting me to do Hester's bidding. So give. All you've told me so far is there are rumours. What rumours? About Hester? About her and Maudesley? What? And then there's the murder. Why did that freak her out?'

Max held up his hand. 'Whoa, Ez. You're losing me now. What murder?'

'Frank Stone's grandfather. He was hanged for murder in the 1920s. Surely she must have told you? Isn't that why you dragged me into this in the first place? To find out about Frank Stone?'

'Oh, that.' Max shrugged. 'Look, I totally get it that to a historian like you, that's all fascinating stuff…'

'So, she did tell you, then?'

Max gave another exaggerated shrug. 'Yeah, but such ancient history isn't exactly relevant to the here and now, is it?'

Esme scowled at him. 'Then why even go there in the first place and engage me?'

Max flicked his hand in a careless gesture. 'It was something she said. Something she wanted checked out, OK? It's no big deal. And I thought, well, worth a punt. Might flag up something.'

'Well it did flag up something, didn't it? And it meant something to Hester, certainly. But what?'

'Look, forget Hester, Ez. I can't answer that. Maybe she'll explain…'

'Yes, but…'

'Yeah, I know, you said. She's not answering your emails. I've said I'll pass on your message and I will, but then it's up to her.'

Esme sighed. Clearly she was wasting her time trying to learn more about Hester's agenda. Maybe Hester hadn't confided in Max the significance of the find. That in itself was odd, being as they were supposed to be partners in this investigation.

Well, there was no point in pursuing that now. Perhaps, if Max pressed her, there was still a chance that Hester would get in touch. And it would be much better to get a full explanation from Hester herself.

'OK,' she said, laying her hands flat on the table, 'let's leave Hester out of it for now. But that doesn't stop you telling me the rest. What's going on that involves you creeping around like a cat burglar?'

Max sniffed and took a breath. 'OK. You win.' He rubbed his hands across his eyes. 'Let's just say it's looking like Maudesley isn't quite the honest broker he's making out he is.'

'Meaning?' Esme said, when Max didn't immediately elaborate.

'Reckon he could be dealing illegally.'

'In what?'

'What d'you think?' Max said, giving her a mocking look. 'Historic artefacts, of course.'

'What? For the museum? Surely you'd not put items on public display which you'd acquired illegally?'

'No, but you might for a private collection.'

'Oh, right. I see.' Esme wriggled on the seat of her chair and crossed her legs as she considered this. 'And this private collection is at his country pile, so that's why you were poking around?' She pulled a sceptical expression. 'Don't tell me you thought if you peered through a couple of windows, you could tell what you were looking at was bought on the black market?'

Max laughed and immediately flinched. 'Bloody paracetamol's taking a while to kick in. You haven't got anything stronger, have you?'

'No. And even if I did, you'd have to wait another 4 hours

before taking another dose.' She leaned forward. 'I'm still inclined to take you up to A & E.'

He gave her a watery smile. 'No need. I'm good. Just looking for the sympathy vote, honest.'

'Trying to get out of fessing up, more likely.'

He inclined his head. 'C'mon, Ez. If I had something concrete to share with you, I'd share it. But, like I said, it's all speculation.' He winced, his eyes glazed over, and for a moment Esme thought he was about to pass out.

'Max?' She got to her feet just in time to reach out and catch him as he keeled over.

He blinked at her and grinned. 'Sorry. Mind drifted.' He stood up. 'Look, I should get going.'

'Are you kidding?' Esme said, blocking his way. 'You'd be lucky to make it to the end of the lane. You don't have a car, remember?'

He pulled out his phone. 'I'll get a cab.' He winked at her. 'Unless there's a lift on offer?'

'If I'm giving you a lift anywhere, it's to the hospital.'

'You're overreacting, Ez. It's not that serious, I keep telling you.' He turned his attention to his phone and began scrolling. 'I've got to head back to London tomorrow. I'll find somewhere to stay near the station.'

'OK, OK, I'll give you a lift,' Esme said, with a sigh. 'But not until the morning. You'd better stay here tonight. At least I can keep an eye on you. I'm still not convinced you're not concussed.'

'Oh, Esme,' Max said, with a mischievous grin. 'I'm touched. Didn't think you cared.' He pocketed his phone and sat back down.

She ignored his teasing and glanced across the room. 'You can bed down on the sofa tonight, though you'll have to contend with the other residents.'

Max looked over to the kittens who were sitting in front of the wood-burner, probably wondering when Esme was going to light it for them.

'I'm sure we'll get on fine.'

Esme took her seat again, wondering if she'd been played and this had been Max's plan all along. Well, it was done now. Besides, she wasn't exaggerating about her concerns and, despite his ability to bring out the worst in her, she wouldn't want to send him on his way only for his body to be discovered in a ditch the following morning.

She studied his wounded face and wondered what other enquiries had resulted in his sustaining injuries. Having a reputation for fishing for what might not even be there must surely mean he'd annoyed his quarries enough for them to dish out retaliation.

'Are you sure this Maudesley thing isn't a complete fantasy?' she said. 'Maybe someone who doesn't like him is spreading these rumours you've heard?'

'Yeah, I might buy that, if it weren't for the fact that I got some intel there was a delivery due.'

'And you thought if you witnessed what it was, and maybe *who* delivered it, you'd have a lead to explore.'

'Something like that, yes. And then,' he jabbed a finger towards his damaged face, 'this happened…'

'Suggesting your suspicions were more likely to be right than wrong,' Esme finished.

'You got it.'

'So what now?'

Max looked around the kitchen. 'Got anything to eat, Ez? I'm starving.'

# 29

Esme fed the kittens and considered what food to rustle up. Something quick and simple. She stabbed a couple of potatoes with a fork and put them in the microwave before grating carrot for a salad. As she beat eggs for an omelette, she tried to assimilate everything Max had told her before she'd sent him upstairs to clean himself up. Tomorrow morning, she'd take him to Barnstaple station to catch the early London train.

Despite what Max had said, she wasn't naive enough to believe he'd set up such an investigation based on just a few rumours. Hester's part in this mystery was a clear indication of that. After all, she worked with Maudesley. So, had Max sought out Hester or had it been the other way around?

Esme was laying cutlery out on the table when Max came back downstairs. She told him to take a seat while she cooked the omelettes. He seemed uncharacteristically quiet and again she questioned her decision to accept his dismissal that he needed medical intervention. Perhaps she should override his wishes and phone for an ambulance. But she could hardly lock him up while waiting for it to arrive. Driving him to the hospital offered no firmer solution. Even if he did agree to get into her car, she'd no guarantee he wouldn't be using it as a ruse and planning to abscond the minute she pulled up at the entrance. No. Far better for him to stay where she could keep an eye on him.

She put his meal down in front of him and took the seat opposite.

Max cleared his throat. 'Appreciate this, Ez. I know we haven't always…'

She picked up the salt cellar, avoiding his gaze. 'Yeah, I know. Just eat, eh?'

He nodded and picked up his knife and fork.

'You know, Ez,' Max said after a few moments. 'When the book came out…'

Esme shot him an angry glance. Hadn't she just made it clear she didn't want to talk about it?

Max held up his hand. 'Hear me out, will you?'

Esme stabbed her fork into a piece of baked potato. 'I'm not sure you've earned the right. You sold me down the river for that book deal. You gave away something that wasn't yours to give.'

'Yeah, I know. I was stupid. I admit that now. I just couldn't see it at the time.'

Esme glowered at him. Was this another of his tricks, just a pretence? If he hadn't been able to see back then that agreeing to cover up a truth she'd been desperate to expose for so long was a betrayal, why should she believe he could see it now?

To her horror, tears formed in her eyes. She blinked them away and forced herself to eat something.

'If it's any compensation,' Max said, quietly, 'the book wasn't the success I'd hoped for.' He gave an embarrassed half-laugh. 'Which is why I'm back to the day job.' He reached out to touch her hand and she snatched it away. 'Look,' he continued, 'it was a bad call on my part. And for what it's worth, I'm sorry I pushed it. I should have backed off.'

Esme looked up at him and sniffed. 'I wonder,' she said, giving him a cold stare, 'if you'd be quite so magnanimous if the book had been a best seller?'

He shook his head. 'I'd lost interest even before it was published.' He poked his fork into the carrot strands and peered up at her. 'Guilty conscience, probably.'

Esme stared back. 'Is that right?' she said. He must know from the tone of her voice that she didn't believe a word of it, but suddenly it didn't seem worth fighting over any more. She sighed and focused on her food. Perhaps that was a good sign she'd come to terms with everything.

Maybe.

Max was looking brighter the next morning, but Esme warned him as she dropped him off at Barnstaple station for a train back to London that he could still succumb to concussion up to 48 hours after an injury.

He grinned at her as he climbed out of the car. 'OK, Mother. I'll try and be a good boy.'

'You do that,' she said, her mock stern expression softening to return his grin.

He thanked her for the lift and slammed the passenger door. As she watched him hurry away across the tarmac, his grubby rucksack slung over his shoulder, she considered the strangeness of the situation. After everything that had happened in the past, if someone had told her that there'd come a time when she'd be concerned about Max's welfare, she'd have dismissed the idea as preposterous.

She turned the car round and set off back home, stopping at the supermarket to stock up. As she pulled off the main road towards the village, she noticed a lorry with the local council's logo on its cab following her. When she turned into her own driveway, it passed her, continuing down the lane, where another local authority truck and two police cars were parked in front of the barriers.

Had something else happened? Or were the authorities ready to remove the cordon at the top of the footpath leading down to the beach? It would be more than frustrating to have just moved into a village with coastal access, only to find it cut off for an indefinite period while an argument raged over who picked up the bill for the work to clear the debris at the foot of the cliff.

She left her shopping in the boot of the car and hurried down the road to see what she could establish, spotting Libby ahead of her.

'Before you ask,' Libby said, as Esme fell in step with her, 'I've no idea what's going on.'

'Be nice to think they're opening up the path to the beach,' Esme said. 'Even limited access would be better than nothing.'

'Maybe,' Libby shrugged. 'It is all a bit OTT at the moment.'

'I'm glad I've seen you, actually,' Esme said, as they walked.

'Oh?' Libby said. 'Why's that?'

'Max turned up at mine last night.'

'Oh, that's a relief,' Libby said, touching Esme's arm. 'I could tell you were worried.' She smiled. 'Despite everything you'd told me about the antagonism between you.'

'Yeah, well, we had the opportunity to bury a few hatchets, as it turned out,' Esme said. 'He was in a bit of a sorry state. He'd taken a tumble in the dark somewhere. So I let him kip on my sofa.'

They arrived at the barrier and stood, looking across at the devastation.

'Looks promising,' Esme said, nodding towards the workmen who'd started clearing the footpath of debris, which they were heaving on to the back of one of the lorries.

'So is Max still with you?' Libby asked.

'No, I took him to Barnstaple station first thing to get a train back to London. He was much better this morning. Hopefully, that's the last I'll see of him.' She grinned. 'I told him he was getting too old for all this mad sneaking around.'

'Sure about that?' Libby said, glancing round at Esme. 'Isn't it a case of once a journalist, always a journalist?'

Esme thrust her hands into her coat pockets and sighed. 'Yeah,' she said with a wry smile. 'Maybe you're right.'

# 30

Libby's comment about Max and the innate nature of journalism played around in Esme's mind as she climbed the hill back to her cottage. From Max's conversation the previous evening, she'd got the impression that the original reason he and Hester had become involved with one another was no longer relevant. Not to Max, anyway. Whatever had been their shared goal at the outset, something had changed.

Maudesley was the common factor between the two of them, and that surely must have been what brought them together in the first place. But under what circumstances? Who had instigated that initial contact? Had the rumours Max had spoken of come originally from Hester? Or had Max heard them and approached Hester for her reaction? If the latter, she'd clearly not dismissed them out of hand and had, perhaps, taken the opportunity to collaborate.

So, where did employing Esme fit in? What had that got to do with anything? Perhaps it had nothing to do with Max's interest at all. His indifferent response to what Esme had uncovered suggested the murder didn't impact on his investigations into Maudesley.

Esme pushed open the front door of her cottage, her eyes alighting on the pillow and crumpled duvet lying on the sofa as she stepped inside. She slipped off her coat and went across the room to collect up the discarded bedding, annoyed with herself that she'd not pressed Max more. But then, what would be the point? Hadn't she made it abundantly clear to Max that she had no plans to get dragged into his Maudesley case?

As she carried the bedding upstairs, she thought of her complaint to him about Hester not returning her calls and his promise to speak to her. Would Hester respond? And did Esme really want her to, given everything she'd just reminded herself about keeping out of it? Wouldn't it be better to let it go, accept that she'd never find out the reason why news of the murder affected Hester the way it did?

With the bedding put away, Esme came back downstairs and went into the kitchen to find herself something for lunch. The day had begun early and she realised she was hungry. She fixed herself a tuna sandwich and put it on a plate, before taking it over to the table and sitting down. She was wasting far too much time dwelling on Max and his Maudesley investigation.

By the time she'd swallowed the last mouthful, she'd made a decision. She shoved the empty plate away. Forget Max, forget Hester and get on with something else. There was that *Photos Reunited* research she ought to be doing, the young woman, Ethel Murray, who'd worked in a hotel.

Esme took the plate over to the sink and swilled it under the tap, washing her greasy fingers at the same time, before returning to the table and opening up her laptop. She brought up Ethel's image on the screen. Maddy and she had agreed Ethel's outfit and hairstyle dated the photograph in the 1920s. The woman Esme had spoken to at the market recalled being told with some pride that Ethel had worked in a prestigious hotel in the county, though she didn't remember which one. Neither did she know if Ethel was a local girl or if she'd come to the area to work. If the latter, one of the places Ethel might have been drawn to find employment could have been Torquay on The English Riviera, a fashionable holiday destination since Victorian times. By the roaring 1920s, it had developed a reputation for glamour, luxury and elegance, advertised on stunning Art Deco tourism posters of the time.

Esme decided that finding Ethel on the 1921 census as a hotel employee would confirm she had the correct person, and from there, having gleaned her date and place of birth, she'd be able to take her search further. She opened up *Find My Past* and navigated

146

to the relevant page on the site, adding in Ethel Murray's name in the search engine and limiting the location to Devon. The list was encouragingly short and once Esme eliminated those who would have been too old or too young, she'd found her.

Ethel had been born in Exeter, and at the time of the 1921 census was residing on Lundy Island. Esme imagined the delight of the lady who'd identified the photograph to have her memories confirmed, and clicked on the image of the original document to find out more. At the head of the list was a housekeeper and Ethel was one of a number of staff employed at Manor Hotel, which in a previous existence had been a large farmhouse.

As Esme scanned down the others listed on census night, her eye fell on the name of one of the staff members, a waiter. Albert Philips. She blinked. Could this be *the* Albert Philips, the murderer convicted in 1923?

She homed in on his details listed in the various columns on the document – his date of birth and where he was born – and confirmed the information fitted. And there was no reason why it wouldn't. It was perfectly feasible that Philips had worked on the island prior to the incident which would lead to his incarceration and subsequent execution. But should she read more into the find? And if so, what?

As she digested the discovery, her phone rang. Still processing the potential implications, she picked it up and made the connection without looking at the screen.

'Esme,' Hester said, with a sigh down the line. 'I owe you an apology. We need to meet.'

# 31

Esme stepped off the street into the entrance of the old building on the quay where she'd arranged to meet Hester and clattered up the narrow linoleum-covered stairs to the second floor. On the top landing, a white-panelled door stood ajar and Esme could hear the sounds of someone shifting things around. She tapped on the door and peered inside.

The room was filled with a sea of boxes, several piled on top of one another. In the middle was a bland grey desk, two office chairs sitting either side of it, and a tall filing cabinet in the corner with an expensive looking coffee machine on top. On the desk sat two larger boxes with cables sticking out of the top of one and computer hardware out of the other.

Hester was standing by the filing cabinet wearing a camel-coloured wool coat with wide collar, reading a leaflet. She looked up at Esme's knock and smiled, relaxing her shoulders, as though Esme's arrival was a welcome distraction from what she'd been doing.

She put down the leaflet and walked towards Esme, holding out her hand. 'I suppose I'd better introduce myself properly this time,' she said. 'Hester Chalacombe.'

Esme shook her hand. 'Pleased to meet you, Hester *Chalacombe.*'

Hester grimaced, her embarrassment obvious. 'Sorry about the… well, you know.' She gave Esme an awkward smile. 'It was Max's idea.'

'Now why does that not surprise me?' Esme said, smiling. 'You're connected with the *Treasures of the Sea Museum* in Bristol, I understand.'

Hester smiled. 'Guilty as charged. It was founded by my great-grandfather, Edward Chalacombe. I've been very lucky to be able to carry on the tradition.'

Esme scanned the room. 'Moving out or moving in?'

'Moving in,' Hester said, pulling the coat tightly around her and surveying the clutter. 'I'll be relocating permanently eventually, of course. But meanwhile, this is a handy base.' She nodded towards a door on the opposite side of the office. 'There's a bedsit next door. So I can be here in the working week, getting plans underway.' She inclined her head towards the window.

'Yes, of course,' Esme said, realising the office overlooked the building site on the other side of the river. 'The museum's new venture.' She walked across the room and gazed out at the skeleton of a building beginning to emerge. Hester joined Esme at the window and Esme got a whiff of her perfume. It smelt expensive.

'I live in Bristol at the moment,' Hester said. 'But I'll settle down here when we open. Well, re-settle, in a way, I suppose.'

'You come from the area?'

'Not personally. But my family's roots are here. My ancestors were ship owners and traders in Appledore back in the 16th century when the ports were the main players in England's maritime industry.'

'When's it due to be finished?'

'A few more months,' Hester said. 'That's if everything goes according to plan. I've plenty to do before then, though – planning the exhibits, packing up what needs to come down from Bristol, arranging the logistics.'

'An exciting time for you,' Esme said.

Hester turned to Esme and smiled, her eyes shining. 'Oh, I can't tell you how much. There's so much people don't realise. Did you know ships were built in Bideford and Appledore as far back as the 14th century? And at the beginning of the 18th century, Bideford imported more tobacco than any other port in the country, other than London?'

'I knew it had an important history, but I'm not very clued up about the detail.'

'And then there's Appledore,' Hester continued. 'Tourists see it merely as a quaint coastal village with winding streets and pretty cottages, but from a seafaring point of view, its importance in history is significant. The naval survey of 1582 recorded 15 ships in Appledore. Fifteen! That's more than three times the number in Bideford. There were also twenty master mariners from Appledore listed too, amongst them my own ancestors.'

Esme smiled. 'You obviously feel a strong personal connection with the project.'

Hester held up her hands, palms outward. 'Oh, I'm sorry, Esme. You're not here to listen to my sales pitch.'

'No, don't apologise. I'm intrigued. Having a whole museum devoted to your own family history must be a dream come true.'

'Oh, it is, believe me. Years in the planning, of course. And if it wasn't for Isaac…' Her voice drifted away, as she gazed out of the window.

'You and he go way back, I'm guessing.'

Hester let out a long sigh. 'Without him, the *Treasures of the Sea Museum* wouldn't have achieved the status it has today. And I'd not be here, my long-term dream within my grasp. I've a lot to thank him for.'

'How did you meet?' Esme asked.

Hester walked away from the window and moved two boxes from a chair, gesturing for Esme to sit down. 'Do have a seat, Esme,' she said, before moving over to the filing cabinet to retrieve the leaflet she'd been reading earlier. 'I was trying to work out how to operate this machine when you arrived,' she said, shaking her head. 'Someone suggested it was a *must have* if I wanted to keep drinking decent coffee now I'd not be working in a big city. But I can't make head nor tail of it.' She looked over her shoulder and gave Esme a wry smile.

'Don't worry on my account,' Esme said. 'We could always go out for a coffee, if you'd like?'

Yes, why not?' Hester threw down the instruction leaflet and came over to take the chair opposite Esme. 'Sorry,' she said, with an embarrassed smile. 'I should have done my homework before you came. Perhaps we could get a coffee later.'

She clasped her hands together and leaned on the table. 'You were asking about Isaac and how we met. He approached me, actually, expressed a passion for what the museum was about. Said he'd love to get involved. He talked about connections to investors who'd be interested in developing the museum and putting it on the global map.' Hester gave Esme a sardonic grin. 'I must admit to having been a teensy bit sceptical, as you might imagine. Anyway, I asked around, you know, and found out he wasn't just a money man, that he'd studied archaeology at university and had been involved in digs in the Mediterranean, including some maritime.'

'Obviously this was before he became a household name?'

'Oh, yes. Though he was quite well known in museum circles. I was flattered, actually, for all my caution, that he'd noticed our little enterprise. It was a modest establishment back then.'

'So, did he invest in it, then?'

Hester shook her head. 'Not to begin with, no. He persuaded others to, though. He was an expert on grant applications, too, so became a trustee. He had a vision, he inspired everyone remotely associated with the museum, and with his input and drive, we achieved it.'

'Sounds like a useful expert to have around. And later, his celebrity status must have helped with getting you on the map.'

'Relating all that to you now brings it home to me how important he's been in my career. Perhaps I'm not...' Hester closed her eyes. 'I don't know. I'm not even sure I should be talking to you.'

'But I thought you had concerns about Isaac. I thought that's why you and Max became involved in the first place.'

Hester slowly shook her head. 'I don't know what to think,

Esme. Yes, the reputation of the museum is a priority, of course it is…'

'And you think it's under threat because of Isaac Maudesley?'

'But what I *think* isn't proof. We've found nothing to suggest my fears are justified.'

Max had talked about there being rumours. Perhaps, as Esme had suggested to Max, there was nothing to find. She cleared her throat.

'There's something you should know, Hester. About me and Max.'

'Oh?'

'I've known Max for a long time. I know what makes him tick, what appeals to him. So his investigating Maudesley adds up. But,' she emphasised the word to make her point, 'it's not what I'm about. I'm not Max's associate, we're not working together and whatever you and he are investigating, that's not on any agenda of mine.'

Hester studied Esme's face. 'How come you know one another?'

'He's a former colleague from when I worked as a journalists' researcher, years ago.'

'So, why didn't he want you to know it was him who'd suggested employing you?' Hester asked.

'He didn't give you a reason?'

'He said you might not approve.'

Esme gave a half laugh. 'Well, that was honest, at least.'

'Though he was less forthcoming about why,' Hester added. 'Are you going to enlighten me?'

Esme felt Hester's eyes watching her, waiting for more. 'Let's say we didn't always see eye to eye on things and we've not kept in touch. So it was a bit of a shock when I found him hunkering down in my outhouse.'

'What?' Hester chuckled. 'I can't say I'm surprised. He's a conscientious sod, I'll give him that.'

Esme rested an elbow on the table. 'Did Max explain why I particularly wanted to speak to you?' she asked.

Hester frowned. 'I thought it was because I'd pretended to be someone else. I felt bad about that. It seems unnecessary when I look back. But Max insisted it was for the best. Like I said when I phoned, I owe you an explanation.'

'Which I appreciate,' Esme said, nodding. 'But there's something else I'd like to understand. Why were you so upset by what I found out? Who's Frank Stone and why is a murder in his family history so significant?'

Hester's face darkened. She swallowed.

'Frank Stone is the reason everything is going wrong.'

# 32

Hester shivered and pulled up the collar of her coat. 'It's not very warm in here, is it? That's something else I haven't fathomed out yet, the heating controls. They don't seem to respond whatever I do.'

'Look,' Esme said, 'why don't we go and get that coffee and warm up? There's a café a few doors away.'

The coffee shop at the bottom of the high street was closed for redecoration, so Esme suggested they walk to the café in the park where they'd met before.

'I'm guessing,' she said, after they'd crossed the road and begun walking along the quayside, 'that Frank Stone is not your partner with a big birthday.'

Hester snorted. 'You assume right.' She gave Esme a dry smile. 'Another of Max's suggestions.'

'So, who is he? And why did you need to know about his ancestry?'

Hester slipped her hands in the pockets of her coat 'He arrived at the museum out of the blue one day,' she began. 'Isaac told me he was a descendant of the Chalacombe family and wanted to join the team. Next thing I know, he's on the payroll. No consultation, nothing.' She threw out her hands in a gesture of exasperation. 'I mean, he just turned up, out of nowhere. He could have been anyone.'

'But Isaac must have known him, surely?'

'What if he did? Bringing him in was all far too hasty in my opinion. I didn't like it and Isaac didn't seem to care less what I thought.'

Esme side-stepped a woman struggling to control her over-exuberant black Labrador straining at the leash. 'And you have no idea why Isaac was so keen?'

'None whatsoever. So, despite my opposition, Isaac completely overruled me. I couldn't even get a straight answer from him about *how* Stone was related, which infuriated me. Then I came across that photo.'

'Oh, I almost forgot,' Esme said, stopping and reaching into the bag on her shoulder. 'I've brought you back your original.' She pulled out the envelope with the photograph inside and held it out to Hester. 'Maddy Henderson has cleaned it up beautifully.'

Hester stared at it warily as though it was contaminated in some way. 'Yes, I saw Maddy's enhanced version in the report you sent me. Did you find out who the woman was? Agnes someone, you thought, didn't you?'

'That's the name Maddy thought was pencilled on the back, but I haven't come across her yet. Any ideas?'

'None,' Hester said. 'But then it's not my photograph.'

Esme looked down at the envelope in her hand. 'So, whose is it?'

'Frank's, I assume. I'd never seen it until a few weeks ago.'

'So, has Frank said who he thinks it is?' Esme asked, as they resumed their stroll.

'No. All I know is he and Isaac think there's something special about the photo.' Hester tugged at the collar of her coat. 'At first, I wondered if he'd shown it to Isaac as some sort of proof of his family credentials, but then I thought even if it was a match with another in the family archive, it proves nothing. He could have got the photo from any antique fair, car boot sale or bric-a-brac shop.'

'And is that what Frank tried to convince you? Is that why he gave it to you?'

Hester gave Esme a sideways glance and grimaced. 'He didn't give it to me. I'm ashamed to say I found it in a drawer in Isaac's office desk. I'd gone looking for something which would give me a clue to who Frank Stone really is, saw the photo he and Isaac had been studying and thought it may lead me somewhere. That's where you came in.'

'I'm not sure I've helped much, though,' Esme said. 'What I've discovered just seems to muddy the waters.'

'That's not your fault, Esme. It was me who asked you to look.' Hester held out her hand for the envelope. 'I suppose I ought to put it back before they work out where it's gone.' Esme handed it over and Hester slipped it into her pocket.

They arrived at the park and walked in through the iron gates, negotiating a wheelbarrow on the path, where a gardener was weeding a flowerbed filled with an array of vibrantly coloured primulas. They made their way over to the café and found a table by the window.

'I'm still curious about one thing, though,' Esme said, once they'd settled down with their coffees.

'I know what you're going to say,' Hester said, interrupting. 'It's my reaction to the murder of Ernest Sanders by Albert Philips, isn't it?'

Esme nodded. 'I usually find people are fascinated by a family scandal – as long as there's enough time and distance – so your reaction threw me completely. I wasn't even sure how to describe it. Shock? Alarm? Panic? Now, with everything you've told me about Frank Stone and how you feel about him, I thought it might offer an explanation. But I'm not really much clearer.' She stirred her coffee, scrutinising Hester over the rim of her cup. 'Unless,' she added, when Hester didn't respond, 'there's something you've not told me about Frank?'

Hester sat back in her chair with a sigh. 'This isn't about Frank,' she said, shaking her head. 'It's about my great aunt.'

'Your great aunt?' Esme inclined her head, puzzled. 'I don't follow.'

Hester picked up her cup and took a sip of her drink before replacing it in its saucer. 'She was called Annie. Annie Pearce. She was my maternal grandmother's older sister and was born in 1902. In her youth, she was an enthusiastic supporter of women's suffrage. I only tell you that so you understand the sort of person she was. Strong minded, determined. And, as it happens, she had a particular love of history.'

Hester leaned across the table towards Esme. 'It was *her* passion for the subject that spawned my own. She drew on her knowledge of our family's past and when I was a child, she'd tell me stories about things which happened to our ancestors, about their lives. I loved it.'

'So you were close?'

'Oh, yes. Very much so. I was heartbroken when she died. I was just about to go to uni to study social history. So sad she never got to see me achieve my ambition and follow a career in a subject dear to her heart, especially as it was she who'd been my inspiration.'

'Did she have children of her own?' Esme asked.

Hester shook her head. 'No, she never married.' She leaned forward. 'And that's at the crux of this situation.'

'It is? How?'

Hester swallowed. 'As a young woman, Annie was engaged. She always implied her family disapproved of the match and I'm almost certain the engagement was a secret between her and her intended.'

'You think the family tried to put a stop to their relationship?'

'That's what I've always assumed. Though it's possible, of course, they may have come round to the idea eventually, had he lived.'

'He died?'

'Yes. And when I tell you his name, you'll perhaps understand my reaction to your discovery.'

'What *was* his name?' Esme asked.

Hester looked up from her latte. 'Ernest Sanders. The man you told me was murdered by Albert Philips in 1923.'

157

# 33

The clatter of crockery and the hiss of the coffee machine echoed around the café as Esme digested Hester's explanation and tried to put it into context.

'So, your great aunt never told you what happened to her fiancé?' she asked.

'Not a hint. Nothing about him meeting a violent death, anyway. I knew Ernest had died and that it was steeped in tragedy, but I'd always imagined it was TB or something like that. Certainly I had no idea he'd been murdered. It could explain why she was bundled off to a relative in Scotland.'

'Which is why you thought the family disapproved of him.'

'Exactly, but in light of what you've told me, perhaps her family *didn't* have anything against him as such, they were just reacting to circumstances. They would have been horrified by her being mixed up in a scandal like murder, wouldn't they?'

'I'm sure they would.'

Hester frowned. 'I did wonder whether she'd never known the truth and that's why she never told me. Is it possible she never found out?'

'It seems unlikely. The case was widely reported across the country's newspapers. She'd have been able to follow what was happening, wherever she was.'

'I wonder if she did, though,' Hester mused. 'If they'd gone to all the trouble of whisking her away, the family might have made sure any information on the case was kept from her. Maybe they hoped she'd forget all about him.'

'Rather a forlorn hope, I'd have thought,' Esme said. 'You said she was a strong character, had a mind of her own. Would she have been so easily persuaded?'

'I'm inclined to agree with you there. Then I thought perhaps they really *were* against him for some other reason, even before he was killed. According to my aunt, he was kind, caring. He couldn't understand their attitude. He was hurt by it.'

'Which suggests their hostility pre-dated the murder,' Esme observed.

Hester nodded. 'Yes, it does, doesn't it? Then, when he was killed, they probably saw it as confirmation they'd been right all along. You mentioned there'd been an argument between Ernest and Albert Philips. They were cousins, you said?'

'Yes. Ernest's mother Betsy and Albert's father John were brother and sister.'

'So, what do you think – a family dispute was at the centre of things?'

'If it was, nothing came out in the trial,' Esme said. 'In fact, it's more definitive than that. It wasn't simply an omission. Philips refused to say what they'd argued about. Maybe owning up to whatever caused the altercation would have brought the family's reputation into disrepute. Something of that nature, anyway.' An idea slipped in to Esme's head and she glanced up at Hester. 'Do you think your great aunt was aware of what was behind it?'

'You're thinking it was why she was bundled away, that her parents were worried she'd be dragged into the court case?'

'Well, I hadn't thought of that, no, I must admit,' Esme said, considering the implications. 'Withholding evidence in a criminal trial is a serious offence, perverting the course of justice. We've no way of knowing whether they believed she did know something and decided it was worth taking the risk, or she knew nothing and they were merely trying to protect her from being caught up in the scandal.'

Hester sighed. 'I can't imagine what it must have been like for her. She obviously buried the whole sad episode deep inside her for years.' She looked across at Esme, unshed tears in her eyes. 'I mean, if she couldn't even bring herself to say how he'd died…'

'Yes, it was just too difficult to talk about,' Esme said. 'Telling would have stirred up the whole trauma all over again, especially as you'd have been bound to ask questions she couldn't answer.'

'And if she'd never understood why it happened, it would only make it even harder.'

'Knowing why is a basic human need,' Esme said, thinking of her own past. 'It drives what we do and determines our emotional reaction. If we assume Annie was unaware of the argument which led to her fiancé's death, and given it didn't come out at the trial, it would have made it difficult for her to come to terms with it and may have haunted her ever after.'

Hester sniffed. 'Poor Auntie. What a horrible thing to live with.' She delved into her coat pocket for a tissue to wipe her nose. 'I always thought it a sad story even before hearing all this. She never married, as I told you, which ironically was probably to my gain. If she had done and had children of her own, they would have taken all her time. As it was, I was the lucky beneficiary of the tragedy.' She gave Esme a sad smile. 'That hadn't occurred to me before. It makes me feel quite uncomfortable, put like that.'

'I'm sure your aunt wouldn't have looked at it that way. More the opposite. She'd have been grateful to have a great niece who shared her passion for history.'

'Yes, you're right. I shouldn't be maudlin, should I? Though it would have been nice if we'd been able to continue to do so for a lot longer. It was cruel to lose her so soon. Yes, I know she was 84, but she was fit and healthy. She should have gone on for years.'

They finished their coffees and left the café through the doors leading back out into the park, heading towards the iron gates and out to the pavement beyond.

'So, what happened to your aunt?' Esme asked, as they retraced their steps back towards the quay.

'She died of hypothermia. She'd gone outside still wearing her nightclothes – no one's really sure why, perhaps to put some rubbish out. That was one suggestion, though that seemed unlikely to me. Anyway, while she was out there, she'd fallen over and hit her head. It must have knocked her unconscious. By the time she was found, it was too late.'

'Oh, I'm so sorry. That must have been so upsetting for you.'

Hester gave a brief nod. 'And to make matters worse, they made assumptions, that she was this doddery old lady suffering from dementia.' She scowled. 'She was an eminent historian, for goodness sake.'

'Dementia's a cruel disease, though,' Esme said. 'Even the best minds aren't immune.'

'Of course, I realise that, but Auntie Annie was in the middle of a major research project, one she was very excited about. She'd written to update me about it only the week before she died. An odd letter, if I'm honest. She seemed to be rambling on about something I didn't understand. So perhaps they were right. Maybe there were signs of dementia I'd not noticed when I'd seen her last. It had been a while, you see.'

She turned to Esme with a sombre expression. 'I've always felt a bit guilty about that. But you know what it's like. I was all set to go to uni and busy seeing friends who were headed off to all corners of the country. I didn't give her the time.'

They reached the quayside and Hester wandered over to the railings overlooking the river. Esme followed and stood beside her, leaning on the top rail to gaze out across the water.

Hester turned her head up river, towards the new museum site. 'She would have been in her element, with something like that.'

'Is that what your great aunt's history research project was about?' Esme asked. 'Related to the new venture?'

'No, it would have been another branch of the family, following up on stories told her by her grandmother. You know, trying to unpick truth from fiction. She used to do that a lot. I think she was close to discovering something which had eluded her for a long time. I can see her now, talking about finding out "after all these years". Her grandmother shared things with Auntie that she was told by *her* grandmother when she was a child, you see, so it would have been a long way back in time.' Hester gave her head a shake and rubbed her temple. 'I feel dreadful that I don't know more about it. I wish I'd been more interested, asked more questions.'

Esme smiled. 'A regret on the lips of virtually every family historian I've ever met.'

Hester sighed and nodded. 'I'm sure you're right.'

Esme chewed her lip, trying to get her head round the implications of Hester's story. 'Do you think Frank Stone knows any of this?'

Hester's head shot round. 'Frank? Why would he? And what if he does? What's it got to do with anything?'

'I'm not sure. But you asked me to investigate Frank's ancestry and it turns out his grandfather killed your aunt's fiancé. Rather an uncomfortable connection.'

Hester gaped at Esme, alarm imprinted on her face. 'What are you saying? That whether Frank knows or not is important?'

Esme shook her head. 'I can't answer that, Hester. I don't have enough information.'

Hester disregarded the idea with a flick of her head. 'It has to be just a coincidence. Why would a murder which took place in the 1920s possibly have any bearing on Frank Stone turning up out of the blue?'

Esme gave a humourless laugh. 'In my experience, it's not always as easy to discount such coincidences as you might imagine.'

Hester peered at Esme curiously. '*In your experience?* You've been in a situation like this before?' Esme gave a slow nod. 'Ah, now I get it,' Hester continued, folding her arms and resting them on the railings. 'That must be what Max meant when he suggested hiring you.'

'Why? What did Max say?'

Hester gave a dismissive shake of her head. 'Oh, I can't remember his exact words. Something about if there were any hidden clues in Stone's history, you'd be the one to find them.' She grimaced. 'Well, you certainly did that, didn't you?'

Esme laughed. 'Hardly. All I've done is expose a tentative connection with something in your own family history. I'm not sure it's got you any closer to solving your problem.'

Hester leaned one elbow on the rail. 'No. But that's rather the point, isn't it? Irrespective of whether Ernest Sanders' tragic death has anything to do with it or not, I still don't understand what Frank Stone's up to.'

Esme sighed. 'No. And I'm sorry I wasn't more help. And I'm also sorry all I seem to have done is stir up some sad memories.' She bit her lower lip, wondering if Hester would ask her to continue digging into Stone's ancestry and how she should respond if she did. If she wanted to avoid getting sucked into Max's investigation, she'd be wise to steer clear. But how would that help Hester? 'So, what will you do now?' she asked.

Hester let out an exasperated sigh. 'The honest answer is, I really don't know.' She turned an anxious face towards Esme. 'I sometimes wonder if I'm making too much of this. I mean, Isaac wouldn't risk his own reputation by doing something stupid, would he?'

'You're the best person to answer that, Hester. You know him.'

Hester balled her fist and pressed it into her chin. 'Perhaps I'm getting this out of proportion. Maybe I need to let it go.'

'Are you still in touch with Max?' Esme asked.

Hester's brow puckered. 'Why do you ask?'

'I wondered if he'd agreed to keep you in the loop, pass by you anything he came across that would make sense of what's happened.'

Hester threw Esme another anxious expression. 'I'm beginning to wonder whether it was a mistake to get involved with Max. If he does learn anything damaging, it's only going to impact negatively on the integrity of the museum and, by default, on me,

163

isn't it? In my desperation to see the back of Frank, I might have made things worse. The law of unintended consequences.'

'Max spoke about rumours, nothing more,' Esme said. 'Perhaps that's all they are. Max may yet find he's floundering in unproductive waters and give up.'

'I hope you're right. Though whether it'll help me with my problem remains to be seen.'

'The Frank Stone problem, I assume you mean.'

'Quite.' Hester pulled back the sleeve of her coat and checked her watch. 'I'm afraid I'm going to have to go,' she said, straightening up. 'I've got a meeting with the architect.'

'No problem. And thanks for telling me about Annie and her story. I hope things work out for you. You never know, Frank Stone might disappear as rapidly as he arrived.'

Hester cocked her chin. 'Maybe.' She reached out and touched Esme's arm. 'Thanks for all you've done, Esme. I'm sorry we didn't find any silver bullet.'

Esme wanted to say she was happy to keep on looking if Hester wanted, but before she could form the words, Hester had wheeled away back to her office.

*

As Esme watched Hester walk away, she realised she'd never asked why Hester and Max had been at the *Roadshow*. Max had said it had been a waste of time, but there must have been a good reason to go in the first place. Well, it didn't matter any longer.

As she turned to retrace her steps back to her car, her phone rang. She pulled it out of her pocket and peered at the screen. Max. She was tempted to let it go to voicemail, but the image of Max's damaged face shot into her head. Perhaps he'd had a relapse and was calling from his hospital bed. She swiped the handset image and made the connection.

'Max? Are you OK?'

She heard him grunt down the phone. 'Sure, why wouldn't I be?'

164

'Oh, only the small matter of a bloodied face and potential concussion, that's all.'

'Nah, it's all good. And thanks for – you know – taking in a waif and stray.'

'Oh, that's all right. Anyway, I'm sure you'd have done the same for me.' She cleared her throat. 'Well, it's good to hear you've suffered no ill effects. I'll let you get on.'

'Hold your horses, Ez. You haven't heard why I'm ringing.'

'Do I want to know?'

'Sure you do. I've got some intel on Stone.'

'Oh, right,' Esme said, walking along the quay back towards the car park. 'Well, Hester will be pleased. You'd better have a word with her. Information on Stone is exactly what she's lacking at the moment. I've just been speaking to her, as it happens. So, I'll let you go so you can phone her. She was heading back to her office for a meeting, but you should catch her if you're quick.'

'Don't you want to know what I've got?'

'Why would I?' Esme said, arriving at her car and pulling out her keys. 'Frank Stone's on your agenda, Max, not mine. And Hester's, of course.'

'Yeah, and it's Hester I'm thinking of. She needs to give him a wide berth. And she also needs to tackle Maudesley about why he's knocking around with this guy.'

'Why? What have you found out?' Esme asked, before she could stop herself.

'Stone's a nasty piece of work, Ez. Been in and out of trouble since he was in short trousers, despite the benefit of his expensive education. And with a violent streak, too.'

Esme shuddered. 'That's bad news. Makes you wonder why Isaac Maudesley was so keen for an unsavoury character like that to come and work at the museum.'

'Ah, my thoughts exactly, Ez. Perhaps Stone's in possession of a little leverage.'

'What do you mean?'

'What d'you think I mean, Ez? Stone knows something that Maudesley doesn't want the world to find out, and is using that knowledge to full advantage.'

Esme gripped her phone. 'You mean blackmail?'

'That's exactly what I'm thinking. And wouldn't we just love to know what that leverage is?'

# 34

Esme drove back to her cottage, mulling over Max's suppositions. Was he right, that Frank Stone had something over Maudesley? Had it something to do with the rumours Max had mentioned? If Max's hunch was true, it was unlikely that the hope Esme had expressed to Hester that Stone might disappear as quickly as he'd arrived would come to fruition. She wondered what Hester's reaction would be to Max's warnings of Stone's reputation. Given Hester's instinctive dislike of the man, it probably would come as no surprise.

She pulled into her drive and got out of the car, buffeted by a brisk sea breeze which played with her hair as she mulled over the plausibility – or more likely, the implausibility – of Max discussing his blackmail hypothesis with Hester. If Hester had begun to question her decision to get involved with Max in the first place, it was doubtful she'd be willing to speculate with him about whether Maudesley had any vulnerabilities Stone could exploit. That's assuming she was aware of any.

Esme stepped through the front door, greeted by the kittens who'd invented a new game of *unravel the kitchen roll* from the dispenser above the worktop. The floor was strewn with long reams of white paper, along with a collection of small chewed pieces scattered all over the hearth rug. She dumped her bag on the kitchen table and began clearing up the mess, her thoughts drifting back to her apology to Hester about not turning up anything helpful to her in Frank Stone's ancestry, only stirring up sad memories.

With the room restored to some semblance of order, Esme sat down at the kitchen table with her laptop to check her emails, but found herself gazing into space. It was hard to ignore the tantalising link between Stone's ancestor and the story of Hester's great aunt. *It's not always as easy to discount such coincidences as you might imagine.* But what would she achieve by digging deeper? Max had made it perfectly obvious that the murder story played no part in his investigation and Esme couldn't conjure up a scenario which challenged that view. So, what did that mean?

It meant just that. This wasn't about Max's investigation into Maudesley, or Frank Stone for that matter. It was about Ernest Sanders and his murderer, Albert Philips, a story Max had readily dismissed as being of no interest to him. But given her affection for her great aunt, and the mystery Annie had left behind, Hester would surely welcome any further information Esme might uncover.

As the laptop booted and the relevant webpage loaded, Esme reflected on what she already knew from her previous research. She'd identified Ernest and Albert's shared grandparents as being George Philips born in 1824 and Lucy Hannaford in 1834. Having already followed the Philips line back into the 18th century, she decided to focus her attention on the cousins' grandmother, Lucy.

Using the online databases, Esme established Lucy's father, Charles Hannaford, born at the very end of the 18th century, was the son of Walter Hannaford and his wife Agnes. Esme stared at the name of Walter's wife on the screen. Agnes. That was the name she and Maddy believed was written faintly in pencil on the back of the photograph Hester had given her. The photograph Hester suspected might belong to Frank Stone.

Esme gave a flippant shake of her head, dismissing the connection with Stone as irrelevant. Whoever the woman depicted in the photograph was, it made no difference at all whether she was on Frank Stone's family tree or not. This was about Ernest Sanders and *his* ancestry.

Esme returned to her search. She located Agnes, wife of Walter Hannaford, still alive and well on the 1851 census, living with her son and his wife Ellen, at the age of 81. Could it be the same woman?

Esme located the file Maddy had sent her of the scans and images she'd made while restoring the photograph and called up the enhanced digital copy. She peered at it, grimacing as she recalled Maddy's conclusion that it was a mortuary photograph, taken at the time of Agnes's death. Esme minimised the image and returned to the database. Agnes had died in 1852, a year after the census, at a time when mortuary photography was most common.

Esme switched databases to *Find My Past* and searched for Agnes's marriage to Charles's father, Walter. She found what she was looking for amongst Devon's Marriages and Banns records. There was an entry for a marriage in 1795 between Walter Hannaford and Agnes Venner.

Esme sat back and blinked at the screen. Venner. In her mind, she was back in John Ford's shop, looking at the painting of Amelia Venner, nee Chalacombe, as Ford related the story of a Thomas Venner, captured by Barbary pirates and enslaved. Was there a connection there too?

Esme closed her eyes and pinched the bridge of her nose. Time for a break. She closed the lid of the laptop and got up from the table. The daylight was fading and she still needed to fill the log basket if she wanted a fire that evening.

She threw on her coat and slipped her feet into her wellies before grabbing the log carrier from the understairs cupboard and heading outside. As she loaded up the canvas carrier in the gloom of the wood store, the haunting image of Agnes Venner's face crept into her head and she placed the old lady on the Philips family tree. Agnes would be Frank Stone's four times great-grandmother, and the great-great grandmother of Stone's notorious ancestor, Albert Philips. And also, of course, the great-great grandmother of his victim, Ernest Sanders, Hester's great aunt Annie's fiancé.

Esme hauled the bag of logs back inside and knelt down by the fireplace to unload them into the basket. As she sat back on her heels, an idea flitted into her consciousness, prompted by something Hester had told her. But what? Was it when they were speculating as to whether Annie had known anything about the ill-fated dispute between Ernest and his cousin? They'd finally concluded not, that it had been not knowing *why* that had haunted Annie. Not only had she struggled to come to terms with her loss, she'd been unable to share the trauma with her great niece.

Esme's face puckered as she tried to work out whether it was that which had stirred her thought. She shook her head. No, it hadn't been that. There was something else. If only she could pinpoint it.

Esme got to her feet and hurled the empty canvas bag back in the understairs cupboard, slamming the door so hard it provoked a yowl of protest from Ally who was sitting washing himself on the bottom stair. Esme went over and sat next to him, stroked his head and tried to track back through the conversation she'd had with Hester.

Had it been later on? Yes, that was it. Hester said her aunt had been excited about a major research project she was involved with, that she was close to discovering something which had eluded her for a long time – *after all these years,* were the words Annie had used.

A jolt of comprehension shot through Esme like an electric current. What if Annie was about to expose that elusive *why*? What if her imminent exciting discovery, which had confounded her for so long, was not another family story passed to her by her grandmother, but the truth behind Ernest's murder?

## 35

The thrill of the previous evening's speculation, that Annie had uncovered the truth behind Ernest's murder, had been dealt a strong dose of reality by the following morning. Even if Annie *had* been investigating her fiancé's story, Esme knew the likelihood of finding out what she had unearthed was remote. That's assuming she'd discovered anything at all. But Esme wasn't yet ready to dismiss the theory completely and considered it was an idea worth passing by Hester.

Building work on her outhouse was due to begin in the next few days, so Esme pushed away any thoughts of disappointment concerning Annie and Ernest to meet with her builder Callum. After they'd discussed logistics and Callum had left, Esme stood in the now empty space with a sense of eager anticipation. Soon she'd be able to de-clutter her spare bedroom and set up her new office exactly the way she wanted. Already, she'd begun to work out what was going where and had decided the 17th century map she and Maddy had found amongst the junk was to take pride of place on the back wall. Maddy had taken the frame away for restoration and promised to have the work completed in time for when Callum and his team finished the renovation.

As Esme came out of the outhouse and locked the door, she heard footsteps and looked round to see Maddy climbing the stone steps from the lane to the front door. Esme hurried down the path to meet her.

'This is a nice surprise,' Esme said, pushing open the door. 'Come on in.'

Maddy jerked a thumb over her shoulder. 'Actually, I really came to have a nose at all the excitement. I just called on the off-chance.'

'Oh, the cliff fall, you mean. Hang on, I'll come down with you.'

Esme pulled the front door closed and they descended the steps and turned towards the beach.

'They've moved the cordon back a bit, now,' Esme explained as they trudged down the road. 'So at least we can get down to the slipway. Though that's about your lot after that. Could be worse, though. I thought we were going to be barred from the beach completely.'

'How long for? These things take an age to sort out.'

They paused at the plastic barriers at the end of the road, pushed to one side, now, to partition the rubble from the route to the beach. Esme pointed to the gap, like a broken tooth, on the top of the cliff from where the cottage had fallen. She shuddered at the sight of the raw and menacing void, which had once embodied the security of someone's home.

'It must have been scary seeing it come down,' Maddy said.

'It was,' Esme agreed. 'The noise was deafening. It would have been absolutely terrifying if it had happened during the night. You'd have thought the world was ending.' She nodded towards the empty space. 'One minute there was a cottage standing there and the next it'd completely disappeared.'

'Sad, isn't it?' Maddy said. 'Another bit of lost history.'

'Jim said it was once lived in by a family involved in smuggling.' Esme grinned. 'I'm not sure if he wasn't pulling my leg, though. Could be a touch of folklore for the tourists' benefit. And as Jim pointed out, the nature of smuggling meant there's not much in the form of written evidence to back up such stories.'

Maddy smiled. 'People like a touch of mystery. Especially in a location like this.'

'Oh, talking of mysteries,' Esme said, 'you'll be pleased to hear that Hester finally got in touch.'

'Oh, that's great, Esme. I'm so glad. So, did you get to find out what her weird reaction was all about?'

Esme nodded and gave Maddy a brief summary of Annie Pearce and her loss.

'Oh, that's so sad,' Maddy said, shaking her head. 'It brings it all home when you know the individual story. So, Hester's great aunt had never told her about the murder?'

'No, she never did. Never even hinted, which was why it was such a shock to Hester.'

'I wonder why not? Then again, it's not uncommon, being unable to voice something that affected you so severely. As it was bound to have done. Poor woman. She wouldn't have been very old when it happened, I take it?'

'About twenty, I think Hester said.' Esme chewed her lip. 'The odd thing is, Hester said her great aunt had been working on a major family history project just before she died. She'd apparently been on the brink of discovering something she'd been trying to get to the bottom of for years, according to Hester.'

Maddy turned to Esme with a sceptical expression. 'And?'

Esme shrugged. 'I was just speculating what her project might have been, that's all.'

'Oh, I see. You think she was looking into her fiancé's murder?'

'Well, why not? It's possible, isn't it?'

'Is it? C'mon, Esme. Just because you like the mystery idea. From what you've told me, Ernest disappeared from Annie's life when she was twenty years old. What would prompt her to start looking into it so many years later?'

'Well, maybe something happened.'

'Like what?'

'I don't know, do I?' Esme said, half wishing she'd never brought up the subject. 'I'm just saying, that's all. It's all academic anyway. I totally accept that we'll probably never know, either that Annie *was* trying to find something out about the murder or, if she was, what it was she discovered.'

'Thank goodness for that,' Maddy said. She checked her watch. 'Well, I guess I should be getting back.'

'Where are you parked?'

'Car park. The sign at the top said residents only.'

'The police put that there after the fall so the road wouldn't become clogged with vehicles of sightseers. I'll walk you back. And while we're on the subject of Hester,' Esme said, as they turned and began walking back up the lane, 'that mortuary photo. I think I might have identified the woman in it.'

'You have? Oh, brilliant. Who was she?'

'Well, if your dates are right, it's possible it's Agnes Venner, born in 1770. I immediately wondered if she's related to Thomas Venner who John Ford told me about.'

'The lad who was abducted by pirates?'

'Yes, that's him.'

'And what's that got to do with the murder?'

Esme blinked. 'I didn't say it had anything to do with it.'

They arrived at the car park and Maddy pulled the keys to her van out of her pocket. 'You might not have said so, but we both know there's a link. Ernest. Annie. Hester.' She cocked her chin, scrutinising Esme's face. 'And Max, too. This isn't straying into dangerous territory, is it?'

Esme gave Maddy an indulgent smile. 'You'll be pleased to hear that Max knows nothing about Hester's great aunt and has already dismissed the murder as ancient history. So you can stop worrying. I won't be having any more to do with the man.'

'Glad to hear it,' Maddy said, climbing into her van.

Esme waved as Maddy retreated up the hill back to the main road before turning for home. Dark clouds were forming on the horizon, meaning rain wasn't far away. Esme huddled into her duffel and hurried down the lane.

A woman wearing a stylish wool coat and a patterned scarf tied around her head was taking a photograph of the tiny Victorian post box embedded in the whitewashed stone wall just above Esme's cottage. As Esme reached her, the woman turned to her and smiled.

'Isn't that the cutest thing you ever saw?' she said, with a mid-

American drawl.

'Yes, it's gorgeous, isn't it?' Esme said, admiring the insignia of the crown moulded into the cast iron between the initials V and R. 'Such a key part of our history, too.'

'Sure is great to see it still in use.'

'Yes, I love it, even if it *is* a bit small to take large envelopes.'

'I just adore the handwriting of that time, don't you? That beautiful copperplate script.' The woman looked back at the narrow red box. 'The lost art of letter writing,' she added, wistfully.

'No, emails don't have quite the same appeal, do they?' Esme said. 'And who doesn't love getting a real letter?'

The woman chuckled. 'Ain't that the truth?'

As Esme continued on her way, the woman's words stirred something in her head. By the time she'd reached her gate, she'd worked out what it was. Hester had mentioned getting a letter from her great aunt the week before she'd died. The letter had been odd; Hester had said that Annie had been rambling on about something Hester didn't understand and she'd eventually dismissed it as evidence that her great aunt had, as was suggested at the time, been afflicted by the onset of dementia.

But what if the letter wasn't the ramblings of an elderly lady losing her mind at all? What if it would have made perfect sense to someone fully aware of what Annie was researching? Could that explain the confusion?

Esme pushed open the gate to her front garden, her thoughts spinning. Hester had no idea at the time she read the letter of the true nature of Ernest's death, so anything within it which related to the subject could easily have been misinterpreted as puzzling or even muddled.

Inside the cottage, Esme hung up her coat and stared into space, forcing her erratic thoughts into some sort of order. Other than the recollection that she'd thought the letter odd, Esme didn't get the impression Hester remembered any detail. Hardly surprising, given how long ago it was and how bewildering it was at the time.

But perhaps Hester still had the letter. And if she did, might they be able to decipher its message?

Esme snatched up her phone and scrolled to find Hester's number.

# 36

Esme stood by the window beside the front door, looking out on the fading daylight. The cloud had continued to build all day, bathing the inside of the cottage with a gloomy light. Now hail had begun battering the front door and Esme shivered as a chill crept around her.

She'd been unable to get hold of Hester, reaching only a disembodied voice on Hester's phone, suggesting the caller leave a message, which Esme did, asking Hester to call back when she was free. She didn't feel she could convey her thoughts concerning Annie's last letter in a telephone message and felt the same about an email.

She pulled the curtains closed on the darkening skies and went over to the fireplace to put a match to the wood-burning stove. She knelt on the hearth rug, watching as the flames flickered and brushed against the inside of the glass doors, throwing a warm light into the room. As the fire took hold, she revisited her theory about Annie's letter. There was some logic that it could hold the key to what had been the subject of Annie's research, but was Esme being too fanciful in believing the search for the truth behind her fiancé's murder was at the centre of it? Or was she, as Maddy had teased, merely captivated with the mystery of Annie's story?

Esme chewed her lip. She had to acknowledge another of Maddy's observations, too, that Ernest disappeared from Annie's life when she was a young woman, so what would make her start looking into his death so many years after the event? Esme had suggested something might have happened to prompt her actions, but had been unable to come up with a feasible scenario.

The kittens circled Esme's ankles, telling her it was time for food. She fed them, and then fixed herself something to eat. By the time she'd finished her meal, she'd decided she must be guided by Hester's reaction. If Hester saw sense in Esme's suggestion, perhaps because it resonated with Hester's memories of the letter, she'd feel justified in pursuing it further.

As she cleared the dishes, her phone buzzed. She snatched up a towel and dried her hands before reaching for the handset from the sofa.

'Hester?' she said, without looking at the screen.

'I thought you two had already been in touch?' said a man's voice.

'Oh, hi, Max,' Esme said, perching on the arm of the sofa. 'I didn't expect to hear from you again. I thought we were done.' What did he want? She'd obviously not made her intention clear enough that she wasn't interested in being a part of his investigation into Maudesley.

'Just thought I'd fill you in with the latest.'

'Look, Max, I appreciate you wanting to keep me in the loop, but I think I'd be wise to let you get on with it now. I've got more than enough on my plate at the…'

'Did you know Maudesley bummed around the Med for a couple of summer seasons during his uni days? Earning a bit of cash working in bars, that sort of thing. Went on a few digs out there, mainly in north Africa.'

'Yes, Hester said something about it.' Where was he going with this? Why did he think she needed to know?

'Seems Stone was out there too,' Max continued. 'In fact, he's spent much of his working life out there.'

She shifted the handset to the other ear. 'Well, this is all very fascinating, Max, but…'

'After that, it all gets a bit hazy. Hey, did you know it's illegal to use a metal detector in Morocco? Tunisia the same.'

Esme couldn't help herself and laughed out loud. 'Oh, come on, Max. Are you trying to tell me that Maudesley's big secret is that he got into trouble for using a metal detector when he was a naive undergraduate?'

'No,' he said, defensively. 'Not exactly. But there *is* a suggestion that Maudesley quit Morocco in a big hurry. Could be they kicked him out of the country or he fled before they caught him and banged him up.'

'You can't seriously think this is the hold Frank Stone's got over him, though?'

'Yeah, but it could be it's just the tip of the iceberg.'

'Or it could be that you're clutching at straws, Max.' She watched the kittens as Ally bopped his sister on her head with his paw and got a wallop back in kind. 'Maybe there's nothing to find.' She grinned as the kittens' antics caused them to roll off the sofa, surprising both of them. 'Maybe Maudesley's as straight as he presents himself. Ever thought of that?'

'Nah, he doesn't fool me,' Max sneered. 'There's something there. And Stone's the key. I'll find it, don't you worry.'

'Well, I wish you luck,' Esme said, standing up. 'And now I'd better get on.'

'Sure, Ez. And don't forget – if you turn up anything juicy in your family history trawling, I want to know. Deal?'

Esme grinned, despite herself. He was such a trier. 'Bye, Max.'

She rang off and stood next to the sofa, resting the phone against her chin, chewing her lip. Was Max also reporting to Hester? She still wasn't sure how things stood between them. Neither was she completely clear how Hester felt about Isaac Maudesley. During their conversation the previous day, Esme got the impression Hester regretted doubting him and getting involved with Max at all. Had it been Hester who had initiated Max's investigation or the other way around? That was another of her questions which had been sidestepped, both by Max and by Hester.

Esme sighed. They were both as bad as one another.

# 37

Saturday's market was frenetic and things didn't begin to calm down until midday. Esme flopped back against the edge of the stall, stifling a yawn as Maddy came to stand beside her.

'You look knackered,' Maddy said, cheerfully.

Esme rubbed her eyes. 'Tell me something I don't know. I should have ignored the phone. That'll teach me.' She'd given up on hearing back from Hester the previous evening and, with an early start due for the next day's market, had gone to bed when her call finally came through. Having reassured an apologetic Hester she hadn't disturbed her, Esme had explained her theory about Annie's letter. Hester's response had been positive. Not only was she confident of finding the letter, she was keen to pursue Esme's idea. After the phone call ended, Esme lay back on her pillow mulling over their conversation and it took some time before she'd finally fallen asleep.

'You should have given me a call. Given yourself an extra hour and come in a bit later.'

Esme raised her eyebrows. 'What, after the rush we've had today? You'd not have thanked me for it.'

Maddy pulled a face. 'Yes, it has been a bit nuts, hasn't it? You stay there. I'll go and get us a coffee. Looks like you could use one.'

She headed over to the market café, leaving Esme manning the stall. While Maddy was away, Esme sold a snuff box to a customer and reorganised the stall to make it look less depleted. At least there was one advantage to the frantic buying spree: it provided a welcome increase in Maddy's turnover.

'You're going to need some more stock,' Esme said, as Maddy returned with their drinks.

'I am, aren't I?' Maddy said, handing Esme a piping hot latte.

'With a bit of luck, I might pick up some stuff at that sale on Monday. You are coming, aren't you?'

'Thanks, I need this.' Esme wrapped her hands around the warm mug. 'Yes, I'll be there. I haven't forgotten.'

'So, when are you seeing Hester?' Maddy asked.

'Tuesday, after the market.' Esme nibbled the ball of her thumb. 'I wish it was sooner, but it can't be helped. Hester's mum has Annie's letter, so Hester's going to see her over the weekend and bring it with her when she comes back to Devon.'

'What does Hester's mother make of it all?' Maddy asked. 'Had she known the full story?'

Esme took a sip of the hot liquid. 'No, she hadn't. She was just as shocked as Hester had been.'

'So this letter, then. Does Hester remember anything at all about it?'

'Not really. She recalls part of it was almost illegible where the ink had smudged.'

Maddy gave a sympathetic tilt of her head. 'Doesn't sound very hopeful.'

'No, so we may fall at the first hurdle.' Esme enjoyed another sip of her coffee. 'The circumstances of Ernest Sanders' murder may for ever remain a mystery.'

*

Esme grabbed a bottle of Shiraz and headed down the lane to Libby's. The new couple Libby wanted to introduce, the reason for the invite, had recently moved into one of the cottages further up the valley. They'd already arrived when Esme got there, ensconced in Libby's ancient oversized leather sofa in the sitting room.

Libby made the introductions. Faith, sporting a cascade of nut-brown hair and an affable smile, was about to return to work after maternity leave, as a casework coordinator for the Red Cross. Dom, bearded with tousled hair and round retro-style spectacles, was a structural surveyor specialising in old properties. They discussed the collapsed cottage and Esme told Dom about Jim's assertion of a smuggling connection. Dom nodded enthusiastically, explaining he was currently working with the owners of one of the oldest houses in Bideford to investigate claims that tunnels existed under the property, allegedly leading to the beach.

'You're joking, surely,' Libby said, as she topped up everyone's wine glasses. 'In the middle of Bideford? I'd have thought it was way too far away to be feasible.'

Dom sat back in his seat, a teasing glint in his eye. 'There's a story of a smugglers' tunnel near Bournemouth that ran inland from the coast for some 4 miles.'

'Now that has got to be a wind-up,' Faith said, turning to her husband and laughing.

'There are tunnels, though, aren't there?' Esme said. 'Maybe not as long as 4 miles, but secret tunnels for smugglers to evade the customs men?'

'Oh, yes,' Dom said, nodding. 'They say virtually every village in southern England had something of the sort. Usually where the smugglers stashed their spoils. Most weren't dug for the purpose, but were convenient fissures in the rock, caves or other channels that already existed. Though, there's one in Hayle in Cornwall which they believe was dug specifically as a smugglers' tunnel. It stretches for hundreds of metres and you can still walk it.'

'Oh, I'd love to do that,' Esme said. 'In the footsteps of history.'

'Any around here?' Libby asked.

'Probably at some point,' Dom said. 'But over time, entrances have been lost or bricked up, so there's not much evidence left these days.'

They sat down to a delicious meal of chicken chasseur, followed by melting chocolate puddings, beautifully cooked by Libby. The evening passed quickly and amiably with much laughter, and Esme again felt her move to the village had been the right decision. Now she had two more people to add to her circle of friends.

The party broke up soon after coffee, Dom and Faith apologising for their early departure, blaming babysitter constraints. They issued an open invitation for Esme and Libby to drop in any time and meet the family of two children, three cats and a dog.

'I'd better be making tracks, too,' Esme said, as the couple headed off into the darkness back up the lane.

'Don't go yet,' Libby said, closing the door. 'You haven't told me the latest antics of your friend Max. Nightcap?'

'Oh, all right,' Esme said. 'But just a quick one. Then I really must go.' She followed Libby into the kitchen, looking around at the debris from the meal and the dishes piled up on the worktops. 'I'll give you a hand clearing up.'

'You'll do no such thing,' Libby said. 'I'll deal with that later. Sit yourself down.' She went over to the large dresser against the wall and opened the cupboard door. 'What'll you have? Scotch? Brandy? I've got some Drambuie in here somewhere, I think.'

Esme sat down at the table. 'Oh, that sounds a nice idea. It's years since I had a Drambuie. Thanks.'

'I think I'll join you,' Libby said, taking out a bottle and two glasses and putting them on the table.

'It was a lovely meal,' Esme said, as Libby poured out the liqueur and slid a glass towards her. 'Thank you for inviting me. Great to meet Dom and Faith, too.'

'Yes, they do seem a nice couple, don't they? They've asked me whether I'd do a mural for their daughter's bedroom wall.'

'That's great. You'll enjoy that.'

Libby wrapped her hands around her glass and leaned across the table towards Esme. 'Come on, then. I know you confirmed he wasn't buried in the pile of rubble on the beach. Anything happened since?'

Esme laughed at Libby's eager expression. 'No, nothing new to report. He's scurried back to London. Like I said before, I think all this hiding in outhouses has reminded him he's getting too old for that sort of investigative journalism.'

'And like *I* said before, once a journalist...'

Esme inclined her head. 'You did.'

Libby took a sip of her drink. 'So, did he turn up anything interesting?'

Esme hesitated. How much should she say? 'Well, that depends on what you mean by interesting. I don't think he learned anything, other than that poking around in people's back gardens uninvited is likely to get you a bloody nose.'

Libby's eyes widened. 'Is that what happened? You said he'd taken a tumble.'

Esme nodded. 'He had fallen over a fence while being chased by a pack of dogs, apparently.'

'Oh dear,' Libby said, sitting back in her chair. 'I see what you mean. Embarrassing. But was he on to something? That's the question, isn't it?'

Esme shrugged. 'I've no idea. I'm not even sure he's...' Her sentence was cut off by the sound of a loud crash from outside.

Libby's head shot round. 'What was that?' She stood up and walked over to the window, peering out into the darkness.

Esme got up and joined her. 'See anything?'

'Not a bloody thing. The security light hasn't been triggered.' Libby grabbed a torch from a shelf and hurried over to the back door. It opened on to the terraced garden behind the cottage from where they'd looked out after the cliff-fall. Libby pulled open the door and stepped outside, Esme following close behind her.

'Where do you think it came from?' Esme said, as Libby turned on the torch and swept the beam into the night.

'Not sure.' Libby took a few steps further into the garden. 'Sounded like something falling over, didn't it?'

'What about up on the terrace?'

They hurried over to the steps, the distant sound of the sea pulsating as they began climbing.

'There,' Libby said, pointing. A chair lay on its side next to the round café table.

'What could have done that? An animal?'

'If it was,' Libby muttered, 'it's pretty big.' She gave a nervous laugh. 'You've not heard that any of Exmoor Zoo's residents have escaped, I hope?'

They reached the terrace and looked around. Esme's eyes had begun to adjust to the light now. Down below, the glow from Libby's kitchen was flooding through the back door, and up the valley, the odd pinprick of light from those residents not yet gone to bed could be seen in the thick blackness.

Something moved in Esme's peripheral vision and she snapped her head round to home in on it, walking slowly towards the large camellia bush on the edge of the patio. She felt Libby beside her and, as Esme bent down to look underneath the shrub, Libby shone the torch on to the ground.

Esme gasped, almost stumbling backwards as, caught in the light of Libby's torch, two eyes looked back at her. But it was not an animal. It was a child.

# 38

Libby crouched down, averting her torch away from the boy's face. 'Hey there, poppet,' she said, 'where have you come from?'

'Don't worry, we're not cross with you,' Esme said, smiling. She reached out her hand. 'Come on, let's get you out of there. It must be really uncomfortable under that bush.'

The boy, a slight frame of maybe 6 or 7 years of age, said nothing, but edged towards them, his large brown eyes flitting from one to the other as he emerged on to the patio. Dead leaves were caught in the tangles of his dark hair, no doubt due to his crawling through undergrowth. He was dressed in jeans and a camel coloured sweatshirt with the face of a bear on the front.

'That's better,' Libby said, straightening up and pointing to herself. 'My name's Libby and this is my friend Esme. What's your name?'

The boy didn't answer.

'You *are* having a bit of an adventure, aren't you?' Esme said. 'Do you live near here?' Perhaps he was on holiday nearby. But it seemed odd he'd chosen to go exploring so late at night. Unless he'd got lost earlier in the day. She imagined his parents sitting distraught beside a phone, the police out searching for him. 'Your mum and dad will wonder where you are, won't they?' Still no response.

'I bet you're thirsty,' Libby said. 'Shall we go into my kitchen and get you a drink while we work out how we can help?'

'Help,' echoed the boy.

Esme detected a foreign lilt to his voice. 'You need help?' she said. 'Is that what you mean?'

'Um,' the boy said.

Esme and Libby exchanged glances. 'Was that an affirmative?' Libby said, under her breath. 'He obviously doesn't speak much

English.'

Esme squatted down beside the boy and laid a hand on his arm. 'You need help?' she asked. 'What would you like us to do? Is there someone we can phone? Your parents? They must be worried about you?'

The boy blinked back at her, but said nothing.

Libby straightened up. 'This is getting us nowhere. We'll have to phone the police.'

At this, the boy shouted, pulling away from Esme's grasp. 'No p'lis.' He pushed past them and began climbing the steep shrubbery towards the woodland behind.

'Oh hell, now what?' Libby said, staring after him.

'You call the police,' Esme said. 'I'll see if I can catch him up. He obviously thinks he's going to get into trouble for being out and about.'

Libby handed Esme the torch. 'Here, have this,' she said, before turning and hurrying down the steps back to the cottage.

Esme switched on the torch and swept the beam of light from side to side, looking for movement in the foliage above her as a clue as to the child's whereabouts. But there was nothing. She set off in the direction he'd run, pushing up between the shrubs, guessing he'd be heading for high ground, perhaps retracing the steps of the way he'd arrived. It was possible she'd find out where he'd come from. There were several holiday cottages further up the valley and while she hadn't seen any evidence that they were occupied this week, the family may have only recently arrived.

But when she reached the boundary wall of Libby's garden, she paused, out of breath, uncertain what to do next. Climbing the stone wall up above her was beyond her, and even if she did, she didn't know which way he'd gone. She sighed in frustration, turning when she heard Libby calling her from below and making her way back down to the small terrace at the top of the steps where Libby was waiting, looking at her anxiously.

'Nothing?' Libby said.

Esme shook her head. 'Far too quick and nimble for me. I'm assuming he's clambered over the top wall, but where he went after that, I've no idea. Did you get hold of the police?'

'Yes, on their way.' Libby wrapped her arms around herself. 'Where d'you think he came from?'

'One of the holiday cottages?'

'Possibly. He obviously didn't speak English. And he seemed pretty scared to me, didn't he to you?'

'That could be because he'd gone AWOL and knew he shouldn't have.' Esme frowned. 'But why did he pounce on the word *help*? He obviously knew what it meant.'

'Yeah, and the word police, too.' Libby jerked her head towards the cottage. 'We may as well wait indoors. There's little we can do out here. He's not likely to come back now, not after I mentioned calling them.'

As they descended the steps, something slipped into Esme's head. 'You don't think he's the figure in the distance we both saw on the beach, do you?'

Libby stopped and looked back over her shoulder. 'What, our little ghost, you mean?' She shrugged. 'It's a thought. Perhaps we should mention it to the police when they get here.'

'Yes, good idea.'

Libby turned back and continued down the steps, Esme right behind her. But as they reached the back door, a child's cry rang out in the distance. They froze.

'Where did that come from?' Esme said, spinning round and trying to home in on the sound.

'Over there, I think,' Libby said, pointing to their left, towards the sea.

'He must have gone back to the coast path.'

She'd barely finished the sentence when there were further cries, followed by a shout in an adult's voice and dogs barking. Before they'd had time to gather their thoughts, there was a piercing screech of frustration, and then silence.

# 39

Esme sat and stared down at Libby's kitchen table, half-listening to Libby remonstrate with one of the police officers who'd responded to her call. Before the police had arrived, Esme had insisted on checking the coast path, despite Libby's concern that it was too dangerous. Esme reassured her that she'd be fine with the torch and Libby needed to wait at the cottage for the arrival of the police.

But Libby had pointed out that it was who Esme might encounter on the coast path which was uppermost in her mind, not that she'd miss her footing in the dark. As a compromise, Esme promised to go only to the cordon of the collapsed cottage and no further. She'd returned to Libby's cottage only a short time later, having found nothing to indicate that a small boy, a large dog and an adult had been on the path a few minutes previously. *What did I think I'd find?* she asked herself in frustration.

Now the bearded police officer, who looked the fitter of the two, was currently retracing Esme's steps on the coastal path and, she hoped, going further along than the point at which she'd turned back. The officers had already searched the garden, despite the women explaining that the child had climbed out and run off. They'd resisted Esme's suggestion to knock on doors and question residents, explaining that they were confident that if any child *had* gone missing, the police would already have been alerted.

'Only if they wanted the police to know, though,' Esme said, provoking a sceptical smirk from the blond-haired officer. She scowled at him. 'And what's that supposed to mean?' she demanded.

He didn't reply and instead turned to Libby. 'Of middle-eastern appearance, you say, madam?'

'Yes, that's right,' Libby confirmed. 'And he didn't appear to speak English, did he, Esme?'

'No. Though he seemed to understand *help* and *police.*' Esme locked eyes with PC Blondy. 'Hearing the word police is when he panicked and ran off.'

PC Blondy tucked his thumb under his stab vest and sniffed. 'Yes, so you said, madam.' He picked up an empty wine bottle from the table and read the label. 'Bit of a party here earlier, then?'

'I had friends round for a meal, officer,' Libby said. 'What's that got to do with anything?'

'And you say you were having a nightcap when you heard this lad outside?' He looked pointedly at the two Drambuie glasses still sitting on the table.

Esme closed her eyes and let out a silent sigh. Oh great. They were going to dismiss the incident as two drunk middle-aged women imagining things. She opened her eyes and stared up at the police officer.

'I thought the police took incidents involving children seriously.'

The officer pulled himself up to his full six-foot-plus height. 'We take all credible reports involving children seriously, madam.'

Esme folded her arms and looked away. *Credible reports.* It said everything. And, perhaps in his shoes, she'd feel the same, given the lack of evidence. Thank goodness Libby had seen it too, or she might have examined everything tomorrow – or later this morning, given the hour – and concluded the whole surreal episode was a figment of her imagination.

Libby showed the policeman out. By the time she came back into the kitchen, Esme was pulling on her coat.

'Sorry, Esme,' Libby said.

'Why sorry?' Esme said. 'It's not your fault.'

'Yes, but if I'd not persuaded you to stay behind…' she shrugged and dropped down on to a chair.

'You still might have heard something, and then there'd only be you as witness,' Esme pointed out.

'True.' Libby sighed and looked up with a reflective smile. 'So, what d'you think, Esme? Have we found our ghost?'

'Maybe. Though he's obviously no ghost. So, who is he? And where did he come from?' She frowned as something slipped into her head. They'd heard dogs. Max had talked about there being dogs guarding Maudesley's place.

'What's the matter?' Libby asked.

Esme smiled and shook her head. 'Nothing. Just trying to make sense of it. Thanks for a lovely meal, Libby. And now, I really should get to my bed. See you tomorrow.'

As she wandered back up the lane to her cottage, the moon cast an eerie light and her footsteps sounded unnaturally loud on the tarmac. She strained to hear the sound of dogs barking in the distance. But all that reached her ears was the faint hiss of the sea behind her as it pushed its way onto the pebbles of the beach below.

# 40

Esme phoned Libby in the morning to thank her for the evening and to enquire whether she'd had any news from the police. Concern about the child's circumstances, not to mention the disturbing connection between the sound of baying dogs and Max's unfortunate episode near Maudesley's property, had dominated Esme's thoughts after she'd said goodnight to Libby. She'd spent a restless night, or what remained of it once she'd finally fallen into bed, trying to make sense of it.

There had been no further contact from the police, Libby told her, and it was clear from her tone of voice that she was sceptical there ever would be.

'They've probably written the whole incident off as an aberration of two middle-aged women who'd had one over the eight,' she said, with a hint of irritation.

'You never know,' Esme said, trying to inject some optimism into the situation, 'someone else might see the young lad and they'll have to take it more seriously.'

Libby gave a dismissive snort. 'I'm not sure the system is that great at joining up the dots, Esme,' she said with a sigh. 'No cross referencing, you see. Every incident logged separately. I've come across it before.'

Libby promised to let Esme know if she did hear anything further and Esme cut the call, wondering whether it was worth putting the word around the village to see if anyone else had more information. Her thoughts turned to Max. Should she ask him if he knew anything, in light of his unfortunate encounter with dogs while he was poking around Dowell Lodge? But lots of people had dogs, especially round here. Why assume the dogs she and Libby had heard barking last night were the same ones as had seen off Max? Besides, she had no desire to contact Max. He'd only see it as an indication she had more interest in his investigation than she'd said. And she certainly had no intention of implying that.

She spent the rest of the morning on household chores, wondering as she worked if Hester had managed to find Annie's letter and what her mother had made of her renewed interest. Perhaps Hester would have some fascinating information to impart when they met on Tuesday.

Esme unloaded the washing machine into a basket and took it outside. As she pegged the items out on the line, she lamented that there were two days to wait before she'd be able to see Annie's letter and conclude whether it held any clues. That was assuming Hester could find it. Esme envisioned an attic full of unlabelled boxes. The task may turn out to be an impossible one. Or, at least, not one that could be managed in a couple of hours on a Sunday afternoon.

Esme returned indoors, recalling what Maddy had said about not getting her hopes up of finding answers in Annie's letter, that Ernest's murder may for ever remain a mystery. So what if Maddy was right and the letter was indecipherable? That wasn't the only route of enquiry. There were others. Finding Albert Philips on the 1921 census was a discovery Esme had not been looking for and, while it was no great revelation, it proved there was much she might glean from other sources.

She dropped the washing basket on to the kitchen floor and went to find her laptop. Once it booted, she sat down at the kitchen table and opened the file she'd compiled for Hester, in which she'd saved newspaper reports of the trial. Had she missed anything in one of those reports?

Most of the articles were of identical wording, as was common when newspapers were society's key source of news across the country. She assumed something akin to a press release would have been passed around the nation's newspaper offices to be printed in local editions. There may, however, be something, an extra sentence, one small snippet of information added in that made one of them reveal more than another.

But having scanned through each of them, Esme concluded that there was nothing more within the reports than she'd originally surmised. There may, though, be others on the database she'd overlooked in her initial trawl. Or, more promisingly, which had been added since her last foray.

She opened up the British Newspaper Archive and entered Albert Philips's name into the search engine, narrowing the search by date. The articles were listed in order of those considered most relevant and she scrolled down through them, identifying the pieces with which she was already familiar. As she reached the last few pages, the search criteria became less focused, throwing up connections with either the name Albert or the surname Philips.

One of these caught her eye. Frederick Philips. Hadn't that been the name of Albert's brother? She flicked back to the family tree and confirmed she'd been correct. Frederick Philips was indeed Albert's brother. He was younger than Albert by six years, born in 1896, though Esme hadn't yet established when he'd died. What she had established, however, was that Frederick had regularly attended his brother's trial.

She returned to the newspaper database and clicked on the article attributed to his name, scanning the page as it came into view on the screen and homing in on the blue rectangle with which the database helpfully identified the resulting searched-for word. She zoomed in closer so she could read the text and noticed it was not a newspaper report, but a letter to the editor of the *Bath Gazette,* the correspondent being Frederick Philips. At first, she couldn't see how this was likely to be of any relevance to her search, until she began to read and realised the letter was some sort of rant concerning his older brother's case.

*Sir – I would be obliged if you would furnish me with the name of the person who supplied you with what purports to be a report of the recent case of The Crown vs Philips. The report is not only grossly inaccurate, but unfairly omits mention of key witnesses called for the defendant…*

Esme altered her search parameters to focus on Frederick Philips by name, revealing the letter to be one of many written by him and sent to the editor's office over a period of time. In exasperation, it seemed the editor had finally decided to publish the correspondence between the newspaper and Mr Philips, including that of the solicitor advising the publication, in an attempt to put an end to the epistolary harassment.

Esme scanned through the extracts. The tone was scathing and nit-picked constantly. In one, Philips threatened to sue the reporter in question for libel, which was clearly ridiculous as Albert had been found guilty of the crime for which he was accused. At the end of the list was an editorial declaring that Mr Philips had taken up enough of the newspaper's time and column space and any further communication would be disregarded. It was obvious that Philips had targeted the newspaper as a vehicle through which to vent his frustration and his anger at his brother's conviction.

The audaciousness of attacking the newspaper in this way suggested to Esme a certain arrogance and self-importance on the part of Frederick Philips. That his brother was found guilty of the murder of an innocent man seemed not to worry him one jot. And it didn't appear that protesting his brother's innocence was his motive for his rant, only that the newspaper had somehow been biased in its account of the trial. She wondered what sort of man Frederick Philips was. Confident, clearly. Arrogant, quite possibly. Assured, most definitely.

She manoeuvred her way out of the newspaper archive and went in search of answers on the Internet, finding to her heightened intrigue that Frederick had been an eminent historian in his day. One claim – unverified – suggested he'd been an associate of Howard Carter and had played a part in the discovery of Tutankhamen's tomb. But his archaeology CV seemed too thin to suggest he'd been anything more than a keen amateur. His biography made more of his work to inspire a love of history in pupils who attended the private school of which he was patron, Garter Abbey.

A quick check told Esme the school had closed in 1983. According to a post on the history of the area, entitled *Place's Schools Then and Now,* Garter Abbey had become economically unviable after it had too few pupils to sustain it. The writer of the article implied this had happened after some sort of crisis, but didn't elaborate as to what the crisis had been. Perhaps the author wasn't aware of the details. The property was now in the care of the National Trust and a browse of their website suggested the school, once a prestigious seat of education and well established by the time Frederick Philips became associated with it, played a major part in their presentation of the building's story.

Esme got up to make herself a cup of coffee, chewing over the information as she filled the kettle. By the time it boiled, an uneasy memory had lodged in her head, something Max had told her about Frank Stone having an expensive education. Could this be the school he'd attended? As Frederick Philips was Stone's great-uncle, it was perfectly feasible, given his association with the school, he might have secured him a place at Garter Abbey.

She poured boiling water into her mug and pushed the thought of Frank Stone out of her head. He wasn't relevant here. Her interest was in Frederick Philips. She was curious about his tirade at the newspaper. He was clearly angry at his brother's conviction – perhaps understandable that he found it hard to accept a loved one being found guilty of a heinous crime, and he may have been merely kicking out at the humiliation the murder conviction had heaped on his family. Surely he hadn't seriously thought the reporter's so-called bias had affected the outcome of the trial?

And yet she sensed it wasn't that Philips believed his brother to be innocent, but that he didn't believe he would be found guilty. Why so confident? Was it merely his arrogance talking? Perhaps he knew of mitigating circumstances which he anticipated would come out at the trial. So why hadn't they? Why hadn't they been used in Albert's defence? And if Frederick knew of such circumstances, why hadn't he brought them to light himself?

The more Esme considered this, the more convinced she was that Albert's brother knew more about what was behind the clash between the cousins than had been made public. If it was true that Annie had been researching Ernest's murder, could *she* have discovered that secret which had been buried since 1923?

# 41

'Any news on the little boy?' Maddy asked when Esme arrived at the sale room where they'd arranged to meet for the maritime collection auction. It was to be held in a rambling Victorian building which had once been important to the town's industry as a collar factory and furniture depository. News of the sale had attracted much interest and it became increasingly difficult to negotiate the narrow aisles in the rooms where the contents of the collection was on display.

'No, nothing,' Esme said, and she told Maddy about Libby's theory that the police had discounted their report as unreliable.

'That's so frustrating,' Maddy sympathised.

'Very,' Esme admitted. 'But I don't see what else we can do. Now, come on. Show me what you've got your eye on.'

Maddy led Esme to the items she'd earmarked as being of interest, pointing excitedly at one very old and grubby wooden box. Esme laughed, giving Maddy a playful dig in the ribs.

'I thought you'd be an old hand at this by now, Mads,' she teased. 'But I strongly suspect you're giving your rivals the heads-up. Aren't you supposed to be poker-faced?'

Maddy rolled her eyes, a grin across her face. 'I know. But it's so hard.' She fingered the box displayed in front of them, thick with grime. 'I mean, isn't this just crying out for TLC?'

'I wonder why it's in such a state when the rest of the collection has been so beautifully restored.'

Maddy nodded. 'Yes, I thought that. I asked the auctioneer. He said it's a recent acquisition. He hadn't had the chance to clean it up.' She looked back over her shoulder. 'Oh, looks like we're kicking off. Let's go and find a seat.'

They shuffled back into the room set out with chairs and found a seat a few rows back from the front. Maddy sighed.

'I hate it when the lot I want is near the end. I'm a quivering wreck by the time it gets to it.'

Esme scanned the room. 'What sort of competition do you reckon you've got?'

Maddy followed Esme's gaze. 'Hard to say. I don't see any of the usual suspects. It would be nice to think most people are here because of the more specialist, expensive maritime items, like spy glasses and sextants, and aren't interested in scruffy old wooden boxes.'

'Fingers crossed you're right.'

The auctioneer brought the room to order and introduced his colleagues, who were either peering at laptop screens or holding mobile phones against their ears. Clearly the sale had attracted interest from much further afield than the buyers who'd come in person.

With introductions done, the auctioneer began proceedings and, with a skill that never failed to impress Esme, he rattled through the first few lots with surprising speed. Maddy clutched her bidder's card on her lap, watching avidly as the auctioneer worked his way down the list.

Esme's phone buzzed and she glanced down at the screen to see a text had come in from Max. *"Call me,"* it read.

Esme typed, *"Can't at mo. Later."* and pressed send. A few seconds later, it buzzed again.

*"It's important. Any chance?"*

She tapped back. *"What is it?"*

*"Too complicated to text. Call me."*

Esme glanced at her watch before replying, *"Half an hour?"*

*"Now's better."* And then, as she scowled at the screen, he added, as an afterthought. *"Please!"*

She sighed. *"OK. Give me a sec."*

She leaned over and whispered in Maddy's ear. 'Max's trying to get hold of me. I'd better go and see what he wants.'

Maddy gave her a flash of irritation. 'That man's got too high

199

an opinion of his own importance,' she hissed.

'I won't disagree with you there,' Esme said, slipping her phone into her pocket. 'But he says it's important so I'd better indulge him, just in case.'

She manoeuvred her way to the end of the row and hurried down the side aisle and out on to the landing outside the auction room. When she made the call, Max answered halfway through the first ring.

'What the hell's this about, Max?' she said, pacing up and down. 'Can't it wait? I'm at an auction.'

'I need your help, Ez. I've hit a snag with Maudesley.'

'Oh for goodness sake, Max. I thought you said it was important.'

'It is. Something doesn't add up. I need your eyes on it.'

Esme closed her eyes in exasperation and sighed. 'Haven't you got the message by now, Max? I'm not interested.'

'Oh, go on, Ez. Do us a favour, eh? It's right up your street. Trust me.'

Esme scoffed. 'Trust you? Are you serious?' The man was a comedian.

'I'll email you the information. Then you can give it the once over. How's that?'

'It won't make any difference. I'm not going there, OK?' Esme leaned her back against the wall of the stairwell and folded her arm across her body. 'Look, Max, we're just wasting one another's time here and I'd really like to get back in the sale room. So if that's all…'

'No, actually. There's something else.'

She rolled her eyes heavenward. 'Isn't there always? Go on, spit it out. Then I'm gone.'

'What do you know about Aidan Garrett?'

'Aidan?' Esme said, blinking.

'Oh, so you do know him, then?'

'Not exactly, no. I've met him a couple of times, that's all.

What's he got to do with anything?' Esme could hear voices in the background. 'Max?'

'Sorry about that. What were we saying? Oh, yeah. Aidan Garrett.'

Esme scowled. This had to be some sort of ploy. He must have got wind of Aidan's link with Maddy somehow. She pursed her lips, irritated with herself. Why couldn't she just cut the call and be done with it? If that didn't get the message across, what would?

'Well, are you going to tell me or what?' she heard herself saying, when Max didn't immediately respond.

'Sorry, just checking my notes. Garrett's some sort of underwater treasure hunter.'

'Yes, I know that. What about it?'

'Working for Maudesley.'

'So? Maudesley has a whole museum full of people working for him,' Esme said. 'Get to the point, Max.'

'Rumour has it there's bad blood between them.'

The image of the confrontational exchange she'd witnessed on Lundy flashed into her head, but she had no intention of giving Max the satisfaction of sharing it with him, thereby falling into his trap.

'Ah, another of those infamous rumours of yours, Max. From what you've told me, they don't seem to have led you anywhere so far.'

'Just need a lucky break, that's all. It's out there somewhere.'

Esme stood upright. 'Well, if that's everything, Max, I'll say goodbye.'

'Sure, Ez. I'll email you later with that stuff.'

She thrust her phone into her coat pocket and strode back to the door to the sale room, turning as she did so at the sound of footsteps running up the stairs behind her. As she pulled open the door, a man in a suit, strands of greasy grey hair curling over the collar of his jacket, pushed past and through ahead of her.

'Excuse me,' Esme shouted after him, but he seemed

oblivious. She shook her head and followed him inside, where people were standing up and conversation was starting to hum. She looked across at Maddy, who was wearing a large grin. She gave Esme the thumbs-up sign and jerked her head towards the front of the room and Esme nodded in response, delighted that Maddy must have secured a deal on the lot she'd earmarked.

Esme sat down on the end chair of the row to wait while Maddy went to pay her dues and collect her purchase. As she watched the proceedings, she mulled over Max's odd behaviour on the phone. Why didn't the man get the message? And what was all that about Aidan, anyway? So, he was going to email, was he? Well, she had no intention of being bounced into helping his investigation. She'd simply delete the email and claim it never arrived.

Satisfied with her decision, she looked up to see where Maddy had got to in the queue and was pleased to see her at the desk paying. Transactions complete, Maddy turned round and began walking away. As Esme stood up ready to join her, she noticed the man who'd rudely pushed past her when she'd come in had waylaid Maddy and was gesturing to her. Maddy looked annoyed and was shaking her head.

Esme weaved her way through the rows of chairs to the other side, navigating the people still waiting in the queue and reaching Maddy as the man handed something to her and walked away.

'Who was that?' Esme asked, watching as he hurried out of the room.

'He wanted to buy the box off me,' Maddy said. 'He said he'd been late and had missed the sale.'

'Yeah, I saw him arrive. He shoved past me.'

'I told him that was his problem.'

'Good for you.'

'Yes, it was lucky he didn't make it in time, or I'd have missed out. He was obviously way out of my league.'

'How d'you know?' Esme asked.

202

'Because he offered me three times what I paid for it.'

'Wow. He's keen. Maybe he'll buy it when you've restored it.'

'That's what I said, but he said he didn't want it restored. He wanted it as it is.'

Esme shrugged. 'Each to his own. I suppose it has a certain charm, the state it's in. So why didn't you go for it?'

'What's the point in that? I like renovating. It's what I do. And anyway,' Maddy added, her face darkening, 'I don't like being bullied. It makes me grouchy.'

Esme laughed. 'Maybe he'll change his mind once it's done. Did you take his details?'

'Didn't catch his name, but he gave me his business card,' Maddy said. She reached into her back pocket and handed a card to Esme. 'Told me to think about his offer and get in touch if I decided to take him up on it.'

Esme looked down at the card, alarm crowding into her head as she read the name printed on it. 'Oh hell, Madds. I don't like this.'

'Why?' Maddy said, peering to see what Esme was looking at. 'Who is he?'

Esme swallowed. 'Frank Stone.'

## 42

'Have you made a start on the new box?' Esme asked Maddy, as they set up their stall at the following day's market.

Maddy's eyes shone. 'Yes, I have. But it's going to take a while, it's got years of dirt engrained in it. So slowly, slowly is the key. I don't want to overdo it and remove all its history.'

'I don't suppose there are any clues as to why Frank Stone was so desperate to get hold of it?'

Maddy shook her head. 'Too early for it to reveal all its secrets.'

Esme straightened up from sliding a storage box under the table. '*All* its secrets?' she echoed, a smile growing on her face. 'You mean you've found something?'

Maddy laughed. 'I'm not talking hidden drawers, if that's what you're thinking.'

'Aw, that's a shame,' Esme said. Maddy's crucial discovery had once helped solve a significant mystery. 'So what sort, then, if not secret drawers?'

'There's an etching of a sailing ship inside the lid under all the grime. I've only uncovered one corner of it so far, but it looks fantastic. Someone was clearly very talented.'

'Is there an artist's name?'

'Not that I can see so far. But the ship's name is on some sort of scroll in one corner. Might give a clue.'

Esme ran her finger along her scar. 'Do you think that's what Stone's interested in?'

'The etching? That it might be valuable or something?'

'Well, there has to be some reason why he's so keen to get his hands on it.'

'I guess I'll have more idea when I've cleaned off a bit more and can have a proper look.'

'You don't intend to contact him, though, do you?' Esme

asked. She swallowed. 'We already know Hester's wary of him and Max told me...'

'Oh, we're taking notice of what Max says, now, are we?' Maddy said, with a mocking smile.

'I'm serious, Maddy. I've already told you – *and* Max for that matter, though it's like talking to the proverbial brick wall – what he does is his business and it doesn't include me.' Max's email had come through, but it remained in her inbox unopened. She knew she ought to delete it before she was tempted to take a look, but for some reason, she'd not been able to bring herself to do so.

She turned back to Maddy. 'What he *did* say which *is* worth taking notice of is that Stone's not someone you'd want to do business with.'

Maddy held up a hand. 'Fine by me. I'm not about to sell, to him or to anyone, at this precise moment in time, so you've no need to worry about it.'

Esme laughed. '*I've* no need to worry. Now you sound like me reassuring you.'

Maddy chuckled. 'Now that'll be the day.' She folded her arms, leaning against the table edge, her ankles crossed. 'Why don't you nip back with me to the workshop when we've done here and see what I've done on the box so far?'

'That's a good idea. I should have enough time before I meet Hester.'

'Oh yes, I forgot you were seeing her. I can't wait to hear what's in her great aunt's letter.'

Esme hugged herself. 'That's if we can make any sense of it. I'm trying not to expect too much, but it's exciting, I must admit.'

'Do you think Hester might have a theory about why Frank Stone is so interested in my box?'

'Why would she?'

Maddy shrugged. 'Just a thought. She knows him.'

'And would rather not,' Esme pointed out.

'True. Might be worth mentioning, though, just in case. By the way, have you told her about Frederick Philips's letters in the press?'

Esme shook her head. 'No, not yet. But if we glean anything from Annie's mysterious letter, the two things might tie in rather nicely.' She chewed the edge of her lip. 'I was thinking about paying a visit to Garter Abbey.'

'That the name of the school he was patron of?'

'Yes, that's the one. It's open tomorrow. Thought I'd make a day of it.'

'Hi, guys.'

Esme and Maddy turned their heads as Aidan approached the stall. Maddy stood upright. 'Ah, Aidan. Good to see you. Hang on a minute, I'll get it.' She slipped behind the stall and began digging around in her bag.

Esme looked quizzically at Aidan, Max's talk of bad blood between him and Isaac Maudesley slipping into her mind. Had they resolved whatever differences they'd had when she'd seen them on Lundy?

'Key,' Aidan said, jerking his head towards Maddy.

'Oh yes, of course. You're staying with Maddy and Harry while you're working on this job.'

Maddy made her way back to them and handed Aidan a mortice key. 'There you go. You can come and go as you please.'

'Thanks, Maddy. Appreciate it.' He smiled at Esme. 'Off somewhere nice?'

'What?' Esme blinked. 'Oh, you mean about having a day out.'

Aidan grinned. 'Sorry. Didn't mean to earwig. Heard you saying as I walked up.'

'Oh, no, that's all right. Garter Abbey. It's a National Trust property.'

Aidan blinked. 'National Trust?'

'Yes, acquired fairly recently, I think,' Esme said.

'Esme's doing some research on it,' Maddy told him. 'Hoping to solve a mystery, aren't you, Esme?' she added, as she and Esme exchanged a knowing grin.

Esme turned back to Aidan. 'Do you know the place? I've never been before.'

Aidan shook his head. 'Me neither. Supposed to be a fascinating place. Must get around to going someday.' He held up the key. 'Well, I'd better scoot. Thanks for this, Maddy. See you later.'

'Yeah, sure.'

'Have a good trip, Esme,' he added. 'Look forward to hearing what you make of the place.'

As he walked across the market hall towards the exit, Maddy jabbed Esme with her elbow. 'Well, that was a missed opportunity,' she said.

'What was?'

'You could have had some company there. If you'd asked him to go with you, he'd have been there like a shot.'

Esme chewed her lower lip. 'Do you think I put my foot in it?'

'No, I'm sure you haven't. Give him a call and invite him along.'

Esme shook her head. 'No, that wasn't what I meant.'

'Then what did you mean?'

'I don't know really.' Esme shrugged. 'He seemed a bit distracted.' Her hand flew to her mouth. 'Oh, Hell. You don't think he was a pupil there, do you? Maybe I conjured up all sorts of bad childhood memories.'

'How could he have been?' Maddy said. 'He said he'd never been, didn't he?'

'Yes, of course he did. You're right.' But there was something.

Esme clicked her tongue, realising what was bugging her. She was reading more into Aidan's reaction than was justified. And why? Because of Max, she thought with a surge of irritation. It was him and his cross examination which had planted suspicions in her head. She reached into her pocket for her phone and navigated to her inbox. She clicked on Max's unread email and pressed delete.

Esme helped load up Maddy's van with the stall's stock and Maddy set off back to her workshop, Esme following in her car. It didn't take long for them to empty the van and store the boxes of stock away.

'Coffee?' Maddy said, going over to the mini kitchen area.

Esme glanced at her watch. 'I'd better not. I need to get over to Hester's.' She glanced around the workshop. 'Come on, then. Let's see this fabulous sea chest.'

Maddy strode across to where the pine box from the sale was sitting on her workbench. She indicated a darker patch on the centre of the lid.

'I think there's something under the grime there. Initials, I'm hoping.'

'I'm surprised you haven't already got to work on that.'

'Well, it was a bit of a dilemma deciding where to begin. But when I lifted the lid,' Maddy said, doing so as she spoke, 'you'll see why I left the top and began here.'

Esme peered inside to see a partly uncovered etching of a ship on the underside of the lid. 'Wow, that's gorgeous,' she said, gazing at the image. Maddy had revealed enough to show it in full glorious sail.

'I've done some research,' Maddy said, 'and I'm pretty certain it's a brigantine, judging by the way the sails are set up on its two masts. In its day, speed would have been its overriding feature.'

Esme ran her fingers along the rim of the box. 'How old is it, do you reckon?'

'The auction blurb put it at 18th century. I'd go along with that.'

'I wonder who it belonged to,' Esme said. 'And what it would have had in it. In the chests on display at the *Treasures of the Sea Museum*, they'd found pewter plates, tankards, shoes, clothes, even dice, counters and a backgammon board.'

Maddy pointed to one corner of the inside lid. 'There's an

apotropaic mark carved into the wood. To ward off evil spirits, I guess.'

Esme could just make out the shape of a daisy set within a circle. 'Makes sense. Sailors were a superstitious lot.'

'Yeah, weren't they just? No whistling on board, as it might conjure up a storm. No setting sail on a Thursday or a Friday as it was bad luck, as was having women on the ship.'

'I suppose you can hardly blame them,' Esme said. 'It's pretty dangerous out there on the ocean. They needed all the help they could get.' She checked her watch. 'Look, I'd better go. Let me know what else you discover, won't you?'

Maddy nodded. 'You'll be the first to know, promise. Oh, and if you get a chance,' she added, as Esme headed for the door, 'don't forget to ask Hester whether she's got any theories on why Frank Stone's so desperate to get his hands on my box. Might give me a clue what secrets I'm looking for.'

# 43

Esme clattered up the stairs to Hester's office, almost colliding on the first landing with a slim man in a well-cut suit, dashing past as though he was on a life or death mission. He came to an abrupt halt as Esme flattened herself against the wall to avoid him, flashed her a radiant smile before apologising and carrying on his way at speed.

'I thought there must be a fire up here,' she said to Hester as she came through the door.

Hester laughed. 'I take it you met my new accountant, Nicholas. Mum calls him Nippy Nick.'

An elderly lady, smartly dressed in a spring green jacket, her hair in a neat elfin cut, appeared from the inner room behind Hester.

'Don't knock him, he's very good,' she said, giving Hester's arm a tap as she stepped forward. 'Which is exactly what you need at the moment.'

'Esme, this is my mum, Pat,' Hester said.

'Good to meet you, Esme,' Pat said, as they shook hands. 'I hear you're helping Hester solve a mystery about research my aunt was doing.'

'Well, that's the theory,' Esme said, glancing at Hester. She wondered how much Pat knew about the background and how they'd arrived at this point. Was Pat aware of Hester's worries about Maudesley and Frank Stone? 'Hester's been telling me how fond she was of Annie.'

Pat gave Esme a wistful smile. 'Yes, they were very close. It was a shock when we lost her, wasn't it, Hester?'

Hester answered her mother's question with a brief nod.

'Hester told me of the circumstances,' Esme said. 'It must have been very distressing.'

'Totally. If it hadn't been the day Jenny, her cleaning lady, came in, who knows how long she would have lain there?' Pat spread her hands. 'Jenny didn't even realise there was anything amiss to begin with. She let herself in as usual, picked up the shopping list and the post and toddled off to the shops, totally unaware that Auntie wasn't there. It was only when she came back and noticed the bedroom curtains were still drawn that she sensed something was wrong.'

'She went upstairs, calling Auntie's name,' Hester said, carrying on with the story. 'I suppose she expected to find the worst, that she'd died in her bed during the night.'

'And all the time,' Pat said, shaking her head, 'she was lying outside in the cold in her nightdress. Goodness knows what she'd been doing out there.'

'There was an inquest, I assume?' Esme asked.

'Yes, though it didn't establish anything. *Who can possibly know what's going on in the head of an old lady?* seemed to be the main theme.' Pat shuddered. 'Makes getting old even more scary, if you're dismissed as ga-ga so readily.'

Hester put her arm around her mother and gave her a squeeze. 'Still hurts, doesn't it, Mum?'

'Well, of course it does. It's bad enough it happened, but not to know the whys and wherefores makes it even harder.' Pat forced a smile. 'Sorry, Esme. You didn't come here to listen to us fret about something that happened many years ago.'

'No, not at all. I totally understand,' Esme said. 'Having any unsolved mystery about your family is difficult. I've been there myself.' Her thoughts drifted to the circumstances concerning her sister, Elizabeth, and her late husband, Tim. Sometimes the pain at uncovering the truth was almost as hard to bear as the uncertainty. Would Hester and Pat ever be in that position?

Pat snatched up a shopping bag from a chair behind her. 'Well, I'll leave you good ladies to get on. I'm off to see what treasures I can find in the town. I hear there are some good independent shops.' She hooked the bag over the crook of her elbow and left the office.

'Thanks for not saying anything,' Hester said. 'Mum thinks we're just carrying on with the family history Auntie was working on.'

'We are, in a way,' Esme said, putting her laptop case down on the floor. Reviewing the files of what she'd uncovered so far might prove useful. 'She knows Ernest was murdered, though, doesn't she?'

'She does now, yes. She was shocked, of course. And in a way, it was because I didn't want to make it worse for her that I decided not to tell her it was his murder we were investigating. Not yet, anyway.'

'Well, it's still only a theory that Ernest was at the centre of Annie's research. We don't know if it's going to lead anywhere.'

'Oh, it's got to, hasn't it? What else have we got?'

Esme hadn't yet told Hester about Frederick Philips and his newspaper correspondence campaign. She slipped off her coat and draped it over the back of a chair beside Hester's desk.

'I've come across something interesting which might prove useful,' she said. 'But let's see where this leads us first, shall we? And if we get nowhere, I'll tell you all about it.'

'OK, fine by me.' Hester gestured for Esme to take a seat. 'Did you want a coffee, by the way? I've worked out how to use the machine since you were here last time.'

Esme sat down, reaching into her bag for her reading glasses. 'Perhaps later, thanks. But don't let me stop you making one yourself.'

Hester shook her head. 'No, coffee can wait. I'm keen to show you this.'

'So,' Esme said, rubbing her hands together and trying to calm the flutter of excitement in her chest, 'have you had a chance to look at the letter?'

'I have,' Hester said, dragging a chair round the desk and

setting it next to Esme. 'But I'm none the wiser.' She picked up a flimsy piece of paper from the top of a filing tray and slid it in front of Esme.

Esme slipped on her glasses and studied the scrap of paper. Annie's final correspondence was more a note than a letter and looked as though it had been hurriedly torn from the bottom of a memo pad. The concession to an address was a house name in the top right hand corner and below it the date, 21 February 1986. There were pencil scribbles underneath Annie's message, which itself was written in a neat distinct hand in royal blue ink, another suggestion that she'd grabbed whatever paper had come to hand. The ink on some of the words was smudged, rendering them unreadable.

'Auntie's letters were normally beautifully written on headed notepaper. And they'd usually run to several pages. So you can see why I found this one so odd.'

'And why you were inclined to go along with the dementia explanation.'

'Exactly.'

'She certainly sounds excited about something,' Esme said, scanning the note. 'Look here. *So thrilled to finally realise, after so many years…* I can't make out the next bit.' She took off her glasses and turned to Hester. 'If only she'd written down exactly *what* she'd finally realised.'

Hester pointed to the end of the note before Annie signed her name. 'And this bit might make more sense if it wasn't just an ink blot. *…will he…* Will he do what? And who is "he"? Unless it's *be* not *he*? *All will be?*'

'It can't be that, there are other words in between *all* and *will*.' Esme slipped her glasses back on and stared down at the letter, her mind racing. 'I read an article recently about enhancing faded ink so it becomes easier to read.'

Hester nodded. 'Yes, there are several techniques we use in museums to enhance old documents. But it's not really faded, though, is it? The words underneath have been obliterated by more ink. It's a completely different problem.'

'Worth a try, though, don't you think?' Esme said, cocking her head. 'We could scan it into my photo software and see what happens.'

Hester pushed the paper towards Esme. 'Be my guest,' she said, standing up. 'I'll switch on the scanner.'

Esme pulled her laptop out of the bag and booted it. They spent a few moments on the technical procedure of linking the two items of hardware before slipping the sheet of paper under the lid of the scanner and selecting the highest resolution possible. Hester pressed the button and they both watched on in silence as the machine hummed its magic. When the image appeared on Esme's laptop, she clicked on it and zoomed in to the enigmatic words at the end of the message. Hester came and stood next to her and they peered expectantly at the screen.

'What do you think?' Esme asked, scrutinising the strange ink blots. 'It's a bit better. You can see the lighter ink more easily.'

Hester shook her head. 'I don't know. *Will he want? Will he write?*'

'Hang on,' Esme said. 'Maybe not *write* but *wrote*.'

Hester pulled a face. 'That makes even less sense than *will he write*.'

Esme tapped the screen excitedly with her forefinger. 'Not if that word is *the*, it doesn't.' She turned to Hester. '*...the will he wrote.*'

Hester looked back at the image. '*...all... in the will he wrote,*' she read. 'She's talking about a will, as in last will and testament.'

'Yes,' Esme said, nodding. 'Has to be.'

Hester's smile faded and she shrugged with a gesture of hopelessness. 'But whose will? We've absolutely no idea who she's talking about.' Hester slumped down on her chair and folded her arms. 'And I don't know about you, Esme, but I can't think of any way of finding out, either.'

214

# 44

While Hester tackled the coffee machine, Esme stood at the window, staring out across the River Torridge to the building site over the water, thinking where they could go from here. Of course, it was pure speculation that Annie had been trying to find answers about Ernest's murder. She could have been just as excited and intrigued by *anything* in her family's past. If, as Hester had explained, much of Annie's research was inspired by stories she'd heard from her grandmother, who's to say that wasn't the case here?

She turned away from the window. 'Who was the grandmother who told Annie all the stories?' Esme said, returning to her chair as Hester brought over their coffees and set them down on the desk.

'On her mother's side, I think,' Hester said, sitting down. 'Mum might know.' Hester rested an elbow on the table. 'Well, it was a nice idea that Annie was digging into Ernest's sad demise. But we don't have any proof, do we?'

Esme picked up her cup and looked at Hester across the rim. 'Don't forget I have that other possible lead.'

Hester's face brightened. 'Oh yes, of course. Tell me more.'

Esme explained about Frederick Philips and his newspaper crusade. Hester gave her head a shake of amazement.

'How extraordinary.' Her brow puckered. 'But I don't see how that's much of a lead, if he didn't actually reveal anything.'

'No, that's true enough. I had hoped that Annie's letter might have something in it which matched up in some way. However, I still have another card up my sleeve.' Esme told Hester about the school and her intention to visit. 'Again, I'm not expecting to walk straight into a major exposé, but simply gather as much information as I can and see where it leads us.'

She wondered if she should mention her assumption that Frank Stone had attended the school, but decided against it. Hester may be spooked by his connection. But her thoughts reminded her of Maddy's parting words.

'Before I forget,' she said, putting her coffee cup back on its saucer. 'My friend Maddy, the one who restored the photograph you gave me, had an interesting encounter with Frank Stone yesterday.'

Hester looked wary. 'What sort of encounter?'

'Maddy bought a wooden sea chest at an auction we were at. I don't know if I explained before, but Maddy restores small items of furniture and so on.'

Hester nodded. 'Yes, you did say. She has a stall on Bideford market.'

'That's right. Well, as Maddy was completing the paperwork afterwards, Frank Stone arrived – later than intended, it seems – furious that he'd missed the opportunity to buy it and began haranguing Maddy to sell it to him.'

Hester scowled. 'Typical of Frank. He's a bully. Did she give in?'

Esme shook her head and smiled. 'Absolutely not. Red rag to a bull, behaving like that towards her. She was still celebrating having won the bid, she was so excited. So, there was no way she was going to hand it over.' Esme leaned towards Hester. 'The thing is, she wondered if you could throw any light over why he was so frenetic about it.'

'What is special about the chest?'

'It dates from the 18th century and it looks like there's an etching of a sailing ship on the inside of the lid. Maddy's only revealed a small part of it so far, but there may be more secrets she's yet to uncover.'

Hester looked thoughtful for a moment. 'There's something Isaac was on about…' Her voice petered out.

'Isaac?' Esme said, feeling a frisson of unease. 'Frank might have been trying to acquire it for Isaac Maudesley, you mean?'

Hester shrugged and let out a long sigh. 'I really don't know, Esme, I'm sorry. If I see Isaac, I'll ask him. That's the best I can do, I'm afraid.'

'No, that's fine. Appreciate it.' Had Stone been under instructions to buy the chest for the museum and, having failed to get to the sale in time, he was merely covering his back? It seemed an unorthodox arrangement for acquiring exhibits and only added to the mystery of the relationship between Stone and Maudesley.

'So,' Hester said, sitting back in her chair, 'what are we going to do about our brick wall? Any ideas how we might pin down whose will Auntie was talking about?'

'The trouble is, we don't have a date or even a time period to whittle things down a bit.'

'Unless we continue with the theory that her research related to Ernest's murder, meaning it could be relatively recent.' Hester sat upright, her eyes wide. 'Maybe it was Frederick Philips. Perhaps he reveals the whole story from the grave. That would be brilliant.'

'From what I've gleaned about him,' Esme said, 'it would be just typical of the man. A last grand gesture, stirring everything up after he'd gone. However,' she went on, with a sympathetic smile, bringing Hester back to reality, 'his will couldn't be the one your great aunt saw, as he didn't die until 1986.'

'Oh, I see. Same year as Annie died. Yes, I see your point. So it must have been earlier. And as you say, how much earlier? And which branch of the family? It's hopeless, isn't it?'

The door clattered open and Pat appeared, laden with bags of various sizes.

'Looks like a successful shopping trip?' Hester said, standing up and going over to help her mother.

'Very,' Pat said, allowing Hester to take the bags from her. 'I solved a couple of birthday presents for friends and treated myself, too. I love your Pannier Market, Esme. Such a beautiful building.'

Esme nodded. 'It is, yes. Pity you missed it when it was open. It was really buzzing this morning.'

'I'd love to see that. Next time, I'll try and time it better. So, how have you two got on? Learn anything from Auntie's note?'

Hester sat back down in her chair and folded her arms. 'We think she found something significant in someone's will.'

'Oh, that sounds interesting,' Pat said, pulling up a chair and sitting down. 'Ah, that's better. I really should have worn more comfortable shoes. Didn't realise Bideford was so hilly.'

'Except we don't know whose will and can't think how to find out,' Hester continued.

'Her notes would tell you that, though, wouldn't they?' Pat said, unbuttoning her coat.

'What notes?' Hester said. 'Don't tell me you've got her notes.'

'Of course I've got her notes. Box files full of them.'

Hester's mouth fell open. 'I never knew that. Where?'

'Oh, in the loft somewhere,' Pat said, flapping a hand. 'All in a complete mess, of course. Well, the two files she was working on are, anyway. She'd left everything scattered everywhere, all over the dining room table. Your father was all for throwing them out, but I was having none of it. Well, I knew how you and she talked history so often. I thought one day you'd want to look at them.'

Hester exchanged an excited glance with Esme. 'You bet I do. Can you get hold of them?'

'I don't see why not. When d'you want them?'

'Soon as possible. I'm back in Bristol on Thursday for a conference on the build. Can you find them by then?'

'I'm sure I can.' Pat smiled at Esme. 'I've always meant to go through them, but you know how it is. They get put away and you never quite get around to it.'

'I'll call in after my meeting,' Hester said, 'and bring them back with me.'

'D'you want all of them?'

'The ones she'd been working on when she died, I'd have thought,' Hester said, looking at Esme. 'What do you think, Esme?'

'Makes sense to me.'

They agreed that Esme would come to the office on Friday and she and Hester would go through the files together. If Hester was seeing Maudesley at the conference, maybe she'd have something to pass on by then about Stone's eagerness to get hold of Maddy's box.

Pat stood up. 'Well, I'll leave you to it. See you at the restaurant later, Hester.' She gathered up her purchases. 'I'm really pleased you're finally going to go through Auntie's fabulous archive. And while you're at it, keep an eye out for her ring in amongst the papers. We never did find it.'

Hester frowned. 'Her ring? Which ring?'

'The one she always wore, of course,' Pat said, hooking the bags over her arm. 'I dared to suggest to the police at the time that perhaps they should consider the possibility that Auntie had disturbed burglars, especially as Jenny had seen a couple of dubious looking teenagers hanging about, but of course that fell on deaf ears.' She shrugged. 'I suppose it could have slipped off her finger at some point.'

'I didn't realise,' Hester said, frowning. 'I assumed she'd been buried wearing it.'

Pat shook her head. 'No, she always promised it to me. Down the female line, she told me. It was the tradition.'

'So it was Great-granny's before?' Hester asked.

Pat paused. 'No, that's the funny thing. It had never been Great-granny's.'

'Then whose?'

Pat glanced between Hester and Esme. 'It was why it was so very precious, d'you see?' she said. 'Ernest gave it to her.'

# 45

Esme turned off the main road and followed the brown tourist signs to Garter Abbey, slowing as she negotiated the narrow lane between the village's neat estate cottages. Finally the lane opened out and the familiar signage of the National Trust appeared in front of her. She pulled into a parking space and turned off the engine.

Since Pat's revelation that Ernest had given Annie a ring, Esme had been mulling over its significance. It certainly suggested Ernest had anticipated a future to their relationship. How desperately sad that tragedy had come between them. Esme imagined Annie looking at the ring in the years following the murder and pining for what might have been. Given her parents' attitude to Ernest, she'd probably kept it a secret for many years before she was able to take it from its hiding place to wear it. Perhaps it had been the ring which had kept her memories of Ernest alive and it was why she'd never married.

Esme climbed out of the car and stood for a moment to breathe in the chilled spring air, gazing across to an orchard of apple trees, the grass beneath them splashed with the soft yellow of wild daffodils and the delicate white blooms of wood anemones. She wrapped her scarf around her and buttoned up her coat before setting off down the tarmacked drive which ran alongside the orchard and towards the property. Wooden tables were set out under the apple trees for picnics on warmer days and at the edge of the orchard was a café, tastefully converted from the original stables. Opposite this, the drive split at a T-junction. Ahead of her was a large courtyard with a series of further outbuildings, beyond which, according to the trust's website map, was a large lake.

She took the turning to the right towards the main house,

which stood some distance away down the drive. The impressive building loomed ahead of her, its long windows staring down at her as she came closer. She tried to imagine how huge and overwhelming it must have seemed to those small boys as they were delivered to the school, probably facing the challenge of being sent away from home for the very first time.

She took the path leading to a giant oak-studded front door where a sandwich board stood, welcoming visitors and inviting them inside. She grabbed hold of the large iron hook handle and turned it, pushing open the heavy door, expecting it to emit an eerie creak as though she was about to walk into a Gothic horror movie. But the door swung silently on its hinges, opening into a wide hall with oak flooring and an enormous fireplace. A woman with a page-boy haircut, wearing a necklace with beads which could have doubled as billiard balls, came over to scan Esme's membership card.

'Welcome to Garter Abbey,' she said, with a sweeping motion of her arm. 'The school was founded in 1179 as an educational establishment, when the monastery's Benedictine monks were required to provide a small charity school by decree of Pope Alexander III.'

'It weathered Henry VIII's dissolution of the monasteries, then?' Esme said.

'The educational aspect did, certainly. The King ensured its survival by statute, funding its renewed status from the royal purse.' She smiled. 'It went through a few more transformations before it was re-founded under Elizabeth I.' The woman handed Esme a printed laminated card. 'Here's information on this room, and you'll find portraits of past patrons and former headmasters hanging on the wall above the grand staircase.'

Esme thanked her and made her way over to the oak stairs on the far right-hand side of the hall, wondering if a painting of Frederick Philips hung in the gallery. She scanned the wall until her eye landed on one halfway up, and then she climbed the stairs for a closer inspection. The small wooden plaque below confirmed it was Philips, noting the sitter was a former pupil and patron of the school. A flabby-jawed elderly man stared down at her, seated and dressed in a dinner jacket, a contemptuous arch of his eyebrow and disdainful twist of his mouth appearing to corroborate Esme's verdict on the sort of man he was.

The woman with the giant beaded necklace, whose name tag identified her as Joan, came over and stood beside Esme. 'Apparently, Mr Philips was found in the attic. That is, his portrait had been removed.'

'He was ostracised, you mean?' Esme asked. Perhaps his brother being a murderer was a scandal too far for the school governors. But that couldn't have been the reason. From what she'd read, Frederick was still involved with the school when it closed down in the 1980s, decades after the murder.

'That's the assumption, yes. It's been suggested he did something to upset the rest of the trustees, though what is not recorded. Perhaps merely being in post when the school's misfortunes led to its closure was enough.'

'So, why did the school close?' Esme asked.

Joan shrugged. 'The same reason most private schools close. Lack of paying pupils. My colleague, Mr Donovan, might tell you more. He's a volunteer steward in the library. He was a pupil here when they pulled the plug.' She glanced around as the front door clunked open and two visitors stepped inside. 'But he's not here today,' she added over her shoulder, as she walked towards the newcomers. 'He only comes in on Tuesdays.'

Esme turned back to the painting, intrigued. If it wasn't anything to do with the murder or his outrageous newspaper campaign that had got Philips's portrait so unceremoniously dumped in the attic, what was it?

She turned away from the image of the petulant old man and trotted back down to the hall to explore the rest of the property.

*

Esme treated herself to a smoked salmon and cream cheese bap from the old stables café, along with a bottle of traditional Sicilian lemonade. She took her lunch outside, preferring to find somewhere with a view rather than sit by herself at a café table. She wandered past the courtyard, where the old outbuilding had been converted into workshops and small retail units selling local crafts, and headed towards the lake.

There were few visitors heading in her direction and by the time she'd crunched her way along the gravel path to the edge of the lake, she was completely alone. She found a sturdy wooden bench on the small beach just off the path and sat down gratefully, gazing out across the dark waters to the woodland which surrounded the lake. In the distance was a rickety wooden jetty and another structure half submerged in the water, which looked like the remains of a boat. She looped her scarf tighter around her neck and put up the hood of her duffel coat before taking her lunch out of her bag and settling down to eat it.

It was fascinating to see what Frederick Philips had looked like and to understand a little about the history of Garter Abbey. She was glad she'd come. But it seemed unlikely that she'd glean anything from her visit which answered any questions as to what Frederick had known about the secret behind the confrontation and Ernest's murder.

She popped the last piece of bread in her mouth and washed it down with lemonade. There was a bin at the end of the beach and she got up from her seat to dispose of her rubbish. As she dropped in the empty bottle and wrappings, she noticed a sign on a pole sticking up above the surface of the lake. *WARNING,* it said in bright red capital letters, *DANGER OF DROWNING.* She stared out across the menacing black expanse, tiny waves lapping on to the shore by her feet. With clouds now building, replacing sunshine with gloom, she couldn't imagine how anyone would be tempted to swim in the lake's dark waters. But perhaps it was more inviting in the summer months.

She shivered and thrust her hands in her pockets. Garter Abbey may not have anything further to reveal, but there were still Annie's notes. What secrets would they hold? And would they offer any proof to back up her and Hester's assumption that Ernest was at the centre of Annie's research?

With one last glance across to the school, Esme turned away from the menacing waters of the lake and began making her way back to her car.

# 46

Esme parked on the quay, close to Hester's office. She climbed out of her car, excitement building as she anticipated what they might find amongst the box files which Pat had unearthed from her attic.

Esme had spoken to Hester only briefly yesterday when Hester had phoned to confirm she and Pat had found Annie's notes. Hester's enthusiasm was palpable and Esme wondered how she had been able to resist delving in right away and searching through them. But Hester explained that one quick look told her Pat was right in saying everything was in a complete muddle. It would take time to unpick the significant from the irrelevant and, busy with meetings and other commitments, Hester said it was best they tackled the job together, carefully and methodically.

Esme had tried to tell her about Garter Abbey and the mystery of Frederick Philips's portrait being confined to the attic, but the tone of Hester's voice changed and she became distracted. Esme could hear voices in the background and assumed business was pressing. So when Hester apologised that she had to go, Esme assured her she understood and cut the call. There would be ample time to speculate over Ernest's cousin when they met.

Esme stomped up the stairs, recalling the last time she'd visited, when she'd almost collided with Hester's accountant. Pat had remarked how good an accountant he was, reminding Hester she needed a competent auditor. At the time, Esme had assumed Pat was referring to the importance of keeping control of finances during a vast building project like the new museum. But maybe there was more to it. Might Hester's concerns about Isaac Maudesley be financial ones? If Hester had confided in her mother on the subject, it would explain Pat's comment.

Esme found herself wondering whether Max's rumour

machine had picked up anything of that kind, but she immediately blanked Max from her mind. She'd not heard from him since he'd sent the email she'd tossed, unread, into the digital dustbin. Hopefully his own investigations were keeping him busy and out of her hair.

She was puffing by the time she reached the top landing and paused to catch her breath. The door to Hester's office was ajar and once her breathing was back on an even keel, Esme tapped the panel and gingerly pushed it open. Hester was sitting at her desk, sifting through papers. Esme spied an old grey box file sitting at the far end, which must contain Annie's research notes.

Esme stepped into the office, greeting Hester with a smile, which faded instantly as Hester looked up. Her face was flushed and her eyes looked sore, as though she'd not slept.

'Is everything all right?' Esme said, closing the door behind her.

Hester laid her hands palms down on the desk and stood up. Her smile looked forced.

'Yes, of course. Just tired, that's all. As you know, I've a lot to do.' She rubbed her forehead. 'It's all feeling a bit overwhelming at the moment.'

Esme swallowed. 'Look, would you rather we do this another day? Perhaps at the weekend, if you're around? You might not feel so worn out by then.' However frustrating it would be to wait, if Hester wasn't well, Esme didn't want to pressurise her.

'That's probably a good idea, yes.' Hester snatched a glance over her shoulder towards the inner room. 'Actually, I've been thinking. It may be wise that we forget the whole thing.'

'Forget...?'

'I've so much on, you see,' Hester pressed on, as though determined to deliver a rehearsed speech. 'I really need to focus on things here rather than get tied up with something else right now. It would just be a distraction, wouldn't it?'

'But I don't understand. When we spoke...'

'I'll pay you up to date, of course. I'm not trying to get out of what I owe you.'

'I never imagined you were.'

Hester flicked another glance towards the inner office. Esme followed Hester's line of sight as a shadow fell across the threshold. She just stopped herself in time from gasping out loud as she recognised the figure who stepped into view, fixing Esme with a cynical sneer.

Esme dragged her eyes away from Frank Stone's relentless glare and turned back to Hester. 'Well, then. I'll let you get on. You know where I am if you change your mind.'

'I won't,' Hester said. 'But thank you.' Esme turned to go. 'Oh, and Esme.'

'Yes?' Esme said, turning back. The message on Hester's face was a mixture of anger and anxiety. She picked up the box file from her desk and held it out to Esme.

'Don't forget your notes. You'd better have them back.'

Esme hesitated only for a moment. 'Yes, of course. Thank you for remembering.' She took the file, hugging it to her, and hurried out of the office without looking back.

# 47

Esme clattered down the stairs from Hester's office, her brain spinning with the implications of what she'd just witnessed. Why was Frank Stone there? And more worryingly, what did his presence have to do with Hester's deciding not to go ahead with any further research? She thought of Max's comment about Stone's violent reputation and shuddered. Was he threatening Hester in some way? But why? About what?

It seemed obvious that Hester's passing over Annie's research notes under the guise they belonged to Esme and she was returning them was for Stone's benefit, debunking Hester's claim of wanting to stop the research. But did it say something more? That Hester didn't want Stone to know they were Annie's notes? So what did *that* mean?

Esme emerged on to the street and took a backward glance up to Hester's office window. She must try and get hold of Hester as soon as she could and find out exactly what was going on.

*

Esme pulled into the driveway next to her cottage and turned off the car engine, her thoughts a jumble of indecision and confusion. She must ask Hester why she was so keen for Esme to have Annie's notes. Perhaps Hester had looked through them after all, despite claiming she'd not yet had time. What if she'd discovered something significant? What significance would she not want Stone to know about? That Hester knew Stone's family history linked him to Annie, via Albert Philips and Ernest? Was there a reason that mattered?

Esme reached over to retrieve Annie's box file from the passenger footwell and climbed out of the car with a sense of purpose and anticipation. Perhaps what was lying inside the file for her to find would answer all of those questions.

She pushed open the front door, the kittens racing over to greet her. She put the box file on the kitchen table and picked them up, burying her face in their soft fur and calming her agitated thoughts. Perhaps a walk down to the beach would help clear her head. But by the time she'd organised the kittens' food and boiled the kettle to make a drink, she found herself staring at Annie's box lying tantalisingly on the table, and she knew it would be impossible to resist opening it up and taking a look.

She took her mug over to the table and sat down, pulling the box towards her. With a rush of excitement, she opened the lid and began sifting through the papers inside. As Pat had implied, the contents of the box file weren't in any sort of order. Some papers were upside down, others half folded or crumpled. Clearly they'd been piled back in hastily with no methodology in mind.

As she picked her way through Annie's meticulous notes, Esme occasionally recognised the names she'd come across in her own research when establishing Ernest's ancestry, the Hannafords and the crucial link with the Venner family. Her brain buzzed at the potential implications. While it was evident that Annie had been researching her fiancé's family history, there was nothing yet to indicate whether his murder was the reason for her work.

Unsurprisingly, given Annie's credentials, there were regular citations to her sources. As her research had been carried out before access to the Internet, these included the volumes of various registers she'd consulted in records offices or, when printed copies had not been available, microfilm reference numbers.

The gentle ticking of the long case clock in the corner of the room accompanied the sound of rustling papers as Esme worked her way systematically down the pile, trying to restore some order to everything to make it easier for future searches. Would there be a will amongst the pile? She thought of the second box file Pat had mentioned. If Esme could find no will here, might it be in that one instead?

Esme's stomach began to rumble and she grabbed an apple to keep hunger at bay. She had no intention of stopping to cook herself anything to eat until she'd reached the bottom of the file.

In the event, she didn't need to get to the very bottom. Nestled about three quarters of the way down she came across a long buff envelope, feeling her heart skip a beat as she turned it over and read what was scrawled on the front. *The Last Will and Testament of William Chalacombe 1743*. This had to be the will that Annie's note had mentioned, surely? *...in the will he wrote...* were Annie's words. So, what exactly had William Chalacombe written in his will and how did it impact on everything?

The phone rang out, making her jump. Was it Hester, getting back to her to explain everything? She'd be so excited to discover Esme had found what they'd been looking for.

Esme snatched up her phone, but the name on the screen was Maddy's, not Hester's.

'Hi, Maddy,' Esme said. 'Guess what...'

'It's gone!' Maddy cried down the phone.

'What?' Esme said, frowning. 'What's gone?'

'That fabulous sea chest,' Maddy wailed. 'Someone's broken into my workshop and stolen it.'

# 48

Esme paced around the room, the phone clamped to her ear. 'Are you sure?' she said.

'Of course I'm sure,' Maddy snapped. 'I was certain I'd left it out and when I couldn't see it, I thought at first I must be getting doolally in my old age. But then it dawned on me.'

'What did?'

'Where it's gone, of course.'

'Which is where?' Part of Esme's brain was still processing the discovery of William Chalacombe's last will and testament, but Maddy's next words shot through her wavering thoughts like a chisel into wood.

'Frank Stone.'

Esme halted her circuit of the room. 'What?'

'Has to be, doesn't it? All adds up.'

Esme sifted through what Maddy was suggesting. 'You think he's come and helped himself because you wouldn't sell?'

'That's exactly what I'm saying. And, he's not going to get away with it.'

'Have you called the police?'

'Not yet. I'm just about to.'

'Do you think they'll take you seriously?' Esme asked.

'They'd better.'

Esme bit into her lower lip. 'But even if they do and they challenge Stone about it, won't he just deny it?'

'He won't be able to if they find it, will he?'

Esme perched on the arm of the sofa. 'Maddy, I admire your optimism, but I can't see Stone being naive enough to let the police find it in his possession.'

'He might if he's cocky enough to think no one knows.'

Esme sighed. 'Well, I see your reasoning and I hope you're

right. But you've got to get the police to act on it first.' She squeezed her eyes closed and rubbed her hand across her face. 'I'd better let you go, then, so you can call them. Good luck. Let me know what happens.'

'Yeah, of course I will.'

'At least you have your photos to show them. Might be helpful.'

'That's an idea. I'll do that.'

'Meanwhile,' Esme said, 'I suppose we could put our heads together and try and work out why he's so desperate to get his hands on it.'

'Good point. And what we find out might help nail him, if the police see a motive. Look, I'll go and make the call. Unless I've got anything to report, I'll see you at the market tomorrow.'

They hung up and Esme sat for a moment, tapping the phone on her chin and chewing over the implications. She hadn't even had time to tell Maddy about Stone turning up at Hester's office, let alone about finding the will envelope in Annie's box. She shuddered. It wasn't a comfortable feeling to find Frank Stone's presence in both situations. She tried to think back to the expression on Hester's face. Had she looked frightened or merely annoyed? Would it be a good time to try and call her now? Surely Stone couldn't still be lurking around. Or would it be better to wait for Hester to get in touch? That's assuming she intended to explain the bizarre circumstances of their meeting.

Esme gave her head a shake and went back to her phone, scrolling to find Hester's number. What had she got to lose? The worst that could happen was Hester refused to speak to her. That in itself would tell Esme how much influence Stone had got over the situation. As to what she'd do about it, or even what she *could* do about it, she'd have to work that one out when the time came.

She stabbed the screen and paced the room as the connection was made. The phone began ringing and Esme composed a message she'd leave if it switched to voicemail. But she was in luck. After a few rings, Hester came on the line.

'Esme, I'm so sorry about earlier,' she said a little breathlessly down the line.

'Are you all right?' Esme asked. 'What was Frank Stone doing there? I assume he's the reason you're pulling out. Why? I don't understand.'

Hester cleared her throat. 'It's complicated. He said...' The sentence petered out.

'He said what?'

'I'm between a rock and a hard place here, Esme. I can't afford to upset Frank and Isaac or they'll pull the rug from under me.'

'What rug? Upset them how?'

'Let's just say, I'm not prepared to put this project in jeopardy. You know how long I've waited for it. I need Isaac's support on this.'

'You mean he's threatening to pull the funding for the new museum? Stone actually said that?'

'That is what I was led to believe, yes. The message is that I need to give it my full attention and not get sidetracked by other issues or it won't happen.'

'What other issues? Are they talking about your great aunt's family history? Come on, Hester. That's ridiculous. It's no business of theirs what you do in your spare time.' Esme stopped, the meaning of what she'd said hitting her like an elbow jab in the side. 'Or perhaps it is.' She got to her feet and straightened up. 'That's why you gave me the file, isn't it? You think they don't want you to dig any further because of something you might discover. Something that your great aunt discovered, perhaps.'

Hester cleared her throat again. 'I don't like being leaned on, Esme.'

'Who does?'

'But I have to make it seem as though I'm capitulating. Which means I'm going to have to rely on you.'

'To find out what that secret is? Is that what you're saying?

233

You think it's somehow connected to Frank Stone's appearance and Isaac embracing his arrival?'

'Will you do it, Esme?'

'Of course I will.' Esme looked down at the envelope lying unopened on the table. 'I've already made the first step. I think I've found the will Annie was talking about. But before you get too excited, I've not read it yet.'

'Will you get in touch as soon as you have?'

'That goes without saying. Whatever it is, Hester, I'll find it.'

'I hope so, Esme, I really do. Just make sure you keep out of harm's way, though.'

'By harm's way, you mean Frank Stone, I assume.'

'Let's just say that my opinion of him hasn't changed. I don't trust him. He knows that and…' Hester took a breath. 'And he's watching me.'

'I understand. And I hope I'll have some news for you soon.'

'I hope so too. Bye, Esme. Take care.'

'And you.' As Esme disconnected, she thought of Maddy's box and her conviction that Stone had stolen it. What would Hester have made of that? Esme chewed her lip. Should she call Hester back and put it to her? Perhaps when she'd got something to report on her findings.

She turned back to the table, her eyes settling on the unopened envelope with William Chalacombe's will inside. But before she had time to pick it up, the phone rang again. Esme snatched up the handset and glanced at the screen, sticking a finger in her ear to block out the chime of the long case clock striking ten.

'Libby?'

'Esme, you're still up, thank goodness.'

'What is it? Everything OK?'

'I'm not sure. I can see lights on the beach. Something's going on.'

# 49

A rustic wooden sign hung on Libby's front door, illuminated by the porch light above, which read, *I'm in the garden*. Esme made her way around the end of Libby's cottage by the muted light spilling out of her kitchen window, and spied her standing on the edge of the terrace, peering out to sea with a pair of binoculars.

Libby started at the sound of Esme's footstep, lowering the binoculars and darting an anxious look behind her, visibly relaxing when she saw Esme.

'I'm so sorry, Esme,' Libby said, as she walked over to her. 'I'm probably making a mountain out of a molehill. But I've not been able to get that lad off my mind.'

'You think the lights are connected to the little boy we saw?' Esme asked, trying to adjust her eyes to focus in the darkness beyond.

'Am I being silly?' Libby said, her face puckering. 'It's just with no explanation…'

'The police haven't come back to you then?'

Libby shook her head. '*Ongoing investigation* is all they'll say. Which means nothing, of course.'

Esme wondered about Maddy's stolen box and what response she'd got when she reported it. Would it also be confined to an *ongoing investigation* category and disappear through the cracks? Or would the police act on Maddy's suspicion of the identity of a suspect?

'So, what did you see, exactly?' Esme said, blinking into the gloom. 'Are the lights still there?'

'I don't think they are now, no.' Libby stretched out an arm and pointed in the direction of the collapsed cottage. 'They were bobbing around over there.'

'One light moving? Lots of lights?'

'At least two, I'm pretty sure.'

'And were they communicating in any way, d'you think? You know, flashing on and off?'

Libby sighed. 'I'm not sure. They were moving, that's for sure, but I couldn't see well enough and by the time I'd got the bins, I'd lost sight of them. So I've no idea whether anyone was sending a message.' She lifted the binoculars back up to her eyes. 'Whoever they were, I think they must have gone now. I've seen nothing for a few minutes.' She dropped the field glasses and turned to Esme. 'I've got you out here on a fool's errand, Esme, I'm sorry. It was good of you to come so quickly. But I just needed someone to confirm I wasn't imagining it all. I can't even do that, can I? Come on, let's go inside. I'm getting cold.'

They retreated to Libby's warm kitchen. 'Can I interest you in a hot chocolate?' she said, slipping off her coat.

'Oh, why not?' Esme said, dropping down on a chair with a smile. 'Might help me sleep. My mind's a right pickle at the moment.'

Libby poured some milk into a saucepan and set it on the Aga. 'Oh, why's that? A research conundrum?'

'Yes and no.' Esme rested her elbows on the kitchen table, thinking of Hester and Frank Stone, and now Maddy's disconcerting news. 'I've got a client with a family history which seems to be straying into dangerous waters, and then I took a phone call from Maddy earlier saying someone's broken into her workshop and stolen her current work in progress.'

'Stolen?' Libby said, looking round at Esme with an alarmed expression on her face. 'Was it valuable?'

'Not particularly, we don't think. But someone was desperate to buy it off her, which she declined as she was looking forward to renovating it, and now she suspects he's decided he's having it by fair means or foul.'

'That's ridiculous. Unless it's just a coincidence. Might she be putting two and two together and making five?'

'I don't think so. It was only that piece taken. Which is why

236

she was immediately suspicious.'

'Yes, I see what you mean. I assume she'll mention all this to the police?'

'Of course, but it's hard to prove, isn't it, unless he's caught red-handed?'

Libby poured hot milk from the pan into two mugs and picked up the hot chocolate tub. 'And what did you mean by a client with a dangerous family history? That seems equally disconcerting.'

Esme watched Libby spoon the brown powder into the milk and whisk it up, wondering how to answer the question. 'Oddly enough, there's a connection between that and Maddy's problem, and I'm struggling to fathom out all the implications.'

Libby put a mug down in front of Esme and took a seat on the opposite side of the table, stirring her own hot drink. 'You're not telling me that Maddy's suspect is also your client?' she said, eyes wide.

'No, nothing like that. Though he *is* a colleague of hers. In a way, that's why I'm in a dilemma. I know it sounds bizarre, but the research I was doing for her has a link to his family history.' Esme wrapped her hands around the warm mug. 'So, I'm thinking, where does it all join up?'

'So in what way is it *straying into dangerous waters,* to use your expression?'

Esme rubbed her forefinger down the scar on her cheek. How could she explain things without it sounding melodramatic?

'Let's just say this individual, the one who Maddy suspects made off with her wooden chest, wouldn't win citizen of the year.'

'Nasty piece of work, is he?'

Esme gave Libby a wry smile and inclined her head.

'So decline the job,' Libby said, with a shrug. 'Don't go there.'

Esme conjured up Hester's anxious face, her pleading eyes as she handed over Annie's notes. 'The thing is, I know how important it is to my client to get to the bottom of this particular family mystery and because of that, I've already agreed to continue my research. I don't feel I can go back on it. She's counting on me.'

'And now, with what's happened to Maddy, you believe something you uncover might help her get her property back, by identifying this man's interest in it.'

Esme nodded at Libby over the rim of her mug, taking a sip of the sweetened milk. 'That pretty much sums it up, yes.'

Libby took a deep breath and sat back in her chair. 'Well, if you think a crime has been committed and your research might expose the perpetrator, why wouldn't you take a look? I mean, who's going to know?'

Esme acknowledged Libby's logic with a brief nod as the image of Frank Stone glowering at her from Hester's inner office materialised in her head. She dismissed it. Libby was right. Why would Stone know what she was researching? He'd be too busy watching Hester.

*

The moon was high in the sky by the time Esme traipsed back up the hill to her cottage, her head buzzing with what she'd told Libby concerning potential connections between Maddy's burglary and whatever Stone didn't want Hester to discover. And what *was* it that he was so keen for her not to find out?

Esme let herself into her cottage and dropped her keys on to the kitchen table beside the unopened envelope lying where she'd left it. She stared down at the date written on the front, 1743, and gave her head a shake, clicking her tongue at her foolishness. Had she not been interrupted by phone calls, she'd have realised straight away that if Annie's exciting revelation had anything to do with Ernest's murder, it wouldn't relate to an 18th century will. And if there was no connection to the murder, it followed that the link between Stone's family history and Ernest was irrelevant.

Or was it?

She snatched up the envelope, lifted the flap and peered inside. The envelope was empty.

# 50

Maddy spent much of the early part of the following day's market session expressing her dissatisfaction with the police's response to the sea chest being stolen.

'They seemed to be more interested in sending their crime prevention officer around to discuss security,' she said, folding her arms with a scowl.

Esme made a murmur of sympathy. Maddy's experience had echoes of Libby's when she'd reported seeing Max in Esme's shed.

'Did you mention Frank Stone?'

'Well, of course I did. Seems a no-brainer to me. But it clearly didn't ring any alarm bells for them. Either that or they were just playing it cool.'

'So, are they going to follow it up?'

Maddy pulled a face. 'They said they'd look into it, but whether that was just a brush-off, I've no idea.'

'Of course, we may be jumping to conclusions,' Esme said, thinking of Libby's rationale. 'If Stone was so keen to get hold of it, maybe someone else wants it for the same reason.'

'Hmm, good point. I hadn't looked at it like that.'

'What do you know about the box's provenance? The auctioneer hadn't had it long, you said, which accounted for the state of it.'

'He said it had been bought from an Appledore family who were clearing the house of a relative who'd recently died. It was amongst a whole load of stuff which had been in the family for years, much of which ended up in a skip, apparently. I suppose we should be grateful the box didn't go the same way.'

'Did he know which family?'

'No, he didn't. And to be honest, if they were glad to be rid of it, they're not likely to be much interested in its history or its provenance, are they? So even if we knew, we'd be unlikely to learn much from them about why it's so desirable.'

'Unless,' Esme said, an idea coming to her, 'that's why it didn't end up in a skip. Someone in the family wanted it.'

'So, why didn't they take it, then?'

'They might not have had a say in the matter. Perhaps whoever was dealing with the estate got ahead of themselves. Then when they found out, they were annoyed they'd been overruled and decided to take matters into their own hands. Might be worth bending the auctioneer's ear and finding out which family he's talking about.'

'Maybe,' Maddy said, without conviction. 'But, even if you're right, we'd be in no better position than we are with Stone. No self-respecting box snatcher is likely to hold their hand up to their crime, are they?'

A flurry of customers and a woman who had information on a photograph Esme had displayed on the *Photos Reunited* board kept the two of them occupied for the next hour. When the activity calmed down, Esme told Maddy about the discovery of the empty envelope.

'Oh no,' Maddy said, her face dissolving into an expression of sympathy and frustration. 'How infuriating. So you can't check what was behind Auntie Annie's cryptic comment.'

'Well, it's not all lost,' Esme said. 'At least I know whose will it is now. I checked the Devon Archives catalogue and they hold a copy.'

'Oh, that's good to know. Have you told Hester?'

'Not yet. I don't want Frank Stone getting wind of it.'

'Stone? Where does he come into it?'

Esme told her about Frank Stone's presence in Hester's office. 'I told you he was trouble. Now he seems to be hassling Hester. She seems to think he has the power to jettison this major museum project if she carries on with researching her great aunt's

240

family history.'

Maddy screwed up her face. 'What's that to him?'

'Exactly what I said at first,' Esme said. 'But when you think about it, it's obvious. We know his family history's linked to Annie because of Ernest. Perhaps Stone's worried Annie disturbed a skeleton or two and Hester's going to find out.' She threw Maddy a glance. 'And now, what with your theft and your belief that Stone's taken it…'

Maddy looked round at Esme with a sceptical expression. 'You're not suggesting that the two are connected?'

Esme lifted an eyebrow. 'Eighteenth century will. Eighteenth century box.'

Maddy gave a dismissive laugh. 'It's hardly conclusive. Stone just likes throwing his weight around to get his own way. He's that sort of person.'

'I wouldn't disagree with that,' Esme said. 'But it was you who thought Hester might have a theory as to why Frank Stone's so fixated on the box. What if that reason is tied in with his fear of what Annie's notes might throw up?'

Maddy balled her fist, pressing it against her chin. 'I can see where you're going with this. Find out one history and it might shine light on another?'

'That's exactly what I'm saying.'

'But you were warning me off Stone only a few days ago. What's changed?'

'Nothing's changed. I'm still of the opinion we should give Stone a wide berth. But unless you're ready to let go of any hope of getting your lovely sea chest back…'

'Not get it back?' Maddy exclaimed.

Esme shrugged. 'Well, I don't hold out much hope that the police are going to come up trumps, do you?'

Maddy scowled. 'No. You're probably right there.'

'Look, Hester's made it crystal clear she wants me to carry on, even if she has to keep out of it because of Frank Stone hovering in the background. So if while digging around I discover the reason for Stone's urgency to get hold of your box, what's not to like?'

Maddy folded her arms and gave a decisive nod of her head. 'Well then. Dig away.'

*

Esme stood in the queue for coffee at the market café, reflecting on what she and Maddy had discussed. Having readily agreed to the challenge, Esme hoped she could deliver. She'd already been through almost all of Annie's box and put the notes in some semblance of order, but so far, only William Chalacombe's will had proved a significant find. There was a chance that now, with a different perspective and Maddy's stolen wooden chest in the forefront of her mind, previously discarded research notes might reveal new information. And there might yet be a gem to discover amongst the last few papers.

As she shuffled closer to the counter, she mulled over the connection between Frank Stone's family history and Annie's research. How had Stone found out? Had Hester challenged him over something Esme had uncovered? Was that what had alerted him? It seemed unlikely Hester would want to discuss anything with Frank Stone, unless she'd let something slip in a moment of frustration. They still didn't know the answer to a question Esme had raised with Hester as to whether Stone knew he was related to the murderer of her great aunt's fiancé. The query had alarmed Hester and she'd asked if it was important. At the time, Esme had said she didn't have enough information to judge. Did she now?

Esme asked herself whether she and Hester were being naive in thinking they could avoid skirting close to Stone, given his family connections. If Ernest and Albert's altercation was over a family feud, and if, as Esme believed, Frederick Philips was aware of the secret which lay behind it, it didn't automatically mean Frank Stone knew anything about what his great-uncle knew.

Even if he had gone to Garter Abbey, the school in which Frederick Philips played a part. And what if he did? How did it have a bearing on anything?

Esme decided it didn't. The idea was to delve into Annie's research files to uncover something which might convince the police to act on the theft of Maddy's sea chest. Exploring William Chalacombe's will was all she planned to do, which certainly didn't involve poking around in Frank Stone's teenage years.

She reached the front of the queue and ordered coffees for herself and Maddy, along with two pasties for their lunch later, and then headed back to their stall.

'You've just missed Pat Chalacombe,' Maddy said, taking her latte from Esme.

'Oh no, what a shame,' Esme said. 'I'd forgotten she might call in.'

'She was in a hurry and apologised for not stopping. She said you'd suggested she pay us a visit.'

'I thought she might be interested in one of your pieces.'

'She said she'd be back another time. Oh, and this, too.' Maddy reached into the back pocket of her jeans and pulled out a scrap of paper. 'Here's her phone number,' she said, handing the folded paper to Esme. 'She said to give her a call. She's found another box of Annie's notes. Thought you might like to take a look.'

# 51

With the additional purpose of helping Maddy to recover her sea chest, Esme returned to her cottage with renewed vigour to revisit all the papers in Annie's box. She'd phoned Pat and left a message to confirm she'd love to have sight of Annie's other box of notes and waited impatiently for Pat to return her call.

After greeting the kittens, she fetched the box file and sat down at the kitchen table. She flicked her way through Annie's carefully recorded notes of parish records, setting the sheets to one side as she worked her way through the papers. As she recalled from her initial trawl through the contents, with the exception of William Chalacombe's will, dated 1743, the itemised lists of Chalacombe baptisms, marriages and burials were all from the early 19th century. But as Maddy's trunk was dated as being from the 18th century, it seemed likely that research from an earlier period would offer more promise of containing something of note. Esme hoped the second box file Pat had found might hold the key.

Nevertheless, Esme was optimistic as she continued her way to the bottom of the box until she came to the last sheet. She scanned it eagerly, but it was a ship's manifest of goods delivered to the port of Bristol in 1894. She added it to the pile, tidying it up ready to return the notes to the box.

As she picked up the heap, she noticed a small piece of white card stuck at an angle in the binding. She replaced the stack on the table before catching hold of the corner of the card, tugging it and pulling it free. When she turned it over, she saw it was a postcard of a painting and she recognised it immediately. It was a print of the portrait of Amelia Chalacombe which she'd seen in John Ford's shop. He'd dated it as early 1700s, before she'd married Richard Venner.

As Esme gazed at the image, her eye fell upon Amelia's fingers, which rested on the richly coloured skirt of her dress. She jumped up and went over to the dresser, rummaging around in the top drawer to find her magnifying glass. She took it back to the table and hovered it over the fourth finger of Amelia's left hand. The ring she was wearing had a heart at its centre, held by two hands, and a crown above. Esme knew she'd seen it before.

She hurried across to the television and switched it on. When she'd spotted Hester and Max on the *Antiques Roadshow*, the expert had been talking about a ring. And if she'd remembered correctly, it was the same design as Amelia was wearing. Was that why Max and Hester were there? Was it about a ring associated with the Chalacombe family? But hadn't Max said their visit had been a waste of time?

The TV burst into life and Esme pointed the remote at it, negotiating her way to the recording she'd made of the television programme. She clicked on the title, fast forwarded to the point where she'd played it back to Maddy and Harry, and clicked play. Her heart thumping in her chest, she sat on the arm of the sofa and stared at the screen.

The camera homed in on a gold ring, almost identical to the one on Amelia Chalacombe's finger. Almost the same, but not exactly. The middle-aged woman owner was replying to the expert's questions as to what she knew about the piece. She explained how she'd inherited it from her grandmother, and it had been passed down to her from her grandmother.

'That's the tradition of a Claddagh ring, which is what this is,' the expert told the owner. 'It would be passed down from mother to daughter.' He turned the ring around and pointed to the raised design. 'You see here, clasped hands around a heart, a crown above. A heart represents love, the crown stands for loyalty, and two clasped hands symbolise friendship.'

The woman nodded. 'How old do you think it is?'

The expert picked up an eye piece to take a closer look. 'There doesn't appear to be any hallmark, so I can't date it exactly, but I'd say late 18th century.'

There was a murmur amongst the people clustered around listening in.

'There was a sort of code as to the way you wore the ring,' continued the expert.

'Code?' asked the woman.

'Yes. Do you recall which finger your grandmother wore it on?'

'Her ring finger,' the woman said, nodding.

'Which way round?'

She frowned. 'I'm sorry?'

Again, the expert pointed to the design. 'It's said that if the point of the heart is aimed towards the fingertips, it indicates the wearer is engaged. If the point of the heart is towards the wrist, the wearer is married.'

Esme turned back to the postcard on the table. The heart was pointing towards Amelia's fingertips. As John Ford had surmised, Amelia was not yet married to Richard Venner, but it suggested they were engaged.

Venner. Agnes Venner. A buzz of excitement surged through Esme's body. She hurried over to her laptop and switched it on.

'Come on, come on,' she muttered under her breath. When the home screen appeared, she opened up the file she'd made for Hester's research and found Maddy's restored mortuary photograph of Agnes Venner. She clicked on it, enlarging the image and scanning around until she found Agnes's left hand.

A Claddagh ring. Identical to the one Amelia was wearing. The heart was pointing to the wrist, indicating Agnes's marital status. So who had Agnes passed her ring on to?

Esme opened up the family tree she'd compiled. Perhaps she could work it out. The diagram filled the screen and Esme found Agnes on the tree and began tracing her finger along possible routes down the generations. Her eye alighted on Ernest's name and Pat's words played back in her head.

*'Down the female line,' she told me. 'It was the tradition.'*

Esme snatched up her phone and dialled Pat's number, her anticipation building as it was answered after two rings.

'Esme, hello,' Pat said. 'I just picked up your message and was about to call you. Yes, of course you can take a look at Auntie's other box.'

'Oh, that's great, Pat. Thank you. I'd love to. But actually, I wasn't chasing you about that. I have a question.'

'Oh, right. Well, fire away, then.'

Esme gazed at the image of Agnes's ring on her laptop screen. 'It's about your aunt's ring. What was it like, exactly?' She held her breath as Pat described it, feeling a flutter of exhilaration as she realised her hunch was correct.

'Well, it was made of gold and had a heart in the centre, held by hands on either side. A pretty little thing it was. It's called something, but the name escapes me for the moment.'

'You mean a Claddagh ring?' Esme said, gripping the handset.

'That's it,' Pat replied excitedly down the phone. 'Have you found it?'

'I haven't found the actual ring, I'm afraid,' Esme said. 'But I think I might have found out who it once belonged to.'

'You mean before Ernest gave it to Auntie Annie?'

'Well, that's just it,' Esme said, sitting back in her seat. 'You mentioned Annie had spoken about the Claddagh ring's tradition of being passed down the female line.'

'Yes, that's what she told me.'

'So why did Ernest have it?'

There was a pause as Pat digested the question. 'Oh, goodness. I see what you mean,' she said, with a gasp. 'You're suggesting it might not have been Ernest's to give?'

'Yes, that's exactly what I'm suggesting,' Esme said, catching her breath. 'If the ring was the reason for the argument between the cousins, I think we may have stumbled upon the motive for Ernest's murder.'

# 52

Esme arranged to meet Pat the following morning in Bideford to collect the second box file of Annie's notes, before Pat returned once more to Bristol. Esme parked on Bideford Quay and walked across the old bridge to Pat's hotel on the other side of the river.

Tucked into the hillside on the corner of what was now a busy junction, the hotel had once been a merchant's home when Bideford was a thriving port. During its eclectic history, it had been a workhouse and a court house, complete with prison cells, before being expanded and turned into a hotel during the Victorian railway era. Visitors would have once arrived by train and alighted at the hotel's own station on the higher level. Trains no longer used the line, which now made way for walkers and cyclists who could join the Tarka Trail that ran between Braunton at the northern end and Meeth, a small village 32 miles away, at the other.

Esme pushed open the entrance door to the hotel and walked in off the street. The clatter of crockery being cleared from breakfast echoed in the distance. Esme stepped on to the plush carpet and looked across to the reception area, which looked as though it had been fashioned from a large ornate fireplace. But before she could approach the besuited young man behind the desk, she saw Pat walking towards her.

'Esme, good morning,' Pat said, smiling. She gestured back the way she'd come. 'Shall we go through here?' She led Esme into an elegant lounge, arranged with armchairs, striped to match the black and white of the carpet, set around small tables. The tall sliding sash windows, dressed with long cream drapes, looked out on to the street and the bridge across which Esme had walked moments ago. She spied Annie's box file sitting on an oval oak table beside the window and took one of the seats beside it.

'No will in there, either, I'm afraid,' Pat said, nodding towards the box.

'Not a problem,' Esme said. 'Devon Archives hold a copy. I've put in a request to see it.'

'That's excellent news.'

A waitress arrived at Pat's side and Esme accepted Pat's offer of coffee. The waitress nodded and retreated.

'It'll help wake me up,' Esme said, laughing. 'I didn't get to bed last night until late, following up on that thought of yours about who might have owned the ring in the past.'

'And did you discover anything conclusive?' Pat asked, sitting down opposite Esme.

'Well, obviously I couldn't say it's conclusive, but my best guess is that at the time of the dispute, it had been in the possession of Ernest's mother, Betsy Sanders.'

'That seems perfectly appropriate. So what could Albert have against it?'

'I can only assume it was the act of Ernest stealing the ring from his mother and giving it to Annie which caused the controversy,' Esme said. 'I'm guessing Albert had anticipated it coming his way, given his daughter Alice had been born that same year.'

'Ah, yes I see.' Pat steepled her fingers. 'So as far as Albert was concerned, Ernest had stolen it from his daughter.'

'I imagine so. Alice would have been the first girl of the next generation, so perhaps it wouldn't have been unreasonable for Albert to expect Betsy to pass it on to her niece.'

Pat leaned over the table towards Esme. 'This matter of the ring being stolen stirred something in my memory that Annie once told me,' she said.

'Oh? What's that?'

The waitress arrived with their coffee on a tray. Esme moved Annie's box so that she could place it on the table. Pat thanked her and the waitress withdrew.

'Hester may have told you,' Pat said, 'that Annie's research often stemmed from stories her grandmother told her, which she'd been told by *her* grandmother.'

'Yes, she did,' Esme said, nodding. 'Annie liked to investigate the stories, and establish what was behind them. Sort fact from fiction, kind of thing.'

'Exactly that.' Pat set out the cups and saucers, slowly and deliberately as if her thoughts were elsewhere. 'It's a shame Hester's too busy to collaborate with you,' she said, in a tone which suggested a degree of scepticism. Pat looked up at Esme, locking eyes. 'At least, that's what she told me. Is that what you understand as well?'

Esme swallowed. 'I know she's under pressure,' she said, wondering how much she should say. If Hester was being reticent about Stone to save her mother undue concern, she'd not thank Esme for revealing the real reason behind her disengagement.

'What do you know about this new man Isaac's introduced,' Pat said, 'this Frank Stone character?'

'I don't think Hester likes him, put it like that.'

Pat pulled a face. 'No, I'm sure she doesn't. What Isaac was thinking of, employing him, I really can't imagine. Anyway, that's as maybe. Where was I? Oh yes, Auntie's family stories.' She reached over to push down the plunger on the cafetière. 'One of the things Auntie's granny told her was there was a ring which she would have inherited – again, coming down the female line – had it not gone missing.'

'Gone missing?' Esme said, something stirring deep in her thoughts. 'So this is nothing to do with Ernest taking the ring?'

'No, it happened a long time before that.' Pat poured out the thick brown liquid into the two white glazed cups, sliding a cup and saucer towards Esme. 'The story of the missing ring had been passed down from Annie's great-great grandmother, Charlotte. And Charlotte had heard it from her grandmother, Matilda.'

'So we're talking…' Esme made a rough calculation in her

head. 'Back into the 18th century?'

Pat nodded. 'Matilda maintained that she should have inherited the ring from her own grandmother, except she never did because somebody stole it.'

'Did she know who?'

Pat shook her head. 'Another member of the family, was all anyone knew, so that's as much as I can tell you, I'm afraid.'

Esme added milk to her coffee. 'In Ernest taking the ring, it was as though history was repeating itself,' she said, picking up her cup and saucer. She glanced down at the box file on the floor beside her chair. 'I wonder if Annie ever discovered this 18th century culprit.'

Pat sat back in her seat, pressing her palms together. 'Oh, I'd love to know,' she said, her eyes shining. 'I do hope you can find out.'

*

Esme walked back across Bideford Old Bridge to her car, mulling over Annie's grandmother's story about the ring. If the ring Ernest gave to Annie was indeed the same ring as Amelia had been wearing in the painting, perhaps the dispute between Ernest and Albert had been about which side of the family had the legitimate claim to it. But while family feuds which stretched over generations could easily become entrenched, even toxic, as years went by, it seemed extreme for murder to be committed over what appeared to be a relatively common gold ring. Then again, perhaps it wasn't common at all, but extremely rare.

She reached her car and climbed into the driver's seat as another scenario occurred to her. Maybe the dispute wasn't about the intrinsic value of the ring, but because it represented something else. But what? Perhaps the answer was buried amongst Annie's notes.

She turned on the engine and headed to the large supermarket on the way out of town. She needed to stock up on a few things,

251

including cat food. The kittens wouldn't forgive her if she ran out of their favourite biscuits.

She was on her way out through the doors and into the entrance area when her phone rang. She manoeuvred her trolley out of the flow of shoppers, parking it against the wall by the noticeboard, and pulled out her phone.

'Hester,' she said. 'How are you? Everything OK?'

Hester's answer was an exasperated expletive down the phone. 'If you mean, have I managed to persuade Isaac to part with Frank Stone, the answer is no. What have you got, Esme? Anything?'

'Well, some, but I'm not sure whether it helps your cause.'

'Can we meet? You can fill me in. Perhaps we can come up with something. I need to, I can tell you.'

'Yes, of course,' Esme said, concerned by the note of desperation in Hester's voice. 'When?'

'Sometime today?'

'Oh, OK. Yes, that's not a problem. I'm in Bideford at the moment. I could call in. I'm only round the corner.'

'No, don't come to the office. We might bump into Frank.'

'But it's Sunday,' Esme said. 'Surely he's off enjoying himself somewhere.'

Hester gave a humourless laugh. 'Enjoying himself includes popping up when I least expect it, just to let me know he's watching.'

'What about coming to mine, then?'

'No, not that,' Hester said. 'He might get wind of it.' She exhaled noisily. 'God, I sound paranoid.'

'Have you reason to be?'

Hester sniffed. 'I'll tell you when I see you.'

Esme leaned on the handle of her trolley, scratching around in her head to think of a suitable venue. 'Well, how about...' Her eye fell on a poster on the noticeboard advertising the afternoon's Bluebell Day at Hartland Abbey. 'Hang on. I've got an idea where we could meet. And I'm pretty sure it's not somewhere Frank Stone's likely to spend his Sunday.'

252

# 53

Esme arrived at Hartland Abbey car park and climbed out of her car. The sky was a wide canvas of blue, dotted with balls of cloud which scuttled along, propelled by a brisk breeze blowing in from the coast. Families were emerging from their vehicles, strapping toddlers into buggies and ensuring other children were sufficiently coated and booted for their walk through the woods and down to the coast.

Esme buttoned up her coat and headed for the small wooden hut to pay the entrance fee. As she came back outside, she saw Hester walking towards her across the car park, wearing a grey trench coat and a felt bucket hat, which she'd pulled low down on to her head.

'Good to see you,' Esme said, as Hester reached her. She looked drawn with little colour in her face. 'Here,' she said, handing Hester a sticker. 'I went ahead and paid for us both.'

'Thank you,' Hester said, putting the sticker on to her lapel.

'Have you been here before?' Esme asked, indicating the expansive stone building stretching away to their right.

Hester shook her head and looked back at Esme. 'Not yet, no.'

'You must come another time and see inside,' Esme said, as they turned to join the other visitors following the path towards the coast and the bluebell woods. 'It's well worth a visit. It's become quite a popular filming venue in recent years. Well, the whole area has been. It's a fabulous spot.' She laid a hand on Hester's arm. 'I'm sorry. You've other things on your mind at the moment.'

Hester acknowledged Esme's comment with a nod and a fleeting smile, thrusting her hands in the deep pockets of her coat. 'Sometimes it feels overwhelming.'

'You'd enough on your plate without Frank Stone becoming a

thorn in your side.'

'I can't argue with you there.'

They reached the lane which ran round the back of the lawns to the rear of the property and crossed over to the track on the opposite side. They passed a couple pushing a toddler in a buggy, who was emitting a low drone and delighting at how the bumpy ground made his voice judder.

'Still no joy convincing Isaac?' Esme said, as they moved ahead of the family.

'I think we both know I'm wasting my time there, Esme.' Hester leaned closer to Esme, lowering her voice. 'Whatever Stone's terrified I'm going to find out, it must be big. That's why he's watching me.'

Esme thought about Max's blackmail theory. But did it add up? It seemed more likely that it was Stone who had something to hide, not Maudesley.

'Do you think Isaac knows what it is?' Esme asked.

Hester frowned. 'Why would he? I think Frank's stringing him some sort of line. Whatever fabrication Frank's come up with, I need something to blow it out of the water. And you, my dear Esme, are my only hope. What have you got so far? Anything we can use?'

Esme sighed. 'I only wish I had. Everything just seems to be a series of tentative connections, and while interesting enough in their own right, they don't lead anywhere. Not the way you were hoping, anyway.' She gave Hester an apologetic smile. 'For instance, I think I have an idea of the argument behind the murder, but I'm not sure what it proves.'

She told Hester about her discovery of the postcard of Amelia Chalacombe's painting, the Claddagh ring she wore on her finger, Pat's family story of the ring being stolen, and the photograph Hester had given her being of Agnes Venner wearing the same ring.

'How much Albert and Ernest knew about the ring's history,

we can't know,' Esme said, 'but it seems likely that Albert took exception to Ernest giving Annie the ring and that's why they'd argued. I'm inclined to think things just got out of control and Ernest came off worse, and so it wasn't the premeditated murder it was portrayed as.'

'I wonder how Albert found out,' Hester mused. 'Annie and Ernest's liaison was secret, remember. I can't imagine she'd wear it openly, not back then.'

'But having unravelled all of that,' Esme continued, 'where does it leave us? Do you see what I mean? It doesn't get us any closer to understanding why Frank Stone is so hostile about you looking into his family's past. I wondered whether Frank having the photo of Agnes is significant – if it *is* his, I mean. But I couldn't see what it proved one way or the other.'

'Yes, I do see what you're saying.'

'I will keep at it, though. It's perfectly possible the answer's buried deeper than we think.'

'But what now? I thought you'd been through all Annie's notes.'

'You haven't spoken to your mum recently, then?' Esme said.

'No, I've been keeping a low profile. She's picked up there's something not quite right at work, but I daren't tell her any more or she'll worry. Why d'you ask?'

'She's found another of Annie's box files. She brought it with her when she came down to Bideford yesterday. I called round at her hotel earlier to pick it up. She's well aware you and Frank aren't getting on, but I just said I knew you were under pressure and tried to give the impression it was work related. I don't think she's fooled, though.'

Hester pressed her lips together. 'No, I'm sure she isn't. Let's hope we can get to the bottom of things before she gets wind of it. Perhaps there'll be more in that other box file.'

'And there's one potential source of information I haven't told you about yet,' Esme said. 'I know whose will Annie was talking about in her enigmatic note. It was William Chalacombe's.'

'Oh Esme, that's brilliant news! What did the will say?'

'I haven't seen it yet. The will itself was missing. But don't worry, I'm on the case. Devon Archives are sourcing me a copy. I'll let you know as soon as I have sight of it.'

They arrived at the start of a narrow path leading them off the main track and up between the trees. 'Let's go this way,' Esme said, pointing. 'The best bluebells are up here.' As they climbed, they became immersed in the heady scent of the stunning rich-blue flowers and they stood for a few moments, absorbing the spectacle stretching out as far as they could see between the trees.

'From what I recall,' Hester said, as they resumed their walk, 'it was William Chalacombe's nephew Nicholas Chalacombe, a clergyman, who inherited both the family estate and the shipping business after his uncle died, and it subsequently passed down the Chalacombe line. Do you think Auntie found something unexpected in the will?'

'Hopefully this week, we'll find out what.' Esme glanced up as the light changed and saw a dark cloud had plunged them into shadow. 'Could be in for a shower,' she said. 'There's a small cabin up ahead. Let's see if we can make it before we get wet.'

They stepped up their pace and after a few moments, the trees opened out to reveal a neat stone building on the edge of the woods. Esme went ahead and opened the brown painted door, delighted to find a fire burning in the hearth inside.

'Oh, bliss,' Hester said. 'What a touching thought to set this up for visitors.' She followed Esme inside, going over to warm her hands against the flames as the sound of heavy raindrops rattled the slates above.

Esme sat on the seat in the narrow bay window and looked out at the rain. After a moment, Hester joined her.

'It seems a million miles away from everything that's going on, doesn't it?' Hester said, gazing out into the woods beyond.

'It must feel like a little bit of respite for you,' Esme said. 'A

Frank-free zone.'

Hester shivered. 'Don't mention his name. I'm terrified you'll conjure him up.'

'What did you mean earlier?' Esme said. 'About being paranoid. I asked if you'd had reason to be.'

Hester looked down at her hands in her lap. 'Frank knows I've been poking around.'

'Well, I assumed as much, otherwise he'd not be warning you off. Which, of course, only confirms there's something he's worried might come out, something which is a threat to him.'

'He crept up on me, you see.' Hester shivered. 'By the time I realised he was looking over my shoulder and slammed the laptop shut, it was too late.'

Esme nodded. 'I wondered how he'd found out. I thought maybe you'd challenged him or something. Well, as you said on the phone, as long as you're appearing to go along with his terms, he should back off and leave you alone.'

Hester swallowed. 'There's something else, though. Something you ought to know.'

'Which is?'

Hester turned to look at Esme, her expression troubled. 'When he came up behind me, I was reading the report you'd emailed me on Frank's family tree.' She took a deep breath. 'You need to be careful, Esme. I can't be sure he didn't see who'd sent it.'

# 54

Back at her cottage, Esme contemplated Hester's warning. Would Frank Stone seriously see her as a threat? Even if he had seen Esme's email over Hester's shoulder, surely Hester's little charade in the office would have convinced him Esme was no longer involved and, by now, would be working for another client. As long as he hadn't realised the significance of the box Hester had passed over. But there wasn't much she could do about that, she just had to hope for the best. And watch her back, of course.

She sat down at the kitchen table and opened up her laptop. Whatever Stone's thinking, she couldn't let it distract her. Even if Hester had asked her to discontinue the research, she had Maddy to consider, and the search for clues that would help her get her sea chest back.

As the laptop booted, Esme debated which route she should follow next. Having arrived at a possible explanation for the disagreement behind the 1923 murder, she felt she'd exhausted that particular trail for now and needed to look elsewhere. Perhaps in anticipation of viewing William Chalacombe's will, she would be prudent to explore other 18th century links.

She decided to pick up with Agnes Venner, born in 1770, and dig further back to find Agnes's parents. She might even be able to establish how the two sides of Hester's family were connected by the Claddagh ring.

She opened up the *Find My Past* database and entered Agnes's name and birth details, clicking on the button to activate the search engine. It led her to an image of baptism records in the parish of Northam, near Bideford, written in a neat copperplate hand. Esme scanned the list for 1770, locating Agnes about halfway down. *Agnes, the daughter of Josiah & Kitty Venner, was baptised on 18th February.*

Josiah. Where had she seen that name before? It was when she'd been researching the Chalacombe family, after she'd visited John Ford's shop.

She located the relevant file on her laptop and opened it up, reading through her notes to remind herself where she'd seen the name. Yes, of course. Josiah Venner was Henry's son and the nephew of Thomas Venner who, along with his brother, had been captured by Barbary pirates. When Thomas had escaped back to England, Esme had reasoned he'd believed Henry had not survived the ordeal and had taken his older brother's family under his wing, indicated by a record she'd found of a daughter born to Thomas and Felicity Venner, Henry's wife.

Esme pulled up the family tree she'd compiled and noted the daughter had been called Matilda. She stared at the name, recalling Pat's story about a stolen ring. Annie's great-great grandmother Charlotte had been told the tale by *her* grandmother… Matilda.

Esme sat back. There was the evidence to connect the two sides of the family right there, surely? According to Pat's understanding, Matilda had anticipated the ring being passed down to her from… from whom? From her mother, Felicity? From her grandmother, Amelia, seen proudly displaying the ring in her portrait hanging in John Ford's shop?

Esme went back to the family tree and studied the branches. Amelia and Richard Venner had only had sons, Henry and Thomas, so if Amelia had followed the tradition of passing the ring down the female line, it was obvious why Matilda would have expected it to go to her as the first-born granddaughter. Given Amelia died shortly after Henry and Felicity had married, Esme noted, it seemed likely she'd passed it to her daughter-in-law. Years later, Felicity's own daughter Matilda would naturally have believed one day it would be hers.

So how had Agnes, pictured wearing the ring in her mortuary photograph in 1852, come to have possession of it? Had Josiah stolen the ring? It was feasible he considered its legitimate route should be via his dead father Henry, the elder of the two brothers. Had he taken the ring to pass on to his daughter? Is that how it had ended up on that side of the family?

As she closed down the computer, Esme wondered if Ernest had been aware of the true origin of the ring. Maybe he'd believed that by giving it to Annie, he'd redressed the transgression of the past by returning it to the correct branch of the family. If so, how tragic that he had paid for his good intentions with his life.

# 55

The email from Esme's contact in the archives came through on Monday as she and Maddy were going through a stock check in Maddy's workshop ready for Tuesday's market. When the alert sounded from Esme's phone that a message had landed in her inbox, she pounced on it.

'Is it what I think it is?' Maddy said, turning to look at Esme over her shoulder as she carried a veneered wooden tea caddy across the room.

'Hope so,' Esme said, tapping her phone. 'Yes, it's Jack from the record office,' she said, smiling as she read the email message. 'Oh, you star, thank you.' She looked up, grinning. 'Apparently all the archivists are intrigued. They want to know what I make of it.'

Maddy put down the box on her workbench. 'Come on, then,' she said. 'Let's have a look.'

Esme fetched her laptop out of her bag. 'I'll get it up on the screen, shall I? Then we can see it properly.' Maddy cleared a section of the worktop and Esme set up the machine, anticipation building as the computer booted and she was able to log on to her email account.

Maddy fetched over two stools and they both sat down in front of the screen.

'OK, go for it,' Maddy said, resting an elbow on the bench. 'Let's see how the illustrious William Chalacombe intended to disperse his wealth.'

'To his nephew Nicholas Chalacombe, according to Hester,' Esme said, as she clicked on the email.

'So Hester hasn't had any thoughts about what revelations her great aunt was hinting at in her letter?'

'None,' Esme said, shaking her head. 'So, she'll be waiting with baited breath. Shame she can't be here right now and see for herself.'

'Will you give her a call?'

'Yes, I will. But not while she's at work. Can't afford Frank Stone to get wind of it.'

'You think he's spying on her?'

'From what Hester's told me, that's exactly what he's doing.'

Maddy folded her arms. 'I wonder what he's so paranoid about.'

'Like I said, skeletons in cupboards,' Esme reminded her. 'Clearly he's worried about what she might find out.'

'But he doesn't think she's looking any more, doesn't he, after your little act in the office?'

'No, of course he doesn't,' Esme said, with as much confidence as she could garner. 'Hester's been very careful not to give him cause to think otherwise.'

Maddy considered this for a moment before nodding at the screen. 'C'mon, then. Get on with it. Let's see what it says. You're doing my head in.'

Esme laughed and opened the email attachment. The screen filled with an image of a document written in a neat italic hand, set out beautifully across the page.

'I love old handwriting,' Maddy said. 'It's so gorgeous to look at. The only sad thing is, I can't usually make head or tail of it.'

'I'm a bit rusty, I must admit,' Esme said, slipping on her reading glasses. 'But at least we have one thing in our favour. It's not in Latin.'

'Oh, don't. It's hard enough as it is. Can you read it out loud? I can follow it then.'

'Yes, of course.' Esme cleared her throat and began to read the document, which started with the usual preamble. "'*In the Name of God Amen in the seventeen hundred and forty third year of our Lord on the second day of the month of March I William Chalacombe of Worthygate in the Parish of Woolfardisworthy in the County of Devon being sick and weak as to my Bodily health but of sound and disposing Mind Memory and*

262

*Understanding do make this my last Will and Testament in manner and form following…'"*

'Why do they never use punctuation?' Maddy groaned. 'It's a nightmare.'

Esme looked round at Maddy over the top of her glasses. 'Yes, I always think that. It's not as though it hadn't been invented. Apparently back in the 3rd century, some Egyptian librarian got fed up with how long it took to decipher scrolls. They didn't even put spaces between words back then, either.'

'Oh, for goodness sake, that's ridiculous.' Maddy gave a flick of her chin before turning back to the laptop. 'We should be thankful for small mercies, then. At least there are a few capital letters to break it up a bit.'

Esme pointed to the text on the screen. 'Looks like this is where the business side of it begins. "*I bequeath…*"' She scanned across. 'Ah, here we are. Hester was right. William's heir was his nephew, Nicholas Chalacombe, the son of his younger brother, John.'

Maddy leaned closer, her eyes chasing across the image. 'Anything to indicate what Annie meant in her note about it being *all in the will?*'

'Not that I can see so far,' Esme said. 'Let's keep reading. "*I give to the…*"' She squinted at the text. 'I can't quite make out that word. *Worst,* d'you reckon?'

Maddy shrugged. 'Could be.'

'Yes,' Esme said, nodding. 'I'm sure it is. OK, I think we might be getting somewhere. "*I give to the worst of men who is guilty of all ills the renegade son of my unfortunate sister Amelia rest her sad soul Henry Venner…*"'

The two women exchanged glances. 'Henry Venner?' Esme said, taking off her glasses. 'He was Thomas Venner's older brother who was captured at the same time as Thomas. It was assumed he'd died a slave.'

'Guilty of all ills? Renegade? It's getting interesting now. Go on.'

Esme replaced her glasses and focused back on the screen. 'Right, where had I got to? "…*Henry Venner who I had in my misfortune thought to make my lawful heir but who renounced his faith for the fires of Hell the sum of five and forty brass halfpence had I known his character this sin and shame I would never have named him thus and made myself unhappy I cannot find it in my heart to give him forgiveness but hope the Almighty affords him a better understanding.*"

'Wow,' Esme said, sitting back. 'He didn't mince his words, did he?'

Maddy blinked, her eyes wide. 'So, what did Henry Venner do to get such a condemnation?'

'I dread to think,' Esme said. 'Hester might know, but I can't afford Stone to get wind of it, having done such a good job of putting him off the scent.'

'Who else is there to ask?' Maddy said, folding her arms. 'We're talking specialist subject Chalacombe, here. Hester's the obvious candidate.'

'Oh, hang on,' Esme said, snapping the laptop shut and standing up. 'I know just the man. John Ford. He seems to be fairly clued up with their family history. He'll be fascinated by this, I'm sure. I'll go and pick his brains.'

\*

Esme hurried down the high street to John Ford's shop and pushed open the door, the bell jangling its melodious signal to its owner who appeared from his inner office. His expression registered a certain recognition, but the accompanying frown suggested he was searching his memory for more.

'Esme Quentin, Mr Ford,' Esme said as she walked towards him, thankful that she'd arrived at an opportune time when there were no customers. 'You bought some old frames from me a couple of weeks ago.'

'Ah, so I did, Mrs Quentin. Have you some more for me?'

Esme shook her head. 'Not today, no.' She turned and pointed to the painting she'd studied previously. 'When I was here before, you told me something of the history of the Chalacombe family. You showed me the painting of Amelia Chalacombe and told me about her son Thomas.'

'Yes, I did indeed. Is there anything more I can help you with?'

Esme slid her bag off her shoulder and pulled out her laptop. 'In the course of some research I'm doing,' she said, looking round for a suitable place to set the machine, 'I came across a copy of the will of William Chalacombe, Amelia's brother. It has some references to Henry Venner in it which I'm sure you'll find interesting.'

'Oh indeed, I'm sure I would.' Ford gestured to a baize-covered card table outside his inner sanctum. 'Perhaps this would suffice.'

'Thank you.' Esme set down the laptop and switched it on. 'There's something curious in it which I'm hoping you might be able to explain for me,' she said, as it booted.

'I'm most intrigued.'

Esme navigated to her emails and opened up the attachment. 'There,' she said, standing back so he could study the screen. Ford bent down and peered at it through his horn-rimmed spectacles.

'Well, well, well,' he said after a moment, 'this is most fascinating.'

'Isn't it just?' Esme said, nodding. 'But what does it mean, exactly? He calls Henry a renegade and talks about the fires of hell. What did Henry do that was so bad he was disinherited? Any idea?'

John Ford straightened up and smiled. 'I think I have a very good idea, yes,' he said, a glimmer in his eye. 'I strongly suspect that our Henry Venner became a pirate.'

# 56

Esme's eye was drawn towards a painting on John Ford's wall of a ship in full sail. She could almost see the skull and crossbones flag flying at the top of the mast.

'Well,' she said, blinking. 'That's something I wasn't expecting.'

Ford chuckled. 'You and me both, Mrs Quentin.'

'Given what you told me last time, about the fear of pirates threatening his ships, it must have rankled William that Henry became one himself.'

Ford inclined his head. 'I'm not so sure it was his piracy that his uncle was unable to forgive. After all, William's own ancestors had been privateers under Elizabeth I. Pirates by any other name, unless you had that crucial piece of paper.'

'Piece of paper?'

'A Letter of Marque, it was called, which would be signed by the monarch. If the country was at war with Spain, for example, and you plundered a Spanish ship, as long as you had the necessary documentation, you were doing so on behalf of His or Her Majesty. That made you a privateer. Sir Francis Drake is probably the most famous. He earned his country a small fortune.'

Esme smiled. 'Licence to plunder. The James Bond's 007 status of its time.'

'Quite so,' Ford said, his face breaking into a grin. 'State-sanctioned piracy stretched back centuries. Before England had any Navy to speak of, she was more than happy to commission pirates, the mercenaries of their day, in times of war. Of course, they risked finding themselves in deep water – if you'll pardon the pun – if England struck a peace treaty. One minute you have the authority to seize ships, the next there was no war…' he shrugged.

'And you reverted to a lawless pirate status,' Esme said, nodding as she grasped his meaning. 'Easy to get caught out, I'd imagine, given it might be weeks before a ship came into port to hear the latest news.'

'Indeed.'

'It makes you wonder why they bothered when their status was so volatile.'

'Well, there were plenty who were willing to take the risk. In the 1600s, thousands of disenchanted and disillusioned seafarers turned to piracy, for one reason or another. Some might have been the privateers I told you about, legitimately making a living capturing the merchant ships of enemy countries. All very well while there was war, but there were fewer options in peace time. Serving in the Navy wasn't a particularly attractive prospect. Conditions were grim. Poor food, pitifully low pay and a discipline regime that would make your hair curl.'

Esme nodded. 'Yes, I've researched a few naval ancestors in my time. Flogging with the cat o' nine tails and being dragged under the ship from end to end, getting gouged by razor-sharp barnacles.' She shuddered, recalling the accounts she'd read of sailors bleeding to death from their injuries after being keelhauled.

'Piracy, on the other hand – if you were prepared to accept the risk of winding up at the end of a hangman's noose, your body tarred and left to rot on a gibbet as a warning to others – at least offered you a modicum of freedom, access to worldly goods you could only dream of and – though I say so with a little irony – a kind of democracy to boot.'

'Democracy?'

'Oh yes,' Ford said, clearly enjoying Esme's surprise. 'In the form of The Pirates' Code.'

Esme chuckled. 'You're kidding me.'

Ford inclined his head with a wry smile. 'That's the theory, anyway. I'm sure not everyone was as diligent to the rules as they might be.'

'So, what was in the code?' Esme asked.

'Well, to begin with, the captain was elected by the crew.'

'Was he, indeed? Interesting. And could he be unelected, too?'

'Most definitely. The usual practice with a captain who'd lost the crew's trust was to set him adrift in a small boat, along with his cronies, or abandon him on an uninhabited island and let him take his chances.'

'Sounds like an idea worth considering for badly behaved politicians,' Esme said, with a wry smile. 'What else was in the code?'

'The spoils of their raids were divided up fairly amongst the crew. The captain had a greater share, as you might imagine, as did his second in command, but the rest was distributed equally.'

Esme wrinkled her nose. 'Even so, it must have been a pretty brutal life.'

'Oh, there's very little doubt about that. And, of course, some pirates were more ruthless than others, as we know from historical accounts. Charles Vane had a reputation for cruelty, torturing his captives to give up their valuables. As for Edward Low, it was said he'd bind his captives in chains, torture them and force them to eat the heart of their captain.'

'Oh, that's revolting,' Esme said, pulling a face of disgust. 'I heard about Thomas Salkeld who declared himself King of Lundy. He wasn't a bundle of fun, either.'

'On the other hand,' Ford said, inclining his head, 'Edward Teach earned the nickname Blackbeard more for his terrifying appearance than for violent conduct.'

'I wonder what sort of pirate Henry was,' Esme said, looking over to the painting of Henry's mother, Amelia. 'And what made him turn to piracy. I still don't understand his motive. Surely he'd have known he was his uncle's heir, so he'd be expecting to become a wealthy man at some point.'

'It may have been a matter of self-preservation,' Ford said. 'Join the pirates who'd captured him or be killed and thrown overboard. A split-second decision.'

'And his ransom potential? You said wealthy families paid handsomely for the freedom of a captured relative.'

'Yes, they did. A very lucrative business model, from the perspective of a Barbary sultan.'

'And yet, despite having the means, it seems Henry's family didn't pay,' Esme said. 'They couldn't have done, could they, or Henry and Thomas would have got home much quicker? Instead, it took Thomas ten years to escape and Henry had to become a pirate to survive.'

'It's possible they weren't seen as candidates for a ransom demand. Or perhaps William didn't have the means. Maybe his business was suffering with all the raids on his ships.'

'Interesting that the account Thomas wrote when he made it back home doesn't mention what happened to Henry. Do you think Thomas knew and deliberately left it out of his story? He might have been wary of admitting having a renegade for a brother. Then again, perhaps he never knew. Not until he returned home, anyway. He may not have even known that Henry had survived.'

'You may well be right,' Ford agreed. 'Pirates would usually take their human bounty back to port and imprison them until they were able to trade them at a local slave market. Obviously, they'd then be sold off to different owners and never see one another again. But even if Thomas had witnessed Henry joining the pirate ranks at the time their ship was taken, he wouldn't have been aware of Henry's ultimate fate.'

'Until he returned home and learned the truth.'

'Which brings us back to this document,' Ford said, indicating the image displayed on the laptop screen.

'Confirming that William Chalacombe found out what Henry had done and changed his will accordingly.' Esme frowned. 'You'd have thought Thomas would have been next in line, given he didn't become a renegade like his brother.'

Ford rubbed his chin. 'Ah, that might have been the case were it not for the other set of circumstances, which brings me back to my earlier comment, that it wouldn't have been piracy per se which William Chalacombe would have found unforgivable.'

'Then what?' Esme asked. 'Henry targeted a ship in his uncle's fleet? That might have been the last straw, especially if it affected his business.'

Ford shook his head. 'No, his words say it all,' he said, pointing to a line in William's will. 'The ultimate betrayal, which society considered worse than robbery or even murder. Henry had renounced his Christian faith and gone over to "the other side". Or, in the terminology of the day, he had "turned Turk".'

# 57

Esme hurried to her car, keen to report back to Maddy what she'd learned, while thinking how fascinated Hester would be to discover this side to her family's maritime history. How frustrating not to be able to head straight over to her office and share what John Ford had told her. She couldn't even email her, as Hester was concerned Stone had found a way to monitor her correspondence. But Esme knew she must make contact somehow – perhaps through Pat?

As she got into her car to drive back to Maddy's workshop, she recalled the words of Annie's final letter, *it's all in the will he wrote.* Did that mean Annie was on Henry's trail? It implied reading the will would explain everything, but what was "everything"? Esme wasn't sure she fully understood yet. Did Annie mean the fate of Henry and his disinheritance? Was that an end in itself? Or was she still missing a vital part of the bigger picture? Perhaps once she discussed it with Hester, things would become clearer.

Maddy was lounging in her old leather armchair, her feet on a stool, eating her lunch. She looked up in surprise as Esme came through the door and sat upright.

'Everything OK?'

'Yes, everything's fine,' Esme said, pulling up a stool. 'You're going to love this.'

Maddy sat wide-eyed as Esme relayed John Ford's information, explaining the reason for Henry's uncle's anger.

'It's like the Crusade mentality of the 12th and 13th century,' Maddy said, shaking her head.

'Exactly that,' Esme accepted a proffered slice of Maddy's pasty and popped it in her mouth. 'In the west,' she went on when she'd swallowed it, 'Islam was "them" and Christianity was "us". Anyone who crossed the great divide was considered a heretic.

But for some of those poor terrified unfortunates who were captured and sold into slavery, "turning Turk" might have given them some degree of protection. Unless they were lucky enough to have their ransoms paid and could return to what they'd see as civilisation. But that doesn't look to have happened to Henry.'

'So he had to adopt his own survival tactics.' Maddy tugged her ponytail, pensively. 'How did William find out, do you think? Did Thomas know what his brother had been up to?'

Esme shook her head. 'If he did, he couldn't have told William. Thomas didn't make it home until 1746, three years after William wrote his will.'

'I suppose Thomas might have benefited from his uncle's will instead of his brother, but at the time William would assume Thomas was dead.'

'Not necessarily.' Esme's phone pinged and she dug it out of her pocket. 'John Ford implied that even if Thomas had made it home by then, William wouldn't have made him his heir.'

'Why not?'

'Because in the account Thomas wrote about his experiences, he talked about a wife and daughter back in Barbary. The assumption is, after they died and he no longer had a reason to stay, it was then he decided to try and get back to England. For him to have married out there, he also would have had to change allegiance.'

'Oh, yes I see,' Maddy said, nodding. 'Thereby putting himself in the same camp as Henry, as far as William Chalacombe was concerned.'

'That's about the size of it,' Esme said, looking at the screen of her phone and breaking into a grin. 'Oh, this sounds interesting. There's another message from Jack. He's found something on Henry.'

'Oh, brilliant. What?' Maddy brushed pasty crumbs off her leggings and stood up, as Esme scrolled to the bottom of the email and tapped on the attached document.

'It's a petty sessions record,' Esme said, enlarging the page so she could more easily read the text. 'What's our Henry been up to, then?'

Maddy peered over Esme's shoulder and read out the offence. '*Unlawfully was in a drunk and disorderly state on a public road and did then assault the complainant.*' She chuckled. 'Assault and drunkenness? Sounds like he was already developing the necessary credentials to become a pirate.'

Esme tapped the screen. 'Look at the date, though. This isn't before he was captured. This is afterwards.' She looked round at Maddy. 'So Henry must have made it home several years before Thomas did.'

'Are you saying Henry *told* his uncle what he'd been up to? Without realising the consequences?'

'I'm not sure,' Esme said, frowning. 'I think we're missing something here. I need to do some digging.'

*

Esme sat in front of her laptop in Maddy's workshop, occasionally stopping to jot down notes on the pad beside her, the pungent smell of polish growing stronger as Maddy worked on her latest project.

'How are you doing?' Maddy said. 'Have you worked it out yet?'

Esme pulled back her arms and flexed her shoulders. 'Yes, I think so.'

Maddy put down her polishing rag and came over to Esme, pulling up a stool to sit next to her. 'Go on, then, fill me in. What have you found?'

Esme slid the laptop out of the way and dragged her notepad closer to her. 'I've drawn up a timeline.' She tapped the pad. 'We know from Thomas's account that the brothers were captured in 1736. By 1742, we know Henry had made it home, as he appears in the records, charged for drunk and disorderliness.'

'What we don't know is when he came back,' Maddy said. 'Had he just got back or had he been back for a while?'

'No, we don't know that. But it may not be relevant for our purposes. Henry pops up a couple more times in the same year with more charges of drunkenness. Then, in 1743, William changes his will, having learned the shocking truth of his nephew's misdemeanours. But, as you said earlier, how did he find out?'

'Mmm, are we thinking the same thing?' Maddy asked, raising an eyebrow. 'Like, he might be boasting to his drinking mates about his exciting life on the ocean waves?'

Esme grinned. 'You can see where I'm going with this, can't you?'

'Word gets back to Uncle and he's not a happy bunny.'

'No, and Henry gets disinherited in favour of Nicholas Chalacombe.'

'And Nicholas was William's nephew?' Maddy asked.

'Yes, the son of his younger brother, John. Hester said Nicholas Chalacombe was a clergyman. John Ford told me that some religious leaders were scathing about those who renounced their faith while in captivity. One Puritan minister in New England was horrified at what he heard and regularly ranted in his sermons about apostasy, citing a lack of moral and spiritual fibre of the captives and accusing them of weakness when the horrors of what they were suffering should have strengthened their beliefs.'

Maddy pulled a cynical expression. 'Easy for him to say.'

'Naturally,' Esme said, with a wry smile, 'his excuse for such a hard attitude was that he was concerned for the captives' souls.'

Maddy folded her arms. 'Nicholas must have thought it was his lucky day when he realised Henry had become persona non grata.'

Esme rubbed a finger down her scar. 'Thing is, I'm wondering if he'd already had his eyes on the prize.'

'Oh yes, of course he would,' Maddy said. 'If everyone

assumed Henry and Thomas were dead, William would have given Nicholas the nod that he'd been selected as the new heir.'

'So you can imagine Nicholas's reaction when Henry showed up.'

'Yeah, can't you just?' Maddy said, nodding. 'A tad awkward to say the least.'

'And being a clergyman,' Esme said, leaning her elbows on the workbench, 'he'd be particularly savvy about the church's views on turning Turk and all that it implied.' She pointed to her timeline where Henry had been charged for being drunk and disorderly. 'Perhaps Nicholas had come to hear about Henry's drunken boasts.'

Maddy narrowed her eyes. 'You think he might have whispered a few choice phrases in his uncle's ear?'

'Well, it's feasible, isn't it?' Esme said. 'William might have initially welcomed Henry back home with open arms, much to the horror of Nicholas, who could see his secure financial future evaporate in front of his eyes. Once he got wind of Henry's stories, he realised that if he could persuade his uncle that William's support of his apostate nephew would result in his own purgatory, he might have been the cause of William's apparent U-turn.'

'Meaning Henry's world was about to fall apart, all the wealth he'd anticipated coming his way slipping from his grasp.'

Esme turned back to her timeline. 'Jack found another little gem in the parish overseer's records which takes us on a couple more years. It seems Felicity, Henry's wife, received poor relief for herself and her young son, Josiah, in 1745. She claimed Henry had abandoned her and,' Esme drew imaginary quote marks in the air, '*returned to his renegade ways.*'

'He went back to piracy?'

'What else could she mean? I know Ford reckoned Henry probably became a pirate for pragmatic reasons when he was first captured, to save himself from being killed, but maybe he got a taste for it. Perhaps it appealed to his sense of adventure. He wouldn't be the first. If he'd been spurned by his family and denied his inheritance, he could have seen piracy as an alternative way to get rich. He might have thought, what had he got to lose?'

'But he *had* got something to lose, hadn't he? His wife and son. Though, thinking about it, she might have been glad to see the back of him. Years of being a pirate could have changed him. It's not exactly a charm school, is it?'

'No, and he might have got worse after being overlooked for his uncle's estate. Maybe she threw him out for bad behaviour.'

Maddy nodded towards Esme's notepad. 'So, do you know what happened to Felicity?'

'Yes, I do. I'd already had a brief dip into Thomas's life after he made it back home and found a baptism record of a Matilda Venner, born in 1749, the daughter of a Thomas Venner and his wife Felicity. My guess, at the time, was that Henry had died, and when Thomas returned home he'd taken on his dead brother's wife and son. Unofficially, I mean.'

'Unofficially?'

'Yes. Marrying your brother's widow was disallowed under ecclesiastic law, but it wasn't actually illegal, back then. I found them living in a different parish, you see, as though they'd moved to a place where they weren't known. Perhaps Thomas managed to get work there and took Felicity with him, along with his nephew, Josiah, who hadn't even been born when Henry was captured. Either they pretended they were married or she presented herself as a widow and they found a sympathetic clergyman to conduct the ceremony. One point of view was that it was better for couples to be married in some form or other, than to "live in sin". In any case, it was better Felicity became Thomas's responsibility or the parish purse would be obliged to find the means of supporting her.'

'Nice to think there was a happy ending.'

'Oh, you old romantic, you,' Esme said with a smile. She got to her feet. 'Well, this is all fascinating stuff and I can't wait to get hold of Hester to tell her about it, but I still don't see…'

'See what?'

'I was about to say, I still don't see how it makes Annie's cryptic remark, *it's all in his will,* any clearer. But perhaps I do.'

Maddy sat forward, resting her elbows on her knees. 'Go on.'

'Right at the start, I remember talking to Hester about Annie being haunted by not knowing what Ernest and Albert had been arguing about prior to the murder.'

'Which is why you were convinced she was trying to find out. And you were right. It *was* about the ring. Ernest gave her a ring which was at the centre of the dispute.'

'Yes, but I think Annie needed to understand *why* the ring was stolen and why it was such a contentious issue. As soon as she read William Chalacombe's will, she *did* understand. The will clearly, and brutally, explained that Henry was disinherited, and that was the catalyst. If Henry had inherited as was intended, the ring – which at the time belonged to Henry's wife, Felicity, courtesy of her late mother-in-law, Amelia – would have legitimately passed down the female line in exactly the way it did, until Ernest took it upon himself to give it to Annie.'

Maddy screwed up her eyes. 'So if that was what should have happened anyway, why did Ernest believe he was righting a wrong?'

'Because Henry abandoned Felicity and she turned to Thomas instead. Felicity clearly believed the ring belonged to her and it was *her* right to decide who she passed it on to. She'd intended it to go to her daughter, Matilda, until it was stolen, as Annie's grandmother told her.'

'Hang on,' Maddy said, cocking her head to one side. 'Didn't we just establish Felicity was claiming poor relief? You'd have thought she'd have been forced to sell it, if she had no money.'

'She may have considered it too precious to part with unless she became destitute and had no choice.'

'Lucky for her that Thomas came back and rescued her. Doesn't sound like Henry left her anything worth having, when he scuttled off back to sea.'

'No, it doesn't,' Esme agreed. 'I wonder what happened to him. Did he really become a pirate, or did he join whatever ship would take him on?' An image flashed into her head of the *Treasures of the Sea Museum* where mariners' belongings had been displayed, along with the wooden boxes in which they kept them. She spun round and pointed to Maddy's laptop on the other side of the workshop. 'Have you got those photos of your stolen sea chest?'

'Sure,' Maddy said, wiping her fingers on a paper tissue and going over to fetch the laptop. She tapped the mouse to bring up the photos on the screen. 'There aren't many, but if the police do ever get their act together and locate it, they've at least got something to identify it as mine.'

Esme watched as Maddy homed in on the first image of the half-revealed etching of the sailing ship. 'Didn't you say you'd started work on the lid?'

'Some. But there's not much to see, to be honest.' She clicked on another image and blew it up so it filled the screen. 'See? There probably *are* letters under the grime but you can't really make them out yet.'

Esme peered at the dark shadow, turning her head one way and then the other to see more clearly. 'What's that, d'you think? An M?'

'MN is my best guess,' Maddy said. 'Although the second letter could be a V.'

'A V?' Esme said, unable to keep the excitement out of her voice. 'Venner.' She pointed to the first letter. 'And it's not M, it's an H.'

'Oh God, Esme,' Maddy cut across her. 'H V. Henry Venner.' They turned and stared at one another.

'Well, that explains Stone's interest in the box,' Maddy said, 'if

278

it really did belong to his ancestor.'

'So, why didn't he just come out and say so?' Esme said, chewing her lip. 'Why was he so desperate to get his hands on it that he had to steal it?'

# 58

Esme sat on her sofa, her legs curled up underneath her, and studied the family tree she'd printed out. One branch showed the descendants of Henry Venner and the other branch was that of his brother Thomas.

Her eye followed the generations down from Henry's son Josiah, his daughter Agnes, pictured in the mortuary photograph, and Agnes's granddaughter, Lucy. It was at this point Lucy's marriage joined her to the Philips family and it would be Lucy's grandsons, Albert Philips and Ernest Sanders, who would trigger the confrontation which would end in murder in 1923.

On the other branch was Thomas Venner and his daughter Matilda, who'd told the story of the stolen ring to her granddaughter, Charlotte – a ring that Charlotte maintained would have, had it not been snatched, passed down the female line of her family. Ernest had ensured, whether unwittingly or otherwise, that the ring did eventually land in the possession of Charlotte's great-great granddaughter, Annie.

Where was that ring now? Had it merely been lost, slipping off Annie's finger when she'd been wandering around outside in her nightclothes on that fateful day? Or was there any truth in Pat's hypothesis when she'd suggested to the police it may have been theft?

Esme wriggled off the edge of the sofa and returned to the second box file open on the kitchen table. She hadn't looked all the way through it yet. There was still a chance she'd find the ring underneath the papers.

She took the file back to the sofa and settled down with it on her knee. Ally got up from the arm of the sofa and padded over to see what she was up to, trying to climb into the box.

'That's not helpful, Al,' Esme told him, picking him up and

putting him on the floor. He sat on his haunches, watching her attentively as she began to offload the papers into a pile beside her. His sister came over to join him and Esme chuckled as their eyes fixated on her task, following every left to right movement like spectators at Wimbledon.

But there was no ring in the bottom of the box. Perhaps Esme had never really expected there to be. Neither had it slipped between the sheets of paper, all of which she had now transferred into a tottering stack on the sofa seat.

The heap became too much of a temptation for Ally. He leapt off the fireside rug, landing right on the top of the tantalising paper pile and the fun it offered. Esme shrieked as Jeanie pounced on her brother and the two of them slithered off the paper mountain as it spewed in every direction, despite Esme's best attempt to grab the contents of Annie's box before it scattered across the sitting room floor.

The kittens shot off in two different directions and disappeared behind the sofa, while Esme dropped to her knees, laughing, and began gathering everything up. She bundled it into the empty box file and stood up to take it back to the kitchen table.

'Well, thanks, you two,' she told the kittens, whose eyes glinted at her from their hideaway underneath the table. 'You've now given me another job to do, sorting through this lot.'

But it was too late to begin now. It would have to wait. Market day tomorrow and an early start.

She closed the lid of the box file on the higgledy-piggledy papers as well as she could and returned to the hearth to close down the wood-burner for the night. As she got up off her knees and turned to head upstairs, she noticed an overlooked slip of paper sticking out from under the sofa. She bent down and picked it up. It was a photocopy of a newspaper cutting. The headline read, *School closes after 800 years.*

Esme's brow crumpled into a frown. Why had Annie been

281

interested in the closure of Garter Abbey School?

Esme scanned the cutting, which referred to dwindling numbers of paying pupils making the school economically unviable, echoing what the woman steward had told her the day she'd visited. The tone of the piece suggested the reporter had taken the opportunity to peddle his own theory for the school's demise, alleging what the private institute offered was out of date and failed to prepare its pupils for the modern world. But buried in the partisan account was mention of an incident at the school some months previously, implying this had been a contributory factor.

Esme grabbed her laptop and switched it on. As she navigated her way to the *British Newspaper Archive*, a comment by the steward slipped into her head. When she had been talking about Frederick Philips's portrait having been found discarded in the attic, she'd also inferred that there'd been blame attributed to him for the school closing down.

The newspaper database loaded and Esme entered the appropriate parameters. The report which she'd found in Annie's box appeared on the list of results, but what caught Esme's eye was another, the headline of which read, *Tragic Accident at Historic School.* She clicked on the entry and zoomed in on the highlighted piece, which reported on an inquest held in July 1982. A pupil at the school, 12-year-old Anthony Milton, had gone swimming in the lake in the grounds and drowned. The verdict was recorded as accidental death.

Esme remembered standing beside the lake after finishing her lunchtime sandwich, thinking it didn't look inviting enough for a swim and reflecting it may have more appeal on a warm summer's evening. But it was clear from what was said at the inquest that Anthony should not have been swimming in the lake, that he'd broken the rules and had died as a consequence. She imagined for a school full of adolescent and pre-adolescent boys, having a lake in the grounds with its potential for adventure must have been too enticing to resist. Had other boys taken the risk and poor Anthony had just been unlucky?

As she mulled over the information in the newspaper report, something puzzled her. She could certainly understand how young Anthony's death may have been a factor in the school's closure, perhaps by undermining parents' confidence in the staff's ability to keep its pupils safe. If parents had then taken their sons out of the school as a consequence, it would explain why numbers were reduced to unsustainable levels. But what she didn't understand was how Frederick Philips fitted into this scenario. What had he done to contribute to the school's downfall and have the blame laid at his door?

As she mulled over the perplexity, she recalled something else the steward had mentioned, that one of the volunteers had been a pupil at the school at the time of its closure. And he, Esme remembered being told, was only on duty on Tuesdays. Tomorrow.

If she wanted to understand why the school's closure was of interest to Annie, as well as what Frederick Philips's role had been in its demise, perhaps it was time for a second visit.

# 59

'It's a must,' Maddy said at the market the next morning when Esme told her about the newspaper cutting and her intention of revisiting the school that afternoon. 'Get off as soon as it starts quietening down, if you like. I'll manage here.'

After grabbing a bite of lunch from the market café, Esme set of for Garter Abbey, promising to report back to Maddy as soon as she learned anything. It was an uneventful journey and she was soon pulling into the Trust car park. She locked the car and hurried towards the main building.

As she followed the wide path to the entrance, she pondered on what she was going to say to the former pupil steward, how to even begin the conversation. Perhaps he wouldn't know enough to be able to help her. Maybe he'd been too young to know what was really going on.

The woman steward with the billiard-ball necklace was not on the entrance desk on this occasion. It was manned by a smart young woman with a blonde ponytail, wearing a black shift dress. Esme explained that she'd been told one of the volunteers was a former pupil and was directed to the library down the corridor.

When Esme came into the room, the volunteer steward, a stocky man with a deeply furrowed face and skin like rawhide, was deep in conversation with a rotund elderly lady, an oversized shopping bag hanging from her arm. Esme ambled around the room, studying the bookshelves which mostly held faded leather-bound classics and encyclopaedias. Thin strands of clear nylon were strung across each shelf preventing over-inquisitive visitors from removing the books. She wondered if the displays had been recreated by the National Trust or whether they'd once belonged to the school. For some reason, it didn't feel like the library of a prestigious educational establishment, but that of an individual presenting his literary credentials to the world through an exhibition of his books.

Esme moved further along, crossing in front of the ornate fireplace. As she glanced up, she caught her breath as she found herself confronting a second portrait of Frederick Philips, peering down at her from above the mantelpiece. She glared back at him.

*What secrets do you hold?* she asked him silently.

Behind her, the conversation between the steward and the visitor drew to a close, thanks were expressed and the bag lady shuffled out of the room. Esme looked over her shoulder as the steward – Gordon Jenkins, according to his name badge – wandered over and stood beside her.

'One of our esteemed patrons,' he said, regarding the portrait thoughtfully, his arms folded across his body.

'Not so esteemed, from what I understand,' Esme said.

The steward looked round and raised a bushy grey eyebrow. 'That's a very curious remark?' he said.

Esme gestured back down the corridor towards the main hall. 'When I was here last time, the woman on the front desk said his hall portrait had been removed from the stairs and dumped in the attic. She seemed to think he may have blotted his copybook somehow.'

Jenkins gave a sardonic smile. 'A controversial figure, I think is how you might describe him. Probably a tad too evangelical for most, about both the views he held and the things which interested him. When he first became involved with the school, I imagine he'd fitted in quite well, but towards the end...' he shrugged. 'Whether that was a sign of the changing times or whether he got more entrenched as he got older, I couldn't say. He was into his eighties by the time the school closed, but was still actively involved.'

'Did you ever meet him? I understand you're a former pupil and were here at the time of the closure.'

Jenkins' mouth twisted into a moue. 'The governors and

patrons of the school had very little to do with the boys, certainly not the new entrants. I only joined the school a few months before the accident, you see, and it closed at the end of my second year.'

'You mean the drowning in the lake? I was reading about that.'

Jenkins nodded. 'A boy in the year above me.'

'It must have been a horrible shock for everyone,' Esme said. 'The suggestion was that the school's closure was connected with the accident.'

'Yes, I suppose it was, indirectly,' Jenkins said, tugging at his earlobe. 'Parents lost confidence in the school. Health and Safety, that sort of thing.'

'Except your colleague implied that the blame for the school's closure was laid elsewhere.' Esme peered up at Frederick Philips hanging on the wall. 'With this gentleman here, in fact. So why *is* that?' She turned to give Jenkins a scrutinising stare.

Jenkins shuffled his feet, the furrows on his face deepening. 'Have you a particular reason for your interest, Mrs…?'

'Quentin. Esme Quentin. I'm a genealogist. I've been researching the Philips family. Hence my interest in Frederick here. When I reported back to my client that their ancestor was seen as responsible for the school's demise, you can understand how we were intrigued.'

'Yes, perfectly understandable,' Jenkins agreed.

'Were you aware that his brother was hanged for murder in 1923?'

Jenkins looked shocked. 'Good God, no, I wasn't.'

Esme watched him. Perhaps her sharing the disclosure might put him in the right frame of mind to reciprocate.

'If it hadn't happened so long ago, I'd have assumed it was that which had upset the school governors.'

'Well, yes, I see your logic. Not a scandal the school would have wanted to be associated with.'

'No. Though he obviously weathered that particular storm.'

'So it would seem.'

Esme frowned as a disturbing idea jarred in her head. 'He wasn't somehow implicated in the drowning incident, was he?'

Jenkins shook his head. 'Not the way you think, no.'

'Meaning what, exactly?'

'I'm not saying he was directly responsible, that he pushed him under the water, or anything like that.'

'Then what *did* happen?'

'I don't know. I wasn't there.'

'But you have a theory,' Esme said, coaxing him. 'You were at the school at the time. You and your schoolmates would have talked about it, come to your own conclusions.'

Jenkins glanced over his shoulder, his body language oozing anxiety. 'Look,' he said, lowering his voice, 'we were just kids speculating. I haven't thought about it in 40-plus years.'

'The official line is the young lad went for a late-night swim on his own. Is that likely? Was he the adventurous sort to do something like that?'

Another shake of the head. 'No, quite the opposite, as I recall. In fact, he was a bit of a target, poor sod.'

'A target for bullies, you mean?'

This time, Jenkins nodded.

'Who was the bully? Frederick Philips?'

'No, not him,' Jenkins said, impatiently. 'Like I told you, he didn't have anything to do with the boys much. Other than his own family, of course. And that's where the trouble lay.'

Family. Esme flinched. Frank Stone. 'His great nephew attended the school, didn't he?' she said. 'Are you saying he was behind the bullying? And Frederick was blamed by association?'

'It may have been the last straw. There's only so much one can get away with, even if one's great-uncle is part of the school hierarchy.' Jenkins' troubled expression suggested he was undecided what more to say. Esme waited, her head inclined, her eyes focused on his face, hoping her eagerness to hear his story would prompt a disclosure.

After a few moments, Jenkins bent his head closer and again lowered his voice. 'There was a gang. *Blackbeard's Brothers* they called themselves. And Philips's little toe-rags were up to their necks in it.'

'Blackbeard?' Esme said. 'As in the notorious pirate?'

'That's right. Pirate obsessed, they were. You might think of it as amusing or quirky, but I can assure you it wasn't.'

A plethora of images flashed around in Esme's head as she grasped the implications of Jenkins' comments.

'They had this old boat they used to meet on,' he continued, his words coming out in a rush as though he was grateful for the release, for being given permission to unleash what he knew. 'Perhaps you've seen the remains of it, down on the lake.'

'Oh yes,' Esme said, nodding. 'I know where you mean.' She bit her lower lip. 'Is that where Anthony Milton died?'

Jenkins jerked his chin in acknowledgement. 'That's the assumption, yes. No doubt poor Tony had done something in the gang's eyes that deserved punishing. They were like that, you see. Saw themselves as gangsters of the high seas, preying on the weak and dishing out their warped version of justice.'

Esme shuddered, wondering what form of punishment poor Anthony Milton had endured. 'So, how many of them were in this gang?'

'About four or five, though it was really the self-appointed captain and his sidekick cousin who were the most obnoxious. The others just went along for the ride.' He scowled. 'Us younger boys kept our heads down as much as we could. If they came across you when you were on your own, that's when you were most at risk of being set upon.'

'And were the staff aware of what was going on?'

'If they were, they turned a blind eye. Even if they'd challenged Philips, he'd have given them short shrift. He was as infatuated by the subject of pirates as the gang, from what I heard. Saw it as all a bit of fun. Which is probably why the school took no action.

288

Until, of course, the gang went too far and Tony died.' Jenkins sighed. 'I often wonder what became of those tyrants.' He shook his head slowly and turned to look at Esme, his eyebrows raised. 'Perhaps in the course of your family history research, you might find them.' He gave her a sad smile. 'Though rather you than me. I'm not sure I'd ever want to come up against them again.'

# 60

Esme wandered back down the drive, digesting what Jenkins had told her. It was obvious this was an episode in Stone's life he didn't want to come to light, which explained why he was trying to stop Hester finding out when he insisted she leave Annie's research alone. And that made sense – Annie's research had led Esme here, hadn't it, given it was the newspaper cutting which prompted her to revisit the school. But how would Stone know it had been in Annie's files? And something else she still hadn't yet worked out – why was the incident of interest to Annie in the first place?

She came to a halt at the junction in the driveway, leading left back to the car park and right to the old farm buildings, beyond which was the lake. She found herself turning right, drawn to the site of Anthony Milton's drowning, heading across the yard to where the cobbles petered out into rough grassland and joining the hoggin path for visitors to explore the wider grounds and woodland beyond.

Being as it was midweek, visitors to Garter Abbey were few. The blustery weather, rain threatening on the horizon, had probably deterred many, so Esme met no one as she headed towards the small beach on the edge of the lake.

She stepped off the path and on to the rough grass, and wandered down to the water's edge. The wind was blowing across the lake, causing the surface to swell into an undulating mass and waves to spit on to the grassy beach. She stood on the shoreline as rain began falling from the dark clouds above, staring out to where the remains of Stone's pirate hideout sat half-submerged in the waters. The rotting boat lay menacingly in the shallows further along the shoreline. There must have been more of it still intact and sitting higher in the water forty years ago for it to be the gang's headquarters.

She turned away and pulled out her phone. Maddy had obviously been poised waiting for news, as she answered on the first ring. Esme relayed what Gordon Jenkins had told her.

'The younger boys were petrified of the gang,' Esme said. 'They seem to have had total autonomy to prowl around the place, terrorising whoever they came across.'

'Well, this *is* Frank Stone we're talking about,' Maddy said. 'Clearly he's never been any different.'

'And it makes perfect sense, too. As I found out right at the start, Stone's grandfather was Albert Philips, brother of Frederick and a descendent of Henry Venner, our infamous pirate.'

'Meaning Stone's also got pirate genes.'

'Clearly Frederick Philips was aware of his ancestral link to Henry Venner, as Jenkins said he was infatuated by the subject.' Esme stared out across the dark waters of the lake. 'I'm guessing he filled the head of his great nephew with all sorts of nonsense, which probably explains Stone's behaviour.'

'What I don't get,' Maddy said, 'is why Stone was fretting so much about Hester getting wind of his bad-boy schooldays. Knowing what he's like, you'd have thought he'd see it as a badge of honour. Proof not to mess with him.'

'Yes, I see your point. But it was definitely something in Annie's notes that made him nervous or why the crackdown on Hester? So if not this, what? We must be missing something.' Esme played Jenkins' words over again in her head. What had she overlooked?

The wisp of an idea floated into her brain, but it melted away as she became aware of someone walking across the grass towards her. She glanced up, catching her breath when she recognised who it was.

'Look,' she said to Maddy, conscious of her heart banging in her chest, 'I've got to go. I'll phone again later.' She cut the call and slipped the phone back into her bag before looping it over her shoulder. She clutched her fingers around the strap, her grip tightening as the newcomer came closer.

He stopped a short distance in front of her. 'Hello, Esme.'

Esme swallowed. 'Aidan.' Her memory slipped back to Lundy and Aidan's remark about pirates and addiction.

'I thought it must be you,' Aidan said. He thrust his hands deep into the pockets of his jacket, his expression serious. 'I guess you want to know what I'm doing here.'

# 61

Aidan sat opposite Esme at a table in the café, cradling a mug of coffee, his gaze lost in the middle distance through the window and across the grass under the apple trees. When she'd accused him of following her, he assured her he hadn't. But when she asked what had brought him to the school, she'd been horrified by his answer.

'Not what,' he'd said. 'Who.' He stared at her. 'Frank Stone.'

Esme's immediate impulse was to turn and run, but something about Aidan's demeanour stopped her. It was then she learned he'd come to the school for the same reason as she had – to speak to Gordon Jenkins in the search for answers. But it wasn't Aidan who'd been a former pupil, as she'd speculated to Maddy, but a relative of his who'd attended the school at the same time as Stone.

Esme reeled. 'Not Anthony Milton?' Her voice was barely a whisper.

Aidan shook his head. 'No, not him.'

Esme sipped her coffee and waited. After a while, Aidan dragged his eyes away from the orchard and looked down at his mug.

'I should explain, shouldn't I? My relative's called Ian Baxter,' he said. 'We might not be close on the family tree, but up until the age of eleven, we saw a lot of one another. My mum knew his from way back – second cousins or something – and when they met up, which they did often, so did me and Ian. I liked him. He was funny and imaginative. We used to have a lot of fun together. Then it all changed when we left primary school. He went off to Garter Abbey and I went to the local comprehensive.'

'So you didn't see one another after that?'

'Not really. From a distance at a couple of big family events, that sort of thing. But I was aware something had happened to him. Overheard muttered conversations between the adults which stopped the minute I came into the room, that sort of thing.' He looked up from his coffee and gave Esme a wry smile. 'You know what families are like.'

'And what *had* happened to him? Did you ever find out?'

Aidan shrugged. 'Not in so many words. All I knew back then was that it had something to do with an incident at the school which had seriously affected his state of mind.'

'We're talking about the drowning?'

'Yes, though I didn't know about it for years.'

'So how was Ian involved?' Esme asked.

'Anthony Milton was his best friend. He saw him drown.'

'Oh no, how terrible for him. That's horrible.'

Aidan stared down into his coffee. 'He suffered with nightmares, extreme anxiety, withdrawn behaviour. These days it would be recognised as Post Traumatic Stress Disorder. Back then the poor sod was told to "pull himself together". He became an embarrassment. Hence the whispered conversations. I'm sure if someone had chosen to get to the bottom of it, the truth would have come out and he might not have deteriorated in the way he did.'

'So what was your take on it?'

Another shrug. 'Well, I didn't really have an opinion to begin with. I mean, we don't, do we, as teenagers? We're too busy trying to get a handle on our own lives. It was just something the adults were wittering about behind their hands.'

'And later on?'

Aidan paused to take a sip of his drink. 'A few years back, Mum said something about Ian's mother struggling with the authorities over his care. I suddenly had an urge to understand and asked her to tell me the whole story. She was a bit dismissive to start with, but when I pressed her, she relented. Putting two and two together, it seems as though Ian said a lot more about what happened than anyone was prepared to admit at the time. I don't think they could handle it, to be honest. It was all too much, too fanciful for them to stomach.'

'Are we talking about the pirate gang, by any chance?'

Aidan looked at her, inclining his head. 'You knew about that?'

'No, not until I spoke to Mr Jenkins in there. But it fits in with something I found out yesterday.'

'Which was what?'

'I'll tell you later. Go on about Ian. You said Anthony Milton and he were best friends.'

Aidan nodded. 'That's right. They reckoned it was Tony's death which caused Ian's problems, that he'd found it hard to accept the loss of his friend.'

'Except it was more involved than that.'

'Yes, much more,' Aidan said. For a moment he was lost in his thoughts, before he looked at her intently across the table. 'He was there, Esme. He knew Tony's drowning wasn't an accident. He'd seen the gang tie him up and drag him under the boat.'

'What?' Esme gasped. 'They keelhauled him?'

'Yep,' Aidan said, a tone of bitterness in his voice. 'Unbelievable, isn't it?'

Esme shuddered at the image conjured up in her mind. There may have been no barnacles on the underside to scrape across the young boy's skin, as on a sea-going vessel, but there would have been rough timbers and rusting nails. The hapless child wouldn't have stood much chance of surviving his ordeal without injury, irrespective of whether he'd been able to hold his breath until the gang pulled him out at the other end.

'But surely there'd be evidence on his body that it hadn't been a simple drowning? Rope marks, or something.'

'You'd have thought so, wouldn't you? Maybe it was explained away, I don't know.'

'Jenkins said the other boys were terrified of the gang members,' Esme told him. 'They'd have been way too scared to stand up and accuse them of being involved.'

'Except Ian did and no one believed him. Pretty obvious why it wrecked his life. He never got over it.'

'And if there was a cover up by the adults, what was one young lad's testimony against that? They may have even threatened him to keep quiet. The poor lad.'

'And that's been the problem ever since. From when Mum first told me all about it, I've been trying to find out what went on, who was responsible. I've tracked down a fair few former pupils, but they've either refused to talk about it or claimed they knew nothing about it.'

'So did someone give you Frank Stone's name?' Esme asked.

'Yeah, as a possible pupil here. But it came with a health warning. So I decided to play the long game. Then I got wind of him turning up at Isaac's around the time I heard there was a job on offer. I've dived for Isaac before, so it all fell into place nicely.'

'So, have you said anything to Frank yet?' Perhaps the spat she'd seen between Aidan and Maudesley had been about Stone. Had Frank seen Aidan's interest as a threat and complained to Maudesley?

'Haven't had the chance. But I sounded out Isaac about it and he reckoned Frank was never at the school. For some reason, I didn't think he was being entirely honest.'

'He wasn't,' Esme said. 'Frank Stone was definitely a pupil here. His great-uncle was one of the school governors.' She leaned across the table. 'And given what I now know, I'm certain Stone was behind what went on.'

Aidan's face darkened. 'So it was actually Stone? He was the head of this pirate gang Jenkins was on about?' Esme nodded. He gave his head a shake. 'Sorry, Esme. It's hard to take it all in.'

'Did Jenkins tell you Frederick Philips, Stone's great-uncle, was as infatuated with the subject of pirates as his great-nephew?'

'No, he didn't. But perhaps having his ear bent twice in one day about what happened made him nervous and he decided he'd said enough.' Aidan took another sip of coffee and replaced the mug on the table. 'You said this fitted with something you'd found out yesterday.'

Esme nodded and explained about Henry Venner and his ancestral link to Stone. As she spoke, her mind drifted, imagining Stone tormenting his victims, spurred on by the knowledge of his pirate ancestor. Again the wisp of an idea came within grasp, but eluded her once more.

Aidan drummed his fingers on the table. 'I've often wondered whether in Ian's case it was that his family didn't believe him, or they didn't want to believe him. Because if they had, they'd have had to act on it, wouldn't they? And they were never going to do that. Not when the person responsible was a great-nephew of one of the school governors.'

'So what will you do?'

'Do?'

'About what you now know. Is there someone in your family you need to tell?'

'Not sure. I've been so long searching for the offender, I've never stopped to think what I'd do when I actually found him.' He downed his coffee and stood up.

'Where are you going?' Esme felt a stab of unease as Aidan pulled his jacket off the back of the chair. 'You're not thinking of confronting Frank Stone, are you?'

His face stretched into a sombre smile. 'You make that sound like a bad idea.'

'It *is* a bad idea.' Esme rubbed her hand across her forehead. 'Sorry, I didn't mean to sound as though I was issuing orders.' She looked up. 'In a way, I have a similar dilemma to you. I'm still reeling about what I've found out about Frank Stone and I'm not sure it answers the question I hoped it would.'

'What question?'

She gave her head a shake. 'It's complicated. But essentially, it's to do with the way Stone's behaving towards Hester. You know Hester, don't you?'

'Yes, I know Hester. So what are you saying?'

Esme put her palms together, resting her hands on the table. 'There's something that connects Stone's family history and Hester's, something we sense could be a threat to him.' She glanced up at Aidan, throwing out her arm in the direction of the main school. 'I don't understand the significance of what happened here, not yet anyway, but if I'm to find out, I don't want Frank Stone to know I'm looking. At the moment, he thinks Hester's left it alone.'

'And you think me challenging Stone will blow your cover.'

'Something like that, yes.'

Aidan gripped the back of the chair. 'Look,' he said, gently, 'Stone and I haven't crossed paths yet. And there's no reason why we'll need to.'

Esme nodded, reassured. 'Thanks. I appreciate it.'

Aidan gave her a cryptic smile. 'Not until I've had time to fully process what I've learned, anyway.'

\*

Esme drove back home in a state of disquiet. As she'd ambiguously explained to Aidan, confirmation that Stone had a violent side and was obsessed with pirates did little to address the core question of why he was so against Hester pursuing her family history. Neither was she sure it gave Hester anything to use to make Stone back off. There was still something bugging her about what she'd learned today and she couldn't put her finger on what it was. Perhaps it would come to her later.

Meanwhile, she hoped Aidan would be true to his word and not seek out Stone to confront him about the trauma his distant cousin Ian had suffered. But he'd also let her know there may be a time limit on his restraint. If she was to solve the mystery, she may not have long left to do so.

# 62

Esme knelt down on a mat on the edge of her narrow lawn in her garden and thrust a trowel into the flower border to lever out a large primrose plant. She laid it down on the top of the soil and teased it apart into smaller plantlets, replanting one section in the garden before nestling the resulting offspring into a tray of compost to take over to Maddy's on Friday for her courtyard garden.

There was something soothing about the task – getting her hands dirty, the earthy smell and the pleasure of being outside on a morning which had dawned as the epitome of the perfect April day. She defied anyone not to wallow in the blue sky, the gentle warmth and the sense of freshness of such a spring atmosphere.

It was also the ideal setting to analyse everything she'd learned the day before and what significance she should make of Stone's misguided youth. It wasn't as if it came as any surprise, Max had already warned her at the outset. It was, however, ironic that she'd deliberately tried to distance herself from Max's investigation, believing anything associated with him was bad news, but she'd still ended up having to negotiate Frank Stone. Albeit covertly – thankfully.

The sound of the latch of the garden gate broke into her thoughts and she turned as a figure came up the stone steps, heading for the front door. Esme scrambled to her feet.

'Hester,' she said, pulling off her gardening gloves and throwing them down on to the grass. 'What are you doing here? Is everything all right?'

Hester spun round, startled. 'Oh, Esme,' she said, shaking her head. 'I hope you don't mind me turning up unannounced. I tried to phone, but…' she shrugged.

'Sorry,' Esme said, crossing the lawn. 'I must have been too engrossed to hear it ring. Come on in.' She pushed open the door for Hester before levering off her Wellington boots and following her inside. 'Tea? Coffee?' she said, padding over to the kitchen to put on the kettle.

'Yes, tea would be lovely, thank you.'

'Take a seat,' Esme said, filling the kettle. 'Then you can tell me what's happened. Has Aidan spoken to you?' she added, flicking the switch and reaching for two mugs and the teapot.

'Aidan? Why would he?'

'Oh, just a thought. Look, forget that for a moment. Let's get to why you're here.'

Hester slumped down on to a chair, dropping her elbows on to the kitchen table and her chin into her hands. 'They've sold me down the river, Esme.'

'Who have?'

'Frank and Isaac. They've cancelled my project.'

'What? They can't do that!'

'They can and there's not a bloody thing I can do about it. I'm being redeployed back to Bristol.'

'But why?'

'Because it's what Frank wants, of course.' Hester sat back in her chair, her arms crossed. 'I've been outmanoeuvred, Esme. Well and truly sunk.' She gave a short, humourless laugh. 'No pun intended.'

Esme poured boiling water into the teapot, before taking it along with the mugs over to join Hester at the table. 'So, what did he say?' she asked, sitting down. 'How did you find out? Have you spoken to Isaac?'

'Oh, don't think for a minute that Isaac's in the dark on this and Frank is operating under the radar. Far from it. Isaac admitted it. He said when Frank proposed it, he thought it was a brilliant idea – a no-brainer, he called it.' She pressed her lips together. 'He might have mentioned it to me, the lying, two-faced…'

'So, what are we talking about?' Esme said. 'I'm not quite clear what they've done.'

'I told you. Cancelled my project. Yes, there's to be a museum, but it's going to be Frank who's in charge now, not me.'

'But Frank doesn't have the expertise on your Chalacombe family and all the history of the ports of Appledore and Bideford. They need you, surely?'

Hester looked up at Esme, a weary expression of desperation on her face. 'Esme, it's no longer going to be about my family and North Devon maritime history. It centres around a baseless fantasy about a lost ship and...' she clicked her tongue and sighed, turning away and glaring sightlessly towards the window. 'I find it hard to even bring myself to say it, it's so ridiculous.'

'Is this about Frank's fascination for pirates?'

Hester's head shot round. 'You know about that?'

'I only found out yesterday.' Esme wondered if it was the time to explain about meeting Aidan and his part in the story, but decided against it. That would be better coming from Aidan himself.

'Yesterday?' Hester echoed. 'So, what happened yesterday?'

Esme lifted the lid of the teapot and stirred the brew. 'I was following up on something in your great-aunt's notes.'

Hester's face creased into an expression of confusion. 'Which notes?' Her hand flew to her lips. 'Oh, you mean her cryptic comment about William Chalacombe's will. You've read it?'

'Yes, that's what led me to discovering Frank's infatuation.' Esme picked up the pot and poured out the tea into the mugs. 'The will mentioned William's nephew, Henry Venner. He was disinherited, partly because of turning to piracy. Henry Venner is a direct ancestor of Frank Stone.' She pushed a mug towards Hester. 'And Frank seems to have developed an obsession with the whole idea.'

Hester nodded, vigorously. 'Yes, yes, it's exactly that. He's completely fixated by it. He told me all about this Henry Venner character, and how he was a descendant. I thought maybe he'd

301

made the whole thing up.'

'From what I've discovered,' Esme said, 'this is not a new fetish. He headed a nasty little pirate gang when he was at school and Maddy's convinced he's behind the theft of a wooden sea chest which she bought at that auction, you remember? Stone had intended to buy it, but he was late for the sale.'

'A sea chest?' Hester said. 'With Henry Venner's initials on?'

'Yes, how did you know?'

Hester snorted. 'Frank told me about that. He's convinced it's going to lead him to the discovery of Henry's hoard of gold, which went down with his ship.'

'What?' Esme laughed. 'A pirate treasure map? He's not serious.'

Hester shrugged. 'He wouldn't be the first fanatic who's convinced there's pirate treasure out there to find. There are still people actively searching for the so-called lost hoard of the infamous Captain Kidd. As recently as 2015, an American explorer claimed the gold bar he'd recovered was Kidd's.'

'And was it?'

'Not according to UNESCO. They dismissed it as highly unlikely. So, you see,' Hester leaned across the table towards Esme, 'Frank thinks he's got everything in place to locate the treasure. In fact, he's claiming he and Isaac already know where it is. And when they recover it, he'll then lay claim to it as Henry's descendant and it'll form the centrepiece of this madcap pirate museum they've got in mind.' Hester gave Esme a cynical look. 'I suspect he also sees it as his way to become a very rich man.'

So that's why Aidan had been employed, to facilitate the dive. Did he know more than he'd implied yesterday? Stone's schoolboy obsession seemed to come as a surprise, and yet comments he'd made to Esme on Lundy Island about addiction and pirate fantasy suggested otherwise.

She turned to Hester. 'Are you sure Isaac's completely behind this?' she asked.

'What do you mean? I've already told you he's endorsed it.'

'Yes, but perhaps he's had no choice.' Esme folded her arms. 'Look, when all this started out, Max sensed Frank had something on Isaac, that he was using it to get his own way.'

Hester shook her head. 'You didn't see him, Esme. Isaac was almost as passionate about it as Frank. I can't honestly believe he'd be like that if he wasn't fully on board with the whole idea. I'm sure I'd have some sense that he was playing a part, but he wasn't.'

Esme bit her lip. 'I know it wasn't what you wanted to happen, Hester, but you have to admit the public would love it. And Henry Venner's mother was a Chalacombe, so not only have you got your own family claim to him, there'll still be a place for the Chalacombe story, which you can be a part of.'

Hester turned to look at her, a dejected expression on her face. 'I don't think so, Esme. I agree with you, the pirate theme would be really popular and a great way to engage people in history. I'm not against that, far from it. After all, it's what I believe in. But I'm not being *allowed* to be a part of it. Frank's making sure of it. And what hurts the most is Isaac's letting it happen, after all our collaborations over the years.'

'Then embrace it, make it yours too. Don't let Frank elbow you out.'

Hester's eyes narrowed. 'You seriously think I could stay involved by working with him?'

Esme sighed and wrapped her hands around her mug. 'I'm sorry. I know what this meant to you. And no, of course I see what you mean. I can't say I'd relish the idea of working with Frank Stone either.'

Esme took a sip of tea, frustrated by Hester's situation – having such a dream which now represented only disappointment and betrayal. What was she missing here? Something wasn't right. And it went further than Hester being ousted from her project.

'So, what are you going to do?' she asked.

Hester shrugged. 'What *can* I do?' She looked at Esme over the rim of her mug, her expression curious. 'Should I speak to Max again, d'you think?'

'Max?'

'You said he had a theory that Frank's using something to lord it over Isaac. Maybe he's found out what?'

'I suppose it's possible. Though he'd have been in touch, wouldn't he?' Esme wondered fleetingly whether what she'd learned would be useful to Max. And more importantly, what he knew and what she knew might combine to offer a chance to help Hester. But having managed to steer clear of him, did she really want to get involved all over again?

Hester stared into her mug. 'I was just thinking where this all started. It was Max who suggested I engaged you to dig into Frank Stone's family history, remember.'

Esme nodded. 'I know, and I feel bad that despite everything we've learned, Frank Stone's still making your life miserable.' She reached out and squeezed Hester's hand. 'Look, I know you've already spoken to Isaac and got nowhere, but what if you took a different tack? Use all that shared history you spoke of and take the softly-softly approach. If Frank really does have a hold over him, Isaac might welcome someone to confide in.'

Hester nodded. 'Yes, I think you're probably right. I have to admit, this isn't Isaac's style. It's not that he'd be against the idea in itself, it's just…' she shook her head. 'I don't know. I can't put my finger on it. But something's not right.'

# 63

When Esme saw Max's name come up on the screen of her phone the following day, her first thought was that Hester had made the decision to contact him following their conversation. She hoped what they'd discussed hadn't given Max the idea that Esme was now willing to get involved. Her second thought, more alarming, was that he was following up on his email, which she'd never read and deleted in a fit of pique.

'Hello, Max,' Esme said, bracing herself. 'How's things?' She stopped herself just in time from saying, *what can I do for you?*

'Oh, you know. Could be better.'

'You're never satisfied, Max,' Esme joked. 'That's your problem.'

'Wouldn't be doing my job properly if I was. Hey, I was wondering if you'd turned up anything interesting at your end in the family history department?'

Esme wandered out into the garden through the open front door. 'I'm always turning up interesting things in the family history department, Max. It *is* my job, after all.' Perhaps Hester had decided against speaking to him and it didn't sound as though he was phoning to ask about his email. Maybe she'd got away with it.

Max laughed. 'Mmm, that's an evasive answer if ever I heard one.'

Esme giggled. 'Just stating the obvious, Max. Have you phoned to tell me something?'

'I'm hoping it'll be the other way round. Have you come across anything about a ring?'

Esme dropped down on to the bench on the edge of the lawn. 'A ring?'

'Yes, one of those things people wear on their fingers. You

might have seen them.'

'Oh, very funny. You know what they say about sarcasm, don't you?'

Max chuckled. 'So, you have come across a ring, then? Oh, come on, Ez,' he said, when she didn't respond, 'we both know if you hadn't, you've have said something like, *no, why?*'

Esme sighed, wishing he didn't know her as well as he did. 'OK, you win. Yes, there was a ring in the story. A Claddagh ring. Passed down the female line. But I don't know where it is now. I'm not sure anyone knows.'

'No, seems not. Stone doesn't, that's for sure.'

'Stone?'

Another mocking chuckle. 'Ah, that got you pinning back your ears, didn't it?'

Esme clicked her tongue. 'Stop twisting things to suit your agenda, Max. I was thinking of Hester, that's all. So, how d'you know Stone's interested?' Should she tell Max about Maddy's missing box and their suspicion Stone was the thief? Another connection?

'He's been asking around amongst dealers, so I hear.'

Something clicked in Esme's head. 'Oh, wait a minute. This doesn't have anything to do with why you were at the *Antiques Roadshow*, by any chance?' she said. 'You and Hester were right next to the expert talking about a Claddagh ring when I spotted you in the crowd.'

Max mumbled something under his breath.

Now it was Esme's time to chuckle. 'Oh, you didn't know?' she teased. 'You're losing your touch, Max.'

'Easy enough to join the dots now, isn't it? Led me a right merry dance, he did.'

'You were following him?'

'Thought I might learn what he was up to. Missed that one, though.'

'And what about Hester? Was she trailing him, too?'

'No, of course not. She was just visiting. I didn't even know she'd be there.'

'So, you've given up on Isaac Maudesley, now, have you,' Esme said, 'and got your sights on Stone instead?

'Oh, you know how these things work, Ez. Stone could be my way in. So, come on. Give me a break. You must have something on him.'

'I already told you about his link to the 1923 murder and you weren't interested.'

'Forget 1923, I'm talking about the here and now.'

Esme rubbed a finger down her scar. 'For what it's worth, I *can* tell you Stone has got a fixation on an ancestor of his, Henry Venner, who was a Barbary pirate, apparently. Hester seems to think he's got this crazy idea there's the stereotypical map with a cross on it out there somewhere, marking where the treasure's buried. Of course, we both think he's off his trolley.'

Max grunted. 'Nice one. If you find this stash before he does, you'll cut me in, won't you?'

Esme grinned. 'Of course, Max. You'll be the first to know.'

'Interesting about the Barbary connection, though.'

'Oh, that's right,' Esme said, recalling something Max had mentioned a while ago. 'You said Maudesley had spent a lot of time in the Med and Morocco in his youth, Stone too.'

'Yeah, they did. But I was thinking of something else. To do with this ring Stone's searching for.'

'Seems to me like another indication that Stone's losing his mind,' Esme said. 'There must be thousands of Claddagh rings out there, what chance does he stand of finding the actual one which belonged to the family?' She thought back to the image of the ring in the photograph and on the postcard of the painting. 'It's quite old, so that might narrow it down a bit, I suppose.'

'There's also an inscription on the inside.'

'That would help,' Esme conceded. 'What's the inscription say?'

'Ah, that no one knows. Not even Stone, it seems.'

'Well, then. Ditto my earlier comment, what chance does he stand of finding the ring that belonged to his family?'

'Thing is, Ez, it's not so much what it *says* as what it *is*.'

'You've lost me, Max. What are you saying?'

'And ditto *my* earlier comment,' Max said, 'about the Barbary connection.'

Esme sighed. 'OK, Max. I admit it. You've got me intrigued. Now spit it out.'

'The inscription is written in Arabic.'

# 64

After she'd cut Max's call, Esme stayed on the garden bench, turning over in her mind what he had said and realising his question had inadvertently given her a more tangible connection between Annie and Frank Stone. The ring. Annie had been wearing the ring up until she died, when it went missing. How it had gone missing, no one was sure, but the likely scenario was that it slipped from Annie's finger and had been lost. What happened to it after that was anyone's guess. Clearly Frank Stone didn't have it or he wouldn't be looking for it. So why did he want it so badly?

Perhaps Stone's search for the ring was prompted by his intention to bring it back into his side of the family. If he'd been close to his great-uncle Frederick, he could have adopted the same distorted view, championing Albert's brutal deed to return the ring to – in his eyes – its rightful place, believing Ernest's fate was the justified payment for his actions. Perhaps he merely intended to continue his great-uncle's quest.

She gave her head a shake, dismissing the theory as implausible. Everything she'd gleaned about Stone characterised someone whose actions were driven by what would benefit himself and nothing to do with family honour.

As Esme stood up to go back inside, it struck her that Stone's fixation on the ring mirrored the one he had for Maddy's trunk. Hester had said Stone believed the sea chest was the key to his finding Henry Venner's treasure. Did he see the ring in a similar light? Was the Arabic inscription another clue to where Henry had hidden his gold?

*

Maddy had earmarked a patch in her back garden for Esme's donated primroses. She led Esme around the modest-sized outside space, enthusing about her plan to create a wildlife-friendly cottage-style garden, filled with a mixture of cultivated plants and wildflowers to attract bees and butterflies. As they knelt down and got underway with the planting, Esme told her about Max's phone call regarding the ring.

Maddy sat back on her heels, her trowel in her hand and a wary expression on her face. 'Whatever happened to, *I won't need to have anything more to do with the man?*'

Esme stabbed at the soil, avoiding Maddy's eyes. '*He* phoned *me*, not the other way round.' She stopped digging and looked up. 'Well, it's difficult to ignore, though, isn't it? There's a direct link with Annie. I'm thinking of your stolen sea chest too, here,' Esme continued. 'We always said solving one side of the equation might help solve the other.'

'Yes, except we've solved that now. Hester's told you why Stone was so desperate to get hold of it. It contains the blueprint to his getting rich.' Maddy looked sceptical. 'If we can believe that.'

'Maybe,' Esme said, as the thought suddenly occurred to her, 'he didn't find a map in the trunk and has switched his focus to the ring.'

'Or,' Maddy said, giggling as she picked up on the theme, 'the map contains a riddle which only the message in the ring can answer, so he needs both.'

Esme grinned. 'I know, it does rather reek of the fanciful, but Hester assures me it's not as unusual as you think. Who doesn't love a finding-treasure story?'

'So, what does Hester make of it? Have you spoken to her?'

Esme picked up a plant and sat it in the hole she'd just dug, pulling the soil around it and firming it in. 'She didn't know of any inscription, but she thought her mum might. She's going to get Pat to give me a call.'

Maddy moved a little further along, pulling the tray of primroses closer as she went. 'How likely is it that it's the same ring?'

'I suppose that depends on what Pat says about any inscription. When the ring went missing around the time of Annie's death, Pat tentatively suggested to the police that it had been stolen, but the final conclusion was it must have slipped off Annie's finger at some point while she'd lain outside in the cold.'

'So it's perfectly possible that someone might have found it at a later date,' Maddy suggested, dropping back to her knees.

'Which brings us back to your sea chest.'

'Does it? How?'

'Something we talked about before, about someone else in the family wanting the chest. Except, unlike the sea chest, no one knows where the ring is.'

'So Stone's worried someone will get to the ring first?' Maddy shrugged. 'Like who?'

'Like someone else in the family who thinks it should have come their way.'

'Anyone in mind?'

'Not yet,' Esme admitted. 'I need to study the family tree, see what other route the ring might have taken had Ernest not intervened.'

They continued to dig and plant in silence, lost in their own private thoughts.

'I'm not going to get my sea chest back, am I?' Maddy said, after a while. 'I'm going to have to write it off to experience.'

Esme looked up. 'But you didn't want to do that.'

'Yes, I know I didn't. And I still don't. But with this Frank Stone character hiding in the shadows, Max reappearing out of the woodwork...'

'But it's only right you get your stolen property back. All we're doing is looking for evidence to tie Stone to the theft.'

'We've done that, in theory, but it doesn't feel like it's likely to get us any further than we are already.' Maddy reached over to pick up another plant, glancing at Esme with a troubled expression. 'I was thinking last night about everything you told me about Stone and his schooldays. I mean, do I want to go there? And now Max is back on the scene, or worse, still digging in the same muddy pool as you are.'

Esme's face folded into a frown. 'You make it sound like I'm going to go round to Stone and challenge him. I have no intention of doing anything other than giving him a very wide berth.'

'And Max?'

Esme shrugged. 'Well, that depends, doesn't it? All he did was ask a question I wasn't able to answer. If either of us comes across anything useful, then we'll pass it on. It's not exactly life-threatening, is it?'

Maddy stood up and picked up the watering can. 'Just be careful, that's all I'm saying.'

# 65

That evening, Esme found herself revisiting the discussion she'd had with Maddy about Stone's interest in the ring and who else in the family might be just as keen to get hold of it. Perhaps it explained Stone's urgency, if he feared they'd track it down before he did.

Esme opened up her laptop, wondering if anything in the file she'd compiled on Frank Stone suggested who that individual might be. She'd already worked out from tracking through the generations how Betsy Philips, Ernest's mother, had come to have the ring. How might it have been passed on had Ernest not given it to Annie?

Esme opened the file and studied the family tree. Frederick Philips, Garter Abbey School's controversial trustee, had never married or had any family, but his brother Albert, before his crime and subsequent execution, had married Hannah Jones and had become the father of twins, Alice and Bradley. As Esme had explained to Pat, Alice would have expected to inherit the ring from her aunt, Betsy, being the first girl of the next generation.

As Esme stared at the tree, she realised she'd never explored Bradley. While the ring would have ordinarily passed to Alice as Betsy's niece, she would only go on to have a son, the odious Frank Stone. So, who in the female line might she have passed the ring on to, had she inherited it? Perhaps, like Betsy, she had a niece. Perhaps Bradley Philips had married and had a girl. Maybe that side of the family had their sights on the elusive ring, and that was what was worrying Frank.

Her phone broke into her thoughts and she cringed when she saw Max's name come up on the screen. Now what? Maddy's words of caution reverberated in her head as she picked up the handset and made the connection.

'Hi, Max. I haven't heard anything back yet about the inscription,' she babbled in an attempt to get rid of him. Why did she have this uncomfortable feeling she'd been caught in the act? She wasn't pursuing any other line of enquiry of interest to Max.

'That's OK. That's not why I'm phoning.'

'Oh? Then what?'

'Wondered if you'd had a chance to follow up on my email yet?'

'Email?' she said, playing for time. So, she hadn't got away with it after all. She should have known it would come up eventually.

'Yeah, sent it about a week ago. Bit longer, maybe. Did you look at it?'

She chewed her lower lip. 'Sorry, Max. I've not seen it.' Well, that was true, at least.

'I'll send it again. Can you take a look and get back to me?'

Apprehension settled in the pit of her stomach. 'Look, Max, what's this about? I'm right in the middle of some research.'

'Oh, just something I could do with you checking out, that's all. My excuse of a researcher can't seem to get past his mother.'

'His mother?'

'Yeah, Maudesley's.'

'Oh, hang on, Max. You can stop right there. Maudesley's your bag, not mine.'

'Thing is, see,' Max continued, as if she'd not spoken, 'he reckons he's hit a brick wall. Couldn't find Maudesley's birth record. Reckons his mother'd been married before and, well, not to put too fine a point on it, he's out of his depth. You're so good at this sort of stuff, Ez. It'd probably take you five minutes.'

'Flattery will get you absolutely nowhere, you know that, don't you?' Esme said, sitting back and crossing an arm across her body.

'Oh, go on, Ez. Take a look, will you? Please?'

Esme felt herself smiling. 'That sounds like someone trying to be very nice and desperately stopping themselves slipping into begging mode.'

Max laughed. 'I have no idea what you mean, Ez. So, am I in luck? Do you think you could just do a quick check?'

'Oh, all right,' she said, sighing. 'I'll give it half an hour. But that's all, mind. If you don't hear from me, it's because I've nothing to report, OK?'

'This is great stuff, Ez. Thanks. I owe you.'

'Yes, you certainly do,' Esme said. 'I'll bill you later. So, have you got any info to give me a head start? Date of birth, parents, siblings?'

'I'll re-send the email. There's everything in it, plus a photo of him at his graduation.'

'OK. I'll see what I can do.'

'Great. I'll give you a call when I get back from Lundy tomorrow.'

'You're going to Lundy? Why?'

'Just following up on a lead.'

'On Isaac Maudesley, of course.'

'Yeah, that's it. Look, I've got to make another call. Speak soon.'

Esme cut the connection and turned back to her laptop with a sigh. What did she think she was doing, agreeing to do Max's bidding? She needed her head testing. She looked at her watch. Well, she'd said she'd give it half an hour and that's what she'd do.

Max's email pinged into her inbox, containing, as he had promised, Maudesley's basic information. Born 1966. Father Daniel, a civil servant; mother Susan with her own small business. Brother Leslie and sister Helen. In the graduation photograph, Maudesley was standing between a middle-aged couple dressed for a special occasion. He was wearing a cap and gown. All of them were smiling broadly into the camera. The caption read, *Isaac Maudesley with Daniel and Susan Maudesley.*

Esme put on her reading glasses and opened up *Ancestry*. She entered the name Isaac Maudesley and his year of birth, 1966, clicked on the search button and waited. The screen refreshed to declare no matches.

Perhaps he was lying about his age. She adjusted the date for a wider sweep, but got the same result. Could be a transcription error.

She changed tack, starting with his parents, altering the name on the form on her laptop screen to Daniel and the date of birth to make him between 20 and 30 years older than Isaac. This time, the page filled with potential hits. Her eye caught a marriage record and when she clicked on it, the details showed the spouse's name as Susan Brickell. The location fitted, as it was a Bath wedding, though the dates would mean Maudesley was born before they married. Perhaps that's why he'd not shown up previously.

Perhaps it was worth trying another angle. She opened up *FreeBMD*, the database set up by volunteers to give free access for family historians to search births, marriages and deaths, and navigated to the search page. If she put in the surname and mother's maiden name and an appropriate date range, all the births of their children should show up. She filled in the names Maudesley and Brickell, selected 1965, the year before the couple's wedding, through to 1975 to ensure a wide coverage. The screen flickered and brought up its findings.

Two names appeared. Helen Maudesley, born 1967, and Leslie Maudesley, born 1969. So where was Isaac? At least it suggested her supposition was correct, that Isaac was born before his parents married and was adopted by Daniel, when he took his stepfather's name. If Susan had had Isaac before she married, his birth would have been recorded under Brickell.

But there was no Isaac Brickell of the right age. Perhaps, as Max had suggested, Susan had been married before, and changed her name back to her maiden name before marrying Daniel, meaning Maudesley's birth would be registered under her previous husband's name.

Esme returned to the screen and began again with Susan

316

Brickell, entering the details into the relevant fields, including a timeframe based on what she already knew, and clicking the search button. The screen refreshed, but after she'd scrolled down the first few on the list, it was clear the options had been exhausted, as no more Susans appeared next to the name Brickell. By the bottom of the page, the name Brickell was being replaced by names like Brickwell, Brickhill and Rockwell.

Did that mean Susan hadn't been married before? Or that she'd been known by a name other than Susan at the time? That the record was missing? Esme shrugged. Well, if it wasn't there, it wasn't there. She'd wasted enough time on it as it was. She was keen to get back to her search for Bradley Philips's marriage and discover whether he'd had any girls who Frank Stone saw as potential competitors for getting hold of the ring. She'd drop Max an email later to let him know she'd hit a blank and to tell him off, too, for being so critical of his young researcher who'd clearly had the same fruitless search as she had.

As Esme switched back to her previous search, her phone rang. Esme assumed it was Max again, checking in to see what she'd found out. Perhaps what he was hoping to discover was pertinent to his trip to Lundy. Her reproach about his being overly critical of his unfortunate young researcher was on her lips until she saw the caller wasn't Max, but Pat.

'Pat, hi. You got my message.'

'Yes, I did. Sorry I haven't got back to you sooner, Esme. It's been one thing after another, you know how it is.'

'No, that's not a problem. I just need to check something with you. It's been mentioned there may have been an inscription on Annie's ring. Hester didn't know and thought you might.'

'You've found it?' Pat said, excitement in her voice.

'Sadly not,' Esme said, despondent at not having better news. 'But if the ring did have an inscription, it might help us track it down more easily.'

'Yes, that does make sense. But I'm afraid I can't help you

there. I never saw the ring other than on Auntie's finger. Certainly if it did have anything written inside, she never said.' She sighed down the phone. 'I wish I could help, Esme, but I just don't know.'

'No, don't worry. It was only a thought.'

'So, how are you getting on with it all? Hester's trip at the weekend sounds interesting, doesn't it?'

'Her trip?'

'Yes, to Lundy. Did she not say?'

'Lundy?' Esme said. 'No, she never mentioned it.'

'Oh, I assumed she'd have told you,' Pat was saying. 'She is quite excited about it.'

'Sorry, Pat,' Esme said, as theories rattled around her head. 'Do you know why Hester is going to Lundy?'

'I'm not absolutely sure, to be honest. Something about the hotel, I think. But I didn't think there was a hotel there any more?'

'No, there isn't,' Esme said. 'But I'm sure she'll report back if she finds anything interesting.'

'Yes, of course she will.'

Esme cut the call and sat back in her chair. What had Hester discovered? And why hadn't she been in touch? *Should I speak to Max again, d'you think?* Hester had asked only two days ago. So, was she meeting him there? Was that her real reason for going? Why hadn't Max said anything? To deliberately keep Esme in the dark? But why?

# 66

Maddy's expression exactly reflected the irritation Esme felt as she relayed the events of the previous evening while they set up at the market the following morning.

'Oh, that's just typical of Max Rainsford,' Maddy said. 'Get his pound of flesh by coercing you to do his research for him, and then not being straight with you.'

'And to add insult to injury,' Esme complained, 'what he wanted me to do was a complete waste of time. I didn't have a chance to get back to our ring query and look at who else might have their sights on it. By the time I'd spoken to Pat, and then tried to get hold of Hester...' she pulled a face. 'Well, I was so annoyed, I just wasn't in the mood, to be honest.'

'And you've still not got hold of Hester, I take it?'

Esme shook her head. 'No. Just goes to voicemail.'

'Too much of a coincidence, though, isn't it? Max on Lundy. Hester on Lundy.'

Esme folded her arms, a grim expression on her face. 'I mean, Max had every opportunity to tell me on the phone last night and chose not to.' She sniffed. 'So I didn't bother to email him to tell him I'd come to the same conclusion as his researcher. He can come running.'

'Well, I understand how you feel. You've been here before, haven't you, when Hester wasn't being straight with you?' Maddy slid an empty cardboard box underneath their market stall and stood upright. 'So, what are you going to do?'

Esme narrowed her eyes. 'Meet them off the Lundy boat tonight and confront them,' she said. 'It's about time they came clean about exactly what's going on.'

*

Esme parked her car and wandered back along the edge of the estuary towards the office of MS *Oldenburg,* just as the ship pulled in alongside the quay. She stopped to watch as the crew moored up and dragged the gangway into position, standing back out of the way as the passengers handed in their boarding discs and filed across to terra firma, dispersing in different directions. Some looked tired after their trip to the island, others energised, chatting excitedly between themselves, laughing and sharing the events of their day.

The procession of passengers thinned until Esme could see only the crew on deck, a couple chatting and joking, another organising what Esme assumed must be Lundy's mail. But she could see no sign of Hester or Max. Perhaps they were inside the cabin talking to one of the staff, following up on the lead Max mentioned during his call. Neither of them knew she was waiting as she'd purposely not let them know of her intention to meet them off the boat, in order to catch them unawares.

She crossed over the gangway bridge and on to the deck. A crew member gathering up a rope looked up.

'Can I help you, love?' he said.

'Are all the passengers off?' Esme said, walking over to him. 'I was expecting friends.'

The guy shrugged. 'I think everyone's disembarked,' he said, scanning around as though pointing out the evidence. 'Maybe they missed the sailing?'

Esme nodded. 'Maybe they did,' she said. 'Thanks. I'll give them a call.'

She returned to the quay and pulled out her phone. Who to phone first – Hester or Max? She tried Hester's number but, as before, it went straight to voicemail. She severed the connection and scrolled down to find Max's details. As she stabbed the screen and put her phone to her ear, she saw a figure coming across the gangway. She cut the call and hurried over just as Max stepped on to the quay. He was better dressed than the last time she'd seen him, having clearly abandoned his down-and-out persona, wearing black jeans and a grey waterproof jacket. A day-pack was slung over his shoulder.

'Esme,' he said, jerking back. 'What are you doing here?'

'Where's Hester?' Esme said, looking behind him along the gangway and beyond on to the boat deck.

'Hester?' Max said, following Esme's line of sight. 'What makes you think Hester was with me?'

Esme scowled. 'Don't come the innocent with me. She was on Lundy today, too. She contacted you, didn't she? She'd been debating about getting in touch with you.'

Max took Esme's arm and steered her away from the boat. 'Ez, I have no idea what you're talking about. Hester hasn't been in touch and I've not seen her. If she was on the boat earlier, I must have missed her. That's if she was there.'

'Her mum said she was going over to check something out.'

'Check what out?'

Esme shook her head. 'No idea. I didn't even know she was going.'

'Maybe she changed her mind. Give her a call.'

'I did, but she's not picking up.'

'Well, can't help you then.'

'So, what are we going to do?'

'Do?' Max shrugged. 'About what? You can't say for certain she actually went. So until you're sure, we'd be wasting our time.' He checked his watch. 'Besides, I haven't got time. I need to be somewhere.' He began walking away along the quay.

'Not yet, you don't,' Esme said, scurrying to catch up and fall in step alongside him. 'You haven't told me what you were doing on the island. And,' she added, pausing for emphasis, 'you haven't asked me whether I dug up anything of interest on Maudesley.'

That got his attention. He jerked his head around to look at her. 'You found something?'

'I might have done,' Esme said, pleased to have a hold over him for a change. She thrust her hands into the pockets of her coat, staring ahead as she struggled to keep up with Max's strides. 'Perhaps we should trade. You tell me what you were doing on Lundy and I'll tell you what I've got.'

Max faltered, stopping abruptly on the pavement. 'You found something? That's great, Ez, you clever girl.'

'I do have my uses,' she said, enjoying her private joke.

'So spit it out,' Max said, as they resumed walking. 'What ya' got?'

'Not so fast. You first. What were you doing on Lundy?'

'I met up with Maudesley.'

'Maudesley? Not Hester?'

'Hey, what is it with you? I already said I didn't meet Hester, didn't I?'

'Yes, you did. OK, if you're adamant that's true, I believe you.'

They arrived at the car park and Max stopped at a dark grey Ford Puma parked beside a concrete container filled with hyacinth bulbs, their perfume making Esme feel giddy. Max pulled a key fob from his jacket pocket and unlocked the car with the customary clunk, opening the rear door and throwing his backpack on to the seat.

He looked round at Esme. 'So, aren't you interested in what Maudesley said?'

Esme swallowed. 'I don't know,' she said, suddenly aware of the black hole of a trap opening up in front of her. 'I was never digging into Maudesley. That's your investigation, not mine.'

'Fine by me. So tell me what you've unearthed, then.'

Esme sighed. 'Nothing. Same brick wall as your researcher.' She jabbed a finger at him. 'So you need to apologise to him and not dismiss him so easily as useless.'

Max stared at her for a moment before reaching inside his jacket pocket and pulling out a document. 'This might stir your curiosity,' he said, holding up the folded paper in the air. 'Might even inspire you to smash down your brick wall and see what's behind it.'

'Why, what is it?'

'You'll remember I mentioned right at the off that Stone and Maudesley spent time in the Med in their student days and that Maudesley'd had to up and leave the country pronto.'

'Which you,' Esme said, a smile creeping on to her face as she recalled teasing Max about his theory, 'attributed to him having used a metal detector illegally.'

'Which I know you found highly amusing.'

'Only because you suggested it was the BIG SECRET,' she drew imaginary quote marks in the air, 'that Stone had over Maudesley.'

'But this,' Max said, handing the paper to Esme, 'is evidence of one very good reason why Maudesley had need to get the hell out.'

Esme took the folded paper and opened it out. It was an official document, in the dual languages of French and Arabic. She scanned the information before looking up at Max who stared back at her with a smug expression on his face.

'Maudesley fathered a daughter?' she said.

Max nodded. 'In 1986. The mother was a Moroccan teenager. Bet her family weren't overly pleased about that. And that's why he ran.'

## 67

Maddy took a chopping board heaped with sliced onions over to the stove and slid the pieces into a pan of hot oil, as Esme stood in her kitchen explaining about Hester's non-appearance off the Lundy boat.

'Do you think I should be worried?' Esme said. 'I mean, she was already nervous of Frank Stone before. What if he's found out she knows about his teenage misdemeanours?'

'Much as I hate to agree with anything Max Rainsford says,' Maddy said, stirring the pan, 'he has a point. You don't even know Hester did go to Lundy. You said Pat was a bit vague about it. Maybe she got hold of the wrong end of the stick.'

'So why isn't Hester answering her phone or emails, then?'

Maddy pointed the wooden spoon at Esme and wagged it like an oversized index finger. 'This isn't you looking for an excuse to join forces with Max on his Maudesley case, is it?'

'No, of course not. I'm not falling for that one. I've told you. Whatever Max thinks he's turned up about Maudesley's long distant past, it's not relevant to us and getting your sea chest back.'

Maddy turned back to her pan. 'I'm beginning to think that's a pretty remote possibility.'

'I'm sorry, Madds. I'm still trying.'

'Yes, I realise that and I do appreciate it.' Maddy looked at Esme over her shoulder. 'Look, if it's any comfort, I'm pretty sure that if Hester had gone out on the *Oldenburg* this morning, there'd be a record of her being on board. And if she'd not come back, the passenger numbers wouldn't have tallied, would they? You said the crew were pretty chilled, so obviously they had no cause for concern.'

Esme folded her arms and leaned against the door jamb. 'I suppose the fact that she's not answering her phone is just a bit disconcerting.'

Maddy grunted. 'Mmm, seem to remember you being here before. Remember? After she went ape when you told her about the murder? You couldn't get hold of her then either.'

'Yes, but we know why that was,' Esme protested. 'This is different. She knows me. She knows I'm there to help. And with Max still pursuing leads and now uncovering something, maybe...'

'Maybe what, Esme?' Again, the wagging wooden spoon. 'Listen to yourself. This is exactly the reason you didn't want to get involved with Max in the first place.'

'Yes, I know that, but...'

'So stop letting your imagination run away with you. Anyway,' Maddy said, turning down the heat and putting a lid on the pan, 'my guess is she'll be in touch sometime soon, if only to tell you she *is* off to Lundy and why. My guess is that Pat got the days muddled.'

'I hope you're right,' Esme said, trying to do as Maddy advised and not read more into the situation than was really there. But she couldn't rid herself of the uncomfortable feeling that she was sitting on her hands when Hester might be in trouble.

Maddy gave her head a shake, impatiently. 'Of course I'm right. Now, are you staying to eat? You're more than welcome.'

Esme shook her head. 'Thanks for the offer, but I really should get back.'

There was the sound of the front door opening and moments later, Harry appeared at the kitchen doorway. 'Hi, Esme,' he said, throwing his keys on to the worktop. 'You stopping for dinner? Aidan's coming,' he added, teasing.

'Don't *you* start,' Esme said, glancing at Harry and Maddy with a mock stern expression. 'No, I mustn't. The kittens will be wanting theirs. Though I'm very tempted. It smells delicious.'

'Esme's fretting because Hester wasn't on the *Oldenburg*. Tell her, Harry. If someone goes AWOL, they check it out, don't they?'

'Yeah, they do. They call the coastguard in if necessary. Do a search of the island, that sort of thing.'

'There you go,' Maddy said. 'So you've nothing to worry about.'

Harry reached for a bottle of wine and stood it up on the kitchen worktop. 'So, what made you think Hester was on Lundy?'

'Her mother told me. She was surprised I'd not known she was going.' Esme glanced at Maddy. 'Maddy reckons if Hester had been planning the trip, she'd have phoned and that I'm suffering from an over-active imagination.'

'Wouldn't be the first time,' Maddy said, winking at Harry.

'Given she'd told her mum all about it,' Esme said to Harry, 'I'd have expected to hear something from her to say what she had in mind. That's what I find odd. No missed calls. No emails.'

'Have you checked your spam folder?' Harry suggested.

'Spam? Why would it be in spam? She's in my contacts.'

Harry raised an eyebrow. 'C'mon, Esme. We're talking technology, here. Mind of its own. As someone once said, *Whoever thought driverless cars were a good idea never owned a printer.*'

Esme laughed and took out her phone, navigating her way to her email account and clicking on the spam folder. Her stomach gave a lurch as she saw a single email languishing there. She looked up at Maddy and Harry and sighed.

'That's why I never saw it. She's used a new email address. Probably to circumvent Stone. She mentioned something about it the other day.'

Maddy put down the wooden spoon. 'Well, put us out of our misery,' she said. 'What does she say? Was she going to Lundy today?'

Esme tapped the email and it opened up on the screen. The soft hiss of the pan on the stove was the only sound as Esme scanned through Hester's message.

'Yes, she was. Pat was right. She says her colleague Clara has dug up something exciting in the hotel records.'

'Who's Clara?'

'I assume she's involved with the liaison between the museum and the new Education Centre. It might have been her I met in St Helen's Church. She lives on the island and Hester mentions here about staying over with her.' Esme groaned. 'Oh no, how annoying I didn't pick it up earlier. She'd actually invited me along.'

'Oh, that's a shame.'

Esme shook her head. 'Well, it's too late now.'

'What's too late?'

Esme looked round to see Aidan coming into the room. She'd not heard the front door open.

'Hester Chalacombe invited Esme to go with her to Lundy today to view some historic records,' Maddy told him.

'But I missed her email and there's not another boat now until Tuesday.'

'Why don't you come with me?' Aidan said.

'With you?'

'Yes. I'm taking the dive boat over to Lundy tomorrow morning. I could drop you off, if you want.'

'That's a great idea, isn't it, Esme?' Maddy said. 'If Hester wasn't on the boat, she's probably stayed over. You'd be able to find her easily enough.'

Esme hesitated, weighing up whether her intrigue in what Hester's colleague had discovered was sufficient to trump her wariness of small boats.

'It's an early start, mind,' Aidan cautioned. 'Need to catch the tide.'

Esme swallowed. 'OK,' she said, forcing a smile. 'Offer accepted. Thank you.'

# 68

Esme stood next to Aidan on the deck of his boat, her eyes fixed on the horizon. Air cylinders stood like sentries in racks along the spine of the vessel and wetsuits hung ready for use, evoking images of extra-terrestrial creatures from a Sci-fi movie. Aidan's colleague Jed, a brawny young man festooned with tattoos and a sunny smile, was at the controls.

When she'd told Libby what she planned, Libby had rummaged around in her understairs cupboard and pulled out a heavy-duty yellow Gore-Tex coat, which she insisted Esme borrow, along with a pair of insulated rubber boots.

'Wear loads of layers underneath,' she told Esme. 'And you'll be as snug as a bug in a rug.'

As Esme peered out from under the coat's hood, her head encased in a thermal beanie hat, she was thankful she'd accepted Libby's kind offer. Even bundled up as she was, putting out to sea at first light in a brisk breeze meant she could feel the fingers of dawn's chill brushing the bare skin on her face.

As they bounced over the surface of the water, heading for Lundy, Aidan talked about how he'd got into maritime archaeology when a childhood fascination for history and learning to scuba dive on a holiday combined to become an obvious career.

'So, who's diving today?' she asked. 'Or aren't you allowed to say?'

Aidan gave her an indulgent smile. 'It's hardly a state secret that Isaac Maudesley's my client. Everyone on Lundy knows that by now.' He looked out across the bow. 'Not for much longer, though.'

'Oh? Why's that?'

He folded his arms, his feet astride on the deck, staring out to sea. 'Well, putting two and two together, I'm beginning to realise it isn't Isaac who's running this project. It's Stone.' He looked round at Esme. 'And I'm not happy with that. Not after everything I've found out about him.'

'No, I don't blame you. Hester felt the same about him.' Not that poor Hester got a say in the matter. 'So when will you tell Isaac?'

'Today, after the dive.'

Esme nodded. 'Have you come across Frank Stone since you found out about his adolescent compulsion for all things pirate?'

Aidan shook his head. 'Like I told you, I'm fortunate on that score. I don't have anything to do with him. Which,' he added, giving Esme a satisfied grin, 'suits me just fine.'

*

Aidan moored the boat at the island's quay and they walked up the track to the village. As they climbed, Esme thought how different her arrival was to last time when she'd been one of a long crocodile of bodies snaking up the steep path.

'So, where will Hester be?' Aidan said, as they passed Millcombe House. 'Have you managed to get in touch with her?'

Esme shook her head. 'I emailed her to say I was coming, but I don't know whether she'll pick it up.'

'No,' Aidan said. 'The island's internet connection is a bit limited, to say the least.'

'I'm hoping if I find Clara, I'll find Hester.' Esme stopped walking to catch her breath, suddenly hot and unsure whether it was from being overdressed or feeling foolish. 'Now that I'm here,' she confessed, 'I'm wondering whether it was a bit rash to come over on a whim.'

'Someone will know where she is. It's only a small island, after all.'

They continued climbing and parted at *The Marisco Tavern*. Having discussed timings for the journey back to Appledore, Aidan strode off to find Maudesley. Esme put her head round the pub door, but the bar was deserted. Clattering noises deep in the building suggested bar staff were busy elsewhere and she decided not to disturb them, but try the island shop instead.

A young lad wearing a white T-shirt with an image of Lundy lighthouse emblazoned across the front was loading the refrigerated shelving with packs of cheese. She went over to him and asked if he knew where she might find Clara. He looked at her blankly for a moment before removing his ear buds and asking her to repeat her question. When she did, he nodded and took her to the door of the shop, pointing away in the distance towards the church and directing her to the old school house, via a path on the other side of a stone wall.

'It's bright blue,' he told her. 'Can't miss it.'

Esme thanked him and followed his instructions, turning off the main track and on to a grassy path. She passed a flat-roofed building and came to a modest corrugated structure with a lean-to extension to the side and a projecting porch in front. As her guide had told her, the whole building had been painted in a vibrant shade of blue.

Esme tapped on the door of the porch, knocking a little harder when there was no immediate reply. When it was clear no one was home, she turned away and returned to the grass path, wondering where to go next. As she retraced her steps, she gazed across the rough undulating grass and out to sea, taking in the bleak beauty of the island around her and admiring the panoramic views across the bay which Clara must enjoy whenever the weather was as clear as it was today. The breeze was surprisingly warm and Esme stopped to pull off her beanie hat. She put it away in her backpack and unzipped her coat, wishing it wasn't so heavy, but reminding herself she'd been glad of it on the boat, and no doubt would be so again on the return trip.

As she set off, the tower of St Helen's church loomed up ahead of her. Assuming it was Clara she'd met at the church on her previous visit, maybe she'd find her there again.

She reached the end of the path and stepped on to the main track, waiting to let a group of climbers go by, ropes looped over their shoulders, hooks jangling metal on metal amid their chatter about whatever rock face they planned to scale. As Esme turned towards the church, she heard the rhythmic beat of a chopper's rotary blades and looked up to see a distant speck in the blue sky. She wandered over to the rough stone wall which enclosed the landing field and watched as the tiny speck grew into the unmistakable shape of a helicopter. The flight must have been a private charter, as she was sure there wasn't usually a service on a Sunday. A number of ground crew in high-vis coats stood together on one side of the field. Beyond them was a parked Land Rover, beside which a small group of people waited to board the aircraft once it had disgorged its current passengers.

The helicopter hovered overhead and Esme braced herself against the downdraught, wincing at the noise and squinting to keep the dust out of her eyes. The helicopter touched down neatly on to the grass, the door was opened and two travellers disembarked, crouching under the rotating blades as they hurried across the field towards the Land Rover. Three people emerged from behind the vehicle and headed towards the open door of the aircraft. Esme's heart jolted as she recognised one of them. Hester.

Esme turned on her heel and ran along the track, over the cattle grid to the entrance to the landing field. One of the men in high-vis jackets spotted her coming and rushed over to intercept her. Esme veered away from him while calling Hester's name over the roar of the engine.

Perhaps it was seeing the steward's reaction which alerted Hester, as it seemed unlikely she'd have heard Esme's voice over the din of the chopper. She turned, saw Esme and stopped, her mouth open just as the ground crew member caught up with Esme and blocked her way.

'You can't be here, madam,' he bellowed.

'Esme,' Hester shouted. 'What the hell are you doing here?'

'Looking for you,' Esme shouted back. She pulled her phone out of her pocket and waved it. 'Your email went to junk!'

The landing crewman looked confused as though uncertain what to do. He placed himself between Esme and Hester, his arms outstretched to create a barrier between the two women.

Hester pointed towards a gaggle of people standing near the Land Rover. 'Go and speak to Clara,' she yelled. 'She'll show you.'

There was a shout from near the aircraft and Hester glanced over her shoulder before turning back to Esme. 'I have to go. I'll call you.'

Hester pulled away and scurried across the field to the waiting aircraft. Esme backed away, conscious of the look of relief on the crewman's face. She retreated to the edge of the track, looking up as the helicopter lifted off the ground and wheeled away towards the mainland.

# 69

Esme watched the helicopter until it became a speck in the morning sky once more. The Land Rover bounced away out of the field entrance and down towards the village, leaving the ground crew behind. A woman in a fuchsia pink fleece, her shaggy hair whipping around her head, stood amongst them, gazing in Esme's direction.

Esme walked across the grass to meet her. 'Are you Clara?' she said. It wasn't the young woman Esme had spoken to last time, but she seemed familiar.

'I am, yes.'

'Hester said I was to speak to you.' Esme held out her hand. 'I'm Esme Quentin.'

'Ah, yes, of course,' Clara said, smiling and shaking Esme's hand. 'I should have guessed.'

Esme inclined her head. 'Have we met before?'

'No, I don't think so. Perhaps you've seen me around. I'm coordinating *The Treasures of the Sea Museum* collaboration with the island's Education Centre.'

'Oh, that's it,' Esme said, nodding. 'I saw you in the church last time I came, while I was looking at the exhibition. Is that why you live on the island, because of the collaboration?'

'Oh, it's only temporary, while everything's being set up.' She laughed. 'It's certainly an experience being a resident, I must admit. But I'm thoroughly enjoying myself. I'll almost be sorry to leave, despite the obvious advantages of being on the mainland.'

'Hester invited me to come over with her yesterday, but I didn't see her email in time.'

Clara nodded. 'Ah, that explains it. She was surprised not to hear from you. Come on, let's bring you up to speed.'

They returned to the main track and, turning right out of the

333

field, walked back towards the old school house. As they walked, Esme told Clara how she'd been able to cadge a lift over to the island after eventually finding Hester's email.

'Hester sounded excited by what you'd found,' she said. 'Something about the hotel, back in the 1920s?'

'That's right, yes. Lundy was in the local newspapers quite often at the time. I've found reports of various soirées on the island, from dances to musical evenings and theatrical productions, often hosted by a certain Miss Sage of the Manor Hotel.'

'I saw her name on the 1921 census,' Esme said, recalling also finding Albert Philips recorded as a member of staff.

They passed the church and took the narrow path to the corrugated iron building where Esme had come looking for Clara a short time before.

'Miss Sage was obviously a *tour de force* for some while,' Clara said. 'People regularly sang her praises in the local press. She took the role for about 7 years, leaving in 1927 when she was awarded a gold wrist watch in gratitude for service.'

They arrived at the neat blue building and Clara pushed open the front door, inviting Esme inside. Esme stepped into a tiny porch entrance and through to a cosy living room. Laid out on a small dining table against the wall were a number of photographs, copies of newspaper pages and other documental paraphernalia.

'Take a seat,' Clara said, slipping off her fleece and hanging it on a hook on the open ledged and braced door to the kitchen. Esme dropped down on to one of the heavy oak dining chairs at the table and Clara took another on the opposite side. Clara sifted through the pile of paper, pulling out a black and white photograph which she put in front of Esme.

'This was what Hester got most excited about,' Clara said, as Esme delved into her bag for her reading glasses. 'Taken at one of those soirées I mentioned, in 1921.'

Esme slipped on her glasses and studied the photo, depicting a number of smartly dressed people – men in bow ties and dinner jackets, young women wearing silk shift dresses and beads reflecting the 1920s era, older ladies wearing the more modest attire of the 1910s.

'Look at this,' Clara said, pointing to the caption along the bottom. '"Those present included Mr, Mrs and Miss Pearce."'

'Hester's great-aunt Annie?' Esme said, looking up at Clara. 'And her parents, here on Lundy?'

Clara nodded. 'And if you read on, you'll see who else was here. "Mr R, E and Mrs Sanders." Ernest and *his* parents.'

'No wonder Hester was so excited,' Esme said, taking off her glasses. 'Perhaps this is where they met?'

'That's what we wondered,' Clara agreed.

Esme put her glasses back on and gazed at the photograph. At the back, half obscured and in shadow, was a young man, evidently not part of the social event, but an employee at the hotel. She tapped the image.

'Is he a waiter, d'you think?'

Clara chuckled. 'Hester said the same. She wondered if it could be Albert Philips who you'd found on the census returns.' Clara took a deep breath. 'She also wondered if it was here that the dispute between them kicked off.'

'Our theory is that they disagreed over a ring, but if this is where Ernest and Annie first met, it would have been too early. There would be no ring to argue over. Not yet, anyway.'

'Unless it wasn't here that they first met. That's what Hester wondered, anyway.'

'I suppose if the parents of Ernest and Annie moved in the same circles, the two lovebirds may have known one another quite well by now,' Esme reasoned. 'Who's to say Ernest didn't take the opportunity on this very occasion to give Annie the ring and Albert somehow found out?'

'Yes, that's perfectly possible.'

Esme sighed. 'Sadly, it hardly matters where the dispute began.

Its tragic end is the same.'

Clara stood up. 'Enough historic speculation,' she said. 'I'm not being much of a host. Tea? Coffee?'

Esme smiled. 'Thank you, a cup of tea would be lovely.'

Clara went into the small galley kitchen, leaving Esme to reflect on what the photograph did or did not tell them. Even if Ernest had given Annie the ring while they were staying here, he could never have done so openly or his mother would know immediately that he'd taken it. But given Hester had said their relationship had been secret, perhaps they'd met up discreetly while on the island. Perhaps Albert had stumbled across their liaison and overheard them. It would answer Hester's question of how Albert had known when no one else did.

Clara appeared from the kitchen with a tea tray and set it down on an occasional table in front of the sofa.

'So, if you're involved with the museum collaboration,' Esme said, 'does that mean ordinarily you work at the museum itself?'

'That's right, I do. And in case you're wondering, I've known Isaac Maudesley for years.'

'Right.' Did Clara mean Hester had confided in her? Or was she merely claiming an association with a local celebrity?

Clara sat down in an armchair and gestured for Esme to take a seat on the sofa. 'Sorry, that was a very clumsy way of letting you know I'm aware you've been trying to help Hester get to the bottom of what's going on.'

Esme left the table and sat down opposite Clara. 'So, do you have any theories as to why Frank Stone has suddenly arrived on the scene?'

'None. I'm as confused as Hester. I'm just thankful I don't have to work with him.' Clara peered at Esme from under her thatch of a fringe and gave her a rueful smile. 'On the few occasions I've come into contact with him, I can't say I've warmed to his charm.'

'No, I'm with you on that one,' Esme agreed. 'He seems to

take delight in making people feel uncomfortable. If you don't mind me asking, given you've known Isaac for years, is he the sort of person to get infatuated by something in the way he appears to be at the moment?'

'He's always been passionate about his subject. I doubt he'd have accomplished what he has if he hadn't been. *Nothing great was ever achieved without enthusiasm,* isn't that what the famous phrase says?'

'There's enthusiasm,' reflected Esme, thinking of Stone's preoccupation during his schooldays and its aftermath, 'and there's out of control fanaticism.'

'History has been Isaac's life,' Clara said. 'His *raison d'être.* In the absence of a family, it's given him a purpose, I suppose.'

Esme thought of the birth certificate Max had waved under her nose. 'I didn't realise he didn't have a family,' she said. 'I thought I'd read somewhere he had a daughter.'

Clara looked puzzled. 'Don't know where you heard that,' she said, frowning. 'As far as I know, Isaac can't father children. It was why his marriage broke up.'

Before Esme had time to absorb the information, Clara abruptly stood up and leaned across the table to peer out of the window. 'What's happening out there, I wonder?'

Esme followed Clara's line of sight to see a gaggle of walkers hurrying across the wide expanse of grass below the cottage. They appeared to be aiming for the main footpath, the couple at the back almost at a run to keep up with the rest of the group.

Clara snatched up her fleece. 'Let's go and be nosy, shall we?'

The two of them left the cottage and followed the narrow grass pathway back to the main track, joining others striding towards the castle end of the island. In the distance, Esme could see a group of people gathered together, their waterproof jackets a patchwork of greens, blues and reds, all staring out to sea.

'What's happening, Rob?' Clara said, turning to a tall, skinny man with a ponytail approaching them from behind.

337

'Emergency callout,' he said, as he scurried past. 'Just spoken to the coastguard.'

'Do we know what sort of emergency?' Clara called, as she and Esme followed in his wake.

'I saw some climbers earlier,' Esme said. 'Perhaps one of them has got into difficulty.'

'Nah, this is on the water,' Rob called over his shoulder. 'Diving accident of some sort.'

'Diving?' Esme felt her stomach tighten. 'Aidan Garrett was on a dive today,' she said, turning to Clara. 'That's who gave me a lift over on his boat.'

They reached the cluster of onlookers and Esme shuffled to the front, looking down at where everyone's gaze was focused. She could see Aidan's boat a short distance off-shore and alongside was the distinct orange of an RNLI lifeboat. As she squinted to see more clearly, she heard, for the second time that morning, the drumming of rotary blades above. The bystanders collectively raised their heads to watch the red and white coastguard helicopter as it circled over them before moving off-shore to hover above the boat.

Esme found herself unable to drag her eyes away from the scene as the winchman descended and dropped into the boat, where he disconnected his rope and the chopper pulled away. What could have happened? Who was the casualty? Aidan? His colleague? Or Isaac Maudesley?

Even though Aidan's boat was too far away to make out what was happening on board, Esme felt compelled to fix her gaze on its location. After an agonisingly prolonged period of time, or so it felt, the helicopter moved back to resume its position above the dive boat. Again the winch was lowered into place, casualty and winchman were harnessed to the line and, with a speed that took Esme's breath away, both were whisked into the air and rapidly drawn upward into the helicopter. The door was dragged closed and the chopper veered away.

Esme slipped back between the group of onlookers to find Clara. 'Isaac was going out there today,' she said.

Rob caught her words and shook his head. 'Nah, won't be him,' he said. 'Mr Maudesley went back to the mainland on the chopper.'

Esme frowned. 'But I came over on the dive boat this morning,' she told Rob. 'I understood he was expected.'

'Changed his mind,' Rob said, with a shake of his head. 'His mate went instead.'

As Rob strode off, Esme looked at Clara. 'Mate?' she said. 'Does he mean who I think he means?'

'Can't think who else it would be, can you?' Clara said, returning Esme's gaze. 'It's got to be Frank Stone.'

# 70

Esme made her way down the hill to the landing jetty with a sense of hope over expectation. Would Aidan's boat be there as arranged? And if it was, would Aidan be on it? Who had been whisked off in the helicopter to hospital? Aidan? His colleague Jed? Frank Stone?

The irony of her conversation with Aidan earlier, his relief that he didn't have anything to do with Stone, was not lost on her. She tried to imagine Aidan's reaction when Stone turned up for the dive instead of Maudesley. Why the change? Perhaps Maudesley or Stone believed Aidan might have declined to take him out had he known in advance.

Relief washed over her when she rounded the corner of the stone track leading down to the beach and saw Aidan's boat in the harbour. She hurried to where the vessel was moored up to the side of the landing jetty, catching sight of Aidan and Jed on deck, deep in conversation as she got closer. Aidan must have seen her approach as he stood up to wave and she waved back.

'Am I glad to see you,' Esme said, as she took his hand and stepped aboard. 'I didn't know who'd be here.'

'Bet that wore good en'ertainment from up thur,' Jed said, grinning.

'You can say that again.' Esme looked between the two of them. 'So, what happened?'

'I'll fill you in on the way,' Aidan said, jerking his head at Jed. 'All yours, Jed.'

Jed disappeared into the cockpit and started up the boat's engine. Esme sat down on a locker in the middle of the deck and Aidan stood beside her, feet apart, bracing himself as Jed manoeuvred the craft out of the harbour.

'I heard Frank Stone turned up,' Esme said, looking up at

Aidan. 'You weren't expecting that, I take it?'

'You know I wasn't. Everything was all set up for Isaac to do the dive.'

'So, how come he didn't show?'

Aidan shrugged. 'Not sure, to be honest. Stone's story was Isaac had said he could have the honour, being as he was so keen.' He folded his arms. 'Stone seemed to have got this idea we were all set to turn up something major and wanted first dibs.'

'And were you?'

'Not that I'm aware, no. Unless someone knows something I don't.'

They'd reached the end of the protection of the harbour and the boat was beginning to pitch a little on the open sea. Aidan sat down next to Esme.

'According to Stone, an ancestor of his had scuttled a ship loaded with gold off the island back in the 18th century. Is this the guy you told me about? Stone's pirate ancestor?'

'Sounds like it,' Esme said, eagerly. 'Henry Venner.'

Aidan nodded. 'Yeah, that's him.'

'Henry became a pirate after being captured himself while serving on one of his uncle's ships. It didn't go down too well with the family, as you might imagine, and he was written out of his uncle's will. The assumption is having lost access to his inheritance, he decided to make his money from piracy.' She frowned. 'So why would Henry Venner scuttle his own ship? Why not land it on Lundy and offload it? You told me yourself it was what the island was famous for.'

'According to Stone, the crew had mutinied. Henry had been killed in the skirmish and his son was lucky to get out alive.'

'So it wasn't actually Henry who scuttled the ship, then?' Esme sifted through what she remembered about the Venner family. 'The son. The one who got out alive. Was that Josiah?'

Aidan grinned. 'I can see I'm wasting my time, here. You know this already.'

Esme shook her head. 'No, I don't. I know the names on a family tree, but I only know so much about the individual stories.' She rubbed a finger up and down her cheek. 'OK, so Josiah got out alive by the skin of his teeth and Stone's saying he returned to the ship later to send it to the bottom of the sea, along with its on-board treasure. An act of revenge to the crew who'd murdered his father.'

'That's pretty much the story in a nutshell.'

'You'd have thought Josiah would've grabbed something for himself before he…' Esme put her hand to her mouth. 'Which of course he did.' She turned to Aidan, excitement growing inside. 'Maddy's box.'

'Maddy's box? The one that was stolen?'

'Yes, which was Henry's trunk. Josiah didn't leave empty handed, he retrieved his father's trunk, and more likely than not, grabbed some gold for himself. But he couldn't take it all, so later, he made a map…'

'A map?' Aidan sat back and laughed. 'You're not serious?'

'It's what Stone told Hester. That's why he was so desperate to get Henry's trunk off Maddy. He was convinced it contained the map of where the ship had gone down.'

Aidan rubbed his chin with his finger and thumb. 'I should say, before you get too excited, I've found no evidence of Henry Venner's ship in the dives I've done so far.'

'You think they're being over-optimistic?'

Aidan snorted. 'Deluded, is the word I'd use. Isaac even wanted me to say I'd found evidence at the dive site of Henry's ship being down there when I hadn't, which I wasn't best pleased about.'

'He wanted you to lie?' That must have been when she'd seen them arguing. 'Why?'

Aidan scratched his cheek. 'That's a good question. And I have another one. Did Isaac genuinely pull out or did Stone bully him to let him take the slot?'

'The latter, knowing Stone.'

'Yeah, that was my first thought. Which puts an interesting complexion on things.'

'What things?' Esme said, frowning. 'You still haven't explained exactly what happened.'

'It was sabotage, Esme. Someone had tampered with Maudesley's dive equipment.'

# 71

Esme fixed her gaze on the horizon as the boat bounced across the waves. She tucked Libby's coat around her, trying to process what Aidan had told her while he went into the wheelhouse to fetch a flask of tea. Now she understood why he'd used the word sabotage.

Aidan and Stone had entered the water and begun their descent to the seabed. But after only a few minutes, Aidan looked across to see Stone thrashing around and heading back to the surface at speed.

'He was behaving like a rookie, panicking,' Aidan said. 'But he's not inexperienced. He's dived for years, in the Med, mostly. I was thinking, *what the hell's he doing? He can't shoot up like that, he'll kill himself.*'

Esme nodded her understanding as Aidan explained about compression sickness, how coming up too quickly causes bubbles of air to form in the blood, with potentially fatal consequences.

'So what did you do?'

'Swam after him and grabbed hold of him. He was all wide-eyed and looked terrified, like he was suffering from a heart attack or something. That's when I noticed his dive belt was hanging off.'

'The thing that holds weights to keep you from floating?'

'That's it, yeah. I assumed he must have released it to get back to the surface quickly, which it's designed to do, of course, in an emergency. But there's a procedure, and he'd already ignored the first rule which is to let your dive buddy know what you're planning.'

'He must have acted first and thought after,' Esme said.

'Yeah, but here's the thing. If that's what he'd wanted to do, he'd have let go of it, where as he seemed to be scrabbling to hold on to it. As though that *wasn't* his intention at all. I'm pretty certain it was the belt slipping that induced his panic. Panic's the worst thing a diver can do, see. Staying calm is key.'

'Well, you obviously got him back to the surface and alerted the emergency services. You saved his life – assuming he recovers from the heart attack, or whatever it was he was suffering from.'

'But that's my point. I'm not sure he was suffering from anything.'

'Then why did he release his belt?'

'According to him, he didn't. He said it came off on its own. Which corroborates my theory that it wasn't a medical emergency.'

Esme frowned. 'Is it likely it would come off on its own?'

'It happens. But Stone claims the webbing had been cut.'

Esme gave Aidan a sceptical look. 'Really? Or is it a damage limitation exercise for his diving credibility?'

'I thought the same until I rummaged through the rest of Maudesley's gear.' Aidan nodded towards the metal locker up against the wheelhouse. Esme stared at the locker before turning back to Aidan.

'What do you mean?'

Aidan raised an eyebrow. 'There was a second belt amongst his kit. That had been cut too.'

\*

Aidan returned from the wheelhouse and handed Esme a beaker of hot tea. She took it gratefully.

'So, what are you thinking? That it was meant for Maudesley?'

Aidan sat down beside her. 'Well, it was his equipment and it was common knowledge he'd been scheduled to come on the dive.'

'When might it have been tampered with?'

Aidan shook his head. 'No idea. I'd done all the usual checks and our gear was all fine. But I can only speak for us. No idea if

Maudesley's as vigilant.'

'So, Stone brought Maudesley's equipment with him?'

'Yeah. Maybe I should have checked it over, but Maudesley's always done it himself.'

'Well, why would you? You were expecting Maudesley, not Stone.' Esme took a sip of tea. 'So, are you thinking this is an attack on the man himself? Or an attempt to stop the dives from happening? Why would that be, though?'

'Maybe someone's not happy in principle. Lundy's a marine nature reserve, remember. Could be there are those who'd rather not see any activity in such a sensitive area.'

'But there are loads of dive sites around Lundy. Dives are happening all the time. Why pick on yours?'

'Bad luck, maybe?'

'Have you reported it yet?' Esme asked.

'Not yet. But I will do.' Aidan stood up and took the beaker from her. 'We're almost there. I'd better give Jed a hand.'

Esme looked around as the boat slowed, watching as the buildings of Appledore's quayside came into view. The sound of the engine dropped to a low drone as Jed steered the vessel alongside the quay and came to a halt. Esme got to her feet as Aidan jumped out to secure the rope, taking his hand to steady herself as she stepped off the boat.

She looked up and saw waiting at the top of the slipway two uniformed policemen. Before she had time to fathom their being there, they marched towards her. She opened her mouth to say something, but they walked straight past. She swivelled around as they reached Aidan, reeling at the words of the taller officer.

'Aidan Garrett. I'm arresting you on suspicion of attempted murder. You are not obliged to say anything, but it may harm your defence if you do not mention when questioned something which you later rely on in court. Anything you do say may be given in evidence.'

## 72

Esme sat at Maddy's dining table, Maddy and Harry on the other side, telling them what had happened as Aidan's boat docked. After she and Jed had recovered from the initial shock, Jed had declared the whole thing was a farce and the police would release Aidan as soon as they realised they'd got their wires crossed. He announced he was off to the pub and Esme headed for Maddy's place.

'And Aidan was certain, was he,' Harry said now, 'that the belt had been deliberately cut?'

'That's what he said, yes.'

Maddy leaned across the table. 'And you're both convinced it's Maudesley who was the target? And Stone only got the treatment because he went on the dive instead?'

Esme made a pragmatic gesture with her hands. 'Well, it's the most logical conclusion to draw, isn't it?'

'So, who's behind it?' Harry said. 'This Stone character? He's someone with a violent past, isn't he?'

'But what's his motive?' Esme said. 'From what I've picked up from Hester, he's got carte blanche on pretty much anything he wants as it is. What would he have to gain by getting rid of Maudesley?'

'Plus the obvious get-out clause,' Harry pointed out, 'that he'd hardly sign his own death warrant by going on a dive with equipment he himself had damaged.'

Maddy tapped the table top with her finger. 'Unless it's some sort of double-bluff. To turn the suspicion away from him?'

Harry looked sceptical. 'Bit of a risk, isn't it? Nah, I don't buy it.'

'No, me neither,' Esme agreed. 'For the reasons I've just mentioned. He has Maudesley in the palm of his hand. Why bother?' She sighed and slumped back against her chair. 'Maybe Max has a theory. He's more the Maudesley expert than me.'

'I hope that doesn't mean you're going to call him,' Maddy said, in alarm. 'You need to stay out of it, Esme.'

'No, of course not. Besides, he doesn't need anything from me. He'll hear about it soon enough on the journalist jungle drums.'

'Well, I wouldn't fret too much,' Harry said, getting to his feet. 'They can't hold Aidan for more than 24 hours unless they've got the evidence to charge him. So unless they come up with any, they'll have to release him.'

\*

Esme felt drained by the time she got home. She fed the kittens and slumped on the sofa to gather her thoughts. Harry's assessment that the police would have to release Aidan soon if they had no evidence was only partly reassuring, given they had no idea what had prompted Aidan's arrest in the first place. Who had instigated the action? Had Frank Stone made an accusation from his hospital bed? Aidan said Stone had been taken to hospital merely as a precaution, and if he was well enough to complain to Aidan that his dive belt had been cut, he would certainly have been well enough to make a complaint to the police.

But had he? From everything Esme knew about him, Stone would have his own way of dealing with a grudge, not turn to the police. Maybe the experience had spooked him.

Esme crawled off the sofa and went into the kitchen to fix herself something to eat. Her energy reserves had been sapped enough as it was, after such a long day, without everything that had happened in the last few hours. She threw together a cheese sandwich and took it over to the sofa. As she sat down, she looked over at the cold wood burner, trying to decide if she had enough stamina to lay a fire, which she'd had no time to do before she'd left home early that morning. The thought of the heartening glow of flames and comforting atmosphere it would create was too hard to resist. She put aside the plate and within a few minutes, the satisfying crackle of burning kindling filled the cottage.

Food and warmth began to have the desired effect and soon Esme was able to relax, to sink into the cushions of the sofa and to reminisce on her day. She realised with frustration she'd not told Maddy about the tale of Henry and Josiah Venner, and how her missing sea chest fitted into the story. She considered phoning her, but it was getting late. She'd tell her tomorrow. And she must talk to Hester, too. She was keen to discuss everything Clara had shared, the photograph and their suspicion that the dispute over the Claddagh ring might have been triggered on Lundy.

As Esme reflected, she was reminded of a question she'd asked herself about how the ring might have been passed on had Ernest not taken it from his mother Betsy to give to Annie. She and Maddy had speculated about Stone being concerned someone else in the family now had the ring, how he may be in a race to get hold of it. Esme had been about to trawl through the family tree to see if she could identify any potential candidates. So, why hadn't she done it?

Of course! It was Max's fault. He'd called to send her off on a wild goose chase about Isaac Maudesley, and then when she'd come up blank, Pat had phoned to say Hester was on her way to Lundy. By then, she'd been too distracted. But there was still time and she might have something to report to Hester when she next spoke to her.

She went to fetch her laptop and brought it back to the sofa, propping herself up against the arm, her feet up and the laptop on her knee. The most obvious trail, which she'd shared with Pat, was via Albert Philips's daughter Alice. If Albert had gone to the gallows defending his belief that the ring should have been hers, it was a logical assumption Alice's descendants still craved what they perceived to be theirs. But Alice wasn't Albert's only child. She had a brother, Bradley Philips. When Max's call came through, Esme had been about to establish if Bradley had married and had daughters, who may also have had their sights on the contentious ring.

Esme opened up *Ancestry* and filled in the relevant information to set the search engine in motion. She tapped the mouse pad and the database displayed its findings. Bradley Philips's name appeared about halfway down the page. She almost dropped the laptop when she saw the name of his spouse. Bradley had married a Caroline Maudesley.

With her heart hammering in her chest, she opened up the *FreeBMD* database. She selected *birth*s at the top of the page, entered *Philips* in the surname field and *Maudesley* in the Spouse/mother's surname box. On the date range, she chose the period between the March quarter of 1966 to the December quarter of 1966. She clicked on *Find* and watched as the screen offered its one and only result. Giles Isaac Philips.

Esme's thoughts reeled as she stared at the screen. Giles Philips had become Isaac Maudesley. He'd used his middle name and his mother's maiden name to reinvent himself. But why? Why had he felt the need to hide his real identity?

As she chewed over these questions, the shocking truth thrust its way into her mind. If Giles Philips, alias Isaac Maudesley, was Bradley Philips's son, it meant that Frederick Philips was his great-uncle. Maudesley and Stone were cousins.

An echo of a conversation Esme'd had with the former pupil volunteer at Garter Abbey slipped into her head. … *The self-appointed captain and his sidekick cousin were the most obnoxious.* Both great-nephews of Frederick Philips were at the school. Both of them were in the pirate gang. Either one of them could have been responsible for the death of Anthony Milton.

But Stone hadn't felt the same compulsion to become someone else, suggesting it hadn't been he who'd been guilty of drowning his fellow pupil in a chilling recreation of a macabre maritime punishment. It had been Isaac Maudesley.

## 73

Esme jerked awake. Her phone was ringing and for a moment she didn't know where she was. As she dragged herself into consciousness, she winced at her stiff neck and the chill of the room. She pulled herself into a sitting position on the sofa and grabbed the offending instrument.

'Hello?' she croaked.

'Esme, I'm so sorry to call so early,' Maddy said, as Esme peered across the room at the clock to read it was just after half past six. 'But I thought you'd want to know they've released Aidan. He doesn't think they're going to press charges.'

Esme slumped back against the sofa cushions. 'Oh, that's good news. Thanks for letting me know.' She wondered what Aidan had told the police about his suspicions that Maudesley might have been the target. Perhaps even now, they'd be taking forensic evidence.

'Are you OK?' Maddy was saying. 'Sorry, stupid question. You're still half asleep. I know I should have waited until later. But I thought you'd be worrying.'

Esme cleared her throat. 'No, I'm glad you called.' She gave a feeble laugh. 'I fell asleep on the sofa. I must have been done in.'

'Oh, poor you. Well, I'll get out of your hair so you can get yourself sorted.'

'No, don't go,' Esme said, sitting forward and perching on the edge of the seat. 'There's something I forgot to tell you yesterday.'

'About what?'

'About your sea chest.' The kittens, stirred by the phone and Esme's voice, were at her feet, looking up at her in anticipation of an early breakfast. 'The story is that Henry Venner's son Josiah took it off Henry's ship before he deliberately sank it in some act of revenge against the crew. But Stone's convinced Josiah recorded the location of the ship somewhere in the trunk.'

'Oh my God, Esme. That's crazy.' Maddy clicked her tongue. 'Pity I didn't have time to uncover its secrets before he snatched it. So, how d'you know all this?'

'Aidan told me. It's what Stone told him on the boat yesterday. Get Aidan to tell you Henry's story. You'll love it.'

'Yes, I will. Definitely.'

'But there's something else, Madds. Something I found out last night about Isaac Maudesley.'

'I'm not liking the sound of this, Esme,' Maddy said, her voice wary. 'What was it?'

Esme explained about coming across Giles Philips and her shock at realising who he really was. She heard Maddy gasp down the line.

'I wasn't looking for Maudesley,' Esme said, as though Maddy was accusing her of something she shouldn't have been doing. 'I was following the ring trail and I stumbled across it.' She took a deep breath. 'So, it looks like Max was right all along, doesn't it? Maudesley's hiding a secret past.'

'Have you told Max?' Maddy said, after a while.

'Not yet, no,' Esme said, clutching the phone. 'I really need to talk to Hester first.'

*

By the time Esme'd had a coffee and some breakfast, she was beginning to feel more human. As she showered, she revisited what she'd learned over the past 24 hours, particularly what Stone had shared with Aidan about Henry Venner's story. Now she knew Isaac Maudesley was actually a Philips, it seemed likely he'd also heard the story passed down through the generations. From his infamous great-uncle, Frederick.

She'd uncovered some of it during her own research. The experience of Henry and his brother Thomas at the hands of the slave traders of Barbary, their return to England and Henry's disinheritance for "Turning Turk". The part Josiah played in Henry's story seemed to chime with the claim of Annie's great-great-grandmother, Charlotte, that the Claddagh ring was stolen by a family member. Had Josiah been that thief? Had he rebelled against his mother, angry that she'd rejected his father in favour of his uncle, Thomas? Had he left the family home as soon as he was old enough in search of his father, his loyalty proving stronger for Henry, despite what Henry had done and how he lived his life? Josiah had, it seemed, embraced that life and joined him on Henry's pirate ship. So, had he taken the ring for its value? Or because, like Albert Philips, he believed the ring should be restored to whoever he saw as its rightful owner?

Esme was puzzled by Aidan's description of Maudesley enticing him to lie about evidence of the ship's existence when he'd found none. What was the point? Unless Maudesley had needed to convince potential investors to raise funds for the new satellite museum. An image of the accountant she'd met on the stairs on the way to Hester's office slipped into her head. Perhaps financial issues had a part to play in this story. Maybe it's what Max would ultimately discover.

Again, she questioned whether she should pass on to Max what she'd learned. Again, she decided Hester had the right to know first, but attempts to call her had gone straight to voicemail.

The kittens' breakfast had used up the last supplies of cat food and with the fridge similarly depleted, Esme reluctantly accepted she needed to do a food shop. She got into her car and headed to Bideford.

The supermarket was thankfully quiet and the aisles uncluttered with other shoppers, which suited Esme, lost as she was in her own thoughts of Maudesley, Henry Venner and Frederick Philips while she struggled to retain her concentration on the job in hand. Finally, deciding that if she'd forgotten anything she'd just have to live without it, she headed for the check-out. After unloading her purchases into the boot of her car and wheeling her trolley back to the trolley-park, she climbed into the driver's seat, wondering if Hester had called or emailed her.

As she pulled out her phone to check for messages, the passenger door was yanked open and someone got into her car.

Esme's head shot round. 'Max! For God's sake. You nearly gave me a heart attack. What the hell are you doing?'

'Trying to confirm what I'm hearing about Stone being set upon by Garrett.'

Esme rolled her eyes. 'Typical journalist hype. That's not the way it was at all.'

'So, what was it, then?' Max said, swivelling round to face her. 'Word has it Garrett was arrested for attempted murder.'

'It's ridiculous,' she said, with an exasperated sigh. 'Stone and Aidan were on a dive. There was a problem with the equipment. Stone surfaced too quick for safety and had to be airlifted to hospital to be checked out. End of story.' She glared at him. 'And he's fine. Just trying to make trouble for Aidan, if you ask me. But then Stone does seem to have a penchant for throwing a hissy fit.' She looked away, watching a young mother clipping a toddler in to his car seat. She was wary of mentioning the damaged dive belt. Why fuel his journalistic fire any more than necessary?

Max drummed his fingers on the dash. 'Rumour has it Maudesley should have been on the dive.'

She turned back to him with a scowl. 'So you knew it was a dive. The way you were talking, you made it sound as though you'd heard it was some sort of street brawl.' She narrowed her eyes. 'A journalistic tactic, I assume, to test the water.'

Max gave her a broad grin, but made no comment.

'Oh, and by the way,' Esme went on, 'your theory that Maudesley fathered a daughter is way off target. He wasn't able to have kids, apparently.'

'Mmm, that's what Hester said when I put it past her,' Max said, folding his arms. 'Even so, it's an interesting one. Got to be something behind it. Because you've seen the document, same as

I have.'

Esme said nothing. Perhaps he'd leave her alone now. But he'd clearly not finished with her yet.

Max took a deep breath. 'So, are you going to give me the full story, whatever you've found out about Maudesley now that you've broken down that brick wall?'

'Who says I've broken down the brick wall?'

'Are you telling me you haven't dug up something about Maudesley?'

Esme turned away. The man was infuriating. 'If I had,' she said, cautiously, 'you wouldn't be the first person I'd share it with.'

Max rubbed his chin. 'No, I guess not. Fair point.' He settled back into the seat, reaching for the seat belt and pulling it across himself to click it into the fastening.

'What are you doing?' Esme said.

'What do you think I'm doing? Strapping myself in.' He jerked his head towards her. 'Suggest you do the same, Esme. The roads can be dangerous out there.'

'Oh, very funny. You know full well what I mean.'

Max made a point of looking at his watch. 'Perfect timing. You can fill us in over lunch and a pint. My treat.'

'Us?'

'Me and Hester. That's who you meant, didn't you? The person you need to tell first.'

Esme stared back at him, blinking.

Max tossed his head. 'Well, come on, Ez. Start her up. We need to be somewhere.'

Esme glowered at him. 'I'm not starting this car, Max Rainsford, until you tell me exactly where we're going.'

## 74

Max directed Esme out of the town and on to the A39, heading towards Esme's home. But they stopped short, pulling off to a large roadside pub, a rambling thatched establishment oozing historic prestige and with a reputation for good food. Esme drove under the archway to the car park at the rear of the property, from where they walked across an inner courtyard, accessing the pub through the back door.

As they entered the bar, Max indicated a small recess area ahead of them. 'You go ahead. I'll get the drinks in.'

Esme made her way over to the alcove, which had probably once been a small room in the former life of the building. Now a table stood in the centre of the enclosure, bench seats running down the sides and a window looking out on the road at the front. As Esme stepped inside, she saw Hester sitting in the corner, a glass of orange juice on the table in front of her.

'Hester, I'm so sorry,' Esme said, glancing back over her shoulder. 'Max outmanoeuvred me. I only agreed to come along because I need to talk to you anyway. What's he up to? Did he set you up, too?'

Hester shook her head, her face pallid and devoid of make-up. 'No, it's the other way around. I demanded he meet me to tell me what he knows. Because he clearly knows more than I do.' She picked up her drink and slid along the bench seat towards the window, allowing Esme space to sit down next to her. 'I got your message, by the way,' Hester added. 'But I thought I'd wait until I'd spoken to Max as I might have something to tell you.'

Esme slid her bag off her shoulder and took a seat. 'You heard about the dive accident?'

'Yes,' Hester said, nodding. 'Clara told me. What's it all about? I don't get it. What's Isaac up to?'

'Indeed, what *is* Isaac up to?' Max said, appearing with a pint of ale and Esme's tonic water. He pulled a couple of menus from his pocket and dropped them on to the table and grinned. 'This is cosy, isn't it?'

Esme ignored him. She passed a menu to Hester before picking up her drink and taking a sip.

'So, who's going to tell first?' she said.

*

Over a simple lunch of pate and toast, Esme told Max and Hester what had happened on the boat.

'And Aidan's conclusion is that it was meant for Isaac?' Hester asked.

'That's what it looks like, doesn't it, being as it was a last-minute switch?'

'Why, though?' Hester said, flicking a bewildered glance at the two of them. 'Who'd do such a thing?'

Max pushed away his plate and wiped his fingers on a napkin. 'First question the cops would ask is did he have any enemies?'

'No, of course not,' Hester snapped. 'All right, so he may be upsetting a few people at the moment – me included – but it's hardly a motive for murder.'

'What about you, Max?' Esme said. 'You unearthed anything which might answer the question?'

'Can't say I have. But you've got something. Are you going to share?' He jerked his head at Hester. 'You said Hester needs to know.'

Esme bit her bottom lip as Hester fixed her gaze on her, her brow knotted, clearly anxious at what Esme had learned. 'You remember I told you about Frank's obsession with pirates stretching back to his schooldays?' Esme said, addressing only Hester.

'Yes, a nasty school gang, you said.'

Esme nodded. 'But it didn't stop there. Things got out of hand.

357

Someone died, drowned when the boys decided to keelhaul one poor unfortunate they took a dislike to.'

Hester gasped. 'Oh my God, that's awful.' She looked at Esme intently. 'Are you saying this was Frank Stone?'

'Yes. And his cousin was also in the gang. And, my guess is he was the main protagonist in the dreadful crime. One Giles Philips.' She looked up, glancing between the two of them now. 'Giles Isaac Philips.'

Hester flinched. 'Isaac?'

Esme nodded. 'And whose mother's maiden name was Maudesley.'

Hester's hand flew to her mouth. 'Oh, mercy me.'

Esme looked at Max. 'That graduation ceremony photo you sent me with his parents. They aren't his parents. They're his aunt and uncle. Daniel Maudesley was his mother's brother. Looks like they took him in and he became part of their family.'

'But why?' Hester asked.

'Obvious, isn't it?' Max said. 'He didn't want to be Giles Philips any more, the person responsible for that kid's death. He wanted to wipe the slate clean and start again as someone else.'

'So, it seems you were right, Max,' Esme said, 'about Frank Stone having a hold over Isaac Maudesley.'

Max sat back, his arms folded. 'Question is, how's he going to use what he knows?'

'What are you talking about?' Hester said, scowling at him. 'He's already using it. It's why I'm having to put up with him as we speak.'

Max shook his head. 'I think he's only just got started. I reckon there's more to come. Much more.'

## 75

'So, what happens now?' Esme asked Max, as the three of them stood in the pub's car park. Max was cadging a lift back to Bideford with Hester and Esme was heading home. 'We've found out what Maudesley was running from, why he hid who he really was and what Stone's holding over him. Why are you convinced there's more?'

Max glanced across to Hester. 'Well, don't look at me,' she said. 'I don't see how any of this changes my position unless I want to go public on it. Which I don't. I've got the reputation of the museum to think about.'

'Will you tell Isaac what you've discovered?' Esme asked.

Hester raised her eyebrows, a look of horror on her face. 'Are you suggesting I should indulge in a spot of blackmail? Use it to get my project back on track?'

'No, of course not,' Esme said, flustered. 'That's not what I meant.' So, what *was* she trying to say? She wanted to put her thoughts in order, but they merged together in a jumble of confusion. 'I thought if he told Frank Stone you knew, Stone might think he didn't have that control any more. Maybe he'd back off.'

Hester made no comment, but turned to Max. 'It's not about whether I let on to Isaac, is it? I'm going to have to brace myself for public scrutiny whatever I do. Your journalist's brain is probably already compiling your sensational news story as we speak.'

'Thing is,' Max rubbed a thumb along his jawline, 'I've got a feeling in my gut there's more to come yet. Still got unanswered questions.'

'Murder not enough for you, then, Max?' Esme said, giving him a hard stare.

Max pursed his lips. 'Manslaughter. I doubt it'd be seen as murder.'

'Well, it was no accident, that's for sure. There was definite intent. And to cover it up, too.' Esme studied Max's face, a picture of contemplation. 'I don't know what more you were hoping to find, Max, but it is what it is.' She thought of the apparently bogus birth certificate and glanced at Hester. Should she mention it? But Max said he'd shown Hester and she'd said the same as Clara. 'And what you showed me before amounts to diddly-squat. Even if he had fathered an illegitimate child, it's not going to cause much of a ripple these days. And if he wanted to refute the claim, he could easily prove he's infertile.'

'Well, I'm not done with him yet,' Max said. 'There's more to that kettle of fish than it seems.'

Esme gave Max a scornful smile. 'Oh, come on, Max, let it go. I don't know what you're complaining about, anyway. All that mad pirate stuff? Tabloid gold, isn't it, if you'll forgive the pun. Readers'll love it. They won't care that Aidan never found Henry Venner's ship. They'll assume it's out there, but just hasn't been discovered yet.'

Max lifted a finger. 'And that, my dear Esme, is my point. Maudesley'll capitalise on it and use it as publicity for the new museum.'

Hester clicked her car key fob and pulled open the driver's door. 'Well, I can't say I'm going to enjoy the next few months. You might be right, Esme, that Frank Stone will lose his grip over Isaac. But all that'll achieve is he won't be best pleased. He'll be like a bear with a sore head.'

'On the other hand,' Esme said, 'he might decide it's not worth hanging around. You might be rid of him completely.'

Hester gave Esme a weak smile. 'I wish I had your confidence.' She looked over at Max. 'Come on then, Max. I need to be somewhere.'

Back at home, Esme found herself unable to concentrate on anything, her head too full of everything she'd discussed with Hester and Max earlier. She'd dismissed Max's gut feeling, that there was more to discover, as disappointment that Maudesley might survive the exposure of his teenage crime. Perhaps for Max, it was all the wrong way around. Instead of the individual under scrutiny being drawn into crime or corruption, it could be argued that for Maudesley, the traumatic events at Garter Abbey had been the making of the man, changing him and shaping his future in a positive way, turning tragedy into a force for good.

Would Max's prediction that Maudesley would turn any revelations to his advantage, rather than them result in his downfall, come true? Maudesley had already tried to persuade Aidan to say he'd found evidence of the shipwreck when he hadn't. Did that mean he was one step ahead? A troubled thought skittered into her head, but vanished before she could grasp what it was.

As for the apparently false evidence that Maudesley had fathered an illegitimate daughter in a foreign country, Esme hadn't yet decided what to make of it. Perhaps Max was right, that there was more to the supposed fabrication than at first appeared. Well, if he did get to the bottom of it, no doubt he'd take great pleasure in sharing it with her to justify his journalist's instinct.

Maddy called during the evening to say Aidan had quit his contract with Maudesley. Esme wondered what reasons he'd given. Had Maddy told Aidan what Esme had uncovered about the real Isaac Maudesley? Aidan needed to know the truth sometime. But she was unlikely to get a chance to tell him now, as with the job cancelled, he'd have no further need to stay at Maddy and Harry's. He may have already moved out.

Esme found herself yawning by late evening and dragged herself off to bed. Her dreams were mismatched images of newborn babies, surfacing scuba divers waving documents in their hands and a galleon in full sail, its timbers creaking as it surged through the surf. Then it became Aidan's boat chugging out of Lundy's harbour. She was standing on deck asking Aidan what he'd said to Maudesley, but she couldn't hear his reply above the rumble of the engine.

The rumble morphed into a pulsating rhythm and Esme woke suddenly, aware that her phone was buzzing on the bedside table, its recurring pattern accompanied by the muted glow of the screen which penetrated the blackness of the night. She dragged herself out of semi-consciousness and turned over to grab the instrument, heaving herself on to an elbow and blinking as she tried to focus on the name of the caller. Libby.

She sat up and swiped to make the connection, noting that it was almost 3 o'clock in the morning. 'Libby? Is everything all right?'

'No, it's not,' Libby said. 'It's the little boy. We have a crisis.'

# 76

Esme scrambled into a pair of jeans and a sweatshirt and hurried downstairs. The kittens looked out from their igloo bed, bemused by her appearance and seeming considerably more awake than Esme was feeling. She told them it was far too early for breakfast and to stay exactly where they were. She slipped her feet into her trainers, snatched up her coat and a torch and went out into the night, checking that no inquisitive feline was following her before closing the door behind her.

She shivered against the chill on her face as she scurried down the lane to Libby's. A glimmer of moonlight pushed its way through a passing cloud and she switched off her torch and slipped it into her pocket. The pounding of her footsteps on the tarmac seemed disproportionally loud in the still darkness, and she felt inexplicably conspicuous, as though her neighbours were peering out through the crack between their drawn curtains to see who was disturbing their slumbers.

Libby's porch light was glowing in welcome and Esme quickened her pace to reach it. Libby must have been watching for her, as the moment Esme mounted the steps, the door opened and Libby ushered her in. She was wearing a dressing gown and slippers.

'Where is he?' Esme said in a low voice, peering over Libby's shoulder.

'In the kitchen,' Libby whispered. 'He woke me up, banging on the door. I couldn't believe it when I looked out and saw him.'

'And it's definitely the lad we saw before in the garden?'

'No doubt at all.' Libby glanced over her shoulder before turning back to Esme. 'I can't make head nor tail of what he's talking about. But he seems desperate about something.'

'He obviously feels he can trust us,' Esme said, 'or he wouldn't come back.'

'My thoughts exactly.' Libby jerked her head. 'Come on.' Esme followed her into the kitchen.

The young boy was sitting at Libby's kitchen table, drinking a mug of hot chocolate. He looked up as Esme came in, wariness in his eyes.

'Here's my friend,' Libby said. 'I told you she'd come, didn't I?' She turned to Esme. 'I explained I was going to call you, that you were the other lady he met last time,' she said. 'I assumed he'd understood as he didn't seem concerned when I picked up the phone.' She turned back to the boy and smiled. 'You mustn't worry. We're going to help you.'

Esme shed her coat and sat down opposite the boy. 'Hello.' She pointed to herself. 'My name is Esme. Do you remember me?'

The boy blinked back at her for a moment before nodding and glancing up at Libby. 'Libbee,' he said.

'That's right,' Libby said, taking a seat beside Esme. 'And your name is Adil.' Again the boy nodded.

'Hello, Adil,' Esme said, watching him as he took another sip of drinking chocolate. 'So, where do you live, Adil?' When he looked confused, she said, 'Your house. Where is your house?' She drew a square shape in the air and used her hands, fingertips touching, to indicate a roof.

Adil stretched out his arms either side. 'Big,' he said, before pointing behind him over his shoulder.

The gesture threw Esme's thoughts into turmoil, forcing her to address her previous suspicion as to where Adil may have come from. Was it Maudesley's house he was describing? She stared at the little boy, at his dark hair, his deep brown eyes and olive skin, the image of a smug Max sliding the birth certificate across the pub table in the forefront of her mind.

She dragged herself back to the present as Libby leaned towards the boy. 'Are you unhappy in the big house, Adil?' she asked, pulling an exaggerated sad expression.

Adil's face puckered into one of anger rather than sadness. 'School.'

'You go to school?'

He shook his head crossly, his expression of anger strengthening. 'No school.'

'But you'd *like* to go to school, is that it?'

His face changed and he beamed. 'Iss. Go school.'

'Well, he seems old enough,' Libby said to Esme. 'I wonder why he can't.'

Adil mimicked Esme's air drawing of a house and balled his fists, before pressing a hand hard across his mouth. Libby and Esme exchanged glances.

'Seems to me,' Libby said, 'he's indicating he's not allowed.'

'I'm sure you're right,' Esme said, recalling the previous incident which concluded with the sound of barking dogs and the poor boy being hunted down like prey. 'And not just school, either. I don't think he's allowed out full stop.'

Suddenly, Adil stood up and gestured in the same direction he'd indicated a moment ago that his house lay. 'Muther.'

'Your mother?' Esme said. 'What about your mother, Adil? Is it your mother who needs help?'

Libby gasped. 'Do you think he's trying to tell us he's a prisoner, along with his mother?'

'Is your mother in the house?' Esme asked him, using the same gesture.

'Iss,' Adil said, nodding. 'Help.' He pointed to himself, and then to the women. 'Adil. Libee. Essmee.' He threw an arm behind him. 'Help.'

Esme stood up. 'Show us, Adil.'

Adil reached out and grabbed hold of Esme's hand and pulled her towards the back door which opened out onto the rear patio. Esme managed to snatch up her coat off the back of the chair and, slipping it on, followed him, Libby trailing along behind.

'Where are we going?' Libby hissed as Adil led Esme around

the side of the cottage and down the steps to the lane. 'I'm not exactly dressed for the outside.'

Esme caught hold of Adil's arm and gave it a gentle tug, pulling him to a halt. 'Adil,' she whispered, with a questioning gesture. 'Where are you taking us?'

Adil leaned towards her. 'Mother. Help. You tell. Say OK,' he said and made the shape of an O with his finger and thumb, before taking her hand once more and urging her to keep moving down the lane.

'Looks like he's heading for the beach,' Libby said, in Esme's ear. 'I'd better go and get some clothes on and catch you up.'

'Good idea,' Esme said, nodding. 'But be quick.'

Libby peeled away and hurried back up the lane. Esme caught up with Adil, who'd stopped at the head of the path to check she was still following. When he saw she was on her way, he speeded up, apparently confident of her commitment.

They reached the bottom of the slipway and crunched their way on to the beach. Esme could hear the hiss of the waves as they broke on to the pebbles. She slowed, scanning around for signs of Adil's mother. Where was she? Had he left her here? But she could see no one anywhere in the watery moonlight. She heard Adil call and looked ahead to see him at the barrier which the local authority had placed after the cottage had collapsed. He was standing, beckoning her.

Esme approached cautiously, looking up into the threatening shadows of the cliff above and wondering whether there'd been any further rock falls since the major rupture which had taken the cottage with it. As she reached the barrier, Adil called her name before disappearing and then reappearing on the other side.

'You can't go over there, Adil,' Esme shouted to him. 'It's dangerous.' But he took no notice, running on further, before turning back to signal for her to join him. As she peered into the half-light, she saw him stop at the base of the cliff, wildly gesturing and calling her name.

Esme glanced behind her. Where was Libby? She couldn't be far behind. It wouldn't take her long to throw on some clothes and come after them. She turned back to the beach and heard Adil call her name again. She sighed. What choice did she have?

She spied the breach in the barrier where Adil had gone and squeezed herself through it. She tried to ignore the looming cliff above her head, picking her way across the pebbles to where Adil was waiting for her. When she got to him, he was standing beside some sort of opening, a black hole below where the cottage had stood. She stared at it, recalling Jim teasing her about secret smuggling tunnels leading down to the beach.

She looked at Adil, who was smiling and nodding, delighted that she'd responded. He pointed into the blackness.

'Come. You help. Muther.'

Esme frowned. 'Your mother's in there?' she asked, nodding at the opening.

Adil nodded, before enacting what Esme took to be his mother's fear. He reached out and took Esme's hand and pulled her towards the entrance before letting her arm drop and disappearing inside.

Esme stood for a moment, uncertain what to do. She assumed his mother had been too frightened to take the same route as her son. But where was she? At the other end of the tunnel? Back in the house? She thought about the dogs and the security that Max had encountered. How had Adil managed to evade them this time? And if she did follow Adil, what or who might she have to confront?

Adil's face appeared again at the entrance, scowling at her for delaying. But how could she follow him? She couldn't see her way. But then she remembered the torch in her pocket.

She pulled it out and switched it on.

'OK, Adil,' she said, sighing. 'I'm coming.'

## 77

A strong smell of brine mixed with a cloying dampness pervaded the tunnel, which had been hewn out of the rock like a Cornish tin mine. The soft sound of waves breaking on the beach behind them filtered into the narrow cave. Esme's torchlight bounced around the walls and roof, highlighting the dripping formations which hung from the ceiling as she followed Adil further into its depths. Low and tight in places, with protrusions of rock strata jutting out into their path, the cave caused her to duck her head and manoeuvre sideways on more than one occasion to get through.

Esme tried to get her bearings and calculate how far into the cliff they'd come, but it was too difficult to judge. Did their route really lead all the way back to the old Chalacombe House, now the Victorian Gothic home of Isaac Maudesley? It seemed astonishing that the tunnel's existence wasn't well known. But maybe in recent years, access to it – perhaps once via the floor of the cottage's cellar – had been blocked off, only now exposed following the collapse of the cliff above and the cottage with it.

A droplet of water landed on the back of Esme's neck and dribbled down her back. She shivered.

'Adil,' she said, her voice reverberating around the passageway, 'how much further?'

He shot her a glance over his shoulder, his dark eyes glinting in the beam of her torch. 'Come more.' He turned back and kept walking.

Esme sighed and traipsed on, apprehension creeping into the pit of her stomach and anxious questions forming in her head. Where was he leading her? What was this all about? And where did Isaac Maudesley fit into this? She immediately thought of Max and his conviction there was more to learn. This had something to do with that birth certificate. Would she find Maudesley's daughter at the end of this trail? But Hester said Maudesley wasn't able to father children. Unless his infertility had occurred later, after his Mediterranean expeditions.

Suddenly, the passageway opened out into a yawning void, vaulting high above Esme's head. Adil slowed and called out, turning to Esme and gesturing for her to shine her torch straight ahead. As she did so, the beam of light fell on a shape – the figure of a woman with long dark hair, sitting on the ledge of a rock. The woman stood up and, holding up her hand to shield her eyes from the glare, shouted something long-winded and incomprehensible at Adil.

Adil turned back to Esme, a sheepish expression on his face. He laid his hand on his chest.

'Bad son,' he said, with an embarrassed grin. 'She wait too long time.'

*

After berating Adil for leaving her for so long in the dark, the woman allowed Esme to coax her back down the tunnel. As they made their way to the beach, Esme's mind was frantic with scenarios of how and why a young woman and her son had found themselves in a situation where fleeing in the dead of night was a solution both of them had been willing to undertake.

Adil's mother had a smattering of English and, with Esme's encouragement, revealed her name as Sahila. Esme thought she'd had good reason to be annoyed with Adil, as waiting for so long had left Sahila chilled. Her hair and clothes – a loose cotton dress and a pair of strappy sandals, offering little protection for the night's escapades – were damp and her slim body shivered as Esme guided her along the narrow route.

As they emerged out of the dank atmosphere of the tunnel and into the cool freshness of the moonlit night, Esme paused to take a breath and saw Libby waiting for them at the barrier. They all trudged across the pebbles towards her, Adil supporting his mother as well as he could, given his slight stature.

'Thank God,' Libby said, as they reached the barrier. 'I got here just in time to see you disappear and I didn't know what to do for the best, whether I should wait or call the police.'

'Police no,' Sahila said, recoiling.

Libby reached out her hand. 'No, luv, don't you worry. I've called no one. Let's get you both into the warm, shall we?'

Back in Libby's kitchen, towels were found and warm drinks were made. Esme studied the woman. Even if Maudesley's infertility was a lie, this could be no daughter of his. She was far too young. His granddaughter, perhaps? No, even that didn't fit.

When Sahila and Adil were comfortable, the four of them sat at the kitchen table and, with halting English, gestures and Adil's childish drawings, the pair slowly told their story. It was one Esme had heard many times in news reports. A promise of a better life, money exchanged, a terrifying journey undertaken, only to arrive in a place where it became clear that the hoped-for freedom was an illusion. They'd been taken to *big house*, as Adil described it, and there they'd been ever since. Sahila, it seemed, had become some sort of housekeeper, cleaning and cooking, when promises of better things to come never materialised.

'Did you know Isaac Maudesley before?' Esme asked. 'Is he family?'

Sahila stared at Esme for a moment before her puzzled expression slipped into one of amusement, as though Esme's suggestion was absurd. She shook her head.

'No family. Him? No.'

'Sorry,' Esme said. 'It was just a thought.' She felt Libby looking at her with similar confusion. 'Do carry on with your story.'

As Esme listened, something Max had said suddenly made sense. He'd been watching Isaac Maudesley's house after a tip-off of a delivery. But it was not smuggled artefacts being delivered,

370

but smuggled people. How had Isaac Maudesley got caught up in such an odious endeavour?

She expressed her fury in Maudesley's deception, but to her surprise, Sahila defended him.

'How can you say that?' Esme said. 'You're a prisoner in his house, a slave with no life of your own.'

Sahila looked down at the table. 'Is true, but worse could be for woman,' she said. 'He not let them take me. He keep me here.'

Esme realised the implication of her words – that Maudesley had intervened to prevent Sahila being sold into the sex trade. So, what was his motive? What was he hoping to achieve?

'One day, he say,' Sahila continued. 'New life.' She reached and grasped Adil's hand and smiled at him. 'For me and for Adil. But too long we wait. Now we go.'

But there was more Sahila had to tell them. Tears filled her eyes and Adil put his arm around his mother as they overflowed and ran down her face. The final leg of their journey had ended in disaster. A few miles off the North Devon coast, they and their fellow travellers had been off-loaded from the hold of a yacht into a small dinghy, just as the weather deteriorated. The inadequate vessel had been no match for the worsening conditions. It rocked alarmingly in the choppy seas and as they approached the shore, a huge wave upended the boat, tipping its human cargo into the water. Many could not swim, many were already cold, dehydrated and exhausted and had no reserves left to deal with such trauma. Sahila and Adil had been the only survivors.

Libby reached across the table and took Sahila's hand. 'You're safe now,' she said, glancing round at Esme, who nodded. But Esme's mind had slipped back to the story of their arrival and something which one of the RNLI crew had mentioned on the night of Maddy's party, that a few months before they'd found a half-inflated boat, but no evidence of it having anyone in it.

'Sahila,' Esme said. The young woman looked up, her dark eyes moist. Perhaps she guessed what Esme was going to ask.

371

Esme cleared her throat. 'What happened to the rest of the people in the boat?'

Sahila swallowed. 'Die in water. All sink in water.'

'Yes, but…'

'Under beach,' Adil interrupted. He began a furious digging action until his mother said something to calm him and he stopped, laying his hands in his lap and staring down at them.

'They were buried on the beach?' Esme said. 'Is that what Adil means?'

Sahila nodded.

## 78

Esme and Libby had a murmured conference in the hall. Sahila was upstairs having a shower and Adil was sitting at the kitchen table drawing.

'Sahila's going to have to report what she knows to the police eventually,' Libby said. 'Despite her reluctance.'

'Yes, I know,' Esme agreed. The image of Adil's enactment of the victims being buried kept playing over and over in her mind.

Libby chewed the ball of her thumb. 'I suppose all she'd need to do is point them in the right direction and they'd do the rest.'

'But she doesn't trust what we're saying,' Esme said, 'that the police will be sympathetic to their situation. That they'll be considered victims of crime.'

'Well, you can understand her being wary. She needs to gain her confidence that she and Adil are safe, first.'

The sound of running water from the bathroom above stopped. Esme fingered her scar and glanced towards the stairs. Sahila would be back down in a moment. They needed to have a plan before then.

'I think your idea of contacting a charity that understands situations like this has got to be our best next move,' she said. 'They'll give Sahila the necessary support and legal advice, that sort of thing.'

'Yes,' Libby said, nodding. 'She can tell her story to them and take it from there.' She moved towards the kitchen door. 'I'll go online and see what I can find.'

'Oh, wait a minute. What are we thinking? We've the answer right here in the village.'

'What d'you mean?'

'Dom and Faith,' Esme said, thinking of a conversation during the meal they'd shared at Libby's. 'Well, not Dom. Faith. She works for the Red Cross. Helping asylum seekers is part of her job. She'll know what to do.'

Libby nodded. 'Excellent idea. Right, I'll see if I can get hold of her.'

'There's one other problem, though,' Esme said, biting her lower lip.

'What's that?'

Esme inclined her head towards the kitchen. 'How long is it going to be before someone realises their birds have flown?'

Libby scoffed and flicked her plait over her shoulder. 'Well, they should be safe enough here. They won't know where to look, will they?'

'No, I wasn't thinking about that, though you're right. I doubt they'd think someone local would take them in. If they did do a search, they'd assume they'd be out there somewhere and go looking for them.' Esme recalled the sounds of dogs barking they'd heard before. Would Maudesley and his cronies try and track Sahila and Adil down? Might that lead them to Libby's cottage? She thought it unlikely, given they'd come across the beach. The tide would be on its way in by now. Surely any scent would have been lost.

'What did you mean, then?' Libby asked.

'What?' Esme blinked at her.

'You said that wasn't the problem you were thinking about. So, what *is* the problem?'

'Oh, yes. Sorry.' Esme grimaced. 'The bodies.'

'What about them?'

'They may assume, quite understandably, that if Sahila is afraid of the authorities, their secret is safe. On the other hand...'

'They might worry Sahila will speak out.'

'And try and dispose of the evidence.'

'Move the bodies, you mean,' Libby said, alarm on her face. 'How horribly gruesome.' She folded her arms and tugged on her plait. 'So, what do we do? If we can't persuade Sahila to talk to the police, maybe we should alert them anyway?'

Esme pulled a face. 'I'm still wincing from their scepticism of our reporting seeing Adil,' she said. 'And if we tell the police about Sahila and Adil, we'll expose them to the very thing we've promised them we won't.'

'So, what do you suggest?' Libby said, flinging her arm out in a hopeless gesture.

'That we find the evidence. That we call it in. That way, we don't involve Sahila and Adil.'

'Evidence? What evidence?'

Esme snatched her coat from the hook by the front door. 'Sahila said they were buried in a cave a little further along the beach from the tunnel entrance.'

A horrified expression came across Libby's face. 'You're not going there?'

'Got to be worth a try, hasn't it? And if I find something, we can get the police down here before Maudesley and his cronies get wind of what's going on.'

'What? And start digging? That's ridiculous, Esme. You can't.'

'No, I don't intend to. But if the cave's above the waterline, like Sahila says, any recently disturbed ground will be obvious.' Esme bit her lower lip. 'Though it might not stay like that, not with this spring tide. It'll come much higher up and could cover it. Which makes it even more imperative.'

'I'm not so sure about this, Esme,' Libby said, slowly shaking her head. 'I'm really not.'

Esme laid a hand on Libby's arm. 'Look, why don't you see if you can get hold of Faith while I go and take a poke around?'

Libby let out an exasperated sigh. 'I can see I'm talking to a brick wall. Well, don't take long. The tide's on its way in.'

Esme slipped on her coat, checking that her torch was still in her pocket. 'Don't worry,' she said, grabbing hold of the door handle. 'I have no intention of being any longer than I have to.'

## 79

Esme hurried along the lane and set off down the steep path to the beach, retracing her and Adil's steps of earlier. All the cottages on either side were dark and silent. There was enough moonlight to see her way, so she slipped her torch back in her pocket.

She crunched her way along the shoreline, further inland now with the tide on the rise. She slipped between the barriers where she'd followed Adil before. Now she did need her torch, as her route took her into the shadows. She pulled it out of her pocket and turned it on, flicking it up against the face of the cliff, looking for the entrance to the tunnel to get her bearings. When she reached it, she stopped for a moment and stared at the heap of rubble which had once been the cottage above. From what she and Libby had understood, Adil had been aware of the passageway from the other end, but it had led nowhere. When the cottage came down, he uncovered its secret – that it led directly to the beach. As the beach was closed to the public, there was little danger of anyone noticing the tunnel entrance. And, Esme realised, little danger of anyone making a gruesome discovery of what was in the cave beyond.

She recalled a comment by the policeman on duty at the barrier the day the cottage went down, that the collapse had taken the experts by surprise. She'd thought nothing of it at the time. After all, it was already marked as a dangerous structure and cordoned off, giving the impression there was an imminent danger of it falling into the sea. Perhaps someone had decided that with the holiday season ahead and the increased risk of someone stumbling upon the cave's terrible secret, a closed beach was the perfect protection against detection and had conveniently engineered the premature fall. Ironic, then, if the action had provided an escape route for Sahila and Adil, and the opportunity to expose their incarceration and the horrific crime evidenced below the floor of the cave.

Esme circumnavigated the rubble pile and continued along the beach, recalling Sahila's faltering instructions and hoping she'd interpreted them correctly. If she had, she should be able to see the cave in question at any moment. She pressed on, scanning the rock strata to her right and conscious of the waves breaking ever closer on her left, reminding her that she mustn't take longer than necessary or she'd find herself cut off by the tide.

The beam of light from her torch picked out a black shadow and her stomach gave an involuntary plunge. There it was, exactly as Sahila had described. Esme stopped walking and stared ahead of her.

Well, if she was going to do this and hadn't just wasted her time coming here, she needed to get on with it. She'd not find out if the cave held any evidence which would convince the police to get down here unless she went in there and looked.

Taking a deep breath, she trudged up the beach towards the entrance.

The enormity of the cave took Esme by surprise. From its narrow entrance, no one would guess what a huge expanse was hidden behind. She flashed her torch around, above and beyond, lighting up the vast roof of the main cavern, and realised it was more than one cave. Further chambers, smaller but just as evocative, led off the central void, some on either side, some stretching ahead, deeper into the cliff side. She stood for a moment, admiring the beauty of the natural phenomenon.

But this wasn't getting the job done. She needed to search each of the smaller caves, particularly those beyond the high tide mark where the sea would not have washed away any signs of digging, thereby obliterating evidence of the crime Sahila and her son had witnessed. Esme ventured deeper into the cave, sensing a difference to the ground beneath her feet. She shone the torch on to the floor and noted the sand was no longer wet and smooth, but drier, scuffed up and uneven. A shiver charged down her spine as she realised other feet before hers had walked this route, feet belonging to vile and despicable individuals with a contemptuous disregard for human life.

She was hit by a sudden sense of despondency. How could she possibly check out every chamber in the short time she had? *And how short is that time?* she thought with alarm. She lifted her wrist to look at the soft illumination of her watch and relaxed. She'd been no more than half an hour. Still plenty of time to look around and get back across the beach before the tide closed in.

She exhaled slowly, telling herself she must keep looking as long as she could. She moved forward, shining her torch into the smaller chambers one by one, making her way around the outer perimeter of the main void. As she peered into each of the inner caves, hope began to fade of finding anything. Until she came to a cavity towards the back of the central cavern which appeared wider and deeper than the rest. She bent her head and stepped inside, sweeping the beam of the torch ahead of her.

As she moved further in, the beam picked out a dark shape on a low spit of rock about halfway into the cave. She stopped, trepidation creeping through her bones, turning to horror as she realised that the shape she was looking at was a body.

But this wasn't the evidence she'd come seeking. It wasn't the remains of someone who'd drowned when their boat had sunk. It was the bloodied and battered body of Frank Stone.

*

Esme stared at the grotesque image in the beam of light, trying to process the implications of what she was looking at, questions swirling around in her head. Who'd done this? Why? Was the killer responsible for trafficking Sahila and Adil? Was this connected to their escape? Did it mean someone knew they'd gone?

Esme closed her eyes and took a deep breath, her thoughts alighting upon the theory that the tampered dive equipment meant someone had wanted Maudesley dead. It had to be connected to Sahila and Adil's situation, didn't it? Maudesley had already prevented Sahila from being taken away and exploited. Had he threatened to expose the traffickers? And what of Stone? Had he also been targeted? And if they'd got Stone, had they also got Maudesley? If she was to explore the cave further, would she find his body too?

She gripped the torch to stop herself shaking. She didn't need to search further. It may not have been the evidence she'd been expecting to find, but it was more than enough. She could now leave it to the police. All she wanted to do was get out of there and raise the alarm.

She spun round and aiming her torch ahead of her, scrambled over the rocks, floundering her way towards the exit from the cave. But as she closed in on her escape back to the beach, a shape appeared at the entrance, a black silhouette against the pale light of the early dawn sky.

Esme cried out, stumbling backwards, dropping her torch as the beam of light caught a figure stepping inside the cave. She blinked in the half darkness as Isaac Maudesley stared back at her, gripping a heavy spade across his body like a weapon.

# 80

Maudesley gaped at Esme as though she was an apparition. For her part, Esme saw a very different Isaac Maudesley to the assured historian she'd seen on Lundy Island. The man in front of her appeared disorientated, defeated and, unless her instincts had deserted her, frightened.

She stared beyond him, her eyes fixed on the cave entrance and her route to freedom, blocked by Maudesley. He blundered towards her and she recoiled, but as a scream formed in her throat, he threw aside the spade. It struck the wall of the cave with an excruciating clatter, Esme wincing at the assault on her eardrums.

Maudesley dropped down on to a rock beside the entrance and hung his head. He looked as though he'd slept in his clothes, the knees of his trousers stained wet and smeared with sand. Esme found herself unable to move as she tried to grasp what had happened here. Had he and Stone been trying to dig up the buried bodies to dispose of them somewhere else and argued? Over what? How had Stone ended up dead?

Esme grappled with her options. To get away, she'd need to pass close to Maudesley, close enough to put herself within his reach. If she was quick, she may be able to push past before he could react. But a sudden action may trigger a response in him to try and stop her. If she'd not dropped her torch, shining the light in his face might improve her chances, but the likelihood of her retrieving it in the dark was negligible. She was wary of doing so, too, given it would mean taking her eyes off Maudesley. Her only solace was that he hadn't sought to attack her. In fact, slumped as he was on the rock in front of her, he looked a broken man.

A sob of panic escaped from her throat, the sound amplified as it echoed around the chamber. Part of her wanted to understand what had occurred, but part of her cautioned herself against revealing what she'd found and what she knew. But Maudesley wasn't stupid. What was she doing there if she was unaware of the secrets he had to hide? He must be asking himself the very same question now. He must also know it was over. Perhaps that in itself would be enough to keep her alive, if he felt he had nothing to gain by hurting her.

Maudesley lifted his head and stared at her. She sensed his eyes boring into hers rather than saw them, given the meagre light spilling in from outside. When he spoke, his voice was hoarse and a little breathless.

'Frank said you'd been poking around. You probably think you've worked it all out.'

'Maybe,' Esme said, keeping her voice steady, alarmed that he knew who she was. 'I might understand more than you think.' She shifted a little closer to the cave entrance, while maintaining the distance between her and Maudesley, her eyes beginning to adjust in the gloom.

He snorted. 'I doubt that.'

'You and Frank Stone were at school together, weren't you? I'm guessing it was your great-uncle who sowed the seeds of your fascination for pirates, filling your heads with stories of your ancestor, Henry Venner.' She dared to take another step. Maudesley didn't move. 'So, did you discover something that suggested there was some truth in those stories? That the spoils of Henry's renegade life might really exist? Was that when Frank came back?'

Maudesley threw his head back and laughed out loud. 'Came back?' he said. The laugh faded and he glared at her, the feeble light creating ugly shadows on his face. 'He never went away. He's bled me dry for years. Each time I thought I'd seen the last of him, he'd crawl out from underneath a stone and hassle me some more.'

Esme blinked into the semi-darkness as the truth hit her. Max had always maintained that Stone had something on Maudesley, but even though they'd discovered what it was, they'd missed the point. Even if both were culpable in Anthony Milton's death, Stone hadn't felt the need to change his name, as Maudesley had done. Why would he? The cover up by the school and subsequent inquest ruling of accidental death gave him no cause. Maudesley, on the other hand, did have cause. Not to hide from his past so much as to hide from Stone. But his cover had failed. Stone had found him – and years ago, it seemed.

Esme frowned. 'But I don't understand,' she said, thinking immediately of Hester. 'You welcomed Stone with open arms. You were in this together. So what changed?'

'I'd had enough,' he shouted into the echoing chamber. 'That's what changed.'

Suddenly, Esme understood. Maudesley had used Stone's obsession for Henry Venner against him, not in a partnership with him. *I'd had enough.* No wonder he wanted Aidan to let Stone believe he'd found evidence of his ancestor's ship in the waters around Lundy, that there was gold buried under the sea bed.

'The whole pirate story was a setup, wasn't it?' Esme said, as the pieces dropped into place in her head. 'You knew Frank would fall for it. You turned the tables. Now it was you in control. Why now, though? Why not years ago?'

The worm had finally turned. *I'd had enough,* Maudesley had snapped. But what had been the trigger?

Maudesley's groan reverberated around the cavern. 'I had to do something. I had to stop him. It couldn't happen again.'

'Again?'

'He came begging, saying my daughter and her son needed help to come to this country.' He tossed his head and scoffed. 'Of course, I knew it was all lies. *His* daughter. Not mine. Never mine. I thought her mother loved me, but she never did. All the time, she and Frank were…' His words fizzled out.

The implications swirled round and round in Esme's head. Sahila was Stone's daughter? How could that be? The same

382

mismatch of dates and ages applied whether Stone was her father as much as had it been Maudesley.

'When she got pregnant,' Maudesley was saying, 'I got the blame.'

'So you left the country.'

'I valued my life!' he yelled, as though Esme was stupid. 'I didn't relish being strung up by her brothers.' He wrapped his arms around himself and began to rock back and forth. 'The only good thing about it was leaving Frank behind. I naively thought that's the last I'd see of him. My mistake. He turned up out of the blue a year or two later, and at regular intervals from then on. Sometimes, I still thought – hoped – he'd gone for good. But it was a false hope. He'd always turn up again, and with increasing demands. And then this.'

'About his daughter and grandson?'

'Yes. So I agreed to the plan.'

'Even though you knew it wasn't true?'

'Yes, because I knew it was *his* daughter and *his* grandson, and if I helped he'd be beholden to me. Figured I could use it against him. Give me some control for a change.'

Something clicked in Esme's head. 'But it wasn't his daughter, was it?'

'No, of course it wasn't. I'd been set up.' He put his head in his hands.

'And you became the unwilling participant in people trafficking.' She wondered if she should tell him that she'd met Sahila and Adil, and knew about the bodies buried somewhere behind her. But perhaps he already sensed she knew. And she did. That had been the trigger. Frank had crossed a line. 'So that's when you came up with your plan, lure him in by rekindling those stories of pirate gold and lost treasure. To achieve what, though?'

'To stop him, of course. If he thought he was going to get rich some other way, he'd have no need to exploit desperate people.'

'But that dream wouldn't last indefinitely. He'd soon realise it

383

was a fantasy. So what then?' She gasped as the horror struck her. 'Oh my God. It was you! You sabotaged the dive gear. Then tricked Frank to go in your place, hoping he'd drown.'

'He had to be stopped, don't you see?'

'But they thought Aidan Garrett had tried to kill him. You were prepared to see an innocent man take the blame to get rid of your nemesis.'

'No, that's not how it was supposed to be. It was meant to look like an accident.'

'And when it didn't work,' she cried, thrusting her arm out behind her, 'you lured him here and…' She swallowed, unable to say more as once again, Maudesley dropped his head into his hands.

Esme stared at him, breathing deeply, struggling to contain her outrage. As she calmed herself, her ear tuned into the sound of the sea somewhere in the distance.

The tide. She had to get back across the beach before the tide cut her off.

'We have to get out of here,' Esme said.

Maudesley looked as though he was lost in his own dark thoughts. 'What?'

'The tide's coming in. We'll be cut off.' She lunged past him, expecting to feel a hand grip her arm, but nothing came. She slithered over stones as the soundtrack of hissing and encroaching waves filled her ears. She burst, breathless, through the opening and on to the beach.

But the beach was almost non-existent. In the early light of dawn, she could see that her way out had been completely covered by the sea. She was trapped.

# 81

Esme stood with her back to the cave, considering her options. There was still some beach in front of her, but it wasn't going to last long before it too would be engulfed in seawater. She recalled Sahila's comment about the bodies being buried above the high tide mark and briefly considered retreating back into the cave to wait it out. But even if she had been willing to share a confined space with Maudesley for any longer than she had already, there was another more significant reason for not taking that option. It was a spring tide, meaning the water would rise much higher than usual and likely flood any areas previously beyond the waterline.

She looked back over her shoulder and into the blackness of the cave. Did Maudesley realise that? Was his plan to stay and emerge at low tide?

She took a half step inside the cave. Maudesley was still sitting where she'd left him. 'It's a spring tide!' she shouted at him, her voice reverberating around the cavernous space beyond. 'You can't stay in there. You'll drown.'

He didn't move.

Esme was alert to the sound of breaking waves behind her. If he wasn't responding to her warning, she didn't have time to wait to see if he'd change his mind. She backed out of the cave entrance and gazed in the direction of the slipway which had brought her on to the beach. Was it possible to wade through the rising waves to reach it? But she knew from the conversation she'd had with Beth, the Lifeboat crew member at Maddy's party, that the firm advice was to avoid going into the water. Not only might she be swept off her feet and out to sea, but her body temperature would fall dramatically and she'd be in danger of succumbing to hypothermia.

But there was another way off this beach, she remembered.

The tunnel. If she could make it to the tunnel entrance, she could follow it back to the house. And she wouldn't have to worry about encountering Maudesley, either. Or Stone, she realised with a shocked memory of what she'd caught in the beam of her torch.

She trudged across the front of the cliff face, glancing up now and again to find her bearings, anxiety growing when she couldn't locate the opening. A surge of water took her by surprise and she had to make a dash away from its reach to avoid getting her feet wet. She stumbled, twisting her ankle as she went down and cursing as she bashed her knee on a large pebble. She staggered to her feet and resumed her journey across the stones.

A few minutes later, she spied the tell-tale overhanging tree which demarked the point where the tunnel emerged from the cliff. But her relief was premature. Ahead of her the surging waves swept into a gully, taking the shoreline higher up the beach and creating a barrier of water between her and her planned escape.

She cursed herself for not getting out of the cave when she should have done. She didn't need to speak to Maudesley, she owed him nothing. And now, there was no way out. She must call for help. She must phone the emergency services and ask for the coastguard.

She reached into her coat pocket for her phone. But her pocket was empty. Her phone was still sitting on her bedside table from where she'd answered it when Libby called. The only thing she'd thought to grab as she'd rushed out of the cottage was a torch. So now what?

Backing away from the waves, which were now rushing at her feet, she turned to look along the beach and at the growing weight of water between her and her exit. Staying out of the water was not going to be an option. If she couldn't call for help, what choice did she have?

She traipsed back as far as she could go to the foot of the cliff. If she chose her moment, she might be able to get beyond the spit of shingle covered in water while the wave was on its way out.

Surely it couldn't be that deep just there. If she made it across, she could then do the same for the next arc of beach, which was still dry. Of course, after that, the stretch of water was wider, much wider than she could traverse in the time it would take for the wave to go out and come back in, but with luck she might still make it across. She had to try. The only alternative was to sit at the bottom of the cliff and wait for the sea to drag her in. And that was not an alternative she relished or was prepared to consider.

She stood on the edge of the water and waited until the next wave was sucked back into the sea. Then she made her move, splashing across the jut of water as quickly as she could, reaching the narrow dry island of shingle beyond. She felt the seawater seep into her trainers, shocked at the level of cold, but relieved she'd made it this far.

She stopped to take a breath, watching the waves as they swayed in and out a few times before bracing herself for the next charge. She repeated the process, a little further than before, but while she felt the incoming wave push at her heels, she managed another successful crossing.

Despite her legs now being wet to the knees, the small triumphs buoyed her. Two more crossings to go and she'd reach the point where the tunnel opened out on to the beach. Of course, there was the wider area of water to negotiate yet, but the important thing was that her plan was working.

As she stood, braced for the next section, her teeth began to chatter. She clamped her jaw tight, focused on the swirling water and, when the optimum moment came, she charged across through it. Again, she felt the pull on her ankles and the water dragging the sand away beneath her. She almost floundered, but managed to catch her balance, throwing herself on to the ground to get out of the water. She dragged herself up on to her feet and took a deep breath.

Made it.

But she knew the next expanse of water would be the greatest challenge. It would take her longer to wade across than it would take the wave to go out and come back in. She had to hope that she had enough strength to keep moving as it swirled around her legs.

She stared into the foamy water and clenched her teeth, waiting for the moment to strike. The wave streamed in and hissed menacingly as it was sucked back out. Esme plunged into the water, dragging her sodden legs through the surf, her gaze fixed on the narrow spit of beach on the other side.

As she'd anticipated, the next wave began to surge back in before she'd got halfway across. She pressed on, but the force of the water was alarmingly fierce. She lost her footing and fell heavily into the water. She forced her head above it, spluttering for air, and tried to stand up.

But the current was too strong. Too weak to fight back, she felt herself being dragged out to the sea.

# 82

The waves closed over Esme's head, plunging her into a muted watery world which invaded her ears and up into her nose. She thrashed around in the surf, kicking out furiously, angered by the situation she found herself in. When her feet made contact with the beach below the surface, it heartened her resolve and she swivelled herself around, digging her toes into the shifting sand to drag herself out of the water. She fell on to her hands and knees and crawled up the beach as far as she could before exhaustion took over.

When she'd recovered a little, she sat up, breathing heavily. What now? Another attempt? Even the thought of it made her feel weary. How would she find the strength? She was also very cold in her sodden clothes and she knew it could only get increasingly difficult to make her limbs do what she wanted them to. She looked back along the beach, which had become so familiar since she'd moved into her cottage. How ironic that her desire to live on the coast would lead to her demise.

She turned her head to gaze out to sea and began to relax. Suddenly, it didn't matter any more. She became absorbed by the way the early morning light flickered on the undulating sea swell and the subdued colours of Lundy Island, barely visible on the horizon. If this was her time, then so be it. There were worse ways to leave this world. She'd tried her best, hadn't she? She couldn't ask more than that.

And then she saw another colour amongst the waves. Orange. She focused on it, fascinated by how it kept disappearing and reappearing, every time getting bigger.

Until the small part of her brain still in touch with reality gave her a hefty kick. It was a lifeboat. And it was heading towards her. Someone must have raised the alarm.

She hauled herself to her feet and staggered towards the water's edge as the boat halted in the shallows and a figure, dressed in the RNLI's distinctive bright yellow kit, red life jacket and white helmet, waded on to the beach towards her, shouting at her to stay where she was.

A plethora of words crowded into Esme's head, thoughts of thanks, of fear and of relief, but the most urgent message she knew she had to convey was that there was someone else. She lifted a weary arm and pointed towards the cave.

'He wouldn't come out. He thinks he's safe in there. He wouldn't listen.'

'We'll worry about him in a minute,' the crewman said, guiding her down the beach. 'Let's get you on to the boat.'

The next few minutes blurred together in Esme's head. She was helped through the water to the boat and felt herself hauled aboard. She heard her rescuer explain to the coxswain that there was another casualty, then he returned to shore while a second member of the crew, a young woman, wrapped a foil blanket around Esme and sat her down on the bottom of the lifeboat. Esme slumped back against the side of the boat, relieved that it was all over and desperately tired. But the crew member kept asking questions and repeating her name, telling her to wake up. Esme's mind drifted. All she wanted to do was sleep, but the woman wouldn't let her.

She was aware of anxious voices exchanging words via radio mics, the sudden roar of the boat's engine and the surge of momentum. The crewman who'd collected her off the beach crouched down beside her.

'Stay with us, Esme,' he said. 'We're heading back to base.'

# 83

Esme stood in her new office, the smell of fresh paint blending with beeswax, after polishing the roll-topped desk she'd salvaged. In her hands she held the old Chalacombe map she and Maddy had found when clearing the outhouse, its frame now beautifully restored by Maddy.

The door opened behind her and Esme turned as Maddy came inside.

'Haven't you got that hung yet?' she said. 'Everyone will be here in a minute.'

'Can't decide which wall,' Esme said. 'What d'you think?'

'That one, definitely,' Maddy said, pointing to the wall opposite. 'You'll see it straight away, every time you come in.'

'Yes, I think you're right. Give me a hand, then, would you?' Esme placed the stepladder against the wall and climbed to the top. 'Have you seen Hester?'

'I have!' Maddy handed Esme a hammer and the picture hook. 'Isn't it brilliant? I never thought I'd see that sea chest ever again. Hester said she couldn't believe it when she found it. Good job Stone hid it in that cupboard in her office or it might have been lost for ever. I can't wait to get back to it.'

'Hopefully this'll do the job,' Esme said, hammering the masonry pin of the hook into the stonework. 'How are we doing out there?'

'Nearly done. Harry's bringing in a couple more chairs and Libby's taken charge of catering. Hey,' Maddy wailed, 'I should have got you a ribbon to cut, shouldn't I? "Esme Quentin's new office is now open." Why didn't I think of it before?'

Esme laughed. 'I think I'll cope with the disappointment, Madds, don't worry.'

The door flew open and Libby arrived carrying a chocolate

cake and an armful of plates. 'Esme! What do you think you're doing?'

'What does it look like?' Esme said. 'Putting up my wonderful map.'

Libby put cake and plates down on the desk and came across the room, flapping her hand. 'Maddy or Harry can do that. You need to come and sit down. You've been on the go all day.'

Esme exchanged a conspiratorial grin with Maddy, who took over as Esme climbed off the steps. Esme knew there'd come a time when she'd need to urge Libby not to fuss, but for now she was happy to let her, not least because Libby was battling with her own trauma and fussing was her way of coping. While it was Libby who'd called the coastguard and instigated the rescue, Esme was aware she still felt guilty that she hadn't come in search of Esme sooner, delayed as she was by alerting Faith to the crisis and explaining about Adil and Sahila.

When Esme had been released from hospital and she'd gone to thank the lifeboat crew for rescuing her, it was only then she appreciated how close she'd been to slipping into dangerous hypothermia. The crew had been seriously concerned and when Maudesley persistently declined their help, they'd aborted their efforts to persuade him and prioritised getting Esme medical attention. She knew she'd been lucky.

Not so Isaac Maudesley. He'd signed his own death warrant by insisting on staying in the cave. But given his state of mind and the crimes with which he knew he'd be charged, perhaps it was his intention. Both his body and Stone's had been retrieved at low tide. Locating the victims buried in the cave had taken longer, but every one had now been recovered and the process of identification was underway.

An inquest would be held in due course, but unofficially, the conclusion had already been drawn that what happened was the result of a toxic relationship between two men. A man who was eventually pushed too far. A man who'd decided he'd had enough.

Esme heard voices outside. She stood up and went to open the door, welcoming everyone and ushering them inside. Hugs were exchanged, glasses of Prosecco issued and Libby's home-made chocolate cake administered.

When everyone was settled, Esme cleared her throat and took a deep breath. 'I'd just like to say a huge thank you to all of you for helping get this place set up. You have no idea what it means to me.'

'Uz's happy to do uz bit, maid,' Jim said, followed by murmurs of endorsement from the rest of the group. Esme smiled and nodded. She wanted to say more, her short speech seemed so inadequate, but she couldn't form the words.

Libby rescued her. She stood up. 'Time for a toast, I think. To Esme.'

'No, not me,' Esme protested. She raised her glass. 'To Esme's lovely new office!'

There was laughter and when her guests had echoed her sentiment, Harry began topping up people's glasses and Libby announced there was still cake left for those who'd like more.

Esme looked around the room, watching her friends chatting amongst themselves. Sahila was shyly helping Libby serve slices of cake and Adil sat at the desk, happily drawing. Libby had taken them into her home while their asylum application was processed, Faith giving expertise and welcome support.

Esme had deliberated about inviting Max, but before she'd made a decision, he'd let her off the hook by announcing he was going abroad on an investigation. Aidan said he'd try his best, but she knew he'd gone back home to Dorset, so wasn't surprised he hadn't made it. They'd spoken briefly soon after her narrow escape from the spring tide and he'd sent her a Get Well card and flowers, but it would have been nice to have talked things over now she was fully recovered. She wondered what he'd made of everything.

Hester's voice broke into her thoughts. 'You all right, Esme?'

Esme turned to look at Hester standing beside her, a plate in her hand and an anxious expression on her face. 'Yes, absolutely fine, thanks. You don't need to worry.'

Hester took a bite of cake. 'Aren't you having any? It's gorgeous.'

'Yes, I will in a minute. But before I forget, remind me to give you back Annie's notes before you go.'

'Oh yes, I will, thanks.' Hester sat down on a stool, beckoning Esme to sit next to her, and lowered her voice. 'There's something I'd like to tell you. It appears Isaac had ring-fenced the finances for the museum in a trust.'

Esme brooded on this for a moment. 'To protect them from Frank getting his hands on them, d'you think?'

'Possibly. But the most important thing is it's all set up so I can continue with the project.'

'Oh, that's great news, Hester. I'm so pleased. And no more than you deserve.'

Hester nodded before giving Esme a sly smile. 'And while I've got you here, I've got some more news. About the ring.'

Esme blinked, her mouth falling open. 'You've found out who has it?'

Hester's eyes shone. 'That's just it. I don't know whose it is. It's been in the museum all this time. Well, that's not entirely true. I can't say how long it's been there. All I know is it's the first time I've noticed it.'

Esme shook her head. 'Sorry, Hester,' she said, frowning. 'I'm not following you.'

Hester laughed. 'Oh, hark at me. I'm not explaining this very well, am I? The ring was in the *Treasures of the Sea Museum* in a display cabinet of personal effects found on a ship which went aground in the 19th century.'

'What ship?'

Hester flapped her hand dismissively. 'The *Sally,* but that's immaterial. It was most definitely not retrieved from the *Sally.*

There was never a Claddagh ring catalogued as part of the effects and, besides, I know it's only appeared recently. But, like I said, how recently, I've no idea.'

Esme considered. 'And you're sure it's *the* ring?'

'Ninety-nine point nine per cent sure, yes. Mum's seen it and she thinks so too.' Hester looked across towards Pat on the other side of the room, who was talking to Jim. 'Mum and I both agree it's the ring Annie always wore.'

'So, how did it get there?'

Hester gave an exaggerated shrug of her shoulders. 'Isaac. Who else could it be?'

'But Frank Stone had been searching for it in every jewellery sale in… Oh,' Esme said, with a heavy sigh. 'Of course. Silly me. I keep forgetting. Isaac and Frank weren't in league as we'd thought.'

'Exactly. So Isaac wasn't going to tell Frank he'd already got it.'

A question shot into Esme's head. 'Max said there was an Arabic inscription inside. Was there?'

'What do *you* think?' Hester said, with a wry smile.

Esme nodded as the answer became evident. 'Another of Isaac's fabrications.'

'Obviously.' Hester took another bite of cake as Pat joined them.

'Hester was just telling me about the ring,' Esme said.

'I know, it's so exciting to see it again,' Pat said. 'That ring's certainly had a chequered history. Stolen, fought over, lost, and then turned up out of the blue. If only it could talk, eh? What I can't work out, though, is how Isaac Maudesley got his hands on it.'

'Guess we'll never know that, now,' Hester said.

Libby came over and handed Esme a slice of cake. 'Here,' she said. 'Get that down you.'

Esme thanked her and tucked into the delicious chocolate

cake. As she ate, Pat's words echoed around her head. *Stolen, fought over, lost.* They triggered a memory of something else Pat had said shortly after Esme had first met her. Pat had been recalling the day Annie had died, the assumption that Annie had wandered outside, collapsed, how the ring must have slipped from her finger and been lost. But also Pat had questioned, though without much conviction, if the ring had been stolen and whether Annie had disturbed burglars, a scenario the police hadn't taken seriously. So, what had prompted Pat to consider such a possibility?

Esme was about to go after her to ask when she remembered something else Pat had said – that Annie's cleaner had seen a couple of dubious looking teenagers hanging about. Esme did a quick calculation in her head. While Maudesley and Stone wouldn't have been teenagers at the time of Annie's death, they wouldn't have been very much older. Could it even be possible that it was them? Was it why Stone was so nervous about Annie's research? If they'd harassed her, Stone could have been concerned she'd written something in her notes which would identify him.

Various scenarios spun around Esme's head. Perhaps they'd approached Annie and she'd sent them packing. Had they come back to try their luck a second time, this time bolder? Maybe Stone, the bully that he was, had grabbed Annie while Isaac took the ring from her finger and pocketed it. Then Annie, furious at their audacity, had given chase and fallen, as the two boys ran off and left her for…

'You OK, Esme?'

Esme's head snapped up to see Hester gazing down at her. For one fleeting moment, she considered sharing her thoughts, but what was the point? It was pure speculation. Too late to verify anything and it would only pile more misery upon what was already a distressing memory. And, of course, she may be quite wrong.

Esme forced a smile. 'Sorry, miles away.'

Hester crouched down and put a hand on Esme's arm. 'You'll

work it out, I know you will.'

Esme stared at her, fighting back the lump rising in her throat. Surely Hester couldn't know what was in her mind? But then she realised Hester was talking about Esme coming to terms with her recent trauma.

'Yes,' Esme said, nodding. 'I'll be fine.'

\*

The afternoon drew to a close. People said their goodbyes and left. Esme shooed away those offering to help clear up, insisting washing up a few plates and glasses was well within her capabilities. But she didn't want to do it straight away. She needed to clear her head.

She donned her wellies and duffel coat before heading out into the lane and turning down the hill towards the sea. As she passed Libby's cottage, she looked up to see Adil on the terrace, kicking a football against the garden wall. Earlier, he'd proudly told her about going to school and she was pleased to hear how well his English was coming on. She called out to him and waved. He grinned and waved back.

Esme took the steep path to the beach, breathing deeply to take in the salty air. As she passed the artists' cabin, she heard her name on the breeze. She stopped and wheeled round to see a man in a mustard-coloured jacket hurrying down the path towards her.

'Hello,' she said, her face breaking into a smile. 'You made it, then? I'm afraid you missed the cake.'

'I'm sorry I'm so late,' Aidan said. 'Traffic. An accident on the 303. I called, but I guess you weren't anywhere near your phone.' He jerked his thumb over his shoulder. 'I saw you coming out of your place so I thought I'd catch you up.'

'Actually, you're not that late,' Esme said. 'Everyone's only just gone. I needed a breath of fresh air.' She cocked her head towards the beach. 'Want to join me?'

'Sure.'

They walked to the bottom of the path and stood by the barriers closing off the beach. Aidan looked up to the top of the cliff.

'That's where the cottage came down, I take it.'

'Yes, that's right. It seemed to take the experts by surprise. But I guess given how unstable it was, there was always a risk it'd collapse before they got round to demolishing it. Some of the cliff came away with it.'

'And opened up the tunnel, allowing the mother and her son to escape?'

'Exactly.' Esme pointed to the distant beach where she and Libby had first spotted their 'ghost'. 'Adil had previously found a way down via an old storm drain, but he's a skinny little kid. The drain was far too narrow for his mum, slight though she is.' She nodded towards the rubble. 'So this cove's cut off until they clear everything away, which is a shame.'

'Convenient for some, though.'

She looked up at him and nodded. 'I know what you're thinking. I thought the same – a good way of keeping people away from places you might not want them to go.'

'And people do love exploring caves.'

Esme shuddered at the memory of that dark, dank space. 'Love the irony, though, don't you?' she said, with a half laugh. 'Block the beach, but expose an escape route.'

'Sorry. Perhaps I shouldn't have said anything,' Aidan said. 'You probably don't want to talk about it.'

'I'll have to eventually,' she said.

Aidan looked troubled. 'At the inquest?'

Esme nodded. 'You know,' she said, daring to let her thoughts revisit that day, 'I don't think Maudesley had thought beyond dissuading Stone away from people trafficking. Once he'd coaxed him into the whole pirate fantasy to stop him doing another run, he realised he was stuck with him. That's when he worked out he had to get rid of him and came up with the idea of Stone drowning on a dive.'

'And if he'd succeeded, it would have been me in the dock,' Aidan said, his jaw clenched. 'Especially if the police decided I had a motive, which they might have done if my connection with what happened at the school had come out.'

'I told him exactly what I thought about him setting you up,' Esme said. 'He was naive enough to think it would be seen as an accident. I wonder what he'd have done if Stone *had* died and you'd got blamed? Would he have confessed his part?'

Aidan turned and gazed out to sea. 'I doubt it. He didn't own up when he was 15, did he?'

'Perhaps he'd have made a better choice the second time around.'

'I was thinking the other day, maybe the 15-year-old Maudesley didn't have any choices.'

'Everyone has a choice, don't they?' Esme said. 'He had the choice to admit to his involvement in Anthony Milton's death as soon as it happened. And face the consequences.'

'Which may have been considerable. A criminal conviction. Youth offenders' institution. His life wouldn't have gone down the route it did, that's for sure.'

Esme remembered something she'd sensed as she'd watched Isaac Maudesley that morning in the cave, that he'd recognised his teenage crime for what it was and tried to atone for it over his lifetime.

'So, what makes you think he didn't have a choice?' she asked.

'Because the school authorities were desperate to cover up the scandal. Even if Maudesley had been prepared to put his hand up, they'd have persuaded him against it.' Aidan folded his arms and gave her a cynical grin. 'I doubt Frank Stone would have taken much persuading to keep quiet, mind. And he'd have loved knowing something to use to exploit his cousin.'

'Well, it came back to bite him in the end,' Esme said, reflecting on Maudesley spending a lifetime trying to get out of

Stone's clutches.

A sea breeze ruffled Esme's hair and pulled a strand out of its clip. She tucked it back in, her eyes drawn to the large lump of rock sitting on the horizon. She turned and saw Aidan was staring at it too. He must have sensed her eyes on him as he looked round at her.

'If when, you know, after you've...' he stopped and laughed. 'What I'm trying to say is, when you feel up to getting on a boat again, maybe we could go over to Lundy and pick up with that walk we never had time to finish?'

Esme smiled. 'I'd love to. Any time you like.'

He nodded. 'Good.'

'Meanwhile,' Esme said, indicating the path behind them, 'shall we go back to mine? I think I might be able to find you a slice of Libby's excellent chocolate cake.'

'Hey, that'd be great.'

'There's just one thing, though,' Esme said, raising an eyebrow.

'What's that?'

'You might find yourself roped into doing the washing up.'

Aidan grinned. 'Sounds like a fair exchange. Lead on!'

# A message from the author

Thank you for reading *The Scourge of the Skua*. If you enjoyed the book and have a moment to spare, writing a short review on Amazon or Goodreads (or your favourite site) would be greatly appreciated. Authors rely on the kindness of readers to share their experiences and spread the word.

# Free ebook

## LEGACY OF GUILT

*The shocking death of a young mother in 1835 holds the key to
Esme Quentin's search for truth and justice for her cousin.*

With the tragedy of her past behind her, Esme Quentin has quit her former career, along with its potential dangers, and is looking to the future.

But when she stumbles upon her cousin in traumatic circumstances, Esme realises that her compulsion to uncover the truth, irrespective of the consequences, remains as strong as ever.

Printed in Great Britain
by Amazon